Departure Tax
A Novel

DARIN COLUCCI

This book is based on an actual event, but in no way is based on actual individuals. Any similarities which may exist are purely coincidental.

Design by Beauty & Brains, LLC

Manufactured in the United States of America

ISBN: 0-578-43475-9
ISBN-13: 978-0-578-43475-

Also by Darin Colucci

Everything I Never Learned In School: A Guide To Success

"Don't confuse activity with achievement."
-John Wooden

CHAPTER 1

Key West 1996

Nick De Julia sauntered down Duval Street with an unmistakable air of self-assuredness. It was the type of confidence that everyone says they dislike but secretly admire. It was real; not some mere contrivance meant to hide a million insecurities. But Nick was far more than strut alone. Brains, drive, wit, savvy, *the look*; he had it all and then some. And in his former profession – the law – that confidence had practical application as well. After all, scaring the hell out of opposing counsel was the foundation of any great settlement. And then there was Nick's tenacity. If he really believed in the merits of a case, he would stop at nothing in its pursuit; which is to say that in addition to his more admirable qualities, Nick also tended toward a rather flexible view of certain ethical cannons. He never felt badly doing the wrong thing as long as it was for the right reasons; an approach that the New York State Bar Association ultimately took issue with.

But if you could see beyond the vagaries of regulatory interpretation, Nicholas De Julia was a star. Noteworthy cases were always concluded with noteworthy victories. And after 17 years of collecting six, seven and eight-figure judgments, there wasn't a defense firm in Manhattan that wanted to face him. Then, like so many other wildly successful untouchables, his last significant accomplishment was to bring himself down. He was unapologetic about it, nothing short of brilliant in his own defense and was actually able to cut himself a deal in the end, but the whole thing was ugly all the same. Even in his wildest nightmares, Nick never envisioned that the last three items on any to-do list would read: Pay fine; sell duplex; head south.

Indeed, southern-most Florida was the perfect place to get lost, a world unto itself where people are left to be who they are without the need to explain; paradise with a bad memory and an un-prying eye. It's been said that Florida is a sunny place for shady people, and Key West seemed to be the destination for the shadiest of all. For most, it's a funky little vacation spot where stress is the first thing that seems to give-way under the searing sub-tropical sun. But for Nick, this particular brand of island life had become a very comfortable way to wait things out.

Despite it being nearly noon, Nick was on his way to work. His daily route took him down the main stretch of Duval Street, past the outdoor restaurants, the bars, the tee-shirt shops and one of the two whorehouses on the island. Everyone knew him as the ex-lawyer from New York but didn't really care one way or the other. To them, Nick was a friendly enough guy who always bought his round; and for Key West, credentials like that qualified him for a legitimate run at political office.

A left-hand turn down Caroline Street brought him aside a number of beautiful "Conch Houses," each tall and narrow in appearance, flanked by palm trees and accented by the intricate latticework that's distinct to Key West architecture. Even the nice neighborhoods had a hint of shanty to them, which made the whole place unique. One more block over to tree-lined Whitehead Street and Nick was at work. The Law Offices of Martin Littrell took up the first floor of a wood-framed building that was the aforementioned hint of shanty on an otherwise desirable street. Still, it was just the way Nick liked it: Unassuming and nondescript. In fact, apart from the lettering on the door, no one would ever believe that the weather-beaten structure housed a law firm. Equally unimpressive were the furnishings. The main office area, which couldn't have been more than two or three hundred square feet, had one old metal desk, three file cabinets, two guest chairs, and a noisy window unit air conditioner that seemed to rattle and hum all day long. The pictures on the wall were from "local artists" who were otherwise known as guys from the bar that Nick felt sorry for.

Just as he walked in, the door to the back room cracked just wide enough so that Marty Littrell could shimmy his scrawny body through. And although he closed the door quickly behind him, it wasn't before Nick heard the uplifting sound of some fast and furious keyboard tapping -- a sure indicator that the phones were ringing. Nothing about the whole set-up screamed law firm —- or legal for that matter, so the back room was pretty much off-limits to "clients."

Nick gave his old associate a warm smile but as usual, added little by way of chitchat. Marty, on the other hand, accepted the fact that after nearly two decades of working together, filling the silent void was his job.

"We're having a good week, Nick. But I guess that's to be expected, huh? I mean it being that time of year and all."

"That's great, Marty," Nick said with noticeable dispassion as he poured himself a cup of coffee and began staring out the window.

"Yeah, thank God. Between the big thing, the little thing and the upcoming thing, we should stay busy for a while," Marty said cryptically as he cautiously lowered himself into one of the guest chairs. Now pushing sixty, Marty was nearly twenty years Nick's senior but looked older. In his heyday, though, he was a solid second chair lawyer. But more importantly, his realist approach to matters was a healthy offset to Nick's gunslinger mentality. "Nick, when you have a chance, I'm gonna need you to look at some things. We got some new business in the offing, and I want you to okay it before we get too involved."

Nick turned around, winked, and then resumed staring out the window.

"What's wrong, Nick? You seem preoccupied --- more than usual, I mean."

Nick ignored the question, clearly intrigued by something going on outside. "Will you look at this poor bastard?"

Marty pushed himself out of his chair and came up alongside Nick. "Which poor bastard?"

"That old guy across the street. The one who's muttering to himself", Nick said with a smirk.

"Maybe he's drunk." Marty took a quick look at the guy then back at Nick. "What do you give a shit anyway? Forget about him." Clearly Marty had not lost the jagged edge to his personality that only comes from a lifetime spent in New York.

"I don't think we're gonna have that option."

"Why not?"

"Because he's walking up our stairs."

Marty looked through the glass portion of the office's front door and saw an old man wearing a wrinkled pair of chinos, a blue tee-shirt, a fishing hat and a blank expression shuffling his way toward the door. Marty tried to wave him off, but the old fellow wasn't looking at anything but the ground in front of him.

"I'm sorry, sir, but we don't do that type of work here," Marty blurted out even before the door had closed behind the old guy.

"What type of work?" The man asked plaintively.

"The type that you need," Marty responded.

"But I haven't even told you why I'm here."

"I don't care. We don't do --- whatever it is."

"I thought this was a law firm," the man said, looking around the room for proof that he had read the writing on the door correctly.

"It is, but we only handle...certain types of cases. Very select stuff."

"Like what?"

"Like the kind of thing that you don't have, alright? Now, why don't we just leave it at that," Marty growled.

The man looked back at him for a long beat and then reluctantly turned to take his leave.

"Excuse me, sir," Nick said with a glare at Marty. "I'm afraid Mr. Littrell is getting a little ahead of himself. Why don't you have a seat?"

Marty walked right over to Nick and leaned in toward his ear, whispering, "This is not a good idea. The last thing we need are strangers in here."

"Would you like a cup of coffee?" Nick asked as he shot a steely, disapproving glare at his friend.

"No, I don't think so. No coffee. No."

Nick tried to act like he didn't notice the man's nervousness and poured himself a fresh cup. "You know I didn't catch your name when you walked in."

"Albert. My name is Albert. Albert Gaffney." The distinct tremor in the old man's voice indicated that he was shaken up about something, so Nick handed him a glass of water and

4

squeezed his shoulder in a friendly, reassuring sort of way.

"Why don't you take a sip of that and try to calm down. And trust me, Albert, whatever it is, we'll sort it out."

"Okay. Thank you." Albert raised the glass to his lips and spilled more than he drank, as his hands shook like he had Parkinson's.

"So, what are you doing down here, Albert? On vacation?" Nick asked with a smile.

"I came down last night from Pompano." Albert tried to take another sip of water. "Just came down to do a little fishing. You know, fly fishing on the flats."

"Really? Catch anything?"

Nick waited for Albert to look up and then stopped smiling when he saw the tears in the old man's eyes.

"No. We never even saw any fish, but something else kind of happened and I don't know what to do about it."

"Oh really. What?"

Albert stared at the top of Nick's desk with a glazed look in his eyes, grasping his hands tightly to stop himself from shaking. "I was out with a guide -- a local kid named Luis something or other. Nice boy; a little chatty, but otherwise alright. We were out fishing near Marquesa. We were kind of in a lee, you know, behind some mangroves. And as I looked out toward the Boca Grande, I could see something off in the distance. I couldn't make it out at first, but there was something about it that kept making me stare." Albert paused for a second. "Did that ever happen to either of you guys? You know...see something that just kinda grabs your attention, and you get this feeling like something's gonna happen?" Albert looked quickly at both men. "Did that ever happen to you?"

"Sure," Nick responded. "I think I know what you're talking about."

"So, you keep watching, and inside you're saying to yourself that things aren't right." Albert's eyes wandered down to the desktop once again. "Yeah, that's what I felt. Definitely. Like something was wrong. And I remember," Albert said, putting his left hand to his forehead, "I shaded my eyes from the sun, and that was the first time that I could make it out. It was a woman --- a pregnant woman, on a raft. Not a real raft, but more like one of those makeshift things that float." Albert took a deep breath.

"And just as I realized what it was, I heard this really horrible horn blast. You know, the kind from a big ship. It kind of caught me by surprise actually. Maybe 'cause I ain't never seen anything bigger than a skiff out there; that whole area is real quiet and remote, so hearing something that loud sort of scared me. So, I dropped the rod and held my ears. And then I started looking all around." Albert, again, held his hands tight to each other, which only made his arms shake.

"What was it?" Nick asked softly.

"It was a Coast Guard Cutter; one of the big white ones with the orange stripe below the bow. It was out a ways, you know, because it's so shallow on the flats it couldn't get too close, but it still looked huge sitting off in the channel. I'm tellin' ya I never seen a boat that big anywhere near that area." Albert took a break to awkwardly gulp down the rest of his water, wiping his mouth with his sleeve afterward. "And then I saw that woman start paddlin' like hell towards one of those tiny islands that are out there. She was lying on her side, and just slappin' at the water like her life depended on it. But the Coast Guard guys had lowered a speedboat into the water, and two or three of them started chasing her. So, I figure, it must be a Cuban trying to get into the states, you know. No big deal. Just a refugee, I figured." Albert's voice trailed off to a whisper. "You know, just a refugee." Albert seemed to drift away in thought momentarily.

Nick stole a glance at Marty who was looking at the floor and shaking his head in apparent disgust.

"Did something happen to the woman?" Nick finally asked.

Albert pushed his white eyebrows far up on his forehead and cocked his head to the side. "Well, she was scared, I imagine. I mean she had to figure that she was about to get caught and all because she dove off the raft and started to run through the shallows toward one of those little cays. But the Coast Guard guys kept closing the gap and you could just see that she wasn't gonna make it. Then all of a sudden, I heard somethin' else, low at first but then a little louder. It was kind of a sputtering sound. So, I looked up and saw this seaplane swooping in real low. I mean, real low, like it was either trying to land or -- hit the speedboat or something." Albert looked at both men real quick. "I'm not kidding. I actually thought the damn thing was dive bombing the speedboat -- for real. And so did the Coast Guard guys 'cause they bailed right the hell out, but their boat kept goin'. Straight as an arrow, right at that poor girl's back. And then, bam!" Albert said as he smacked his hands together. "The boat clipped her from behind. And she went down hard like she'd been shot. So, I'm thinking, you know, she's dead." Albert's voice cracked as he swallowed back some tears. Then, in a raspy voice, said, "But a second or two later, right there in the boat's wake, I see her pop up and start to stumble toward land again. She had all this blood running down her face, and all down her front." Again, Albert paused to compose himself. "So, my eyes are bouncing back and forth between the Coast Guard guys, the woman, and this plane, when all at once...everything on our boat started to rattle, and..." the old man slowly tapped his fist against his chest. "I felt this...boom...hit me right in the chest. I mean, it was so loud that it knocked me right off my feet into the well of the boat." Once again, Albert momentarily drifted off into memory. "Scared the shit out of me," he muttered as a tear ran down along the grooves of his wrinkled cheek. "I didn't even want to look, but it...it...flew right over us."

Nick leaned his head down until he made eye contact with Albert. "Another plane?"

"It was a fighter jet."

"A fighter jet?" Nick repeated in a slightly disbelieving tone.

"Yeah, you know, like Top Gun shit." Albert shrugged his shoulders and felt a wave of embarrassment as if he had stepped outside himself and could hear how crazy it all sounded. Forgetting about Marty for the moment, he decided to plead his case to Nick, raising his voice up a few decibels for effect. "I'm telling you, it was a fighter jet. It went screamin' over the whole area in a tight turn then came right up behind the seaplane. I swear it."

"It's alright, Albert, I believe you. Go on," Nick said, feeling Albert's worry.

"So, the little plane starts going like this..." Albert motioned with this hand.

"Banking?"

"I don't know what you call it, but it was kind of going sideways trying to get away. But the jet just came up behind it, and they both headed off toward the open ocean." Albert wiped some imaginary sweat off his forehead with the back of his hand. "So, for just a second, I looked over toward where the woman was, and

I saw one of the Coast Guard guys tackle her in about a foot and a half of water. Bam, just like that. And I remember that she fell right on her stomach and sort of...bounced on her side. And that's when...I heard..." Albert's whole demeanor darkened.

"Heard what?"

"This god-awful, hiss ---- and then this massive explosion. It all happened so fast. By the time I looked around, all I saw was the seaplane, on fire, slamming into the ocean." The old man seemed to be in a trance, clearly reliving every detail of the incident as if it was playing out all over again right in the office. "Pieces of the plane shot in every direction when it hit. Water sprayed up like a fountain." Albert ran his hand through what little gray hair he had left and then looked directly at Nick. "The tail was the last thing to go down. And I could see the number as it sank: H022028." His voice had a hint of pride at this detail before emotion swept back over him and he buried his head in his hands.

The whole room fell silent, as no one really knew what to say. So, Nick gave it a minute, hoping that Albert could compose himself enough to answer a few questions.

"Sir, I'm just a little curious about one thing. Mind you, I'm not in any way calling you a liar, but how is it that you remember the tail number so clearly? Seems like a kind of odd thing to remember given all the other things you say you witnessed."

Albert shrugged his shoulders, looked at both men and said with a slight trace of a chuckle. "It's...my birthday."

"What's your birthday?"

"February 20, 1928." Again, Albert glanced at both men. "2-20-28."

Nick nodded with a smile and then Marty, who was busy brushing lint off his trousers, didn't even bother to look up when he asked, "What happened to the woman?"

"There was another speedboat which picked all of them up. I didn't really see it, but I assume they arrested her."

"What do you mean, you didn't really see it?" Marty said mockingly.

"We were kind of...hiding...on the floor of the skiff. I mean after the little plane got blown up, I guess you could say I panicked."

"Did you see anything else, Albert? Anything at all?" Nick asked.

Albert nodded his head, "yes", but didn't say anything for a long while. "I looked up one more time and saw the Coast Guard guys pulling a body out of the water. I figure it was someone from the little plane, but I can't say for certain."

Nick thought for a second and only had one follow-up question. "What happened to the jet?"

Albert just shook his head and turned his palms toward the ceiling. "You got me. I never really saw it again after the little plane got it. I assume it just got the hell out of there. And so did we. The kid guided us back, but I think he was in shock, too. I don't think a word passed between us until we got back to the dock. We both agreed to keep our mouths shut, but now I feel funny about the whole thing."

As ten seconds turned into a minute, the three men just looked at each other through what had quickly become an uncomfortable silence. Not surprisingly, it was Marty who actually decided to break the ice. "Like I said when you walked in here, we don't handle matters like this. I'm sorry. But thank you for stopping by, and we certainly wish you better luck on your next fishing trip."

"Will you knock it off?" Nick said in a biting tone.

"No, I won't," Marty shot back. "Now I don't know who the hell this guy is or what any of these alleged events have to do with us, but we are not in the business of getting involved in…" Marty searched in vain for the proper term. "… shit like this. We don't need it, Nick. We just don't."

Nick, ignoring everything that Marty was saying, just kept rubbing his thumb and index finger over his bottom lip.

"Yo," Marty shouted and then waited for Nick's attention. "We just don't."

Nick let go of his lip and drummed his hands on the arm of his chair. "So where are you staying tonight, Albert?"

Albert thought about it for a second or two, apparently surprised at the sudden change in subject. "I guess I'm just gonna head home. Unless you think that I should do something else."

"Like what?" Marty asked sarcastically.

"I don't know; like go to the authorities, maybe."

"And say what? According to you, it was the authorities that shot down the fuckin' plane. And we are talking about the Florida straits here, right? I mean, God knows that there's never any type of criminal activity going on in that particular stretch of water." Marty waited for his sarcasm to bore its way into Albert's consciousness. "Did you ever stop and ask yourself, Albert, why in the hell the government might be shooting at a plane over the Goddamn Florida Straights? I mean really, if you had to take a wild guess, what do think was really going down out there?" Marty wrinkled his eyes at the corners. "Sounds like they were putting a stop to some sort of well-financed drug smuggling operation if you ask me. And as for the woman, it seems pretty clear that she was either in on it, or just a refugee in the wrong place at the wrong time because she apparently chose the wrong tide; plain and simple. So, what are you really looking to do here, huh? Sue the federal government for ruining your fishing trip? You want to go down in the annals of legal history right next to the lady who spilled coffee on herself and then blamed Ronald McDonald? Is that what you're eager to do?"

"Alright," Nick interjected. "That's enough. Albert, I think going on back home is a good idea. Obviously this whole thing has been upsetting to you, and perhaps home is the best place for you."

"Look, I don't even know why I came in here. I'm not looking for anything and I sure as hell don't want to be thought of as some kind of crackpot like he's talking about," Albert said, pointing at Marty. "It's just that I've never seen anything like this before and I didn't know if I should do something. That's all."

Nick got up and started to escort Albert to the door. "You didn't do anything wrong by coming in here. Hell, I used to tell all my clients --- consult your lawyer first. And that's all you did. No harm done."

"I mean, I sell car insurance for chrissakes, you know? I deal with the general public and sure, some of 'em can get pretty nasty, but I never have to deal with stuff blowing up."

"And...I'm very glad for that. Are you gonna be okay to drive?"

Albert exhaled loudly. "I think so. I might need to sit in the car for a minute or two, but I think I'll be okay."

"Alright, sir, you take it easy."

"Do you need my address or anything?" Albert asked as he hit the front porch.

Nick thought about it and then looked over at Marty who was still within earshot. "I don't think we will, sir. But I'll remember your name and that you sell car insurance in Pompano, okay?" The old man smiled for the first time.

"Actually, I can take care of all your insurance needs."

"And as soon as it's time to re-up any of my policies, you'll be my first call."

Nick walked Albert down toward the street to a point where he was certain that Marty could no longer hear him. "You know, Albert, maybe you should give me your phone number." Nick put his arm around the old man. "Just in case."

"Okay. Just let me get a pen, and I'll write it down for you."

"No, that won't be necessary; I'll remember it."

"Are you sure?

"I'm sure, go ahead."

"It's 804-835-5198." Albert spoke slowly in an apparent effort to help Nick digest the information.

"Thanks. Now go on home." Nick took a step or two toward the office but turned back toward the old man one last time. "And, Albert --- I wouldn't discuss this with anyone else. Know what I mean?"

Albert nodded. "Are you sure you don't want me to write down my number for you?"

Nick smiled at the old man. "Don't worry; I got it."

Nick went back to work but really didn't do much. Marty, on the other hand, never stopped. He slammed file after file on his desk, opened the mail, made his daily phone calls and conspicuously avoided any talk of the old man or his story. Nervous energy fueled his attack on the mounds of paperwork that kept coming out of the back room. Occasionally, he'd glance over at Nick who was deep in thought, which scared the hell out of him.

At five o'clock, Marty stuck his head into the back one last time, walked out onto the porch, and waited for Nick. The afternoon trek over to Captain Tommy's bar was sacrosanct, and something the two of them had been doing since they came to the island. In fact, despite his apparent machine-like tending to business, Marty had been anxiously awaiting five o'clock ever since the old man walked out of the office. If he had any hope of dissuasion at all, his argument would have to be well thought out, succinct, and presented over several empty glasses of scotch and soda.

Nick and Marty stepped off Green Street and right into old

world Key West. Captain Tommy's grubby little bar had more history than anyone would admit to. The Captain himself was still walking around barefoot, slinging drinks, telling stories and trying to pick up any woman who'd have him. And for a haggard, wrinkled old seafarer, he did remarkably well, a fact that he loved to make known at every opportunity. He did admit, albeit reluctantly, to a slight lull during his late seventies but claimed that things had significantly improved since he hit eighty.

The décor, if it qualified as such, consisted of thousands of business cards and pairs of lady's panties, each of which had been stapled to every square inch of wall and ceiling space. No one, not even Captain Tommy, could remember how either tradition got started, but like all other things in Key West, no one really seemed to care. The bar itself smelled of stale beer because that's the way Captain Tommy wanted it. According to Key West lore, Captain Tommy, on the day he bought the bar some forty odd years ago, took five cases of Bud and dumped it all out on the floor. Instant atmosphere was what he allegedly proclaimed just as the last drop fell.

Nick and Marty took their usual seats at the far end of the bar and were immediately besieged by the regulars. There was Patsy, the former luggage salesman; a terrible bore who never could seem to recover from the Vuitton family's decision to sell out to a group that would never again use brass fittings on the steamer trunks. Mo, Joey B., and Rocco were all widely recognized as Captain Tommy's cronies who got every other drink for free so long as they verified as true any story the captain might tell. A portly gentleman Nick nicknamed, Wahoo, was a frustrated singer who always positioned himself next to the pool table and would usually break out into song in between shots. And then there was Bra, a frail-looking, white bearded charter boat captain who only referred to Captain Tommy as Junior. No one actually knew just how old Bra was, but some of the more educated guesses ventured into triple digits. Truth be told, these fellas along with the endless stream of tourists are what really gave the joint atmosphere.

Marty threw a half-hearted wave to the Captain who quickly slid down some drinks. And as per usual, Nick kept to himself, more interested in carefully cutting his cigar than exchanging the same old same old with the regulars. Cigars were a passion that stemmed back to his New York days. Originally, Nick subscribed to the Jeffersonian philosophy that one should never skimp on books or liquor; it wasn't until a little later in life that he added cigars to arrive at his own holy troika.

"So, you never told me, what do you want to do about the new client?"

Nick hesitated for a second. "Which new client?"

"The guy that contacted us yesterday from the Bahamas. The one I told you about who wants us to, you know," Marty quickly glanced around the bar, "cover his interests."

Nick took a long swig of his drink. "I don't really give a shit, Marty. I'll go along with whatever you say."

"Oh, if only that were true."

"What are you talking about? I mean it; whatever you decide to do is alright with me."

Marty smiled, nodded and said, "Stop it."

Nick looked at the ice in his glass as he rattled it, and then took a casual sip, clearly nonplussed by Marty's non-sequitur. "Stop what?" He inquired through a winning smile

"Hey, I have no interest at all in waltzing around this thing anymore, okay? So why don't we just dispense with the bullshit and move right on to what's really pissing me off."

"Which is?" Nick's smile dimmed but only slightly.

"That you need to grow up and put this whole ridiculous situation right out of your mind."

"I don't know what you're talking about, Marty," Nick said unconvincingly. "I'm just sitting here drinking my drink."

"Look, Nick, you can take that babe of the woods routine and shelve it, alright? I know exactly what you're thinking, and it's beyond stupid. The way I see it, the Feds busted up a drug drop, end of story."

"Let me ask you a question, Marty — did you believe him?"

"You are missing the point, Nicky. I'm saying that I couldn't care less whether it was true or not. And I can't understand why you would."

Nick shot him a skeptical look. "You weren't the slightest bit curious about all that? Come on?" Nick asked in a mocking tone.

Marty held out his hand and closed his thumb and index finger until they were a quarter of an inch apart. "Not even this much. And even if you do, did you forget that pesky little disbarment issue?"

"I was never disbarred," Nick shot back.

Marty knew that he was treading on sensitive ground, so he chose his words carefully, trying to take any hint of anger out of his voice. "No, but you don't exactly have an up-to-date license to practice either."

"Yet again, Marty, you flaunt your ignorance." Nick polished off his drink on his third pull. "My license was never even suspended. I accepted a private reprimand in exchange for a private assurance that I would no longer practice law in New York."

Marty dipped his head for a moment and then placed his hand on Nick's shoulder in a fatherly sort of way. "Let's just take a step back for a second, ok? I know you, Nicky. I know how you operate, and I know what makes you tick. It's the challenge you love. Not the money, it's the challenge. And even more than that is your desire to be loved by your clients. That's what no one really understood when you had your...problem. You didn't do it to win and you didn't do it for the payday —- you did it so your client would love you. But in the end no one stood up for you. You were just painted as a shyster who thought he was above the law."

"Hey, that son-of-a-bitch doctor paralyzed that kid for life. --- LIFE! And then he lied through his fucking teeth just to save his deductible. There was no way that I was gonna let him get away with it."

"You bribed a resident to testify against the doctor."

"I paid the resident to tell the truth...huge difference. If I had paid him to lie, then you'd have something to give me shit about."

Marty put both hands up and shook his head. "Okay, so your heart was in the right place — what did that get you in the end? And I know, whether you want to admit it or not, that you've been looking for a way to redeem yourself." Marty waited in vain for a response. "Go on, call me a liar."

It wasn't often that Nick pulled back the curtain on his thoughts or emotions, but he had the look of someone who really did want to say something real. "Maybe you're right, Marty. Maybe I am hoping to make amends someday. Or maybe I'm just sick and tired of not caring about anything." Nick looked Marty dead in the eye. "All of our days are the same lately. It's become so rote that it's barely worth getting up. Then out of nowhere some old man wanders in and says that someone was killed in really odd circumstances. I mean when you strip it all away, that's what happened. And that doesn't intrigue you at all?"

Marty just shook his head slowly. "I've got nothing left to prove; none of it matters anyway because we couldn't get involved even if we wanted to. And I keep coming back to: Why would we ever want to?" Marty dropped his voice to a whisper. "We're making more money than we could ever count, and I don't mind telling you that I've grown pretty fond of the cushy life we have because of it. We do not need this. And forgive me for saying it, but you are deluding yourself if you think that redemption lies in helping some old guy find out why his fishing trip got ruined."

Nick sighed, shrugged his shoulders and said unconvincingly, "Maybe you're right." He slid off the stool and threw some money on the bar. "I'll see you tomorrow."

Marty decided to try one more tactic. "What about standing?" Nick stopped and looked at him. "I know it's been a while but you remember the concept of standing, right? You need standing to bring any type of lawsuit. I don't see how you would have it to begin with."

Nick turned his palms to the ceiling and shrugged his shoulder one more time before walking away. He had barely passed Marty when Patsy dropped himself down into Nick's vacated stool. "You know, I can't really figure that partner of yours out."

"That makes two of us."

"But I bet he's got some great luggage. I picture him with grade A stuff, you know, real classy, top-end pieces. Am I right?"

"Oh, mother of God." Marty let go of his temples just long enough to push Nick's hundred in front of Patsy. "All you have to do is shut the hell up and it's yours."

Patsy smiled at the old curmudgeon, and never even looked at the money. "What's got you so ticked?"

Patsy followed Marty's gaze and joined in staring at Nick, who was now sitting in a booth with his sometimes girlfriend, Iris. "Look at him, Patsy, and tell me what you see. – And your answer better not have anything to do with luggage."

Patsy studied Nick for a long moment, intent on answering Marty's question. "I see a confident, great looking guy with money to burn who's gonna wind up going home with the girl who, in my opinion, has the single best ass on the island."

Marty nodded. "Okay. Now tell me what he's thinking."

"I would imagine...he's thinking about...what he's gonna do to that ass once he gets home." Patsy looked back over to Marty, who didn't so much as grin.

"Right now, at this second, he's got about a million scenarios going through his head. He's solving problems, running contingencies and otherwise figuring out exactly how he's going to get from A to Z in the most efficient way possible."

Patsy looked thoroughly confused. "I don't understand."

Marty downed his drink and signaled for another. "The worst possible thing happened today, Patsy."

"What?"

Marty picked up his empty glass, stared at it, and let out some disgusted air. "Nick got curious."

Iris was in her mid-thirties but looked much younger, primarily because of the way her curly blonde hair landed softly on her shoulders. Although she didn't have the cover girl-type beauty that most of Nick's past girlfriends enjoyed, her body was competitive in any league. Endless hours at the gym and strict dieting, coupled with excellent raw material had yielded a physique that no man drawing breath could ignore. Add in an entire wardrobe that could succinctly be described as short and tight, and you had a woman who just oozed sex appeal.

Iris and Nick had been a quasi-couple for nearly a year, and although he enjoyed the stress free nature of it, she had grown increasingly unhappy with the *quasi* part.

"How was your day, Honey?"

"It was fine. Same old stuff." Nick never volunteered to talk about his day, a trait that Iris despised.

"I see," she said before taking a quick nip at her water with lemon. "And how was your day, sweetheart – Oh, thanks for asking, Nick. Well, let's see, I worked out, had lunch with my roommate, and then shopped for this dress." She ran her thumb under the spaghetti strap that lay on her tanned shoulder. "I felt pretty confident that you'd just love it."

Nick looked at Iris and promptly apologized. "I'm sorry, Iris. It's beautiful," Nick said with a sad smile. Try as he might, he couldn't muster any genuine feelings for Iris, a fact that they both knew and ignored in equal measure. She was willing to try anything to change that fact, and he felt awful that nothing she did ever seemed to make a difference. He liked her but couldn't even fake anything beyond that.

Nick quickly downed the rest of his shot as he clearly spotted someone he wanted to talk to. "Iris, would you mind terribly if we just met up later at the house? I really have to speak to that guy over there."

Iris dutifully nodded and said, "Sure," through a fake smile. She lovingly kissed him on the cheek and walked out of the place leaving a trail of craned necks in her wake.

Nick moved back over to the bar and leaned into Captain Bra's good ear. "How would the fishing have been out at Marquesa today?"

The old seafarer didn't hesitate or ask why Nick wanted to know. "Nonexistent — wrong tide."

Nick patted him on the back and then sidled up next to a young Hispanic kid that was sitting a few stools away. "Hey. How are you tonight?"

The kid, who couldn't have been more than twenty-one or two, gave Nick a long stare, a terse "'sup," and nothing more.

"Can I buy you drink?"

Again, the kid looked at Nick skeptically, and again, a one-word response followed. "Whiskey."

"Whiskey it is." Nick caught the Captain's eye and motioned for two short ones. "So, what is it that you do, kid?"

"Why?"

"No reason really, just trying to make conversation."

"Oh, okay...Why?"

"Hey kid, why so unfriendly? It's not like I'm trying to hit you up for money or anything. I just know that you live on the island, --- I live on the island --- and I thought that maybe we should be on a first name basis with each other. Is that so terrible?"

The kid looked down at his shot but didn't make a move for it. "Luis."

"That's your name, Luis?" The kid nodded. "Nice to meet you. I'm Nick." The two exchanged an unenthusiastic handshake. "So, what is it that you do, Luis?"

"I'm a fishing guide."

Nick noticed that Luis had begun to nervously twirl his still full shot glass. "No shit. What type of fishing?"

"Mostly flats stuff. You know, fly fishing."

"Really? How was the action today?"

"There were quite a few around, but we couldn't get any interested."

Nick smiled at him with an almost imperceptible disdain. "So, I take it you like being a guide?" Nick studied Luis closely.

"It's alright," Luis said in a disgusted tone. "Look, mister if you're looking for a free trip you can forget it. I'm in this to make money."

"I'm sure you are. And believe me, the last thing that I'd ever do is trample on someone's entrepreneurial endeavors."

Luis wrinkled his face and looked at Nick for an extra beat. "What the fuck does that mean?"

"It means that I'm not interested in a free fishing trip."

"Oh…Good." Luis said, showing the first signs of softening. "Actually, I don't fish much anyway."

"I thought everyone on the island fished."

"Well, it's not the actual fishing that I don't like."

"Well, what then?"

"I'm just not that crazy about the water."

Luis laughed and finally sank his shot. "You don't like the water and you live on a spit of land that's not even three miles long? You're not too bright, are you?"

"Should've stayed in school, I guess." Nick and Luis laughed a little more and ordered a second round, which led to a third, and then fourth. Nick noticed that the more Luis drank, the more talkative he became. So even before he'd finish one, Nick had another on the way.

The conversation varied from local stuff to women and back again; anything to keep him talking.

"So, you're a fishing guide, huh?"

"Yeah. Well, you don't have a lot of choices when you live here and you're my age, you know? I mean if you really think about it, what is there: Bartender, waiter, or fishing guide."

"Yeah, absolutely. I know exactly what you're saying."

"So, given the three, I chose guiding. I mean, who the hell wants to be a bartender anyway?" Luis looked down and saw two full shot glasses in front of him. "I'm fallin' behind here," he said before throwing one back. "What was I sayin' again?"

"Bartending."

"Oh yeah...screw that. Guiding is much better."

"Gotta go where the money is, right, kid?"

"You got that straight."

"And I'm sure you get to meet interesting people from time to time."

"Yeah, some."

"And you must see some amazing things if you're spending a couple hundred days a year on the water."

"Occasionally, that's true."

"Tell me one."

"What do you mean?" Luis suddenly looked a little less drunk and a little more serious. "Why would you ask me a question like that?" he slurred.

"No reason. I just figured that you must see some fascinating things out there. That's all."

Luis consumed his remaining shot, but never took his eyes off Nick. "I'm not really sure what you're gettin' at."

"Oh, come on, there has to be some event that sticks out in your mind."

Luis wiped his mouth even though it was dry. "I guess I'd have to say...yeah...one time I saw a hammerhead shark throw a tarpon fifteen feet in the air only to finish him off as soon as he landed." Luis paused for a second. "Yeah, definitely that one. It was some messed up shit, man," he said with a wide smile.

"That does sound like an interesting thing to have witnessed; I'll give you that. But, putting myself in your place, I don't think that I would have enjoyed it."

"Oh, I love that stuff. I always pull for the predator, you know."

He gave Luis a steely glare, "I guess that's where we part company, kid; I always pull for the prey." Nick got up from his stool without saying another word and walked right out of the bar.

CHAPTER 2

Nick, coffee cup in hand, waited not so patiently for the clock to strike eight. He had been awake since 5:30 and memorized the phone number but still needed the place to officially open.

"Good morning." Iris always tried to have a smile in her voice whenever she was around Nick. "You made the coffee – that's a switch."

"It's an all new me."

"I'd love to believe that one," Iris remarked as she poured herself a cup wearing nothing but a tiny, white cotton robe. "You're not going to work this early, are you?"

Nick never wanted to be rude to Iris and knew that he had been the night before. So, he folded up his newspaper and gave her his full attention. "No, not exactly. In fact, I might not even go in at all today."

"You're gonna miss work?" Iris looked stunned. "Maybe this *is* a new Nick De Julia." The bottom of Iris's robe fell to the sides as she crossed her legs, a move that she had mastered several years previous. "So, do you want to spend the day together? We could go to the beach or something."

"I don't think that I'm gonna be able to do that, sweetheart."

"And back the pendulum swings to the Nick that I recognize," Iris said sarcastically.

"It's not that I don't want to, it's just that I might have to go out of town for a couple of days. You know, business related."

Iris spied Nick's luggage in the hallway. "When did you

decide this? I don't remember you saying anything about it before."

"It just came up yesterday and I didn't have a chance to tell you."

All moments like this felt to Iris like a referendum on their relationship, and it never seemed to be encouraging. "How long will you be gone?"

Nick heard the clock begin to chime and immediately got up. "I have to make an important call. Why don't you have your coffee on the deck, and I'll be out in a minute." Iris couldn't hide her disappointment. She could deal with love or hate, but Nick's unique blend of charm and ambivalence was just so confusingly painful. Initially, she had convinced herself that Nick just needed time to come around, thinking that at minimum, he'd learn to appreciate what the two had together. But like any lacking relationship, there comes a point where you either have to accept it for what it is or move on. Problem was -- she wasn't conflicted in the slightest. She loved him, plain and simple. Iris never told him, though, knowing that pressure like that might make him end it, but she loved him all the same.

"Iris," Nick said as he bounded onto the deck. "I have to go."

"Wait...go where?"

Nick walked right back into the hallway and picked up his luggage. "Key Largo."

"What's in Key Largo?"

Nick rushed past her in the other direction, retrieving his wallet from the counter. "Business."

"Do you want me to go with you?"

"No, but I appreciate the offer, sweetheart." Nick reached into his wallet, pulled out three hundred-dollar bills and threw them on the kitchen table. "Here. Buy yourself something nice. I'll be home in a couple of days and we'll go out or something, okay? I'm sorry but I have to go." Nick kissed Iris on the top of the head, mussing her hair a little, and then rushed out the back door. Iris stayed in the hallway for moment or two to contemplate what had just happened, and then slammed her coffee mug onto the counter as she unsuccessfully fought back tears.

Nick took Eaton Street out of Old Town and over to Roosevelt Boulevard where he pulled over for gas, something which he hadn't done in nearly six months. As he nervously drummed his fingers on the pump handle, he glanced to his right and saw that Marty had pulled right alongside him in his cherry red, 1967 Corvette.

"I take it you're not coming to work today?" Marty said with a distinct note of resignation in his voice. And even though he knew the answer, he waited for Nick to shake his head, 'No'.

"Would you mind telling me where you're heading at five past eight in the morning?"

Nick slowly forced one corner of his mouth up into a half smile and said in a sort of an embarrassed way, "To get some standing."

Marty closed his eyes tight for a second, having his worst fears confirmed. "Well, I know that I can't talk you out of it, so I'm not even gonna try. But just know that I'm shutting it all down today."

"There's no reason to do that, Marty."

"There's every reason to do it. You're going out to actively court the one thing that we don't need: Attention. Now maybe you don't care, but I do. As of right now our partnership is over, and the business is no more." Marty pushed a pair of Ray-Bans onto his face and put his car in gear. Nick watched Marty speed away toward the office for ostensibly the last time, losing sight of him just as the pump bucked and pulled back from the tank.

CHAPTER 3

US 1 is quite possibly the most scenic highway in the southern United States. Predominantly a two lane road, it winds through and connects all of the Florida Keys in an almost poetic sort of way. Some stretches are no more than forty or fifty feet wide with travel-brochure quality views of endless turquoise water on either side. Sections of now decrepit trestles and obsolete railway tracks run parallel to certain portions of the highway, suspended far above the water, providing a rustic backdrop reminiscent of simpler times. But in actuality, Nick saw none of it. He was far too busy grappling with the nagging feeling that he was driving more toward ruination than redemption.

He flew past those poor souls who didn't have 500 turbocharged ponies under the hood and really dropped the hammer whenever he found some running room. In all, he made amazing time, reaching Key Largo in just under an hour and thirty minutes. He had set his dashboard GPS somewhere around Islamorada, and it now guided him right to the rather impressive front gates of 1 Ocean Lane. Knowing that confidence was the key that unlocks just about every difficult situation, Nick pushed the button like he owned the place and waited for a response.

"Can I help you?"

"Yes, I'm Harry Greensboro, and I'm here to see Mr. Randolph Charlton." Nick heard a high-pitched hum and noticed that a video camera had been directed at him.

"Is Mr. Charlton expecting you?"

"No, but it concerns one of his assets. I'm afraid that there's been an accident involving a plane that he owns." Nick paused for a second and added. "I hope to God that my information is accurate and that he wasn't involved in the crash?" Nick, not knowing the answer, waited nervously during a very long pause.

"No, Mr. Charlton is still with us, and will see you." Two clicks and a long buzz later, Nick was driving up to one of the most magnificent homes to dot the Florida coastline. Done in a Mediterranean Style and painted a pale orange, the home just reeked of money. From the height of the front doors to the ornate fountain, to the grandness of the sculptures that stood guard over the grounds, it was quite obvious that Mr. Charlton was a rock star, a titan of industry, or the idiot son of one or the other.

The door swung open and a uniformed servant greeted Nick. "Please come in. Mr. Charlton is by the pool. If you would follow me, sir."

Nick walked through the museum like living room toward the rear of the house, which boasted a two-story glass wall leading to the pool area. Charlton was sitting under an umbrella with a stogie sticking out of one corner of his mouth and a cell phone glued to his ear, screaming about some deal that was apparently on life support.

"I don't give a good Goddamn what the hell you think, I want the thing signed by Friday. Friday!" he repeated for emphasis. "Because if it isn't, I'm gonna come up there personally and bitch slap every last one of you. You hear me?" Charlton took the cell phone from his ear and squeezed it in his right hand as if trying to get juice from it. He then slammed it down onto the table and turned toward Nick.

"And who the hell are you, some overly crafty process server who rented a Porsche for the day? Well congratulations, son. Just leave it on the foyer table on your way out."

"Sorry to disappoint you, but I don't have a subpoena or a summons for you. I'm just here to ask you a few questions."

"Really? And why the hell would I answer them?"

"My name is Greensboro, Harry Greensboro, and I'm a special investigator with the FAA. And please let me say at the outset, that I'm very glad to see that you're well."

Charlton put both palms to his chest. "And please let me thank you for your concern," he said facetiously. "Now why am I listening to you?"

"Because according to our records, you are the registered owner of a plane with the tail number H022028, are you not?"

"Yeah, what about it?"

"I'm afraid that your plane crashed yesterday about twenty-five miles south of Key West."

Nick was more than a little surprised when he saw the wide smile slowly cross Charlton's face.

"You're shitting me, right?" he muttered through his stifled laughter.

"No, I'm quite serious."

"Did it crash in the water?"

Nick hesitated, still uneasy with Charlton's reaction. "It did."

"And we're talking — it's on the ocean floor?"

"Yes, we are."

"Well I'll be a son-of-a-bitch," he yelled, clapping his hands to punctuate his happiness. "You see, sometimes you just get lucky in life." Now Nick looked confused. "I've been tryin' to dump that damn rust bucket for two years. Do you have any idea how hard it is to sell a plane in this economy? I mean if it were a Gullwing or a Gulfstream it would move, but a jet that old? Damn thing's been like an albatross around my neck ever since I bought it. Hanger fees, maintenance fees, not to mention you people and your Goddamn FAA safety bullshit that I have to pay for every fucking year. I say to hell with it. I'm glad it's gone."

"Perhaps it hasn't yet dawned on you, but kindly allow me to point out that your plane crashed with people in it."

Charlton's smile dimmed, but not entirely. "Oh shit, I wasn't thinking. Was it the Cuban guy?"

"We have no idea who was aboard, and that's the reason for the visit. We need a name and an address, so we can properly notify his family."

"So, I take it he didn't survive?"

"I'm afraid not."

Charlton picked up his cell phone and hit speed dial. "Hello, Ed. It's Randy. Hey who rented the plane yesterday? I know it didn't come back – who had it?" Charlton took a pen from his breast pocket and scribbled down some information. "Thanks, Ed. No, I don't think so. And tell the airport guys that we want to cancel our hangar space as of today. Right."

Charlton handed the slip of paper to Nick, but clearly couldn't have cared less about *the Cuban guy*. His lack of compassion pissed Nick off so much that he decided to screw with him just for fun.

"Now, Mr. Charlton, I advise that you wait to file an insurance claim until our investigation is concluded. And I estimate that a final report won't issue for ten or eleven months."

"Why the hell not? I didn't do anything wrong."

"Well I'm sure you didn't, but please allow me to remind you that the standard aviation insurance policy exempts from coverage: any craft if damaged or destroyed while in the process of being operated or otherwise used for illegal or illicit purposes."

"Look, I had no clue about anything they were up to. I think I only spoke to that Cuban guy once or twice. I mean he was a nice enough, clean-cut looking fellow and I can't imagine he was up to no good. But if he was, I sure as hell didn't know anything about it. I just rented him the plane a couple of times a month."

"Well precisely what he was doing has yet to be determined, but we'll stay right on it. But like I said, we strongly advise against filing until a final report issues."

Charlton took off his sunglasses and squinted suspiciously at Nick. "And who the hell are you again?"

"Greensboro, Harry Greensboro, special investigator for the FAA's crash unit."

Charlton finally stuck out his hand and Nick obliged. "Well it's nice to meet you, Mr. Greensboro. And anything you can do to speed up the process will be greatly appreciated."

"I'll do my best. Thank you for your time."

Nick could see that Charlton was not quite convinced that everything was as advertised, so he wheeled around and tried to beat a hasty retreat.

"Hey, Mr. FAA, you mind if I ask you a question?"

"It's not mine."

"What's not yours?"

"The car. It's my brother-in-law's. My Taurus is in the shop and he loaned me his car for the day."

Charlton nodded. "'Cause I was gonna say --- I didn't think government work paid that well."

"It doesn't, trust me."

Nick's mind whirred with ideas, plans, and problems. He reviewed what little he knew but was awed by the totality of what he needed to know. One thing was absolutely crystal, however, he needed help. If this matter was in New York, Nick would enjoy a distinct home court advantage, but Florida was a different story. He scanned his memory bank for any contact but came up blank. The local attorneys that Nick either knew or knew of, were all too high profile and/or egocentric to stay below the radar long enough to allow for proper planning. He needed someone that no one would see coming, an unassuming type preferably with connections. Then one potential candidate did come to mind, but Nick couldn't even remember the guy's first name or in what city he practiced. So, with tremendous reluctance, he dialed a number that he hadn't hit in over three years.

"Good morning. Collinsworth, Laughton, and Levin. May I help you?"

"Hello, Nancy. It's Nick De Julia."

"Mr. De Julia, it's so nice to hear your voice. How are you, sir?"

"I'm fine. How are things at the firm?"

"Nowhere near as good as when you were here, sir. We all miss you very much."

"I appreciate you saying that."

"So whom can I connect you with?"

"Is Aldo Cicero in today?"

"I believe he is. I'll put you right through to his line."

"Thank you, Nancy, and please take care of yourself."

"You too, sir."

During Nick's tenure at the firm, Aldo Cicero was the second smartest lawyer in the building. He was a Yale graduate and a Rhodes Scholar with a legendary, and for the most part warranted, ego. Known within New York legal circles as the man with the million-dollar wardrobe, Aldo was a player who privately reflected upon Nick's departure from the firm as a red-letter day which brought him one step closer to the top of the letterhead.

When the intercom buzzed, Aldo was seated in his gold leather captain's chair, which he had positioned slightly away from

27

his antique Chesterfield table desk. His thinning gray hair was slicked straight back, acting to feature his large yet stylish, tortoiseshell eyeglasses. Aldo always wore Trafalgar suspenders, and this day was no exception. This particular pair was made of silk and had as its design a continuous series of silver dollars, one on top of another, running the length of the braces. His tie was Armani, as was his suit, which was beginning to wrinkle beneath the weight of his secretary. And even though Cindy had just found her rhythm, Aldo answered the call anyway.

"Aldo Cicero."

"Hi, Al. It's Nick."

"Nicky D? Do my ears deceive?"

"No, it's me."

"It's been a long time, my friend. What gives?" Aldo said above the rhythmic squeak of his chair.

"I hope I'm not interrupting anything?"

"I actually just got into something, but I'm not so far along that I can't talk." Aldo said as he motioned for his secretary to continue riding him. "So, what have you been up to?"

"A little of this a little of that."

"So, to what do I owe the honor?"

"I need a favor."

"Anything."

"Didn't you once tell me that you had a brother down here practicing, what was it…immigration law or something?"

"Yeah, Lenny."

"Lenny Cicero. I couldn't remember his name for the life of me. Where's his practice set up, Al?"

"His office is in downtown Delray Beach. I don't know the actual address off the top of my head, but I'm sure you can look him up."

"Where's Delray?"

"Just north of Boca. What's goin' on? Are you practicing again?"

"No. A friend of mine has an immigration problem and I told him that I'd try to find him a good lawyer."

"Well, Lenny's no me, but he's alright, especially if you need something wired. You know what I mean? You never met anyone so plugged-in, he knows everybody."

"That's precisely what I need."

"Does your friend have any money?"

"Why? Is your brother expensive?"

"No. But if your friend does pay him, make sure you tell Lenny that I'll be expecting a referral fee."

"That's very brotherly of you."

"I am a prick, aren't I?"

Nick nodded in silent agreement. "I'm sorry to have bothered you, Al."

"Not at all. Hey, Nick?"

"Yeah."

"You're not thinking about coming back to the firm, are you?"

Nick thought about Aldo's question for only a second. "You took my office, didn't you, ya bastard?"

"Well, it seemed like such a waste for it to just sit there, unoccupied. And when the big boys offered it to me, I just felt like I had to accept."

"I'm sure it was a tough call. But at any rate, the answer to your question is 'yes'."

"You're coming back to the firm?"

"No --- I meant "yes" you are a prick. But, that fact notwithstanding, I have no present plans to rejoin the firm, so I guess you can tuck right in, Al."

"I appreciate that."

"Great. Oh, and make sure you tell your wife that I said hello."

Cindy immediately stopped bouncing and dismounted. "I'll do that," Aldo said sadly. "Thanks a lot, Nick."

"No problem."

CHAPTER 4

Nick stood in the doorway, unsure whether he should cross the threshold or run back downstairs. The Delray Beach office of Lenny Cicero looked more like an unemployment office than a law firm. Disparate folding chairs lined the walls of the poorly lit reception area. Ten or so people seemed to be speaking five or so languages. A hastily scrawled sign, written both in English and Spanish, explained office policy concerning smoking and personal checks, both of which were most emphatically *Prohibido*.

Nick walked up to the receptionist who ignored both him and several ringing lines, choosing instead to continue with a rather personal call. Nick smiled politely once, but it had no effect. He then leaned over the counter and calmly disconnected her call. "Lenny Cicero, please."

The receptionist looked at Nick defiantly at first and then slowly gave him a flirty smile. "He'll be with you in a moment," she said meekly as she put the receiver down. "And can I have your name, please?"

"Nicholas De Julia."

"Nicholas De Julia," she repeated, making certain her pronunciation did not offend. "Would you mind?" The young girl asked, pleasantly reminding Nick that his finger was keeping her phone in disconnect mode.

"Not at all," Nick said, as he calmly relented.

"Thank you." The young girl activated the intercom and a second later, Nick heard Lenny Cicero's rasp for the first time.

30

"Yo."

"Mr. Cicero, I'm sorry to interrupt, but there is a Nicholas De Julia here to see you."

"If you're calling me 'Mr. Cicero' he must be dressed nice." The young girl winced knowing that Nick heard her boss's comment.

"Can I send him in, sir?"

"'Sir?' Is this guy from the IRS?" Lenny asked in a stage whisper that was broadcast to everyone in the office. The receptionist promptly turned the intercom off and motioned that Nick should just go right in.

Lenny Cicero, all five foot six and 200 pounds of him came out from behind his desk to greet his guest. Lenny welcomed Nick with a vigorous handshake that lasted a "good-friends" duration.

"How you doin'? How you doin'? I'm Lenny Cicero." he said, continuing to pump Nick's hand.

"I'm Nicholas De Julia."

"Nice to meet you, Nick. Care to take a seat?" Nick finally pulled his hand away and Lenny, realizing his gaffe, laughed hardily. "Why don't you sit here?" Lenny pulled one of his guest chairs away from his desk and slapped its green vinyl seat cushion twice. Nick didn't move right away; instead, he decided to take in an eyeful of Lenny Cicero. To say he was portly would be extending a courtesy; he wore a short gray beard, rectangular eyeglasses and an enigmatic smile. He had kind of a Kris Kringle sans the velvet look about him. Clearly, Aldo had been the first one in and the last one out of the Cicero gene pool. "Go ahead, sit down already. Make yourself at home," Lenny said as he scampered back behind his desk.

Nick looked around Lenny's disheveled office and began to smile to himself. A mountain of paper rested on his desk, the top layer of which fluttered every time the electric fan perched on the windowsill would oscillate in that direction. Every picture hung askew except Lenny's diploma, which he had nailed to the wall, proudly displaying that he was a graduate of Universitas di Aruba Law School. Eventually, Nick's eyes returned to Lenny whose broad smile had yet to ease.

"So, what can I do for you, Nick?"

"I got your name from your brother, Aldo. We used to work together."

Lenny let out a tremendous sigh of relief and slumped onto his desk. "Thank Christ. I thought you were a Fed." Lenny took another cleansing breath and resumed smiling. "God, that was a close call."

"I'm sorry I scared you."

"No problem," Lenny said, tapping his chest at about heart level. "So, you know my brother, Al?"

"Yes. I actually spoke to him this morning."

"Yeah? How's he doin'?"

"Seems like he's doing fine. I told him that I have a potential case that I'm looking into and that I might need the help of a local attorney. And that's when he told me about you."

"Really? Did he say anything else?"

"Yeah, he wanted you to know that he'll be expecting a referral fee if anything comes of this."

Lenny laughed faintly. "Well, once a prick, always a prick, I guess." Within a second, Lenny stopped smiling entirely. "So what kind of case are we talking about? Slip and fall, divorce, car accident, dog bite...I love dog bite cases."

Nick glanced up once again to the beach scene on Lenny's diploma. "I'm not really sure this is going to work out, Lenny."

"What? You're firing me already? Don't let the old Aruba sheepskin fool ya. I passed the bar on the first crack, my friend." Lenny straightened out one piece of paper on his desk and pushed his glasses back up against his eyebrows.

"It's nothing personal."

"Didn't you see the sign out there? The initial consultation is free. What have you got to lose?" Lenny asked as he pulled some wax paper with a half-eaten sandwich across his desk and into a wastebasket. Lenny's smile reappeared but Nick remained un-swayed.

"Was that the remnants of today's lunch?"

"No, no, not at all. I'm pretty sure that was yesterday's. I don't know --- yesterday, the day before."

"Well, then what do you say? I'll buy." Nick wasn't hungry, but if nothing else, lunch with Lenny was certain to be entertaining.

"Terrific." Lenny leapt up and jogged around to the front of his desk. "I know a good place just up the street."

"What about all those people in your reception area?"

"Don't worry about it," Lenny said with a wave. "Most of 'em are from countries where all they do is wait around; they're used to it. Come on."

Nick followed Lenny into the waiting area and watched as he smiled warmly at his prospective clients. Somewhat remarkably, they all smiled back and offered friendly waves as Lenny walked out the door.

"Do you mind if we walk? I really need the exercise. I tell ya, I had an ice cream sundae last night and I could actually feel my arteries clogging." Despite his steadily expanding girth, Lenny had a lively step. Nick had to break into a canter just to keep pace. Even more impressive, though, was that everyone on the street seemed to love Lenny. Time after time horns would honk and passersby would offer effusive hellos to the cherubic lawyer with the island education. The same was true at the restaurant. From the owner to the cook to the busboys, everyone treated Lenny like their best friend from the old neighborhood. And he responded in kind, liberally dispensing handshakes, hugs, and backslaps to all he encountered.

Finally, free to study the luncheon specials in this questionable-looking, undersized Mexican restaurant, Lenny was a king in his court.

"I can see why you like this place."

"Oh, the food's very good here."

"I'm sure it is, but I meant that you seem to be very popular with the staff."

Lenny took a clumsy sip of his water and tried to smile while swallowing. "The owner is a very good friend of mine, Nick, and so, I come here a lot." Lenny took another gulp of water and Nick noticed that although he had a loud way about him, Lenny always seemed to speak in hushed tones.

"Hey, Lenny," the waiter said enthusiastically, "how's it going, man?"

"Good, good. I keep puttin' on weight but otherwise okay."

"Hey, you know that thing you helped me out with?"

"What thing?"

"The thing --- you know, man."

"Oh, yeah. How did that turn out for you?"

"Terrific, man. Thank you."

"It was nothing, really."

"And no argument. Lunch is on me, man!" the waiter

exclaimed.

"You don't have to do that..."

"No, no, no, no. I won't hear of it. Lunch is on me. And put those menus away. I'm gonna have the cook make you guys something special."

"That's awfully nice of you, really. Thank you," Lenny said with his toothy smile. "You're a good guy."

"I'm just trying to pay you back, man."

"Gracias."

"De Nada."

Nick waited for Lenny to turn towards him. "You have no idea what his name is, do you?"

"It begins with an 'S', I'm sure of it." Lenny continued to think for another moment. "Sanches...Sancho...It doesn't matter... It'll come to me."

Nick took a moment to grapple with how oddly comfortable he felt around Lenny. The beloved always fascinated Nick; those chosen few people in life who inexplicably inspire love and loyalty from all those they meet, the type that bank on and receive the benefit of every doubt. Even when the beloved go awry it's hard to hate them. And in such cases, where the rest of us would be considered bastards or scoundrels, they are euphemistically knighted as "loveable rogues". And such was definitely the case, Nick determined, with Lenny Cicero.

"So, Nick, you never told me what type of case we're talking about."

"To tell you the truth, Lenny, I wouldn't know where to start."

"I've got time. Start wherever you like." Lenny placed both elbows on the table and looked straight at Nick with as much concentration as he could summon while chewing on tortilla chips.

"Well, it's a potential...wrongful death claim, I guess. Yesterday morning I learned about a ---" Nick hesitated. "--- an incident that occurred about twenty miles outside of Key West at a place called Marquesa Key."

"Okay, an incident. Okay," Lenny muttered while constantly adjusting and re-adjusting his glasses.

"Based on an eyewitness account, it seems that this woman, most likely a Cuban refugee, was trying to make it to the states on a raft. From what I've been able to deduce, somehow the Coast

Guard was made aware of it, and showed up to try and apprehend her." Nick studied Lenny's intent glare for a second. "You with me so far?"

"Yes, yes, absolutely. A woman on a raft, absolutely."

Nick laughed a little at Lenny's manner, but continued, nonetheless. "Well, it would seem that a chase of sorts ensued, and ..." Nick started to feel like Albert, almost embarrassed to be telling this seemingly disjointed tale. "Then something else happened. And I haven't been able to determine if this next thing is related to the pursuit of this refugee or not."

"Go ahead, I'm with you."

"At just about the time that the Coast Guard started closing the gap on this woman, a small propeller plane began to buzz the area."

"And?"

"And then a military fighter jet armed to the hilt burst onto the scene and allegedly engaged the little prop plane."

Lenny waved his hands in the air. "And by engaged, you mean...?"

"Blew it to hell."

"Oh dear." Lenny thought for a minute before quickly dipping his chip in some salsa. "And people died?"

"Two, I think."

Lenny pulled at his beard with his mouth slightly agape. "Did they get the girl before she reached a land mass?"

"Yeah, actually, they did. Why do you ask?"

"No matter." Lenny sat back in his chair. "That sounds awful, Nick. Really awful." Lenny shook his head in disgust and then picked at remnants of some chips in his teeth. "But --- so what?"

Nick was taken somewhat aback at Lenny's terse response. "Well, like I said, I'm considering looking into the matter as a potential wrongful death matter."

"And do you actually know someone affiliated with Brothers of Freedom? I mean, is that how you got the case in the first place?"

Nick sat back in his chair and stared a bit at Lenny, taking a moment to rub his own chin. "I'm afraid I'm not familiar with that group. Who are the Brothers of Freedom?"

"It's a group of Cuban-Americans who try to help Cuban

defectors. They take turns flying seaplanes over the Florida Straights looking for rafters. And if they see one, they land the plane and pick 'em up."

"Which is obviously illegal."

"Well, yes, it's illegal for the guys operating the plane but it's the best thing that ever happened to the rafters. You see, the current immigration laws state that if a Cuban can make it to land they can stay in the country as a legal alien. But if the Coast Guard can nab them in even an inch of water, they're immediately sent to prison. They aren't charged with anything and there's no trial, they just get sent to a military prison in, of all places, Guantanamo Bay, Cuba. How's that for irony."

Nick was actually impressed that Lenny used the word irony correctly. "For how long?"

"Forever. Well, that's not quite accurate. They're given the choice of staying in prison or being returned to Cuba, where they will undoubtedly be put to death for an act of treason against the Republic; hence, they're in jail forever."

"So, if the woman had actually made it to Marquesa Island, she wouldn't have been arrested?"

"No, she still would have been imprisoned."

"I don't understand. You just said ..."

"They have to make it to the continental United States. The southernmost part of the continental US that will trigger the sanctuary provisions of the immigration code is Key West. Those smaller, uninhabited Keys don't count. The woman clearly knew of *the law* but didn't read the statute closely enough, I guess."

Nick leaned away from the table as the waiter brought the first course. And although he didn't even look at the food, Lenny dug right in.

"It doesn't make sense. Why would the military shoot down a plane even if it was connected to this Brothers of Freedom operation?"

Lenny chewed while he thought. "Well, technically, they would be guilty of smuggling."

"Smuggling what?"

"People."

"But they wouldn't have attacked the plane for that."

"No, probably not. But maybe they were smuggling something else too. You know, guns, drugs, whatever." Lenny finally swallowed. "How well do you know the guys who got killed?"

"I didn't know them at all."

"Okay, alright, okay. I see what you're saying here. But then I find that I'm a little confused about one thing."

"Go ahead."

"Okay." Lenny paused, furrowed his brow and placed his fingertips together, trying to strike as contemplative a pose as possible. "Then why," Lenny paused again, searching for just the right turn of phrase, "if you don't mind me asking, of course…do you…give a shit about any of this?"

Nick thought for a moment while Lenny tore into seafood nachos. "I'm not sure I do. But for right now, it just doesn't sit right with me."

"I see, I see. Well, then, I guess the more appropriate question is: Why should *I* give a shit about any of this?" Lenny reached across the table and took hold of Nick's water. "Do you mind?" Lenny asked, politely waiting for Nick's permission.

"If, for whatever reason, I do decide to look into this, I'm going to need someone who knows his way around the Florida court system. I may also need someone who has the ability to get --- information. Do you understand what I mean by that? The kind of information that is usually hard to come by. Something tells me that's your wheelhouse, Lenny."

Lenny put down his silverware and pulled up tight to the table -- or as tight as his prominent paunch would permit. "With all due respect, Nick, -- and I hope I can speak freely?"

"By all means."

"Thank you." Lenny struck his pose once again and Nick prepared himself for another pearl of insight spoken through half-chewed food. "Nick, this doesn't cry out to me as a situation that really needs…," Lenny said using air quotes, *to be fucked with*. Do you know what I'm saying? And without casting any aspersions or making any judgments mind you, the guys in the plane, were apparently doing --- something --- that sufficiently pissed the government off to the point where --- well --- they blew 'em up." Lenny said with his hands in the air. "Does it really matter why?" he asked plaintively. "Do you really want to stick your neck out to protest US immigration policy?" Lenny waited, but didn't get a response. "Why don't you pick a cause with more wide-spread appeal? Like, Save the Whales. Everybody loves whales and the government rarely kills anyone trying to save one."

"I can give you five thousand dollars a week."

"Goddamnit, these people need help. And let me ask you: Is there anything better than when principle coincides with profit? I think not."

Nick stood up and threw a fifty-dollar bill on the table to cover the tab despite the waiter's generous offer. "I'll decide what I'm going to do within the next day or two. I'll call you either way." Nick turned his back on Lenny and headed for the door.

"I'll wait for your call, Nick." Lenny had to yell as Nick seemed in a hurry. "Take your time deciding what you're gonna do. But I really think we have to get into the fight on this one. Am I right?"

CHAPTER 5

Nick stopped at the mailbox and un-wrinkled Randolph Charlton's note to make sure that he was at the right address. Unfortunately, in a not so nice section of Miami, he had indeed found the home of Jorge Diaz. Nick crushed the scrap of paper and shoved it back into his shirt pocket. What seemed like a practical necessity only a few hours before, now felt like an obligation that usually comes by way of a short straw.

As he approached the front door, Nick decided to stall by looking around the neighborhood. It seemed quiet --- too quiet; almost somber. He couldn't tell if the neighborhood was truly in mourning or if he was just projecting the apparent pallor given the unpleasantness of the task at hand. In either event, the only discernible sounds were from some young boys clamoring around his car. Nick couldn't help but wonder if they were the ones that would be growing up without a father.

"May I help you?"

Nick peered through the wire-mesh portion of the screen door and was startled to see a fairly attractive woman wearing a smile. She was in her mid-thirties, with dark brown hair that hung just above the straps of a pale-yellow dress. "I'm looking for a Mrs. Diaz."

"I'm Maria Diaz," she said, nudging the door open an inch.

"And are you the ---- wife --- of Jorge Diaz by any chance?"

"Yes, I am," she responded through the tiny slit between the screen door and the jamb. "And may I ask who you are, sir?"

Nick ran his hand through his hair and paused as long as he could. "My name is Nicholas De Julia, and I'm a lawyer. I've come to discuss an accident which —- may have involved your husband."

Nick saw Maria swallow hard, as her bottom lip began to quiver. "Well it's nice to meet you, Mr. De Julia, but I'm afraid that I really don't have the time to talk to you right now. Please accept my apology. Perhaps you could come back some other day?" she said, trying to sound unaffected.

Nick looked behind the bravery of Maria's smile and saw a woman who was far more comfortable with uncertainty than the prospect of reality. "Are you certain, Mrs. Diaz? I have come a long way to speak with you."

"I really don't think it's a good idea. My sons are going to be home soon and you being here would just make them ask a lot of questions. I think it best if you leave but thank you for stopping by." Maria closed the door abruptly and retreated through the living room and into the kitchen. Nick wanted to call out to her, but a sense of propriety gagged him. If she wasn't ready to talk, he wasn't going to force the issue.

Nick turned for his car and glanced across the street where a young father was teaching his son to hit a baseball. He watched as the boy's dad positioned the bat over his son's head and then guided him through the mechanics of a level swing. The father then stepped away and watched his boy strike an awkward stance with the bat unsteadily swaying above his head. The boy then demonstrated his swing three or four times, with the weight of the bat nearly pulling him over at the end of each cut. Sufficiently impressed with his son's progress, the young dad reminded his boy to "keep his eye on the ball", stepped back, and tossed him an underhand pitch. Just as the little boy made his first contact, the Diaz's screen door closed behind Nick. Unannounced, he entered the house and trespassed his way through the living room and into the kitchen where he found Maria slumped over the sink, crying.

"I want to help find out what happened to your husband --- and that's the only reason why I came here today."

Maria spun around, her eyes red with anger and her face wet from tears. "Nothing has happened to my husband. Do you hear me? Nothing! He's alive and well."

"It's possible, but not probable." Nick's directness and

confidence scared her, but she tried not to show it.

"How dare you come into..."

"It's also possible," Nick said, speaking over Mrs. Diaz, "that the United States government murdered your husband."

Maria was momentarily stunned but quickly regained her defiance. "I already told you that I don't want to hear this. My husband is alive, and I don't want to hear another word about it. Now you get the hell..."

"It's true." Nick said barely above a whisper. "I have no reason to lie to you. I spoke to someone who was there." Nick gave Mrs. Diaz a moment to prepare for his account of the events that would forever change her life. "Your husband's plane was shot down near Key West. A man who witnessed the incident also told me that he saw members of the Coast Guard pull a body from the water."

Maria's voice suddenly lost all its anger. "This person actually saw a body? What did he look like? What was he wearing?" Her questions caught Nick by surprise, and for a fleeting moment, he considered lying to buoy her spirits, but couldn't bring himself to do it.

"I don't think he could see that type of detail from his vantage point."

"Well, what did he see? Please tell me." Maria asked desperately.

Nick chose his words carefully. "He saw a small plane get hit by some type of projectile; he saw the plane hit the water; and he saw a body being taken out of the water by the Coast Guard. And that's all I know, I swear it." Maria had heard enough. She stepped around her kitchen table and threw an open hand punch that caught Nick flush, just inside his left ear. And although he saw it coming, he didn't do anything to avoid it. If it was something that Maria needed, he was happy to oblige and made no effort to touch or rub where she had hit him. "Now you listen to me. My husband is alive. I feel it. I feel it in my heart, deep in a place where only he can touch. So, don't you stand in my house and tell me that my children have no father. I won't stand for it."

"Mrs. Diaz, --- something very strange happened out there, and it may have --- and I stress -- may have -- cost your husband his life. Now, it was not my intention to come here and upset you. I just thought that you would want to know. I also thought that you may have citizenship issues, or ---" Nick stammered, not wanting to offend, "other concerns that might make it difficult for you to inquire about such a situation. So, I'd like to make the necessary inquiries on your behalf."

Maria wiped her nose with the back of her hand while she mulled over Nick's offer. "What are you saying?"

"Well, the only way to find out exactly what happened to your husband would be to --- petition --- the government, for lack of a better word, for information. I mean, we know they have him," Nick paused trying to be compassionate, "one way or another."

Maria looked at Nick with pleading in her eyes. "Are you certain," she whispered, "that this witness saw the Coast Guard retrieve only one body from the water??"

Nick quickly ran through Albert's account in his mind so as not to make a mistake. "That's what he said." Maria shut her eyes tight, but that only forced more tears to rush down her cheeks. "Your husband wasn't alone on the plane?"

Maria shook her head. "No, he was not." Maria looked at Nick through the blur of her tears. "So, sir, how do you propose to petition the sea for information on whichever body it has?" Nick pulled out a kitchen chair, took a seat, and reached out to hold Mrs. Diaz's trembling hands.

"Look at me." Even in soft tones, Nick's words were commanding. "I don't care how many people were on that plane. No private plane should ever be shot down in America."

Maria pulled her hands from Nick's. "How do you know what my husband was doing? Maybe his plane was filled with cocaine or guns. He is Cuban, you understand, so he must have been doing something awful, right? I'm sure the papers will say that he was connected to some Columbian drug cartel or some South American war lord."

"But we both know the truth, don't we?"

"And what truth is that, Mr. De Julia?"

Nick needed a break, so he decided to bluff. "That your husband was risking his own life to save someone he never even met." Nick watched as Maria's expression softened, telling him that Lenny was on the mark. "Or at least that's what I've heard." Maria felt the weight of a great burden lift from her conscience. "I need your authority before I can dig into this thing. Now, my intention is to keep this quiet and away from all media attention, but, of course, I can't guarantee that'll happen." Nick hesitated and then added. "And in reality, it probably won't happen. More likely than not this type of thing will eventually lead the nightly news."

Maria put her hand over her mouth and muttered, "I don't know what to do."

Compassion is not ordinarily the hallmark of a good lawyer, but Nick summoned all that he had. "I'm asking you to please let me do this. And if you really think about it, what's your alternative --- to just forget it ever happened?" Nick tried to get Maria to look at him. "Could you even do that?"

"It's something that we discussed a million times. I just never believed it could happen." Nick kept his composure but wasn't entirely sure he understood. "We have sons and that was always our number one goal. I can't jeopardize their future."

"Isn't that all the more reason why you should want to learn what happened to their father?" Maria was at a crossroads that perhaps only she understood, so Nick decided to subtly alter his approach.

"When I first told you this horrible news, your initial, gut reaction was that your husband was still alive. You absolutely believed it when you said it. And in that moment, even I felt how much you believed it in your soul. So maybe that type of feeling shouldn't be ignored. Maybe, and I pray this is true —- you're right. But the only way to find out is to let me find out for you."

Even in her deepest upset, Maria reached over and touched Nick's hand as if to say, thank you. "But what Jorge was doing was illegal. We both know that. And courts don't ever look the other way when someone does the wrong thing for the right reasons. This is the only home our sons have known, and I can't risk it being taken from them." Maria began frantically wiping all sadness from her face when she heard her sons come in the back door. They were loud with laughter as children often are. They each yelled an "hola" to their mother as they passed by the kitchen and into the living room. She returned the pleasantry without even a trace of sadness in her voice.

"Mrs. Diaz, to be perfectly frank with you, I'm not really sure what the hell your husband was up to, so I can't look you in the eye and say that no harm would come to you if I go nosing around, especially where the government is the would-be defendant. But still, this whole thing just --- seems crazy. And I just think ..."

Words rarely escaped the great Nicholas De Julia, but Maria Diaz had gotten to him. There was a real sincerity to her fear, rational or not, and Nick felt it. Yet he wanted to persevere. Nick had always been coolly analytical, but now he was acting anything but. It was as if he was on autopilot, being urged forward, and it made him feel alive and vital. And like an addict, Nick only cared about obtaining the objective, which in this case was Maria Diaz's assent to take the next step, whatever that was.

Nick tried to think of something so persuasive that Mrs. Diaz could not ignore it, something so profound that she would have no choice but to conjure the necessary courage to risk it all. In essence, Nick needed a one-sentence closing argument; one clear, cogent thought that would make an impression on Maria Diaz's soul. He needed to be the Nick De Julia of old.

"Mrs. Diaz, if there's one thing about this country that separates it from the rest of the world, it's that one single individual, with the courage of his or her convictions, can change the law for everyone."

"I'm not interested in changing the law for everyone. I just want to protect my family." Clearly, Nick was rusty.

"What if I told you that I could protect your family and still find out what happened to your husband? Would you let me go forward then?"

"You just said a minute ago that you couldn't promise me that."

"I know what I said, but I'm telling you that I'll think of some way to do it. And I promise you that I won't move forward until I check with you and give you the game-plan."

Mrs. Diaz pondered Nick's remark to the backdrop of her children happily playing Nintendo but gave not the slightest clue as to which way she was leaning.

"I know that you have no reason to, but if you could just trust me, then maybe..." Nick let his incomplete thought dangle for a moment or two

Maria took several deep breaths, nodded with her eyes shut, and said, "Okay."

Okay was the last word Nick expected to hear. And in a very real sense, it frightened him. "Are you sure?" he asked cautiously, fully aware that he had no plan at all.

"No, but you have my permission anyway, as well as my

gratitude. I just hope you know what you're doing, for all of our sakes." Maria got up and walked over to the counter. She stuck her hand in a drawer and pulled out her checkbook. "How much will this cost, for you to help us?" Nick waited for Maria to sit down before he leaned over and gently took the checkbook from her. Carefully, he ripped off the top check, folded it in half, and stuck it into his pants pocket. "I haven't signed that yet, Mr. De Julia."

"You don't need to." Nick stood up and extended his hand to his new client. "I'm going to head back to Key West now. It'll probably take me a day or two to decide just how I want to proceed, but I'll be in touch after that. And please don't worry – we have an agreement. I won't do anything major without checking with you."

"And what should I do in the meantime?"

"Just let me know if you hear anything that might be of interest." Nick turned to walk out.

"Thank you, sir."

"Don't thank me yet. Thank me when your husband comes home." Nick smiled at Mrs. Diaz who appreciated the optimism, even if insincere.

CHAPTER 6

As Nick pulled into Old Town, he couldn't help but allow himself a brief smile. Despite having been gone less than a day he missed the uniqueness of the island and the eccentricities of its inhabitants, both of which were on full display in the late-day sun. Even the barefoot bums, some of which were undoubtedly former lawyers, turned to look at the car with the throaty growl as it glided by. The Georgian architecture along the lower end of Simonton Street, surrounded by lazily waving palm trees seemed equally welcoming. Perhaps Key West had become home.

Thankful for the turbocharger in his car, Nick had made it to Key Largo to meet Charlton, Delray Beach to meet Lenny and Miami to meet Maria all before sunset. With the whole of Route 1 South now separating Nick from the sadness in Maria Diaz's eyes, he began to feel the first pangs of ambivalence; and of all things, it was Lenny's un-urbane question which now ricocheted through Nick's mind: Why, Nick thought, do I give a shit about any of this? Maybe Marty was right, Nick thought. Maybe I'm just weak and want to be loved...by anyone...and everyone. Or worse yet, he pondered, maybe I am looking for redemption.

The prospect of becoming embroiled in this struggle did have some positive attributes, though. For one, he was enjoying a budding sense of purpose. There was work to be done. On the other hand, Nick's stomach pain reminded him that he was most decidedly back in the law.

Many years ago, Nick swore that he would never make a

major life decision without at least forty-five minutes of calm reflection and a quality smoke. So, Nick proceeded to his part of the island, made one final turn and pulled his car onto the crushed stone that was his driveway. A flood tide filled the air with the salty-sweet aroma of accomplishment and financial independence, and Nick breathed deeply. The late afternoon trade-winds had cooled off the day and Nick was suddenly struck with the desire to reacquaint himself with Iris before heading for the humidor.

Nick left his bag in the car and leapt up the porch. All seemed normal until he walked in and saw the concern on Iris's face. For a split second, he thought that she was still annoyed at his abrupt departure. But as one second turned into ten, Nick knew that something else was up. There was a palpable tension, as the two stared at each other without uttering a word. Nick stayed absolutely still until Iris very deliberately moved her eyes toward the back hallway and, with a subtle head tilt, motioned that Nick should leave. Understanding fully what she was trying to silently convey, Nick didn't waste a single second as he walked through the house directly toward what Iris had hoped he would avoid. Nick picked up speed, turned the corner, and stopped short when he saw an older man, dressed like a tourist, standing in the hallway inspecting one of Nick's paintings.

"Who the hell are you?" Nick asked angrily.

"I'm Adrian Olin," the man responded calmly. "Is this an original Miro?" he asked, tilting his head backward to make use of the bottom half of his bifocals.

"That's none of your Goddamn business."

"It's striking, absolutely beautiful. I particularly like the intensity of the brighter colors juxtaposed to those that are more muted."

"Look pal, you've got about five seconds to get the hell out of here."

"You never answered me -- is this an original?" For an intruder he was incredibly calm and polite. Nick reached over and yanked the man's attention away from the art. In full face, Adrian Olin did not seem too frightening; he had a soft appearance, with deep blue eyes that looked brave but friendly. And in spite of Nick's battery, he still had a pleasant smile. "It's a pleasure to meet you, Nick." Olin shifted a tan paper bag to his left hand, offering his right for a handshake, which Nick cautiously accepted. I'm sorry to meet you like this, but it's kind of important that you and I speak for a minute. Would you mind asking the young lady to leave?"

"I would mind and I'm not at all interested in having a conversation until you tell me who you are and what you want."

"No problem at all, but could we at least go somewhere that's a little more private? I think that it's in both of our interests." Nick stared down his guest but couldn't dim the pleasant look on his face. A few seconds later, Nick gestured toward the rear of the house and Olin obediently walked clear to the far railing of the observation deck. "What a view. My God, that's breathtaking."

Nick wasn't gentle about closing the double glass doors behind him. "Alright, enough with the horse-shit. Who are you with, the FBI?"

Olin took one last gaze and then turned back around. "I'm sorry --- what did you say?"

Nick was quickly losing his patience. "I asked if you were with the Goddamn FBI."

"No. I tried to get in there early on in my career, but they wouldn't take me. They said I was too overweight, but that's another story. No, I'm actually with the INS."

"The INS?"

"That's right. And this is for you, my friend." Nick took a step backward as Olin raised the bag up and pointed it at him. Nick stared at the bag, trying his best not to look frightened. "I said I was with the INS not the KGB. Take it easy, will ya?" Olin tossed the bag to him. "Go ahead and open it. You'll be happy; I guarantee it." Nick continued to hold the bag away from himself, unsure what was going down. "Go on already."

Like a father watching his son open a Christmas present, Olin waited for Nick's reaction. As the bag fell to the floor, Nick looked down and saw an unopened box of his favorite Petit del Punch cigars with the official green and white seal of the Cuban government unbroken and in the appropriate corner. "I told you you'd be happy, Nick. What do you say we crack the seal on those and enjoy a couple. I mean, I know it's old hat for you but I've never smoked one in such a beautiful setting. You're not gonna deprive me of that, are you?"

It was rather clear that anger wasn't intimidating Nick's guest, so he decided to employ a new tact. With a deep sigh and a phony smile, he tried to appear won over. "I wouldn't think of it. Why don't you have a seat?"

"I appreciate that," Olin said, as he dragged two deck chairs next to each other. For his part, Nick expertly pulled the finish nail from the top of the box, slit the seal, and offered his guest first choice. "Thank you." Olin ogled the little cigar from top to bottom, paying particular attention to its red and gold band. "That is a fine-looking cigar. Excellent construction, wouldn't you agree?"

"I would," Nick said matter-of-factly as he pulled one from the box. "Here you go," Nick said as he tossed Olin a solid gold, S.T. DuPont torch lighter. "There's a cutter hinged to the back. Just flick it out."

"No thanks." Olin flipped the lighter back to Nick. "I'm a lowly civil servant, Nick. We don't get gold lighters until we retire." Olin then bit the end off the cigar and held up a book of matches. "And even then, they're never really gold."

"Suit yourself." Both men lit up using their implement of choice and took a seat. The fact that Olin showed up with a box of Nick's favorite cigars was not lost on the host. But Nick acted as though it had gotten by him. Olin clearly wanted to convey that he had done his homework, and Nick clearly wanted to convey that it didn't phase him.

Nick assumed his usual smoking posture, taking several smooth pulls from his cigar. Olin, on the other hand, inelegantly puffed on his while continuing to make believe that he appreciated the view. "Damn good, huh, Adrian?" Nick said with a little dab of sarcasm.

"Absolutely. You just can't beat a Cuban cigar. But you already knew that, didn't you, Nick?"

"Who's your source for these things?" Nick asked through his own smarmy smile, unrepentant for his very illegal habit.

"You're kidding, right?"

"Not at all. I'm always interested in finding a new supplier."

Olin laughed and took another few puffs. "The supplier in this instance would be me. I'm out of the country a lot and rarely have to bother with any pesky Customs requirements when I return. Perk of the job, I guess."

"Would you mind picking me up a few boxes of these on your next trip? I wouldn't mind paying a premium for any inconvenience it causes you."

"We could arrange that. That's very possible, indeed."

"I would appreciate that sincerely." Now it was Nick's turn to feign interest in the reddish glow shimmering in front of the southernmost sunset. And at that moment, Olin knew that he had his hands full. Nick was trying to wrest control of the conversation, but Olin would have none of it.

"Say, do you ever hear from that beautiful ex-wife of yours?"

"Only on the back of my checks."

Olin tried not to but couldn't help laughing. "That's very witty, very witty indeed. I heard you were very smart."

"Don't get too excited, it's from a Michael Franks song. So, I guess you're gonna have to break into his house and blow smoke up his ass."

"Maybe tomorrow. But for now, I'm content just sitting here talking with you."

"I'm afraid you're about to find out that I'm not much of a conversationalist."

"That's okay. I'm pretty good at getting people to talk."

"Really...and is that another perk of the job?"

"Is what a perk of the job?"

"Persuading people to talk. I thought that was more the CIA's thing?"

"No, I'm pretty good at it too. Olin widened his smile. "What can I tell you --- I'm a people person. I love to chit-chat."

"And what is it that you'd like to talk about?"

"Marquesa." Now both men were looking out over the ocean pretending to enjoy the view. "I'd like to talk about Marquesa."

Nick took a long pull on his cigar, held it for a moment, and exhaled a slow, confident stream of thick white smoke that only comes from the very best Cubanos. "Marquesa... Great place to fish; or at least that's what I hear."

"That's true, that's true. But I'm a little more interested in discussing what you think may have happened out there recently."

"I have no idea what you're talking about."

"Oh, come on, sure you do."

Nick snapped his fingers and pointed at Olin. "Oh, excuse me, I do think I know what you're talking about. Marquesa – yes. Isn't that where a couple of Cuban-Americans were recently murdered in an unprovoked attack by representatives of the United

States government?" Nick let his quizzical look slowly fade into a glare before continuing. "But then again, you already knew that, didn't you, Adrian?"

Olin tapped his cigar several times on the arm of the chair until all excess ash was gone. His lips were pursed and he shook his head from side to side; apparently, he did not appreciate Nick's sense of humor. "You know, Nick, I love to study people. I really do. Maybe that's why I got involved with government law enforcement. And you know one thing I've learned about people such as yourself?"

"What's that?" Nick asked, content to play along for the moment.

"Whenever someone has mastered some very tiny aspect of the universe or achieved real excellence in one area of concentration —- they're always arrogant enough to think that they know everything. People like you never even leave open the possibility that you could be missing the bigger picture."

"Is that a fact?"

"It's an absolute fact. You see, people like me are trained to be circumspect. Do you understand what I mean by that?"

"'Careful to consider all circumstances?"

"Well, have you done that in this instance, Nick? Have you considered all possible consequences of your actions?" Nick didn't respond; he just took another draw on his cigar and brushed some wayward ash off his leg. "No, you haven't done that. Do you know why you haven't done that?" Again, Nick appeared more interested in his smoke than Olin's soliloquy. "Because you have no fucking idea what you're involving yourself in. You couldn't even begin to fathom the global implications that could stem from yesterday's events. Are you listening to me, you smug little prick?"

Finally, looking far less aloof, Nick temporarily ignored his cigar and turned to face Olin. "So, what do you want from me?"

"All we want is for you to forget about this whole thing and enjoy your very early retirement. It's as simple as that. I mean, come on, look at all this. I can't imagine it's hard to be happy here, especially with that knockout in the kitchen."

"That's all you're looking for, ---for me to just walk away?"

"And you'll be taking the gratitude of your government with you; not a bad chit to have, my friend."

"I'm afraid you're gonna have to do a little better than that, my friend. And for starters, I'd like to know why you shot down a private plane."

"I'm afraid I can't discuss specifics with you, Nick. All I can tell you is that the entire incident is a matter of national security."

"National security," Nick said mockingly. "Then how come someone from the National Security Counsel or the CIA isn't paying me a visit bearing gifts?"

"To be honest with you, we're hoping that that doesn't become necessary. But, of course, that's up to you. As far as we're concerned, though, this is a matter of national security and, as such, I'm not permitted to discuss specifics with you or anyone else. I'm sorry to hide behind that, but that's the way it is."

"And what do you expect me to say to the dead guy's wife, 'Sorry, but you'll never know why your husband was murdered because that's the way it is'?"

Olin raised his eyebrows high onto his forehead and shrugged his shoulders.

"Look, Nick, I'm sorry for Mrs. Diaz's loss but ---"

"But what?"

"Let's just say that the United States Government --- your government --- didn't murder anyone out at Marquesa, okay?"

"Oh, it was self-defense? That F-16 thought that the tiny, unarmed prop plane was a threat to the homeland out in the middle of the open ocean? Is that the idea? Or are you trying to tell me that the sputtering Cessna had missile lock?"

"I'm not trying to tell you anything. I said what I wanted to say--- more, in fact. You can believe it or not. I really don't give a damn either way. All I am really interested in knowing is whether or not you're prepared to serve your country."

"Trite references to patriotism aside, you want me to keep my mouth shut."

"What we are asking you to do is simply understand that this is a highly sensitive matter that requires containment --- informational containment in the name of national security."

Nick shut his eyes tight for a moment and then looked out over the ocean, unsure what to do. Different scenarios ran through his head, but nothing seemed workable. He thought of Maria Diaz and still felt like he owed her his best efforts, even under the evolving circumstances. He thought of Marty and how he predicted that looking into the matter would spell disaster. "I'll tell you what I'm willing to do: I'll drop the matter if you return the bodies for a decent burial."

"That's not my department, Nick, and I'm not here to negotiate. I just need to know whether or not you're willing, for the good of the country, to forget about what you think happened out there and put all this unpleasantness behind you?"

"And if I'm not?"

"Then you'd be making a very foolish mistake."

Nick was no longer glib, he was concerned at the seriousness in Olin's tone. "Is that a threat?"

"Not in the slightest. If anything I've said or intimated here today has left you with such an impression, please accept my apology. But, that said, you should know that we will do whatever's necessary to contain this situation." Olin paused so his words could fight their way through the lingering fog and into Nick's deliberations. "So, my friend, can we count on you?"

Nick turned to Olin and waited for an uncomfortable amount of time. He looked away for a moment and then extended his hand. "Yes, you can."

"That's a good man. And your country appreciates it. Thank you, Nick." With that, Adrian Olin stamped out his cigar on the arm of Nick's white, Adirondack chair and headed for the door.

"Hey, Adrian?"

"Yeah."

"How do I find you when I want to call in my marker?"

Olin held up his card and dropped it on top of Nick's humidor. As he headed for the front door, Olin paused only to tip his Miami Dolphins cap to Iris as she ran by him toward the deck. By the time Olin had sauntered across Nick's front lawn and reached the street, his driver was waiting.

"Well, boss, is he gonna play ball?" Young Agent Fletcher asked.

"Not a chance in hell," Olin rasped through a disgusted look on his face. "Get on the phone, call Washington and tell 'em that we have a problem. Have one of our lawyers placed in the Dade County DA's office and the United States Attorney's office in the Miami Federal Court. Activate the taps at all four locations and get an eye on him and that little beach bunny in there. All reports go directly to me, understood? I want each previous day's transcript in my hand by 7:30 every morning." Unable to control his anger any longer, the burly Olin took off his cap and slammed it on the dashboard. "Fletcher, did you hear me?"

"Of course I heard you."

"Well, then, say something, like 'I've got it' -- 'okay, boss' -- 'yeah'. Give me some sign of acknowledgment so I don't think I'm talking to the Goddamn wind."

"I'm sorry. I mean, I heard you. It's just that ..."

"What, what?"

"Shouldn't we turn this over to the FBI or the CIA? I mean, jurisdictionally..."

"I don't give a shit about jurisdiction. I finally got a high-profile assignment and I'm gonna handle it."

"Okay, boss. I'm sorry."

"Oh, shut the hell up." Olin waved off his rookie's mea culpa. "You make me sick, Fletcher. Just take me to the hotel you useless idiot."

By the time she reached the deck, Iris found Nick lounging as comfortably as ever, enjoying his cigar. She knelt down in front of him and sweetly asked if everything was alright. Nick nodded reassuringly and as he lifted his cigar to his mouth for the next draw, ever so slowly placed his index finger across his lips telling Iris to remain quiet. Nick then stood up, took her hand and led her down the stairs and onto the beach. Both kicked off their shoes and walked until they were ankle deep in the surf. Tiny waves curled a few feet in front of them and then dropped right where they were standing. The green, foamy water would then spill past them and sizzle against the white sand of Nick's backyard. The two were facing the last five or so minutes of the descending sun. Nick put his arm around Iris and pulled her close; she, in turn, placed her head in the crux of his neck.

"Sweetheart," Nick whispered.

"Yes."

"I don't want you to move or show any emotion at all. Just stay right here and act like we're in love." Iris didn't need to act, but smartly, she kept that fact to herself. "Do you understand?"

"Yes."

"We're being watched right now. And the house as well as the phones, I imagine, are bugged." Nick kissed her on the forehead, pulling her even closer. "So, I want you to listen to me and do exactly as I say without any questions, okay?"

"Of course, Nick. I'll do whatever you want."

"Good. Do you still have some of the money that I left you?"

"All of it."

"And you still belong to the gym, right?"

Iris pulled a few inches away from Nick and motioned toward her own body as if to say, obviously.

"Good. Now, listen carefully, please. Take the money with you when you leave tonight, but otherwise, go about your normal routine. Tomorrow morning put on one of your sundresses and a pair of heels, but throw the money, a pair of jeans, a pair of sneakers, the ugliest top you have, and a baseball cap in a bag." Nick thought a little deeper for a minute. "And make sure your roommate goes along with you."

"Tammy?"

"Yes, Tammy," Nick said tersely. "Does she have a car?"

"Sure."

"Alright, I want you to take the bag and go to the gym. I want it to look like you're just going for a workout. Go right into the locker room and change. Leave your sundress and the bag in the locker. Have Tammy pull up to the front door of the gym about fifteen minutes later. Are you getting this?"

"I've got it. Go ahead."

"Pull the cap down tight over your eyes, tuck all your hair up under, and walk directly to her car. After you get in tell her to drive away slowly, okay? No tire screeching."

"Then what?"

"I want you to go to the mall and use the money to buy three flip phones. Put them in your roommate's name and make sure I can tell which phone number goes with which phone."

"Got it."

"And then have her drive to the Boca Cheeca boat landing. It's at mile marker 182, about fifteen minutes out of Key West."

"And then?"

"That's where I'll meet you."

"How are you gonna get there?"

"Don't worry about it. Just try to be there by 9:30."

"Okay, I'll be there."

Nick pulled slightly away from Iris and faced her. "Don't you even want to know who's watching us, or why?"

Iris stood up on her perfectly painted toes and kissed Nick as another tiny wave brushed past them. "I don't care 'who' or 'why'. I just want to help you."

"I appreciate that, sweetheart," Nick said sincerely. "I really do."

CHAPTER 7

Iris stepped from her car looking particularly gorgeous. She had on a short yellow dress that demanded attention, thick brown sunglasses, and a pair of white, open-toe shoes with a clear plastic heel. And slung over her tawny shoulder was a black, nylon bag.

"Will you look at that ass? It's perfect."

"Knock it off, McGregor."

"I'm serious. When have you ever seen an ass like that? Or legs like that? She's unbelievable. This De Julia guy is straight up crazy. If I was him, I'd live in the bedroom and never come up for air."

"That's enough. Just keep an eye on her."

McGregor kept the binoculars pressed hard to his face. "Oh, crap."

"What is it?"

"She's goin' to workout. And with a body like that, you know she's gonna be on a Stair-master for three hours. You better call in and tell them we're stuck."

"Boss, this is Ericson and McGregor."

"What is it?"

"We're with the girlfriend."

"Where is she?"

"At a place called Workout Plus. She's probably going to be a while."

"How did she get there?"

"She drove herself."

57

"Okay. Keep a wide perimeter but stay with her."

"Roger that."

Several minutes later, a boyish looking Iris swung open the gym door and calmly walked up to her roommate's car. She didn't get in right away, choosing instead to lean in through the passenger window as if having an impromptu conversation with a friend. Thirty seconds later she and Tammy were on their way to the mall as McGregor and Ericson began wasting their time staring at the tinted gym windows.

Looking every bit like the cover model for Fly Fisherman's Quarterly, Nick walked along captain's row, rod and reel in hand, concentrating on those boats that looked familiar to him. He asked a few guides about the possibility of a charter but begged off when he found out that in each instance there would be other clients on board. No, he needed a two-man skiff, but most of those were run by the island's young guns, and that, Nick had decided, was out as well. For this day's run he needed a more sea-seasoned guide, preferably a conch. That was his best chance.

As Nick stood panning the boat slips and his dwindling options, he noticed the futile sound of a motor that was not about to turn over any time soon. Several slips away, and mostly obscured by a number of larger, more impressive skiffs, stood a very old man inside a very old boat. It was Captain Bra, the regular from Captain Tommy's. He watched intently as the wizened skipper alternated between priming the motor and unsuccessfully tugging on the engine's ripcord. It was clear that the motor, the boat, and its aged captain had each seen better days. In short, Nick had found his man.

"Can I give you a hand there?" Nick asked.

The now winded captain peered through his fingers, trying to shield his eyes from the bright sunlight at Nick's back, and politely waved him off. "Thanks anyway but she'll kick over. It just takes a while sometimes." Four more quick pulls produced nothing except four puffs of black exhaust.

"Are you sure I can't help you out? I'm pretty good with

motors."

The captain looked the motor over one last time, hoping to recognize the problem on his own, and then checked to see if any of the younger captains were watching. With noticeable reluctance, the captain smiled and said, "I certainly would be obliged for the help."

Nick had seen Bra a hundred times before but never really looked him over. Although some people look very good in a beard, the captain wasn't one of them; in fact, he had the distinct appearance of someone who couldn't afford a razor. The skin on his face and the exposed parts of his arms were loose and sallow; his white hair was long in the back, bushy at his sideburns and wet from sweat. But his most defining feature was the thick, black bags beneath his eyes. He looked more homeless than heroic, but Nick was convinced that there was no better choice for what he needed.

Nick popped off the engine's plastic casing and began to pinch, twist, and pull at the engine's circuitry. "Have you got a screwdriver?"

"Flat or Phillips?"

"Flat."

"Here you go."

"Thanks." Two clockwise turns and one pull of the ripcord later, the senior member of the marina was back in business. "And there you have it."

"Hey, hey, that was pretty impressive, Nick. To be honest with ya, I thought she was dead."

"No, it was more like a reversible coma."

"How do you know so much about boats? I always heard you were more of a land lover."

"Back when I was a lawyer, I handled a case where a guy got injured when one of these blew up. So, I had no choice but to become kind of a half-ass outboard expert."

"Isn't that something? And you really got to know motors because of a lawsuit?"

"Well, the wheels of justice turn pretty slowly, and I made damn sure they did in that case because I was getting paid by the hour." Nick said with the warmest smile he could muster.

"Very shrewd."

Nick took a second to look at the inside of Bra's boat in detail. Everything was old, corroded, and discolored, but seemed operational all the same. The boat's radio was held together with what looked like a combination of super glue and duct tape, but hisses, squeals and the occasional voice blurted out of it with regularity.

"I even have an older one if you can believe it," Bra said, referencing the radio. "I actually keep one next to my bed at home and run it all night. Can't seem to sleep without it in the background." Bra shrugged. "Plus, the only people I ever talk to are boaters, and it's a helluva lot cheaper than having a phone."

Nick nodded and threw the old timer a smile. "Say, are you booked today?"

"I wish. I'm afraid it's been a while since I was booked. My eyes ain't what they used to be. And, to be honest, poling a skiff has always been a young man's game."

"Then how come you're still out here?"

"What choice do I have? At my age it's wear-out or rust-out; there ain't much in the middle, know what I mean?"

"Ah, come on, you're not that old."

"Are you kidding? I tell everybody that I came with the place when the US bought it from France." Nick laughed, taken by the old man's self-deprecating charm. "Are you interested in going fishing?" Bra asked skeptically. "Never heard of you spending any time on the flats."

"Well I'm looking to try it, so I figured why not start out at the top. Can you take me out today?"

Bra seemed instantly energized. "Absolutely... I'm your man. I run both half and full-day charters."

"What are we talking?" Nick said as he rubbed his thumb against his index and middle fingers.

"A half a day is $375, and a full day is $450."

"A half a day doesn't seem like much of a bargain."

"That's the general idea behind the pricing structure."

"Very shrewd yourself."

"Thanks all the same, but I'm pretty certain I didn't invent that concept."

"Well, I hate to waste money, so I guess I'll take a full day."

"Great. Is there any place in particular you'd like to go today?"

"Marquesa."

"Are you sure? You don't mind crossing the Boca Grande

Channel?"

"Not at all. Especially since I have no idea what that is?"

"It's a pretty nasty confluence of where the Atlantic Ocean meets the Gulf of Mexico. Makes for some severe chop."

Nick shrugged his shoulders. "Does it scare you?"

"Are you shitting me?" Bra said defiantly. "I could cross that bath water in my sleep."

"Well, alright, then, but I would like you to do something for me before we leave." Bra waited to hear what it was. "Do you know the harbormaster?"

"Of course. I've known Teddy for years. He was one of the first..."

"Whatever." Nick said, rudely interrupting. "Why don't you go in and tell him that you've booked a client and that you'll be running out to Marquesa today."

Bra did not seem to like that suggestion at all. "Look, I know you're new and all, but I don't know of any captain who announces where they're going for the day. It just ain't done. Ol' Teddy will think I finally lost what little of my mind I have left. That kind of information is what you might call propriet." Nick knew he was shooting for *proprietary* and saw no reason to correct him. "If I advertise where we're headin', every young captain will run right out there after us. I might be half blind, but I still know where to find 'em, and they all know that."

"I appreciate you looking out for me, but all the same, I'd like you to just tell good Ol' Teddy where we'll be fishing today."

Captain Bra mulled over the closest thing to an ethical dilemma he had faced in the last quarter century. "I won't be doing you any favors, you understand?" I guarantee ya, it'll look like an armada out there by noon."

"I see. Okay, how 'bout this, do it... and I'll double your fee."

"The money's got nothing to do with it. I mean, I'm already feelin' guilty that I'm chargin' you full after ya fixed my motor and all. I'm not trying to be a pain in the ass to ya, but is there anything I can say to talk you out of this? I mean, I've been doing this a long time and ..."

"Please don't worry about it. Just do this for me, okay?"

"I'm sure you got your reasons."

Nick grabbed hold of Bra just as he was preparing to exit the boat. "But I don't want him to know that I put you up to this, understand? Make him think that you're just mentioning where you're heading, okay?"

"Sure. Ol' Teddy's gonna think I have a fever but what the hell." Captain Bra steadied himself on one leg for a second before climbing onto the dock. "Why don't you stow your gear. I'll be back in a minute." Captain Bra hobbled along the dock and into the harbormaster's tower for a brief chat. Nick took the rod and reel that he bought the night before and two small travel bags into the boat and pushed his hat off his head to get some sun.

"Okay, we're all set. Are you ready to catch some fish?"

"I am."

"Well, let's hit it then." Happy to be guiding a full day's charter for what could be twice the usual fee, Captain Bra loosened his boat's stern line and idled his fare out of the harbor and toward Garrison Bight. Behind them, standing at the edge of the dock, was a very young and very bewildered INS agent. He pulled out a cell phone and hit only one number. "Boss?"

"Yeah."

"It's Fletcher. De Julia just got on a boat. What should I do?"

"I don't want to talk to you, Fletcher. Where's Stein?"

"He's in talking with the harbormaster."

"Well go get him and put him on."

The first-year agent ran the length of the dock and flagged down his partner as he was exiting the tower. "It's Olin. He wants to talk to you."

"This is Stein."

"What the hell's going on, Ira?"

"Hey, give me a break, will you, Adrian? De Julia chartered a boat to go fishing. What do you expect me to do, swim after him?" You told us to play this guy loose so I didn't set up any contingencies."

"After twenty-seven years in this business you'd think that I'd learn. Every time we do something half-assed it inevitably becomes a cluster."

"Be that as it may, what do you want us to do?"

"Is he with a local captain?"

"Yeah, some guy named Bruce Sanders. He's been a guide down here for fifty something years. They call him 'Captain Bra.' I have no idea if that's a nickname or a fetish."

"Stop screwing around, will ya, Ira. What kind of boat?"

"It's a decrepit wooden skiff. Fifteen feet with a single outboard."

"Do you know where he's going?"

"I'll give you one guess."

"Marquesa."

"Yep."

"What the hell is that son-of-a-bitch looking for at Marquesa?"

"I don't know. Maybe he really wants to fish."

"No way, Ira, not this guy. He's up to something. Alright, to hell with the kinder and gentler approach --- get on the horn to C3; have them raise the aerostats from Shark Key forward and fix each on Marquesa. Tell them to check in with you when they get a visual."

"Don't we have to get the CIA's okay for that?"

"Just call and do it. I'll take responsibility for it."

"If you say so. Do you want the Coast Guard involved?"

"No. Tell them to keep a crew ready, but to stand down unless you give them the go ahead. Let's try to find out what he's up to before we move on him."

"Is that it?"

"Yeah. But make sure you call in hourly."

"Roger that."

"And keep an eye on the kid, Ira. Fletcher worries me."

"Will do." Stein and Fletcher crossed Roosevelt Avenue, walked over to the Attocchia Sub Shop parking lot, and got into their car. Stein picked up the radio and made a series of efficient calls to set up the needed surveillance. Fletcher sat quietly until his partner was through.

"Ira?"

"What?"

"Can I ask you a question?"

"Of course."

Even for a first-year INS agent, Anderson Fletcher seemed awfully unsure of himself. "What's an aerostat?" he asked reluctantly.

Ira Stein remembered what it was like to be a rookie and took pity on the kid. "It's the most sophisticated, land-based surveillance equipment we have."

"Yeah, but what is it, precisely?"

"Well, technically, it's a radar platform. You've seen 'em down here. They look like little blimps. They're only ten or so feet long, filled with helium and tethered with Teflon cable. Anyway, they're actually under the purview of the CIA, but we use them from time to time whenever we want to take a closer look at something."

"I noticed them on the ride down here from Miami. I even asked Olin about 'em, but he said they were some type of weather equipment."

"That's the bullshit line we feed the general public."

"Son-of-a-bitch. And it," Fletcher stammered, hoping to frame an intelligent question, "can see a lot of stuff?"

Ira Stein rolled his eyes before answering. "The correct term of art is *look down capacity*. And the answer to your question is yes, each aerostat has a tremendous look down capacity."

"How good are we talking?"

"Put it this way, the ones we have down here in the Keys can tell us what kind of cigar Castro is smoking when he leaves his house in the morning." Stein glanced over at his smiling partner. "I'm dead serious. The aerostats are that powerful. Anyway, the information is transmitted to a top-secret army facility called C-3. I've never been there personally but I hear it's buried in some mountain in California."

"And what happens then?"

"Somebody with a considerably higher pay grade decides how the information is to be classified and/or dealt with."

"So how long until we hear something?"

"It takes about an hour to raise the things to the proper height and feed in the correct coordinates, so it should pick up De Julia just about the time his boat gets situated in the Marquesas."

"So, what do we do in the meantime?"

"We notify the Coast Guard to stand down --- and then we wait."

Captain Bra pulled a thermos out of the center console and

offered Nick what would be his fourth cup of coffee of the day, which, of course, he accepted. The two men sat side by side as Bra's antiquated boat, the Cross Your Heart, idled through the "no wake" zone. For a fishing guide and a new client, the "no wake" zone is like the first few awkward minutes of a blind date; neither person knows exactly what to say but feels the need to try.

"So, I take it from your gear that you're a fly caster? Is that what you'd like to concentrate on today?" Bra looked at Nick, who was staring over his shoulder at the mouth of the marina. "I said, would you like to fly fish today?"

"I don't think so," Nick said, still fixated on the tail end of the boat's wake.

"Is something wrong back there?" Bra asked with a squint toward the boat's wake.

"No, everything's fine."

"Are you hearing a problem with the motor?"

"No, she sounds good actually."

"I'm glad. To be honest with ya, I thought I was gonna be forced to finally retire this morning before you came along and patched her up. She's been sick as hell all winter, and I sure can't afford a new one. It's become a race to see which one of us dies first, I guess." Captain Bra's joke dissolved into the morning mist without any reaction; clearly, Nick remained far more interested in the view from the rear. "Okay, you might want to hold onto your hat because I'm gonna try to kick her up now."

"Hold on there, Captain."

"Problem?"

"No, but I think I've changed my mind. Instead of fishing out at Marquesa today, why don't we try the backcountry?"

"Oh, I really don't think that would be very productive today. And, while we're on the subject, I really don't think that Marquesa is an ideal place to fish this time of year either," Bra said in a respectful tone of voice intended to spare his client's feelings. "I mean, I'll take you anywhere you want to go to be sure, but if you're looking for the benefit of my experience, I'd suggest we try the flats around Woman Key. It's a much shorter run and a pretty reliable place to find tailin' fish this time of the morning. Plus, it gives you good cover from the wind and that can really help if you do wind up fly casting."

Nick suddenly felt guilty that he had tricked the old man into thinking that they would really be fishing. And he felt even worse when he finally took the time to notice how proud and happy Captain Bra was to be working. This elderly seafarer was actually looking forward to the prospect of spending the next eight hours pushing a boat along an edge so someone else might enjoy the opportunity to catch a fish. Nick nervously peered over his shoulder one more time and decided that someone with yester-generation's work ethic deserved at least half a truth.

"Captain, I really don't have a whole lot of time to explain this, but I need to get to the boat landing at Boca Cheeca. I'm supposed to meet some people there in about forty-five minutes, so I'm afraid we're not gonna be able to fish today. I hope you can accept my apology for that."

Captain Bra gave Nick a different kind of smile but, true to the Key West code, didn't ask any questions. "You better pour that coffee over the side. If we're gonna make it to Boca Cheeca in forty-five minutes, I'm really gonna have to open her up. I wouldn't want you to spill that on yourself."

Nick put his hand on Bra's small shoulder and a squeezed it. "I appreciate that."

"Oh, I don't give a rat's ass about you, to be sure. I just don't want you to spill coffee in my boat." Captain Bra's regular smile returned as he started to turn his boat to the north. A moment later, Nick reached over and grabbed hold of the wheel.

"I'm really sorry about this, and we will fish together soon --- I promise you that."

"That's good to hear, but we do have to get moving. Hold tight."

Captain Bra and Nick stood next to each other directly behind the boat's center console. Each leaned in against the rushing wind as the boat picked up speed and began to weave its way along the pale blue water of the channel toward the backcountry. The Captain, who just figured that Nick was hiding from someone, stayed away from open water whenever possible, choosing instead to cling tight to the mangroves and make use of strategic lees and inlets. He brought Nick through streams and cut-throughs that only a 1930's rum-runner would know of, and he did it while exhibiting expert boatmanship. Nick quickly realized that the self-satisfaction that comes from showing-off apparently survives the aging process, as Captain Bra reveled in his abilities as a boat pilot.

At one point, the Captain steered the skiff between two stretches of mangroves that were no more than fifteen feet apart, and as the boat pushed on, the motor seemed to get louder as the light grew dimmer. Nick looked up and noticed that the tangled tops of these thick mangroves had grown together in a way that created a natural ceiling, letting very little light through even at its entrance. Despite rapidly decreasing visibility, the Captain kept his speed up until the very last of the natural light had faded away. Even though Bra had cut the power to near an idle, the motor's roar fought to survive as it raced away from the boat, bouncing off the leafy green walls of this tropic cave. Unable to see even one foot in front of him, Nick concentrated on the echo until he was only hearing it in his mind. Soon, the squawk of birds just in front of their flapping wings and the emphatic splash of tarpon striking at prey thrust him back into the present and made him grasp the console a little tighter. Even the water gently lapping the sides of the skiff was much louder than normal and created a faint, hollow echo of its own. Neither Nick nor the Captain said anything as the boat floated through this dusky estuary toward a funnel of light which was coming from a bend in this living cave fifty or so yards away. At one point something flew dangerously close to Nick's head and actually picked off his cap, but he still said nothing. Clearly, Captain Bra was helping him out by keeping the boat obscured and the loss of a fishing hat was hardly worth complaint. As the light grew closer, the Captain slowly but steadily tapped up the throttle to full power. Nick looked at him quizzically, having never experienced anything like the tunnel that was now behind him.

"It's called the Green Room," Bra yelled to be heard. "Not too many people know about it."

"I'm very impressed," Nick screamed back.

After fifteen more minutes of full-tilt running, there were no more secrets that lie between the skiff and the Boca Cheeca boat ramp. The Captain pulled tight to a quarter-mile stretch of US Route 1 that was unavoidable and began racing right alongside the endless stream of rental cars heading back toward Miami. The children fishing with hand-lines along the water's edge gave youthful protest to the boat's inconsiderate path which, they knew, would stymie their efforts for at least the next thirty minutes. All Captain Bra could do was yell, "Sorry," through a barrage of high-voiced jeers.

Finally, the Captain broke off to the right and went around several channel markers. He quickly cut the power, causing a backflow of foamy white water to rush over the stern, soaking his client. Again, Nick knew better than to lodge any objections.

"Is this Boca Cheeca?"

"Up there on the left about seventy yards. Can we just pull right in or will we have to get inventive?" Bra inquired.

"No, we should be okay. Famous last words, right?"

"Boy, you can say that twice. If I had a nickel for every time my daddy crossed over from Havana with a hull full only to get nabbed in the marina..."

"You'd be a rich man?"

"No, I would have been rich if he made it. But the nickels would have paid for a new motor, I'll tell you that much."

The Captain threw the motor into reverse and stopped the skiff just at the corner of the last row of mangroves. He grabbed hold of the trees' water-level roots and brought the boat to a complete halt. He crawled onto the bow, grabbed hold of the roots once again, and slowly edged the boat forward to a point where he could just peer around the corner. Nick felt like he was in the presence of bootlegging greatness. "Yellow Honda? Two girls?"

Nick gave a wink and a nod, and then Bra, with a deliberateness that only comes with age, crawled back off the deck, resumed his position at the helm, and guided the boat toward the slanted concrete apron that was the Boca Cheeca boat ramp. Nick jumped into the knee-deep water and waved to Iris. He then handed a folded wad of money to the Captain. "Nine hundred dollars I believe we agreed on."

"Oh, hell, why don't you just give me the regular pay for a half day, and we'll call it square."

"No way. I said I would give you nine hundred dollars for a full day's work and a full day is still what I need."

"I'm not following." Bra said with a head tilt.

Hoping that there still was honor among thieves, Nick decided to be straight. "I need to buy a little time, Bra." Nick motioned for Iris to wait a moment. "There are gonna be some guys waiting for you at the marina when you get back. And they're gonna panic when they see that I'm not with you. I just need them," Nick paused, moving his head from side to side, "not to panic until, say, five or six o'clock?"

The captain took the money, shoved it into his back pocket and nodded. "And I want to make this perfectly clear: You don't owe me a thing. So, when they ask you what happened today, you tell them the truth. All I will ask is that you forget you ever saw the young ladies. They're doing me a favor and I don't want to get them in trouble, okay?"

Bra just nodded and extended his hand. "Thanks for fixing my motor."

"No problem. Just don't retire before we get a chance to go fishing together, okay?"

Bra flashed a brief, semi-toothless smile, gave Nick a subtle wave goodbye and, obeying the 'no wake in the basin' rule, began idling the skiff back toward the canal.

There was no time to waste. Nick sloshed through the water and ran up the ramp, peeling off his clothes as he moved. "Any problems?"

"None."

"Were you followed?"

"I don't think so."

"How long since you left the gym?"

"About an hour and ten minutes."

"We have to hurry then. Did you get the phones?"

"Just like you said --- We got three phones and I scotch taped a piece of paper to the bottom of each with that phone's number written on it."

Nick, now down to his underwear, peeled that off too, reached into his fishing bag and pulled out a towel and some dry clothes. "Did you put the phones in your roommate's name?"

"Yes, she did," Tammy interjected angrily. "And her roommate is none too pleased."

"You must be Tammy."

"Yes, I must," she said sarcastically. "And you must be the one who's gonna mess up my credit." The five-foot nothing Tammy was built like a bulldog, and twice as tough. "I don't know who you think you are, but this is bullshit."

Nick turned to Iris. "Oh, I don't have time for this."

"Tammy, I told you last night that this wasn't gonna cost you a dime, so just knock it off."

"Easy for you to say Iris, you're not the one who's gonna be gettin' fifteen phone bills next month."

Nick had heard enough. He dug into his bag and yanked out a stack of money, which he then halved. "Here's a six-month advance against the Goddamn phone bills." Tammy dragged her thumb across the top of the stack several times. "Satisfied?"

Tammy, finding it difficult to control her excitement, uttered a restrained, "I guess."

"Good. Now can we go, please? We don't have a lot of time."

"Where to?" Iris asked sweetly.

"Tropic Rental Car, it's about three miles up US 1."

Tammy's face showed sudden concern. "And I take it that the car's gonna be in my name too? You can forget it."

"Tammy...."

"No way Iris, screw this. First, I'm Verizon's best customer and now I have to worry about whether to take out supplemental collision coverage on some piece of shit Hyundai. No freakin' way."

Nick grabbed Tammy by the back, a little more firmly than gently, and guided her into the rear seat of her own car. Iris barely made it to the passenger side before Nick stood on the accelerator. It took the majority of the ride and a slightly smaller stack of cash to convince Tammy to help a friend in need, but she finally agreed. Forty minutes later, Nick threw his bags full of clothes and money into the front seat of his new ride and placed his collection of cell phones in the back. It wasn't a Porsche Twin Turbo, but it would do the trick.

Nick neither had the time nor inclination for a tearful farewell. He thanked Tammy for having a price, and then turned his attention to Iris. Her beautifully groomed blond eyebrows were lifted high on her forehead; her blue eyes sparkled even under the shade of her cap. Overall Iris beamed like a child who had been allowed to help the grown-ups with a project. Nick tapped her hat back and kissed her on the cheek. Nick told her to get back to the gym as quickly as possible, wet her hair, and change back into her regular clothes. With a glance at his watch and some quick calculations, Nick determined that, as far as the Feds were concerned, Iris would have been working out for about two hours and twenty minutes, which was a reasonable amount of time for a young girl with a perfect ass, and a circumstance that shouldn't give rise to suspicion. If all else went well, by the time Bra docked at the city marina, Nick would be holed up in a Miami hotel room, pulling all the strings necessary to set his plan in motion.

CHAPTER 8

"Alright, let's go over this one more time. Why was your boat towed into the marina?"

"How many more times am I gonna tell ya? I ran out of gas. I forgot to fill the tank before we left this morning and I ran out of gas. My radio is busted so I had to pole the boat for hours until we reached the nearest place with a phone, which was Stock Island. From there I called a friend who came and towed my boat back to the marina. How hard is it to understand?"

"And why wasn't De Julia with you when you pulled in?"

"Like I've said about twenty times now, if 'De Julia' is the guy I took out this morning, he was pissed off that we ran out of gas and that we spent the majority of the day just floatin' around. When we finally got to land, he bummed a ride off some guy he knew at Stock Island and that's the last I seen of the guy."

"So, you had intended on fishing the backcountry?"

"Again," Bra said, exasperated. "He wanted to go to Marquesa, but I convinced him that it wouldn't be productive. Just go ask any other guide worth his salt and he'll tell you the same thing. Marquesa would have been a waste of time today. I told him that backcountry would be good for the morning and that Woman Key would be perfect for the afternoon tide. And that's what we would have done if I hadn't run out of gas."

Olin stared at Bra who looked thoroughly bored. "Just sit tight for a few minutes." Olin said as he exited the room.

Olin slammed the door behind him. "What have you got, Ira?"

"It all checks out. The boat was out of gas when it reached the marina and the guy who towed him in said that this Bra character called him from Stock Island around 3:30 and said that he had run out of gas."

"What about the boat's radio?"

"Dead."

"Did you check with the phone company?"

"Yeah, they confirmed it."

"Why didn't he just trailer the boat back to the marina? It would have been a helluva lot quicker."

"Neither Bra nor this other guy owns a trailer; they both keep their boats at the marina."

"Ira, are you trying to tell me that this old bastard, who's lived here since the Taft administration, doesn't know one guy with a boat trailer?"

"No, Adrian --- I'm telling you that neither he nor the guy he called owns one. Now, is there anything else, because this isn't getting us anywhere."

"Did you talk to anyone from Stock Island who may have seen them?"

"Fletcher's doing it now, but you know as well as I do that we're not gonna come up with anything. Face it Adrian, we screwed up. De Julia paid this guy off to feed the harbormaster a line of horseshit about how they were gonna fish out at Marquesa. He knew that we'd buy it and waste our time looking in the wrong place."

Agents Olin and Stein looked through the two-way mirror and watched Captain Bra scratch his crotch over his heavily-stained fishing trousers. Olin's jaw clenched ever tighter, and Stein could actually hear his boss's teeth grinding. "What's on your mind, Adrian?"

"I'm just wondering what the going rate is for an alibi in Key West?"

For a fleeting moment, Ira considered treating the question as rhetorical but knew he was better off coming clean. "Seemingly, nine hundred and fifteen dollars. At least that's what he had on him when he reached the marina."

Olin laughed in a kind of disgusted way. "Do you think the girl had anything to do with this?"

"No. She was never out of sight. She went to the gym for a

73

few hours and then went home. She's at dinner now in a local place with a friend. But I told the guys to stay with her. I assumed you'd want it that way."

Olin nodded. "I'm through messing around, Ira. I want you to ask for help from any agency necessary to get surveillance on everyone who ever knew Nick De Julia, including Methuselah in there. I want wire taps and all mail monitored. Cancel his credit cards, freeze his bank accounts and see if we can get the IRS to pull his returns for the past ten years. He may have gone under for the moment, but he's got to come up for air. I want to make sure that we're there to plug up his blowhole when that happens. Understood?"

"Adrian?" Stein took a pause. "If you're okay with asking other agencies for help, maybe we should just turn the whole thing over to somebody better suited for this sort of thing?"

"No chance in hell. This is my show. Just set everything up the way I want it, understood?"

Stein shook his head. "I got it." Neither man had taken his eyes off the captain who was now winding his watch. "So, what do you want me to do with him?"

"Let him go. And make sure he gets his nine hundred and fifteen dollars. God knows he's earned it."

CHAPTER 9

Nick sat at the tiny desk in his grimy hotel room and pounded away at his laptop's keyboard. Both his travel bags were open on the bed and, except for the hole left by the computer, displayed the end result of some precision packing. Nick had folded, rolled, attached, and otherwise generally condensed, three changes of clothes, one suit, one tie, three pairs of shoes, two belts, a shaving kit, a travel humidor and seventy-five thousand dollars in cash into two undersized bags. Nick felt confident knowing that he had taken care of the most crucial items on his mental to-do list with the twenty or so phone calls he made during the three-hour drive to Miami, but what was he overlooking? And now, although he appeared engrossed in drafting the necessary filings, the question bit at him just as it always did the night before a trial. Adding to his general stress level and increasing stomach pain was the fact that the cab driver was now late. Nick had offered him an exorbitant amount of money for his best effort but held back half to ensure it. Nick looked down at the five-thousand-dollar titanium IWC chronograph attached to his wrist and saw that it had been two hours and thirteen minutes since he dispatched the foul-smelling cab driver and time was growing tight.

Nick continued to type although his mind now wandered in a different direction. He thought of Captain Bra pulling into the marina alone and the firestorm of activity that it was sure to create. It was ingrained into Nick's thinking to always overestimate your opponent, which in this case meant that both Lenny and Maria

Diaz would be under surveillance within minutes after Bra stepped onto the Key West City Dock. Nick glanced at his watch again and took note of the time: 6:17. Finally, he leaned away from the computer, unable to concentrate any longer. He parted the nearby window blind with two fingers and peered out onto the steamy streets of Miami's Little Havana district, but didn't see any cabs parked in front of the hotel. The cheap window treatments snapped back into shape with a tinny ping as Nick angrily pulled his fingers away and walked over to one of his bags. He took out the compacted roll that an Armani suit was never meant to comprise and unfurled it onto the bed. He then reached into one of his Bugatti loafers, pulled out a small travel iron, and plugged it in before returning to the window; still no cab.

Nick, not even aware that he was doing it, pressed his right hand against his stomach as the pain gnawed at him ever harder. But as he had mastered in his former life, he showed no trace of it. He was too busy mentally abusing himself with endless second-guessing. There's no way I could have called them, he thought. Their phones had to be tapped. How else could I have gotten word to them? Nick scoured his mind for any questions he forgot to ask himself, and although none materialized, he knew they were out there. He must have overlooked some small matter that would turn out to be critical. There had to have been a better way, Nick mulled, I just didn't think of it. Then, mercifully, the knock came. Nick righted and steadied the iron and then jerked the door open.

"Señor Henderson, I am Manuela, the hotel manager. Welcome to the Abundos Mundos. Would you like a wake-up call in the morning, Señor?" This was not a four-star hotel. In fact, it would have difficulty getting even half of a star from an easy-going critic on the take, so it seemed out of place for a hotel manager to be personally inquiring about a wake-up call and it made Nick more than a little concerned.

"No, thank you. I'm good."

"Very well. Buenos noches, Señor."

"Good night." Just as Nick started to close the door, he heard the chime on the elevator. With some hope, but more trepidation, he looked back at the only window in his room and decided that if he had to jump, his prospects were not good from the fourth floor. He turned back around and peered with one eye at the elevator. As the door slid slowly from left to right, Nick saw in succession, the young cab driver, Lenny, and finally Maria Diaz. He stepped into full view and motioned for them to hurry while scanning the lengths of the hallway. He then put his hand out and stopped the young cab driver at the threshold. To save time, Nick had segregated the additional money he had promised the young man but pulled it back at the last moment. And then in perfect Spanish, Nick told him to keep his mouth shut. The cabbie said "Si", and asked if there was anything else he could do for Señor Henderson. "No," Nick said with the Spanish pronunciation and handed the young man his money. "Vamos." Nick gave a quick head tilt toward the elevator, and the young man was on his way.

Nick closed the door behind him and saw that Maria Diaz was already seated at the desk, and Lenny was seated squarely on Nick's suit. "Lenny, for chrissakes, I just ironed that."

"Oh hell, I'm sorry, Nick. I didn't notice." Lenny laughed loudly as was his style and, with no care at all, lifted himself slightly off the bed and pulled Nick's suit aside. "Alright, we're here. Now, what's with all the undercover shit?"

Nick shot a disapproving look at Lenny who, showing himself not to be a complete Bohemian, did mutter a sheepish apology for his earthy use of language in mixed company. Nick stared at him for an extra second to reinforce the point and then turned his focus to Maria.

"I'm afraid we no longer have the luxury of 'should we' or 'shouldn't we'. I got a visit from the government yesterday and, cutting right to the heart of it, we're all in trouble. I've been under surveillance since at least yesterday and unless I miss my guess, they're making arrangements right now to place both of you under as well. And that's going to include wiretaps and, most likely, bugs in your homes, cars, and certainly your office, Lenny."

"You mean they're listening to us right now?" Lenny whispered.

"No, I shook them back in Key West, or at least I think I did, but it won't last long. We're no match for the government's resourcefulness. If we bide our time and try to move around quietly, we're playing their game, and it's one we can't win."

"Which branch of the government?" Maria asked.

"I really can't say for sure but the guy who came to see me said he was from the INS."

"What did he say?" Lenny asked with what seemed like genuine interest.

"He made a couple of veil threats, told me to leave it alone and generally pissed me off, but not much beyond that. He did mention you by name, Maria, so he obviously knows that your husband was on that plane."

"So, what do we do?" Maria asked gamely.

"The way I see this we only have one workable choice: Go right at them."

"'Go right at them.'" Maria repeated.

"That's right. We have to be the aggressors. We have to knock them off balance and keep them off balance." Nick looked around the room and could see that neither Maria nor Lenny was following his thinking. "It's nothing more than basic school-yard logic. The only way to deal with a bully is to act like you're not scared... and hit them first."

"Let me see if I have this straight," Lenny interjected. "You want us, the three of us, to pick a fight with the GODDAMN GOVERNMENT? Are you crazy?"

"That's exactly what I'm suggesting. Lenny, engaging them is the safest thing we can do under the present circumstances."

"Yeah, I guess that could be true," Lenny said sarcastically. "Or, of course, the other thing that could happen is that we wind up pissing them off, and they in turn, could --- oh, I don't know --- kill us?"

"Lenny calm down. I don't think the INS is gonna kill anyone."

"The INS is only the beginning of it. You know that, Nick. Today it's the INS, tomorrow it's the CIA or, God forbid, the IRS! And you expect me to calm down? I'm a sole practitioner. The only time I see the inside of a courtroom is when I'm defending myself in a legal malpractice suit, and now you're asking me to take on the Feds? They'll dice my chubby ass up for brunch. And for what? Five thousand lousy dollars a week? I mean, no offense, lady, but no one I know died out there. You see what I'm saying?"

"I'll bump it to ten thousand but that's it, you greedy little bastard."

Lenny took a beat. "Cash?"

Nick raised his eyebrows to seal the deal, he knew that convincing Lenny would be the easy part. Now it was Maria Diaz's turn to weigh in.

"Mr. De Julia, can I ask a question at this point?" Maria spoke with unexpected calm.

"Of course."

"Do you have a plan?"

"I do. Well, to be completely frank, it's a work in progress; but generally speaking, yes, I do."

"Can you explain what you have so far?"

"It's a good question, Nick." Lenny said in his best CNN correspondent's voice. "Just how do you plan to use our plucky little band of counter-intelligence operatives to provoke and then vanquish the United States Government?"

"By shining a very bright light on ourselves and what happened out at Marquesa."

"And how do we do that?" Lenny asked in a more respectful tone.

"I've already taken care of everything. I just need you both to meet me on the steps in front of the Federal Courthouse at 8:45 tomorrow morning. Lenny, you're going to be presenting a motion to admit me to the Florida Bar pro hac vice."

"How do you expect me to file and argue a pro hac vice motion when I don't even know what the hell pro hac vice means?"

"Well, on the off chance that was the case," Nick said, trying to be diplomatic, "I took the liberty of drafting the motion for you." Nick handed Lenny a thumb drive. "It just means that you'll be asking that I be allowed to practice law in Florida for the duration of this case. That's all."

Lenny turned his palms to the ceiling. "What case? There's a case?"

"There will be tomorrow at 9:00 a.m. I'll be filing the case of Maria Diaz as mother and next friend to three minor children against the United States Navy."

"And what's the, ah...." Lenny tapped the top of his head, searching for the term... "the ah... Oh, hell, what do you call it, Nick?"

"The cause of action?"

"Yeah, that's it. What's the cause of action?"

"It's a personal injury suit. We'll be claiming that Jorge Diaz's children suffered loss of their father's consortium due to an intentional battery inflicted upon him by the United States Navy, and whatever else I can think of before tomorrow; provided, of course, that you agree to all this, Maria."

Maria suddenly looked angry and flatly ignored the tears

beginning to trickle down her face. "You are suing for money?" she asked with incredulity. "You want me to bring a personal injury action, like this was some car accident? Is that what you think I am about, money?"

"Absolutely not. Money is not the issue here and never will be, period." Maria's jaw slowly unclenched, and she wiped one of the tears that stubbornly hung from her chin. Nick needed her to understand, "The suit itself is nothing more than a mechanism which entitles us to information. We need to find out what happened, and this allows us to ask questions. That information is the primary benefit. But a secondary one is that it will draw attention to the incident itself and, hopefully, sway public opinion in our direction. That's key. A public outcry protects us and cripples the government's ability to stonewall our demands for complete disclosure." Nick dropped his head down a few inches to evaluate the expression on Maria's face. Her brave facade was giving way to resignation. Unwilling yet to answer Nick's stare, Maria closed her eyes as if praying to stem her rapidly metastasizing despair.

"I never heard you say that Jorge could be brought home." Maria said in a controlled whisper.

Nick sat silently until Maria opened her eyes. "I haven't worked that part out yet but bringing Jorge home is the ultimate goal."

Maria wiped her remaining tears with the back of her index finger. "I appreciate your honesty, as always, but..."

"But nothing." Nick's tone had just a little bite in it, he quickly composed himself. "I don't believe that you have a choice anymore. This is it. This is your only option. You either take the fight to them or forget about ever learning what happened to Jorge." Nick ran his hand through his hair several times waiting for it all to sink in. "I do apologize for my directness, but I want to make certain that you fully understand the urgency of the present situation. The only reason that you haven't been questioned or worse, is because they don't want to risk drawing any attention to your family and, by extension, the Marquesa incident. But that won't last forever. And Lenny's right about one thing: Up until now we've only had to contend with the INS, which is like dealing with the cub scouts. But it's only a matter of time before this situation gets turned over to the real professionals. And that's a group that we don't want to mess with. They play for keeps and there's never a loose end. Do you understand what I'm saying, Maria? We have a very small window of opportunity here. If we don't make you famous right now and shine a bright light on your husband's case, you're gonna find yourself surrounded by suits, separated from you children, and wishing you had listened to me." Maria's tears flowed a little more freely now. "So, that said, you've got to let me take this to the next level."

"Absolutely." Lenny's enthusiastic endorsement was not quite what Nick was looking for.

"Maria," Nick said softly. "I need you at the Federal Courthouse tomorrow morning at 8:45, and I need you to bring your children."

Maria forced a closed-lip smile. "We'll be there."

A terrific relief washed over him. "Great."

"I'm in too, Nick," Lenny said brightly.

"There was never a doubt in my mind, Lenny." Nick got up and retrieved two of his recently acquired cell phones. He gave one each to Maria and Lenny. "From time to time I may need to speak to one of you, and for reasons I previously explained, privacy might be a little hard to come by."

"Once you're her lawyer, the Feds can't tap any of your conversations. That would violate the attorney-client privilege." Lenny looked over at Maria and nodded with pride that he had remembered something of substance from the bar exam.

"Call me crazy, Lenny, but I don't think that admissibility is their main concern at this point, you know?"

"You're right. Better to be safe than sorry."

"I'm tickled that you agree. Anyway, keep the phone with you at all times, but don't ever use it for any reason except to call me, and only then if it's absolutely necessary. The number for my phone is taped to the back. I'd much prefer that you memorize it as opposed to leaving it attached to the back. Now, this is important so pay attention: Don't ever use the phone in your home or your car or from any place you frequent. Understood? Now, if your phone rings, it's me. I'm the only one who knows your phone's number. So, if the phone rings and you're at home or in your car, don't answer it. Just head for a park or a supermarket or a movie theater, any place you don't normally go. I'll call back every fifteen minutes until you answer. Same goes for me. If you call and I don't answer, call back every fifteen minutes until I pick up. Understood?" Lenny and Maria both nodded. "So, go home and try your best to act normal. Remember that your conversations are most likely being monitored so steer clear of anything even remotely connected with the case or our meeting today. Now, Lenny, tomorrow is business as usual for you. Grab your briefcase and drive to the courthouse."

"Okay, Nick."

"Maria, your situation is a little different. It wouldn't seem normal for you to be heading to Federal Court and I don't want to take any chances. If they dope out what's going on, they might try to move on you, so I want you to call for a cab at exactly 8:00 a.m. Now, the dispatcher's gonna ask you for a destination. Pick an appropriate place for you to be going under the present circumstances, and make sure that it's twenty or more minutes away from your home. About ten minutes later, go outside and a Blue Cab will pull up. The driver will already know to take you to the Federal Courthouse. Alright?" Maria nodded. "Then that's it. I'll see you both tomorrow."

Nick walked the twosome to the elevator. He shook hands with Lenny and then Maria, holding onto her hand a little longer. "Maria, what was the name of the gentleman who was with your husband on the plane?"

"Juan Altea, but he prefers to be called John. Why?"

"No reason. You should try to get some sleep tonight."

"I don't think that will be possible."

"Well, look at it this way, starting tomorrow morning at 9:00 a.m., there's hope." Maria found no solace in the comment; she was too scared to engage in optimism leaving Nick feeling like a lawyer in a low-budget cable TV commercial. Without another word passing, Maria stepped onto the elevator with Lenny who gave Nick an effusive thumbs-up just as the door squealed shut.

Nick went back to his room and straightened the mess Lenny made of his suit. He then reached into his other Bugatti loafer and pulled out a garment bag that had been reduced to a six-inch by six-inch block of plastic. He placed his suit in the bag, hung it on the shower rod and closed the bathroom door. A quick pause at his travel humidor and Nick was ready to relax.

He sat at the desk and hit two buttons on his laptop. A moment later, Michael Franks' jazzy rendition of "Fool's Errand" began to seep from the computer's minute speakers. He lit his cigar and turned his chair parallel to the window. Nick's hands were steady as he lifted the Petit del Punch to his mouth. The condensed streams of smoke he exhaled turned from white to bright red and back to white in unison with the hotel's flickering vacancy sign. A trace of a smile emerged and slowly widened, as Nick was now free to revel in the joy competition brought him. Despite what he told Lenny and Maria, he loved matching wits with the government, and he wasn't about to stop. His sustained smile became a little laugh as he held his tiny cigar in his right hand and shook a bottle of Maalox with his left. He gulped down a gob of the thick chalky liquid, took another, and then resumed his smoke. The fight had begun.

"City Taxi."

"Hello. I live at 26 Riverdale Road. I need a cab to take me to Santa Lucia Church in North Miami."

"Is that on West Seminole?

"Yes."

"I'll send someone right away. Should be no more than fifteen minutes."

"Okay, thank you."

Agent Edwards was as young as Anderson Fletcher but not nearly as timid. "Chief, this is Edwards, come in."

"Go Edwards."

"Chief, I'm at the Diaz house and she just called for a cab to take her to Church," he then peered down at his watch, "at 5:30 in the morning. Do you want me to stay with her or keep an eye on the house in case De Julia shows?"

Adrian Olin had been on the job so long he never needed to hesitate. He always knew the right thing to do, by the book and otherwise. "How are you dressed, Edwards?"

"Appropriate to the neighborhood, which is to say lower-middle-class shitty."

"Could you pass as a cab driver?"

"Absolutely."

"Did you get the name of the cab company she called?"

"Yeah, City Taxi."

"Alright, call City Taxi and intercept the cab driver two blocks from the home. You drive her to church, watch the door until she comes out, and tail her home. I'll send in someone else right away to watch the house. Once she arrives back on her street, you can consider her handed-off to the replacement team."

"Roger that."

"Get moving."

Agent Edwards made his calls and drove to the hastily arranged meeting spot. Shortly thereafter, an angry Haitian pulled up next to Edwards and began to yell in a language all his own something about the loss of a day's pay. And his green card was obviously up to date because neither Edwards's badge nor tough talk had any effect on him. Just as Edwards was really about to lose his temper, he heard Adrian Olin screaming his name in his earpiece. He turned his back on the irate Haitian and walked several steps away.

"This is Edwards, go."

"It's Olin. Get back to the house immediately and arrest her. Now."

Edwards told the Haitian what to do, employing a combination of universally understood gestures, and jumped back into his car. "I'm en route. What the hell's going on chief?"

Olin was feverishly scanning the morning edition of the *La Cubano Journal*, an independent, low circulation Miami paper for the Spanish speaking. Attached to the front page of the paper was a translation done by an INS field operative working within the Little Havana community. Olin's face turned from crimson to purple as he speed read through what could have been his undoing with the agency. "Where are you, Edwards?"

"I'm one block away."

"I want you to arrest her and put her on a plane to Guantanamo immediately. Screw the paperwork. Do you read me?" Olin yelled. "No processing, just get her the hell out of here."

Edwards floored the accelerator and fish-tailed onto Maria Diaz's street. He pulled in front of her house and screeched his car to a halt, nose to nose with the replacement team of agents. Three men with guns brandished ran onto Maria Diaz's front porch. Without so much as breaking stride, the largest one of the three lowered his right shoulder and splintered the Diaz's front door. Edwards and the other agents entered like storm troopers, screaming wildly and swearing profusely as they moved from room to room. It took no more than ten seconds for them to realize that Maria Diaz was gone.

"Chief, this is Edwards, over."

"Have you got her?"

"She's gone."

"What the hell do you mean by that Edwards?" Olin said softly.

"I mean she's gone. She must have slipped out when I went to make the switch with the cab driver." Olin was in utter disbelief. "Chief, are you there?"

"Of course I'm here, you idiot."

"Do you want us to stay with the house until she gets back?"

Adrian couldn't even bear to open his eyes for this conversation. "Did you do any damage?"

"We broke down the front door."

"Have it repaired immediately."

"And then what? Should we start looking for her?"

"No, I know where she is."

"Where?"

"Federal Court."

"What?"

"It doesn't matter; we're gonna be off the case within the hour."

"There's got to be something we can do, chief?"

Olin winced like he just got hit with a tremendous wave of pain and then whispered. "Just get the door fixed, Edwards, so I have one less thing to answer for."

CHAPTER 10

When Nick stepped from his cab he took a well-earned moment to behold his work. Four-foot-high metal barricades set twenty feet apart ran from the curb to the front door of the courthouse, creating a makeshift pathway. At least fifty policemen in full riot gear stood in front of the barricades facing hundreds of unruly Cuban-American immigrant protesters. Many of them held hand-scrawled signs: "Justice for Juan and Jorge", "Viva los Hermanos", and "Libertade and Justice for all?" were but a few.

Lenny, leaning forward over his gut, cautiously ran down the rows of concrete steps from the front of the courthouse to where Nick continued to survey the scene. As usual, Lenny's unique blend of patterns and colors offended Nick's commitment to style. Lenny's commitment, Nick now realized, was to be covered as opposed to dressed. But, regardless of the day, date, weather, or event, Lenny was always smiling. And even though it didn't seem possible, Lenny could actually take any smile to a higher level when necessary. True to form, he dug deep for a look of thorough contentment as he approached Nick. "What do you think? This is six o'clock news shit, you know what I'm saying?"

"Lenny, for chrissakes what the hell's with that outfit?"

"What are you talking about?" Lenny said while checking himself out. "What's wrong with this?"

"Are you serious? A blind man getting dressed in someone else's closet would have come up with a better outfit."

Lenny smiled through Nick's insult and then turned his attention to the unruly crowd. "How did you pull this off?"

Nick ignored Lenny's irrelevant question. "Is this the only entrance to the building?"

"I don't know if it's the only entrance, but it's the main one. Why?"

"Because I'm starting to worry about Maria; she's late."

"There's no way they're gonna mess with her today. Not with all this attention. I get it now --- the bright light and all. You're one smart son-of-a-bitch, I'll give you that."

"Well then where the hell is she?" At that moment, Lenny grabbed Nick and shoved him two feet forward onto the sidewalk just as a Blue Cab slid in behind them. After inertia was through having its way with Maria and her children, they stepped from the cab and into the melee.

"Any problems?"

"They were watching me, but I did what you said. We've been driving around for 3 1/2 hours but I don't think we were followed."

"It doesn't matter anymore. We just had to get you here and, theoretically, at least, you should be safe from now on." Nick looked down and noticed Maria's children. The three boys ranged in age from eight to four. Each had jet black hair, deep brown skin, and dark eyes. All three looked handsome and uncomfortable tugging at the ties Maria made them wear. Nick squatted down to their level and introduced himself as their lawyer. He shook hands with each of his new clients and asked if they were ready to be men. Each whispered "yes" but seemed to be preoccupied with the screaming crowd. "Don't worry about them," Nick said confidently, "They're with us."

Maria held her two youngest sons' hands and Nick put his arm around the oldest boy. As they started up the stairs, the discordant din eased and then morphed into a more orderly applause. The crowd seemed to intuitively grasp that the handsome man in the finely-tailored suit had to be the lawyer from New York rumored to be helping the widow and her three children. The protesters closest to the barricades reached out and patted Nick and Maria on the back, while others made the sign of the cross as they passed. Lenny trailed the entourage handing out his business cards with the speed and dexterity of a Vegas dealer. It took several minutes to get beyond the well-wishers and to the front door of the courthouse, but when he did Lenny still had a handful of cards left and, seeing no reason to blow a marketing opportunity, threw them high in the air before he too disappeared into the hallowed halls of justice.

––––––––––––––––––––

A gaggle of reporters were impatiently loitering outside of Court Room 7 waiting for the arrival of Nicholas De Julia. And these were not just local journalists. The major news organizations had picked up the story over the wire once the Cubano Journale story was finally realized, and immediately dispatched their best to cover the proceedings. After all, it's not every day that planes are shot down in Florida. The entire atmosphere changed once Nick, Maria and her children came into view. The reporters and news personnel mobilized quickly and pushed for positioning. Maria initially tried to shield her face from the glare of the television lights, but Nick, as always, had a firm grasp of the bigger picture and leaned close to remind her that publicity was not only good, but essential. They stopped just shy of the courtroom door and Maria lowered her hand away from her face.

"I respect that each of you has a job to do," Nick paused, waiting for complete quiet, "and we intend to answer all of your questions in due time. But these wounds are fresh, and Mrs. Diaz now asks for your patience while she tries to come to grips with this wholly unnecessary and thoroughly avoidable tragedy. However, we do want to make perfectly clear that this case we will be filing today is nothing more than an expedition for the truth. And we will not stop until the whole truth about this horrible act is known and Jorge Diaz, or his remains, is returned to his family. That's all I can say at this time. Thank you." The reporters resumed yelling questions as court officers ushered the group into the courtroom.

When Lenny's motion was called, Nick wondered why another lawyer accompanied him through the rail and sat at what was traditionally considered defense counsel's table. Nick had purposely waited to file the actual case until immediately before Lenny's motion was heard so it would go forward unopposed. Still, the fifty-ish man in the three-piece gray suit, which was completely inappropriate for Florida climes, continued to unpack his briefcase. If such a thing is possible, the man looked smart. He was thin but not skinny, balding in a lawyerly way, and wore his half-spectacles just below his eyes. His shoes were conservative but had a military shine and his files, which now lay in two neat piles on counsel table, did not have any shreds of paper hanging from them the way Nick remembered files, looking back when he practiced in New York. And worst of all, until Lenny's motion was allowed, Nick did not have standing to even speak in a Florida court. Unfortunately, the game was already on the line and Nick had it all riding on a player who was only known for being a good guy to have around the clubhouse.

"All rise. This Court is now in session. The Honorable Constance Fabre presiding."

Judge Fabre was the most attractive of all the Federal Judges east of California. She was known for always wearing the highest of heels and never wearing a skirt that hung below the drab black robe her lofty position required.

"What's first up on the docket today, Madam Clerk?"

"Your Honor, we have a motion to admit counsel pro hac vice to the Florida Bar. Moving party, please introduce yourself to the Court."

"Yes, good morning, Your Honor. My name is Leonardo Cicero and I am the moving party here today."

"Mr. Cicero, I thought I made myself perfectly clear the last time you were before me." At this, Nick rolled his eyes in despair and slowly dropped his head into his hands.

"You did, Your Honor, you certainly did. But I thought you wouldn't mind if I came back here for this particular motion. You see, Your Honor, the whole purpose of my motion is so that someone other than myself will handle the case we have filed here today. Said another way, Your Honor, if you grant this motion, you'll never have to see me again."

"Do you swear?"

"Oh, yes. I swear," Lenny said, placing two fingers over his heart.

"That was rhetorical, Mr. Cicero."

"I thought it might be, Your Honor, but I'm reluctant to take chances knowing full well just how much you hate me."

"Actually, that's clear thinking on your part. But then you also understand, I take it, that whomever you're proposing for admission to The Florida Bar has two strikes against them because you're the one proposing their admission to The Florida Bar, correct?"

"Absolutely, Your Honor, yes."

Judge Fabre read through Lenny's motion and then the court filing that Nick had prepared. "I should have known. So, Mr. Cicero, you are in some way connected to that riot which caused me to park several blocks from the courthouse on this extremely humid morning?"

"Not if you sign that paper, Judge. Then it will be Mr. De Julia's riot."

"Your Honor? May I interject?"

"And who would you be?"

"My name is T. Dalton Lowe, and I am a United States Attorney recently assigned to this circuit. And before this goes any further, I would like to request a lobby conference."

"Have you filed an appearance on behalf of the government, Mr. Lowe?"

"No, Your Honor. We only found out about this situation several hours ago and haven't had the time to draft a responsive pleading. I can assure you, however, that any further discussion on the plaintiff's motion, or concerning the underlying case for that matter, is best done in chambers."

"Any objection, Mr. Cicero?"

"I don't think so, Your Honor," Lenny said while looking back at Nick, "but I would ask that Mr. De Julia join us."

"The government has no problem with that, Your Honor."

"Wonderful. I just love it when we all get along," Judge Fabre said sarcastically as she tapped her gavel once. "Let's go, boys."

Nick glided through the rail and right over to T. Dalton Lowe. "Excuse me." Attorney Lowe turned around but didn't utter a sound. He just stared blankly at Nick. "Do you mind if I ask you a question?" Again, Lowe remained inscrutable. "Is Jorge Diaz dead or alive?"

"I beg your pardon?" Lowe said with incredulity.

"Did you have difficulty understanding that question, Mr. Lowe? Because if you did, I'll be happy to speak more slowly: Is - Jorge - Diaz - dead - or - alive?"

A smirk crept onto Mr. Lowe's face. He then tapped Nick on the shoulder. "I'm afraid you'll have to excuse me, my good man, I'm wanted in chambers."

"As am I, but we can talk on the way in, can't we?"

"I'm afraid I have nothing to say to you, sir."

"I'm very sorry to hear that." Nick extended an open hand. "After you, sir."

"That's right, come on in fellas. Have a seat." Judge Fabre unzipped her robe and tossed it over her chair. Everyone, the bailiff, Lenny, Nick, and even T. Dalton himself checked out the Judge's legs before they swung behind her desk. "Now, would someone, other than you, Mr. Cicero, like to tell me just what the hell is going on?"

"Would it be acceptable if I were to cut right to the chase, Your Honor?"

"That would thrill me, Mr. Lowe."

"Very well. The underlying event which purportedly gives rise to the instant action is one which directly affects our national security."

Judge Fabre flashed a beautiful, almost seductive smile. "That's your idea of 'cutting to the chase', Mr. Lowe?"

"Pardon me, Your Honor, but I am well versed in matters of national security as well as executive privilege, both of which unfortunately require a certain vagueness."

"Says who?"

"Says your employer: The United States Government."

"If all inquiries stopped there, Mr. Lowe, Richard Nixon would have finished his second term. Now, I'll ask again: What's going on?"

"I'm sorry, Your Honor, but I am not at liberty to say."

"I see. And how long a jail term will you require to be at liberty?"

Mr. Lowe's smirk re-emerged as he smoothed-over an imaginary mustache. "You might want to take caution in your exuberance, Your Honor; a cavalier attitude tends to be rather dangerous when it trifles with our country's safety."

"And smart-ass retorts tend to upset the judicial branch, Mr. Lowe. So, I suggest you unwrap yourself from the American flag and stop sparring with me." Judge Fabre winked at the U.S. attorney and then read the plaintiff's complaint. "This is a well crafted filing, which tells me, Mr. Cicero that you signed something that you didn't write," The Judge peered up at Lenny's widest smile, "or read most likely."

"Guilty as charged, Your Honor." Lenny crinkled his face for emphasis.

"I take it that you drafted this, Mr. De Julia?" Nick nodded almost imperceptibly, which was consistent with his usual courtroom demeanor. Nick found subtlety to be far more commanding than chest beating. Stillness, he once told a protégé, scares the shit out of people. "I don't think I've ever seen this done," Judge Fabre said as she flipped to page two of the complaint. "You're bringing a tort claim action against the United States Navy for the 'personal injury to or death of' Jorge Diaz? Mr. De Julia, death is usually not an iffy proposition, either he is, or he isn't."

Nick shrugged his shoulders. "I realize that it's an unusual way to plead, Your Honor, but I saw no alternative. The government is refusing to reveal whether my client is a widow. As recently as two minutes ago I asked Mr. Lowe about the status of Mr. Diaz's life, but..." Nick shook his head from side to side, "I guess that too is a matter of national security."

Judge Fabre finished reading the particulars of the complaint and then redirected her beautiful glare toward the government's counsel. "Mr. Lowe, even if the underlying event has been classified as highly sensitive, common decency would dictate that you disclose whether Mr. Diaz was killed as a result of the incident. I cannot imagine any set of circumstances where disclosure of that fact would impact our national interests or safety. Or, put another way, if you don't come clean right now, I'm going to allow Mr. De Julia to tell that throng of salivating reporters all about how the government is torturing three small children by withholding information concerning whether or not they still have a father." Judge Fabre stared at Lowe with an intense resolve. "So, what's it gonna be, ace?"

Lowe rubbed his lip a little harder while he weighed his options. He then opened one of his files and read directly from the first page. "'One body was recovered at the site of the wreckage. The man was injured but survived. He was found to be an illegal alien and, as such, sent to the U.S. prison at Guantanamo Bay, Cuba in accordance with U.S. immigration law, where he shall remain indefinitely as a detainee.'"

"Well, is it Mr. Diaz or not?" Nick asked pointedly.

T. Dalton Lowe closed his file and looked right at Nick. "We had reliable intelligence that both occupants of that plane were illegal aliens. So, given that fact," he said, taking a cruel pause, "we had no need to ask the survivor his name. We just followed the law and sent him to prison. Of course, Your Honor, he will be given the choice to remain at our prison in Guantanamo as a detainee or return to Fidel Castro's side of the island. It makes no difference to us. And since we're on the subject, we are also aware that Mrs. Diaz is an illegal alien, subject to arrest and deportation at any time. So, she might want to think twice about the wisdom of maintaining this action. Because the minute we arrest her, she loses any right to access the courts. Not to mention the effect such an eventuality would have on her boys."

"All of whom were born here, Mr. Lowe." Nick responded calmly. "Which makes each one of them United States citizens. And even if you are comfortable with, for all intent and purposes, orphaning them, you won't be able to block their legal right to maintain this suit and find out what happened to their father. The whole messy truth is going to come out, my friend, one way or another."

T. Dalton Lowe seemed to be enjoying the competition. "With all due respect to your bluster, Mr. De Julia, I'm not concerned."

"You should be."

"And why is that?" Lowe said with a grin.

"Because I'm the worst combination imaginable: a smart, rich guy who has nothing better to do with his time."

"I suddenly find myself awash in testosterone." Clearly, Judge Fabre had decided to reestablish herself as the one in charge. "Why don't you uncock your pistols, boys, so we can figure out where this leaves us."

"Your Honor, the government requests an immediate dismissal. But if The Court should fail to see the prudence of such a ruling, we ask that the case be stayed indefinitely."

"Mr. De Julia?"

"Your Honor, we haven't even served the complaint on the defendant. In fact, and correct me if I'm wrong, Mr. Cicero, Florida Law gives us 90 days to effect service. And until that's done, the would-be defendant lacks standing to move for dismissal, a stay, or anything else for that matter. Regardless, I would like permission to travel to Guantanamo to meet with and interview whichever man survived. He's either my client's husband, or a percipient witness to the event which claimed the life of my client's husband. In either respect, I have a right to speak to him."

"Need I state the government's obvious objection to such a request?"

"As a matter of fact you do."

"Your Honor, how many times must I say it? Mr. De Julia is trespassing in the area of national security. We simply cannot allow a compromise in this regard. The ramifications could be catastrophic."

"Mr. Lowe, did the Navy or any other governmental entity shoot down that plane? And I don't want to hear the words 'national security' come out of your mouth. Whatever is said in response to that question will stay in this room." The judge looked at all in the room. "Call it a limited gag order, if there is such a thing," the judge muttered. "So, I will not accept the government's position that such information cannot be disclosed to The Court. Now, answer my question. Yes or no: Did the government shoot down Mr. Diaz's plane?"

T. Dalton Lowe adjusted his glasses and dragged the back of his right index finger across his lip only once. "No."

"Are you prepared to explain precisely how allowing Mr. De Julia's request would adversely affect our national interests?"

"I believe I've said all that I care to say."

"Very well. Mr. Cicero, your motion to admit Mr. De Julia pro hac vice is allowed. Accordingly, I wish you well and hope never to see you again. Mr. De Julia, you can go to the prison at Guantanamo Bay to meet with the survivor. You will have to do so, of course, at your own expense. Further, I agree that until the plaintiff serves the complaint, there is no defendant in the strictest sense, and therefore the government's motion is premature. As concerns my gag order: I fail to see why it's necessary, but I'm going to leave it in place all the same. So, I guess that's it."

"Your Honor, there is one more issue I'd like to discuss."

"Are you sure you want to press your luck, Mr. De Julia? I mean we've only known each other for five minutes but you seem so much brighter than that."

"Unfortunately, I'm gonna have to risk it, Your Honor. Despite Mr. Lowe's representations here today, it remains our belief that the government fired upon Mr. Diaz's plane and caused it to crash.

I would like The Court's permission to begin efforts to locate and hopefully raise the wreckage. A forensic evaluation of the plane's remains may be the only way to determine what happened. And, not insignificantly, one of the plane's occupants is obviously still missing. It's distinctly possible that the body is strapped into what remains of the plane. And since the government didn't allocate any resources to recovering that body, it would only seem appropriate that some effort be made."

"I assume that will be an extremely expensive undertaking, Mr. De Julia. Is Mrs. Diaz in a financial position to foot the bill for such a thing?"

"I'm gonna pay for it, Your Honor."

Judge Fabre looked at Nick for a long moment. "How rich are you?"

"Are we talking liquid assets or on paper?"

"Never mind. Mr. Lowe, it's not that I'm ignoring you, but I already know that you object to Mr. De Julia's request. However, he does not need the court's permission to search for a downed plane. As long as he obtains whatever type of permit one needs obtain to do such a thing, it's okay with me. Now, is that it? Good. Please leave."

Several police officers in full riot gear escorted Nick, Lenny, Maria, and her children down the courthouse steps to awaiting cabs. While Nick yammered a recap of events to Maria along with a litany of instructions, Lenny, seemingly caught up in the moment, thrust his fist into the air to signify victory. The crowd erupted in happiness, but Nick was infuriated. Self-congratulatory fist pumping only comes from the uncouth and those who are unaccustomed to success, and Nick was neither. Maria, on the other hand, didn't even notice; everything seemed to fade into oblivion once Nick told her why he would be traveling to Guantanamo Bay. To her, it was nothing short of a miracle that she now had legitimate hope. Elated, Maria kissed Nick's hand several times as he shouted reminders about the rules for using the cell phones. Finally, as if small pieces of carry-on luggage, Nick tossed each of Maria's boys into the back of a cab as she made her way around to the front. Nick then grabbed Lenny and shoved him in as well. "Stay with her as long as you can, ---I'll call you on the cell phone in five minutes, okay?"

"You got it."

"And keep your fist out of the air, we haven't won anything yet."

"Taxi, Señor?"

Nick nodded, and calmly placed his briefcase on the far side of the back seat. The cheers from the crowd grew louder and a spontaneous burst of applause sent a twinge through Nick's spine. No award, fee, nor tribute he ever received meant as much to him, and he was embarrassed that he felt that way. Only the weak need a constant diet of reassurance and acknowledgment, and Nick was anything but weak. In this rare instance, though, Nick felt compelled to respond. He took off his suit coat and laid it over the back seat to buy a moment or two, and then turned back toward the crowd, which, only made them cheer louder. He stood tall and looked at the faces crammed in together behind the barricades. Then, uncharacteristically, Nick gave an elegant, half salute of thanks for a job well done.

"Where would you like me to take you, Señor?"

"The Abundos Mundos Hotel."

"Si. It will be an honor. And please allow me to thank you for all you are doing for that poor woman and her children. I believe I speak for all Cubano exiles when I say that we appreciate your efforts."

Nick gave a closed lip smile to the driver. "Could you step on it, my friend?"

"Si, Señor."

Nick stared out the window as the cab weaved its way through the steaming streets of Little Havana. And although he had the relaxed look of a tourist taking in the local color, his thoughts were actually two hundred and fifty miles south, to a place he and every other American civilian could only guess at. Either Jorge Diaz or Juan Altea was rotting in a small section of Cuba which the United States had graciously deeded to itself as compensation for helping the Cuban people during the revolution of 1890. Now it was used primarily to imprison terrorists. Nick would be traveling to Guantanamo Bay, a mere fence line away from one of the last surviving communist regimes in the world. Under different circumstances a trip to a taboo land would have been something that appealed to the adventurous side of Nick's spirit, helping to temporarily quiet his discontented inner voice. The voice that taunted him away from the security of success years earlier, the one that now urged him to help Maria find out what happened to her husband. But as Nick contemplated his next move, he found that his own thoughts, fears, and wants were no longer part of the equation. The pending trip was nothing more than a necessary part of a case; something that had to be done and done right.

Clearly, at this point in the game the objective was information. Springing the crash's sole survivor from jail was still many moves away; so, Nick began to formulate two distinct sets of essential questions, one for Juan and an entirely different set for Jorge. He took care to place the questions in order of importance in case he found himself pressed for time, and then committed the series to memory. Nick would do his job, but now it was time for Lenny to start putting his talents to work. So, Nick promptly flipped open his new cell phone and made use of the speed dial.

"Lenny Cicero here." Nick rolled his eyes as he learned that Lenny's telephone voice had a smile all its own.

"Lenny, it's Nick. Is everything alright?"

"Of course. I'm here with Maria and her boys and we're just cruising along. Our cab driver," Lenny took a moment to squint at the man's license, "Rahib, is doing a fine job. Nothing unusual."

"Terrific. Now, Lenny, I need you to do a few things while I'm gone."

"Absolutely, shoot."

"At the end of every day, around 7:30, I want you to call a guy named Captain Otis Scarborough. His phone number is 919-835-5198. Have you got that?"

"I'll remember it."

"No you won't. Write it down." Nick could faintly hear Lenny asking Rahib for a pen. "Are you set?"

"Okey dokey, thank you, Rahib. Now what was that number again?"

"919-835-5198."

"...5198, got it."

"Where did you write it, Lenny?"

"On my hand."

Nick thought for a second or two. "Write it on your pant leg too, just to be on the safe side."

"Okay." Lenny tilted his eyes downward to make use of the bifocal portion of his lenses. "And .... we're set. Now who the hell is Captain Otis?"

"He's gonna be in charge of trying to locate and raise the plane. By tomorrow morning he should have his boat, The Atlantis, in place out near that section of the Boca Grande where Jorge's plane went down. He and his crew are going to stay out at sea until they find it. I just need you to check with him every night and get a progress report. Now, remember, make the call from some place other than your home, or your ..."

"Office, or my car. I get it already."

"Hey, Lenny, don't screw around. We can't afford any mistakes. Just make sure you call from some place you've never been: like a dry cleaner's, for example."

"You're hilarious, Nick. Anything else?"

"Yes. I need you to earn all that money I'm paying you."

"What do you call what I've been doing so far?"

"A whole lot of nothing. Your job starts now. I need you to find out what the hell happened out at Marquesa. Get on the phone, call in your markers and get me some information, a lead, anything. I specifically sought you out because of your contacts. Your brother told me that you were wired into the community down here. That's true, right?"

"I do have a lot of friends."

"Well start doing whatever it is that you do to make people love you so much. Work any lead you can get. Do you understand what I'm asking you? Forget about what I told Maria. We're never gonna be able to get any meaningful information through the usual process. Our only chance is to find a leak, a snitch, a rat, something. Have you got it?"

"Absolutely."

Nick took a beat. "I'm counting on you, Lenny. Don't let me down."

"I'll do my best."

"Tell Maria that I'll call her the second I get back from Guantanamo."

"Okay. But what about...."

"Lenny, I'm getting another call."

"How's that? I thought that the only people... Hello. That son-of-a-bitch cut me off."

"Nick De Julia."

"Have you lost your Goddamn mind?"

"Irving --- How the hell are you?"

"Confused, Nick. Very confused."

"I take it you got my Fed-Ex."

"Oh, I got it alright. And after reading it for most of the morning in utter shock, I've narrowed the situation down to two possibilities: 1) You're being blackmailed by some broad; or 2) you've sustained a significant closed head injury. Now which one is it?"

"Neither."

"Well then, do you mind telling me just what the hell is going on? I mean, all of a sudden you're spending money like you inherited it."

"Oh, come on, Irving, it isn't that bad."

"Not bad? Are you delusional? You want me to send $10,000 per week to a lawyer named Leonardo Cicero; $75,000 to Atlantis Marine Search and Recovery; $25,000 to a lady named Maria Diaz; and I quote 'a brand-new Mirage fishing skiff with teak decking and a deluxe Evenrud 350 motor' to a man named Bra Sanders?" Irving said in a tone of disbelief. "Look, Nicky, I'm an accountant not a psychiatrist, but I do think that you've lost your freaking mind. No offense intended, of course."

"Oh, none taken, Irving, I'm sure you meant that in the best possible way. Now look, the account number for Maria Diaz should be accurate; I copied it off one of her blank checks. All the same, make sure you verify it before you make the deposit. And I want Bra's boat delivered to slip 39 at the Key West City Marina. And make sure that it has the latest instrumentation. You know, radio, GPS, the works. But don't call ahead, it's kind of a surprise."

"I'll bet."

"And one more thing, I closed out all my accounts and liquidated the stocks."

"Naturally."

"I've opened an account in the Caymans. I put the account

number on the back of the instructions."

"I see two account numbers on the back."

"The first is for the Cayman account; the second is for a kind of reserve fund I set up in the Bahamas. That one is strictly in case of emergency so be judicious."

"'Judicious'. You're telling me to be judicious? Hey, Nick ... GET HELP, you hear me?" Irving screamed.

"I hear you, Irving. Oh, one more thing..."

"No, Nicky, no more things. I can't take any more things. I'm a conservative Jewish accountant; this type of spending gives me angina."

"I wrote down this cell-phone number on there as well, but don't ever call me from your office phone. Only use your cell phone and only call from some place outdoors." Irving looked at the receiver as if it was an advanced calculus proof. "Have you got it?"

"Yeah, I got it, 007. Trust me; nothing to worry about here."

"Terrific. Take care, Irving."

"Get Help!" was Irving's last piece of advice before hanging up.

Only after Nick pressed "end" on his phone did he realize that the cab was screeching to a halt in a garage. Before Nick knew what was happening the garage door was yanked down behind the car and the once polite cab driver now had a gun pressed hard against Nick's forehead.

"You move and I kill you. Out of the car. Now!" Before Nick had a chance to react, the door flew open and he was brutally pulled from the backseat and thrown onto the trunk of the cab. The assailant then grabbed hold of Nick's hair and slammed his face against the hot metal in rapid succession until he could see a dent. The man felt Nick's body go limp and allowed it to slide down the back of the car, leaving a long smear of blood which trailed him all the way to the dank garage floor. The assailant and a third man then pulled Nick to his feet and held him up straight, so the scrawny cab driver could pump a few short uppercuts into his stomach, punctuating each blow with some Spanish expletive. The nasty little bastard began to tire so he stepped back to watch as Nick struggled to lift his head off his chest. If not for the two burly Cubans holding him upright, Nick surely would have collapsed. The cab driver's gun reappeared, and Nick heard him cock the hammer.

"You t'ink you so smart, right? That you gonna get famous from helping the poor little Cuban widow and her children. Well, guess again, you prick." The cab driver peeled Nick's chin off his chest and stuck the gun right in his mouth. Nothing shocks a man back into consciousness like impending death. The sound of Nick's teeth clicking against gunmetal as he strained to open his mouth ever wider seemed to entertain the would-be murderer. Nick could barely see through the haze of fear and perspiration. Even worse, he couldn't breath due to the fact that he had a large metal cylinder in his throat and gobs of blood in his nose. Nick's senses were on danger overload but he could hear the cab driver laughing and understood his every cruel word. "What do you t'ink will taste worse, huh? The gun or the bullet?"

"That's enough."

The cab driver looked off to the right, but Nick concentrated only on trying to keep his mouth as wide open as possible, despite starting to turn purple from a lack of oxygen and a gag reflex which was now in spasm. The voice was calm but authoritative. The disappointed cab driver didn't argue. Seconds before Nick would have certainly passed out, the meanest of the four Cubans scraped the barrel of the gun slowly against Nick's teeth as he withdrew it. The gun's sight had barely passed Nick's lips when he projectile vomited a smattering of blood and bile ahead of a desperate gasp for air. Nick didn't have the strength to spit, so the vile goo just hung from his bottom lip and leaked off his chin. The two Cubans who still had hold of him tightened their grip to make Nick stand up straight, as the calm one stepped out of the darkness. Nick looked up and saw an older man in a blue silk shirt and white linen pants carefully trying to avoid the vomit that lay between him and Nick. He had silver hair, dark skin, and an unmistakable look of reluctance. "Can you see me, Mr. De Julia?" The man lowered his head a little so he would be in Nick's line of sight. Nick tried hard to blink the blood out of his eyes but didn't make much progress. "I'm afraid I'm having a little trouble."

The calm one motioned for the two Cubans to loosen their stranglehold on Nick and then he extended a handkerchief. "Go ahead." Nick took it and wiped at the vomit on his chin. His arms were free but the two men to his rear still had a firm hold on him. The man in charge dragged over a couple of folding chairs and motioned toward them in a gentlemanly way. "Have a seat, please." Nick complied because he saw no future in defiance. "My name is Diego Martin, and I very much want you to know that we are not a violent organization."

"You could have fooled me."

"Perhaps I should rephrase:" Diego Martin spoke perfect English, free of any accent other than a slight southern drawl. "Our actions today are at odds with our life's mission. I mean," Diego looked around the filthy garage, "this is not who we are, but I am afraid that you are leaving us with no choice."

"I hope I'm not speaking out of turn here," Nick said as he continued to dab at the blood coming from his mouth, "but if this isn't who you are, then who the hell would you be?"

"We are members of a fraternal organization dedicated to helping any Cuban who flees from Communist terror. We refer to ourselves as The Brothers of Freedom. We fly planes over the Straits of Florida looking for refugees attempting to flee Cuba. Jorge Diaz and Juan Altea were part of the brotherhood, and like the rest of us, they knew of and accepted the possible consequences. And I'm afraid a lawsuit against the United States Government was not something that was ever contemplated. I'm sure a man of your intellect can understand why we must avoid publicity. A trial would bring much too much unwanted attention to our cause. Which, by the way, we believe to be wholly moral, but so too, realize that it is most definitely illegal. You must see our point. It's hard enough trying to finance our work and evade governmental interference as it is. A lawsuit is simply untenable." Nick wanted to debate the point but felt as though he was at a decided disadvantage since he had dried vomit on his chin, not to mention the Cuban holding his hands behind the chair, and another pointing a gun at his temple. "You can speak freely, Mr. De Julia."

"That's kind of a Castro-esque statement given the setting, wouldn't you say? Telling me to speak freely with a gun to my head and all." The man in charge nodded to the increasingly discontented cab driver, who then uncocked his gun and pointed it at the floor. "Thank you." Nick ignored the torque being applied to his arms, the pain in his stomach, and his impending death, concentrating only on Diego Martin's face. And when he finally spoke, Nick did so without the slightest waver in his voice. "With all due respect, you seem to be living in some sort of dream world. Do you really think for one second that you are operating out of the shadows? That the government is unaware of your existence? I mean, come on. That Coast Guard ship was not out at Marquesa by accident. And the government is not in the habit of firing missiles indiscriminately at civilian planes. I'm sure that a man of your intellect understands that." Nick paused, his comments hanging in the air like cigar smoke on a humid day. "Your comrades were sold out. Somebody tipped off the Coast Guard and the Navy that Jorge and Juan were gonna be in the area. But firing on a civilian plane to strike a blow against illegal immigration seems a bit drastic to me, wouldn't you agree? I mean, a missile, as a countermeasure to immigrant smuggling — it doesn't add up."

"What does the whole event say to you then?"

"I won't lie to you, I don't know yet. But isn't it clear that something else is going on here? Isn't it odd that I've been under surveillance ever since this thing started? And guess what? They've had you under surveillance for a whole lot longer." Nick whispered, "I mean, come on man, you're obviously the brains of the outfit. You must realize that this place is bugged. No doubt about it. I'll bet you anything that they're parked right down the street in some piece-a-shit Chevy Lumina laughing their asses off, unable to believe their luck. This pain-in-the-ass De Julia guy is about to be killed by those assholes from the Brothers of Freedom." Nick's face turned deadly serious. "With one bullet you're gonna wipe away all their problems. I'll be dead, the four of you will be in jail, all future refugees lose their ride, and the government gets away with murdering your friends." Nick's expression turned cynical. "And this makes sense to you?" Nick looked around the room as if dumbfounded. "It's a wonder four guys that stupid could even get together in the first place."

"I think I've heard enough." The man in charge stood up and slid his chair back toward the darkness. He then nodded to the husky Cuban who placed his arm around Nick's throat and lifted him right out of the chair.

"One of them is alive." Nick blurted out.

"What did you say?"

"It's true. I just found out that one of the two, Jorge or Juan, survived the crash." Nick began talking much faster. "One of them is being held in prison at Guantanamo Bay. I've received permission from the court to go and interview him. That means no one but me can ever go to see him." Nick lied, as the big Cuban tightened his hold. "This whole situation can be the best thing that ever happened to your organization if you really think about it, my friend." Nick's voice was starting to crack as the big Cuban really started to put the hurt on him. But instinct told Nick to keep talking. "I mean, this is really the chance of a lifetime for you guys."

Diego Martin seemed to be studying Nick's comment, which gave him a glimmer of hope. "What do you mean?" Emboldened, Nick launched into an impromptu speech aimed directly at Diego as if they were the only two in the room.

"Let me tell you something: rights are not conferred at birth in the United States. I know that's the correct answer on the citizenship test, but in reality, it's bullshit, trust me. A person's inalienable rights only kick in once he makes the news. The government can do anything it wants to you as long as 60 Minutes doesn't get wind of it, there's no paper trail, and no video, you know." Nick figured he'd keep talking until they killed him or let him go. "Remember that poor bastard Rodney King? The one who got beat up by the cops? If not for the video no one would ever have cared. Well, don't fool yourself, there are a hundred other guys who also got beat by the cops, but you've never heard of them because it wasn't captured on video. Do you see what I'm saying? Ask yourself this: Why were the cops originally chasing that guy?" Nick waited only a second. "You don't know, do you? Of course you don't. You know why? Because it's not important. The only thing that matters is that they got caught abusing their power. And that's what'll happen here if you just let me see this thing through. Don't you see, it's a real-life drama and you're the good guys. Once CNN gets a hold of it, they'll have you guys on par with those marines who planted the flag at Iwo Jima. This whole thing will go on until Jorge or Juan is released from prison to a war hero's welcome with a parade, a band, a sneaker contract, --- you know, the works. And one of you could be the odds on favorite to become some involved congressman's liaison to Latino affairs. Who knows, with a little luck you may even land a cabinet slot." Nick finally paused. "Or, alternatively, you can just kill me and go to jail for the rest of your life. It's your choice."

With Nick's speech finally concluded, the cab driver re-cocked his pistol and put it in Nick's ear for a change of pace. As he bored in a little harder, Nick winced and expelled an involuntary groan. Fear was finally starting to tighten the screws on his mind, making it impossible for him to come up with any more thought-provoking banter. His argument had ended and now it was time for the jury to decide.

"Mr. De Julia," It seemed like an eternity before Diego Martin spoke, and even then, he took an additional, torturous pause, ----- "what exactly ---- are you proposing?"

CHAPTER 11

As the Director of the most prestigious intelligence agency in the world, former Five Star General and former Chairman of the Joint Chiefs of Staff, Harrison Glendale, was not particularly fond of embarrassment. In fact, even in minute doses, it made his gums bleed. Throughout his long military career and brief bureaucratic foray, his approach to any problem was simple: Contain it; engage it, and then eliminate it. This fit hand and glove with his foresworn avoidance of all gray areas. With General Glendale it was black or white, right or wrong, attack or shell 'em first and then attack with ground forces. Even his appearance was in perfect synergy with his personality. He shaved his head because it seemed neater. And he worked out incessantly despite being in his late 60's, because a formidable chest was needed to support his medals. The General's shark-like stare was now fixed on Adrian Olin, and his questions were never rhetorical nor cryptic.

"What the hell happened?"

Despite being an accomplished public servant in his own right, Adrian Olin was clearly intimidated by General Glendale's air of authority. About the only thing that Olin knew for certain, was that Director Glendale still preferred to be called General. "General, we, meaning the INS, as part of a joint anti-Cuban-refugee effort with the Coast Guard, had intelligence that a situation was likely to occur on the 23rd, and we ...."

"I read the intelligence, Mr. Olin, and I'm fully aware of what happened out at Marquesa, but that's not why we're here." General

Glendale spoke softly, and his comments were measured, but a seething anger was evident all the same. "I want to know how my order that the situation be contained resulted in the present fiasco."

"The situation crossed departmental jurisdictions causing a breakdown in communication which led to insufficient action."

The General thought about Olin's remark for a long moment, and then he thought about it some more. He gave it every consideration during the extended silence, construing it from every angle, and only then said, "I have seen all the works that are done under the sun, behold, all is vanity."

"I beg your pardon, General."

"Ecclesiastes 1:14, Mr. Olin. It appears clear to me that you have lost sight of business. Collectively our main responsibility is to protect our country; singularly our mandate is to do that which is required of us, and not venture out in the name of self-aggrandizement." Olin looked down at the floor, wilting under the General's stare. "The INS should have immediately turned this information over to CIA or the NSA, and you know it."

Adrian Olin put his hand over his mouth as if trying to prevent any stupid comments from escaping. "It was an egregious error, and one that I'm responsible for."

"I read your file, Mr. Olin. You've been an exemplary government servant, but unfortunately, our business doesn't allow for a simple *my bad, let's move on.*"

Again, Olin looked down in embarrassment. "I understand, sir."

"Why were the two eye-witnesses even permitted to leave Marquesa without some form of debriefing?"

"General, only the Coast Guard was present at the time of the altercation, and they had no idea what was going on. And I only learned the full details of the incident a short time ago. Originally, all I knew was that there was an 'incident' witnessed by a fisherman who later conveyed his story to this Nicholas De Julia fellow. My orders were to prevent further dissemination. And given the more important national security concerns we have around the globe, I guess I didn't give it due thought."

The General shook his head over and over again. "If the Coast Guard was even out there, then intelligence existed on some level that an event was in the offing. Why was that information kept from the appropriate agencies?"

"It was only passed on to those directly involved in the joint anti-Cuban immigrant effort I mentioned earlier."

"So, in other words, you were able to confine this piece of highly sensitive and confidential information to a couple dozen, low-level people who lack grade 1 security clearance. The General yanked down hard on his vest to straighten his look. "Continue."

Olin stared back at the General. "I'm not sure what you're looking for, General. That's all I know."

"Tell me the particulars of the current situation," he said, growing impatient.

"We have satellite surveillance on De Julia and wiretaps and bugs on everyone else. We've already learned that he has contracted with a marine salvage concern to locate and raise the downed plane. He's also received court permission to interview the survivor at the Guantanamo prison and is set to fly out of Miami International in the morning. He chartered a private plane which we've wired and, of course, inserted our own crew."

"What for?" The General asked dryly.

"For obvious reasons?" Olin responded meekly.

"Prepare to listen to two hours' worth of silence, Mr. Olin. We're not dealing with an idiot here. I'm afraid it's going to take a little more creativity to probe the depths of this particular individual's knowledge."

"Do you think we should try to --- prevent --- De Julia from meeting with the survivor, sir?"

General Glendale decided at that moment that Adrian Olin's intellect made him a liability. "Mr. Olin, there's nothing the prisoner can tell Mr. De Julia that he doesn't already know. And I'm afraid the opportunity to prevent him from doing anything has passed due to your inexpert handling of the situation; a circumstance that will not be risked again. Mr. Olin, you are hereby relieved from any further responsibility in this matter."

Adrian Olin looked at the General's fierce steel blue eyes and saw that the decision was irrevocable. He felt embarrassed and inadequate, but also thankful that he wasn't being involuntarily retired. Not wishing to give the General any time to rethink his position, he stood up promptly and quietly withdrew. Harrison Glendale pulled on his vest once more and made certain that his A line was acceptable. The only other man in the room was Deputy Director Ken Anderson, the person in whom the General placed the most trust.

"Do you believe this, Kenny?"

"What part? This guy ignoring his mandate or the President of the United States allowing something like this to happen?"

The General motioned back as if to say: Both. "Did you get everything I asked for?"

"I did." Deputy Director Anderson spoke as succinctly as the General, which was part of why the two got on so well — accomplished men rarely have time for anything extraneous.

"So, what do we know?"

Anderson opened his file and started right in. "The naval air force base in Key West was immediately alerted as to what was happening and had more than adequate time to intercede. They were told, however, to stand down. General Ridgely at NORAD was also alerted of the situation via satellite intercept but was also instructed to stand down."

"By whom?"

"POTUS, by way of an aide. General Ridgely was also told to shut the entire grid down so as to backstop against any automatic response."

"Unbelievable."

"It would appear, General, that for a period of close to five minutes, the United States of America, the most powerful nation in the world, was defenseless. Our multi-trillion-dollar early warning system was disabled." Anderson took a breath but continued. "After the attorney was given permission to prospect for the downed plane, we sent a team out to recover and remove it. So whatever time or money he expends will ultimately be wasted."

General Glendale sat in his massive office in utter disgust. "I never wanted to be someone who thought his generation was better than another, but do you think for one second that Ike, or Harry Truman, or Ronald Reagan, would have allowed something like this to happen?" Deputy Director Anderson shook his head no. "Not a chance in hell. Our boys would have been in the air two seconds after their first blip hit the screen. Instead, our Commander-in-chief gives the green light to come on in and start firing in our air space." The General could not believe what he was about to say next. "I swear to heaven that if the truth weren't so God-awful embarrassing, I'd be half pulling for this DeJulia guy. Say what you want but at least the boy's got some cast iron south of his belt buckle."

"What is it that you would like me to do, General?"

"I imagine you should pray that no one ever finds out that the President doesn't always protect the citizenry against all enemies, foreign and domestic."

Anderson did not respond at all, stoically waiting for his orders.

"Put the best lawyer in the Agency on the case, debrief all the Coast Guardsmen, and just 'keep an eye' on Mr. De Julia."

"And if the attorney proves problematic?"

"I'll take care of Mr. De Julia," the General said confidently. "He'll feel the pressure, believe me. We'll dissuade him from taking this crusade to the next level. Or else we'll have to take it to the next level. In the meantime, make certain that you contact every branch of the military as well as every governmental agency and instruct them that their resources, including radar platforms, aerostats, and satellite surveillance technology is to be made available to us on an as-needed basis. The handling of this situation has been given a rating of Priority 1."

Anderson always knew when to depart, another trait that General Glendale loved, so he stood up, nodded an acknowledgment and headed off to begin containing the situation.

CHAPTER 12

Nick hustled through the "D" terminal at the Miami International Airport, aware that two men were tailing him. They had been watching him since he left the hotel and now did little to obscure their presence. He was fairly certain that the cab driver was also Agency, but it really didn't matter; everyone knew where Nick was headed so misdirection was no longer necessary. Nick wanted to call Lenny one more time before he left, though, and kept looking for some place along the concourse where he could duck in for two minutes' privacy. He looked back and saw the two men about ninety feet away, moving quickly and dodging unsuspecting tourists so as not to lose sight of him. Nick took a quick look around spying a shoe shine guy, several ticket agents, and some baggage handlers in close proximity; none were looking at Nick, but, then again, experienced CIA agents wouldn't. There was no way to tell who was who in such a vast place. Nick decided that his best bet was to turn completely around and face the charging agents who had closed the gap to within a few feet.

"How are you guys doing this morning? Beautiful day for a plane ride, huh?"

"From the looks of your face I'd say we were doin' a whole lot better than you." Special Agent Ted Hundley replied.

"You mean this?" Nick said as he pointed to his nicked-up nose and the bruises on his face. "I slipped in the shower."

"Really? That's funny because to me it looks more like you got your ass kicked by some angry Cubans who'd rather you just leave well enough alone."

Nick gave a look as though he were impressed. "And you would be Special Agent...?"

"Hundley. My name is Special Agent Hundley, and this is my partner, Special Agent Lamonica."

"It's a pleasure to meet you both."

"I'm afraid we can't say the same. We both know that we weren't sent here to become friends."

"I'm a lawyer, pal. Nobody wants to be friends with me." Nick calmly turned around and walked over to the first TSA agent he spotted. "Excuse me, sir. I don't believe these gentlemen have tickets, but I am fairly sure that they are carrying pistols. You might want to check them out." Both Hundley and Lamonica pulled out their credentials and were waved through the security checkpoint as if they were expected.

Nick walked over to Marlin Charters and announced himself. The girl behind the desk, who also happened to be a CIA agent, sweetly thanked Nick for choosing their airline and told him that the plane had just finished refueling.

"Thank you," Nick replied. "And could you tell me how I, and your two colleagues here, can get out to the tarmac?" Nick asked with a smile.

"Through that door," the young-looking girl said dryly.

"Thank you. Come on, boys." Nick headed for the door and stepped onto the exterior stairway flanked by two men with brown suits and earpieces. It was the kind of South Florida day that the Arizona Tourist Board loves. The oppressive heat and wet, stagnant air made mere breathing a cardiac stress test. And as Nick walked toward his charter, the exhaust from the various other planes notched up the heat to an ungodly level. Nick had to pause twice during the eighty- or ninety-yard walk across the tarmac to wipe the teeming perspiration from his face. The agents, on the other hand, despite their woolen suits, showed no outward effects from the weather. Apparently it was agency policy not to sweat.

Knowing that the crew was an Agency plant, the two men escorted Nick right up to the plane and stayed until he actually walked up the jet's stairs. Only then did they begin double-timing it back across the runway to their own awaiting plane. Nick hung tight until the agents disappeared into the jet and the staircase was retracted before he stuck his head in the cockpit to introduce himself to the two pilots.

"How are you fellas today?" Each man responded in a friendly way. "How long a flight can we expect today?"

"It's a short hop, Mr. De Julia. Forty, fifty minutes."

"Great. By the way, neither of you are affiliated with the Central Intelligence Agency or any other governmental entity, are you?" Nick said as he flipped open his cell phone and hit recall 2. He had dialed Lenny twice from the cab, hanging up both times after only one ring thinking that perhaps Lenny would pick up the signal and go to a remote location and await Nick's real call. Knowing that he would have thirty seconds at most, he prayed that it worked.

"No, sir. We both just work for the airline."

"Then you wouldn't mind it I stepped out onto the tarmac for a moment? And I'd appreciate a little privacy, this is a personal call."

Both men looked at each other for a second and, knowing their orders, merely said, "Not at all."

"Thanks." Nick ran back down the plane's stairs and glided over to the starboard engine. He kept his eyes trained on the plane that the first two CIA agents had disappeared into. Sure enough, that plane's door opened, and both men jumped out before the staircase was fully lowered. Nick continued to watch as the two tried to evade taxiing planes as they ran toward him. A second later, although barely, Nick heard Lenny's smiling voice.

"Lenny?" Nick screamed to be heard over the engine. "Are you some place safe?"

"Yeah, I've been walking down Ocean Boulevard for the past thirty minutes waiting for your Goddamn phone call, but I can hardly hear you." Lenny stuck his finger in the ear that didn't have the phone pressed up against it. "What's the racket?"

"It's a plane engine."

"A what?"

"A plane engine!" Nick screamed.

"You're playing hangman? Why the hell are you playing hangman?"

"No, it's a ... forget it. Look, I need you to meet with a guy named Diego Martin. Have you got that?"

"Yeah, Diego Martin, I got it. And, as per usual, I'm forced to ask: Who the hell is Diego Martin?"

"Don't worry about that. Tomorrow at noon he's gonna charter a boat called the Caballero out of the Southern Miami Boat Club. He'll meet you at the gas pumps. Don't tell anyone where you're going, don't wave to Martin when you get there, just jump on the boat and let him take you for a ride. He'll explain everything once it's safe." Nick looked up and saw that the two agents had side-stepped the last plane and had a clear path to him. "Have you got that, Lenny?"

"I think so. What was the name of the boat club again?" Lenny yelled.

"Southern Miami Boat Club. Got that. Southern Miami." The men were within a hundred feet. "Now look, I don't want your head to explode or anything, but I mailed some things this morning that may cause…. a bit of a stir…. but I don't have time to discuss it, Lenny I've got to go." Nick slammed the phone shut, ducked under the wing, and hurried up into the plane just ahead of the sprinting agents. Both men came to a skidding halt five or so feet from the plane, smoothed their wind blown ties back under their unfashionable suits, and watched as Nick sealed up the cabin. Nick again stuck his head in the cockpit. "Thanks. You can wait until those fellas get back to their plane. I wouldn't want to make them run anymore. It's too damn hot out there." The pilot smiled at Nick and told him to have a seat.

General Glendale sat in his office with Deputy Director Anderson watching the direct feed from the six high-tech surveillance cameras and microphones on the plane. Another two sets had been placed in the lavatory in case Nick needed to sit or stand when using the facility. For the first half of the flight, the United States taxpayers shelled out a ridiculous sum of money to watch a man look out of a plane window. It was what he expected but hoped to bait Nick into a mistake. The General leaned toward his Deputy Director, "Tell them to close the cockpit door."

Anderson pressed one button on the console in front of him. "U2 this is command. Why don't you give the man a little privacy?" The co-pilot leaned back and slid the cockpit door shut. Nick immediately opened his briefcase and pulled out his laptop. He plugged in a small speaker and hit the play button and the plane was instantly filled with the smooth jazz guitar of Norman Brown. Only then did Nick put the phone to his ear.

"We got something," the General yelled. "Get the reader. ---

Stupid bastard isn't that smart after all." The lip reader employed for such occasions was in another room but watching the same feed. Although the mics weren't picking up anything but Norman Brown's *Just Chillin'*, the General was hopeful on a number of levels. "What have you got?"

"I don't have anything; he's shielding his mouth with his hand."

"Get him at another angle." The technician punched up every other camera view, "Anything?"

"I can't see his lips. He's got his hand cupped over his mouth entirely. He must know that he's being watched."

"I want a direct feed from every angle at the same time," the General barked. "Is there any way you can segregate his voice from the music?" The General didn't want to lose what looked like a golden opportunity for some possible intel. "Well? Can you?"

"We can, but not through a direct feed. We can run the digital recording we're making through a de-scrambler once he's finished, but it could take a few hours to segregate all the sounds."

"I'm afraid there's nothing we can do at the moment, sir." Anderson said calmly. "But I'll make sure that it's sound segregated the minute we can pop the tape."

"Find me wherever I am the minute you have it. Do you hear me? Who is his cell provider?"

Showing his competence, Anderson had the answer, even though it wasn't what the General was hoping for. "He canceled his service several days ago. We believe he's using a prepaid phone so there is no way to track that call."

After what seemed like a twenty minute conversation, Nick finally clipped his cheap phone shut, tossed it into his briefcase, and opened up his computer. Again, General Glendale leapt to his feet. "Get me an angle of the screen so we can see what he's typing." The technicians pulled and pushed their high-tech joysticks in every direction to adjust the surveillance cameras, but all they saw was a darkened screen.

"What-in-the-hell is going on?" The General demanded of his second-in-charge.

"He has apparently dimmed the screen."

"Well, un-dim it."

"I'm afraid we can't do that, sir, but we can do the next best thing." Deputy Director Anderson leaned forward and placed his hand on the shoulder of the nearest technician. "Give me a camera angle focused entirely on the computer's keyboard." Everyone watched as the young tech nudged the camera into place. "We'll be able to recreate everything by tracing the keystrokes when we play the tape back."

"Smart, Kenny. Very smart." The General proclaimed.

General Glendale was always a pragmatist. He drew on that side of his personality to help him look away from his present nemesis and focus on the advantages of the classified technology used by the world's premier counter-espionage and intelligence agency. Nick's phone call and computer diddling would read like a novel and offer the agency some badly needed insight. But until that time, the General would have no option but to silently endure Nick De Julia's cocky smirk, as well as an impromptu smooth jazz concert.

From his perspective, Nick couldn't stop himself from smiling even if he wanted to. Just the surrealistic image in his mind's eye of the entire CIA war-room filled with a smooth jazz version of *That's the Way That Love Goes*, was simply too delicious. The added bonus image of minions running to and fro trying to figure out what the hell Nick was up to was mere frosting on the shit-cake he was force feeding them. Low-tech misdirection remained the game plan. The more time and resources the government expended on chasing shadows the more time Nick would have to find the smoking gun that lurked in every case; the bargaining chip that evens the odds; the leverage that brings the other side to the table. But, as with all dealings with the CIA, staying alive was the lynchpin to all hopes for success.

CHAPTER 13

Nick stepped off the plane and learned the difference two hundred and fifty miles makes when closing in on the equator. The heat at Guantanamo Bay was of the blistering variety. There wasn't an American born meteorologist with an expansive enough vocabulary to adequately describe the sheer intensity of heat that routinely seared the Guantanamo desert. It didn't make him long for a New York winter, but it was incredibly uncomfortable all the same.

Nick undid several buttons on his shirt as he hit the sandy, pockmarked runway and walked to an awaiting jeep. As expected, the two CIA agents from the Miami airport were already in the back seat. They had shed their brown suits in favor of camouflage fatigues but effectively maintained constipated expressions that were seemingly required by the Agency. In addition, two jeeps filled with US Marines toting serious firearms would be escorting the entourage to the prison, just in case any Cubans along the fence-line decided to lodge an objection to the new world order. One thing was immediately evident; however, Guantanamo Bay was not an inviting vacation destination.

Nick said hello to his two old friends and offered an unaccepted handshake to the driver just before the whole operation pulled out. The Marines in the lead jeep locked and loaded their weapons and turned toward the fence that separated Cuban owned soil from American owned Cuban soil. This was not a large, impenetrable appearing fence someplace off in the distance, but rather a regular looking cyclone fence that was, at times, no more than twenty or so feet away. The sweltering heat-therms rising from the fallow ground gave the landscape an out-of-focus appearance that was unnerving when trying to spot snipers. But the Marines, and Nick for that matter, stayed trained on the fence-line nonetheless, while the two automatons in the back seat stayed trained on Nick.

The road was dotted by check-points which were nothing more than small, wooden structures, each manned by two soldiers and a bevy of weapons. There was never a salute offered by anyone along the route as a matter of common military courtesy; appearing important was considered unhealthy when driving along the Guantanamo Bay fence-line. But there was a war-front mentality about the soldiers there, and it was palpable. Each tight-faced Marine had the look of absolute readiness to engage the enemy if need be. They were instructed to respond immediately and harshly to enemy aggression, a term which was given flexible meaning at Gitmo.

Twenty miles passed slowly over unpaved and potentially hostile roads, and by the time the group finally saw the Marine Corps base emerge out of the desolation, Nick's stomach pain was inching steadily toward severe. It seemed his previous meeting with Diego Martin had kicked, or rather punched, his usual pain level up a few notches.

Once the jeeps entered the compound, the caravan came to an abrupt halt. Nick found it difficult to climb out of the jeep and had to straighten up in stages. He took a couple of weak steps forward and then paused to gather himself again. His deteriorating condition was so obvious that Special Agent Lamonica grabbed Nick by the arm, held him up, and asked if he was alright. "Hell, yeah," he replied through a shallow groan. Lamonica continued to hold on through another evident wave of pain and allowed Nick to get his legs beneath him before letting go.

Nick took the moment to look around and notice that the military can even make a desert look neat. Pathways lined with white stones cut through the compound leading to handsome looking wooden structures that had louvered shudders propped open over every window. A bright white flagpole stood aside a gunmetal gray cannon and a pyramid of gold painted cannonballs. Troop transport trucks with their canopies folded down buzzed by, and chanting Marines in camouflage fatigues jogged in tight formation right by Nick, never once looking at him. Gitmo was impressive.

Nick blotted his face with the sleeve of his shirt. "Alright then, let's get going." The Agents filed in behind a listless Nick De Julia for what would prove to be a very long, very slow walk. Without any military escort at all, the three shuffled their way across the sand toward a prison that more closely resembled a POW camp than a correctional facility. A squatty concrete bunker sat in the middle of a lifeless swath of earth surrounded by cinder block walls and topped with razor wire. The building had no visible bars or windows; its roof was metal, and its walls were comprised of rotting wood and peeling plaster faded gray by the sun. A single watchtower loomed high over the yard. A marksman, who only now looked away from surveying Castro's side of Cuba, signaled to another man to open the gate so the three sweat-soaked individuals who just crossed the Guantanamo equivalent of Death Valley could enter. The two CIA Agents then walked in front of Nick and motioned for him to wait at the doorway. Hundley and Lamonica pulled handkerchiefs from their pockets, placed them over their mouths, and stepped into the building. Several feet away, a single, bare light bulb hung over a small metal desk --- this unofficially comprised the reception area. The agents reluctantly lowered their handkerchiefs to have a word with what had to be the lowest ranking Marine in the Corps.

They spoke in tones unbefitting men with guns but were successful in keeping their conversation confidential. Occasionally, one of the men would look back and squint at Nick's silhouette set against the white glare reflecting off the sand, but for the most part, they seemed to be negotiating over some language on a piece of paper laid out over the desk. Nick didn't much mind the delay; he used the time to memorize every aspect of his new surroundings. In the time it took the two agents to complete their talk, Nick noticed that there were no sign-in sheets nor metal detectors; no clang of bars nor common areas. The only natural light came from each end of an extremely long corridor that ran the length of the building and separated the rows of "cells" which seemed to run parallel to each other like horse stalls. But from Nick's vantage point, the single most defining quality of this particular hellhole was the silence. It was absolutely still. On the few occasions that Nick had to visit a client behind bars it was always the noise that he hated most. The reverberating shrieks and inhuman howls of the inmates that bounced off the concrete floors, the barking prison guards, the chilling sound of metal against metal, it all went right through him. But there was none of it here. Not a sound. The silence was so deep that it made Nick wonder if the cells had any prisoners in them at all.

After smoothing out a few more details with the desk officer, Lamonica gestured toward the door. From Nick's first few cautious steps into the dank building, he was struck with an eerie assurance that he was about to enter a lesser world, death seemed to hang suspended in the still air. But what he didn't know was that reality would far outdistance even the darker meandering of his imagination.

Both Lamonica and Hundley were coughing into their respective handkerchiefs as Nick approached, and within a single inhale, he learned why: the smell was so vile that Nick, like a fighter who took a stiff right to the chin, stumbled backward and turned away. He balled up the bottom of his shirt and pulled it up over his nose and mouth to stop from vomiting right where he stood. It was a stomach-turning blend of rotting flesh, infection, must, excrement, urine, body odor, and despair, all brought to a boil. The low ceiling and lack of ventilation seemed to conspire with the stench to create the disturbing, claustrophobic feeling. The experience was ten seconds old and Nick already felt weak; his legs were unsteady, and his field of vision began to narrow into a tunnel of white. He paused and dabbed at his sweat, realizing that his only chance to remain erect was to breathe through his mouth, the idea of which didn't thrill him either, but was certainly preferable to passing out on the prison's dirt floor.

"Announce yourself," the Marine on duty demanded using boot camp like volume.

"Yeah, how ya doin'? I'm Nick De Julia, and I'm here to see my client," he said through his Canali shirt.

"Your client is in the fifth cell on the right. You may proceed to the cell with Special Agent Hundley for your interview. I have been instructed to tell you that your interview has been limited to no more than five minutes and Special Agent Hundley must be present at all times."

Nick moved the shirt away from his mouth, gave a long

exhale, spit, and then rasped, "Bullshit."

Nick turned to the two CIA agents. "Hey, what the hell is going on here? I have a court order that permits me to meet with my client. And the order isn't limited in any way, okay?" Nick had to breathe through his shirt once or twice more before continuing. "It doesn't say anything about supervision or any time restraints."

"Those are our orders," Special Agent Hundley said matter-of-factly.

"Well I'm afraid that it's unacceptable. You either let me see my client, alone, right now, or I go right the back to Miami, inform Judge Fabre of what you're trying to pull, and get a Court order that not only straightens this out, but prohibits you from following me next time." It wasn't much, but it was the only bluff Nick could come up with in his weakened state. He pulled his shirt back up to his mouth and took a much needed breath through his new GQ air filter.

"Orders are orders. We're not free to alter them."

"Then I'm afraid we have to head back to Miami. I respect the position, but I'm not willing to relent on mine."

The two agents huddled and then one took a cell phone from his breast pocket. "Give us a minute." Eventually, he shoved his phone back in his pocket, and gestured for Nick to proceed down the hallway. "Cell 5," was all he said.

Nick had put on his best performance, but it didn't do anything to improve his physical state. His stomach pain was as bad as it had ever been and worsening, as the horrid odor caused Nick to repeatedly gag on the bile pushing up to the back of his throat. He moved his makeshift mask several times to spit, but that was more out of nervousness than anything else. And even though his gait was as unsteady as his stomach, he pressed on.

The first cell was about ten feet by six or seven men. There was one backed-up toilet in the far corner with fecal matter spilling over the top covering it in an oozing, brown sludge. A single light bulb hung from a fraying wire in the center of the cell, providing the only light. The inmates, all of whom wore dirty, tattered clothing, sat virtually shoulder to shoulder on the dirt floor lining the cell's perimeter. It was an appalling sight, but Nick couldn't just walk by. He was compelled to stop and take in the full measure of squalor these men were forced to endure. Each inmate looked up at the new face, but none of them moved beyond that.

One man, directly below Nick, sitting with his back against the bars, was urinating through his crud encrusted shorts. Urine soaked the crotch and then ran down his legs and dripped onto the dirt in front of him, but he never took his eyes off Nick. And Nick looked back --- at all of them. Their eyes were dead, lifeless, filled with a resignation that only comes from a soul abused by neglect. It was obvious that these men lacked the one essential emotion needed to survive prison life: Hope. Nick could see it in their vapid expressions and hear it in their silence. They were each beyond tears. There was no visiting day to anticipate. There would be no credit for time served or for good behavior, there was no parole board, no pending appeals. They were each alone, waiting to die without dignity on a dirt floor next to another's excrement. But still, Nick looked. He removed the shirt from in front of his face because in a strange way he thought it insulting. He got as close to the bars as he could and forced a smile. The oldest appearing of the prisoners offered Nick a slight acknowledgment and feeble wave "hello". Nick returned the gesture and realized that even convicts in America don't know how good they have it. Then he reminded himself that he wasn't in some third world nation. He was, regrettably, in a detestable piece of America kept deliberately hidden so as not to tarnish the shining example of freedom so often referred to during presidential campaigns and monument dedications.

Finally, with a wink to the old man, Nick silently excused himself, and continued on through the long corridor of horrors. Each cell brought a new group of men who were suffering the same fate. Nick saw some men who looked seventy and others who weren't seventeen. It didn't really matter, though, because in each face Nick saw the same look of utter dejection. Nick had no idea what any of these men did to land here but felt certain that none of them deserved the sentence of being forgotten.

Mercifully, Nick reached cell 5 and found it to have the fewest number of inmates --- four. Each man was in his late thirties or early forties. There was no other place to look. This was Nick's only chance. "Are any of you fellas Juan Altea or Jorge Diaz?" Nick's voice broke the silence in a harsh way. His question seemed to bounce off the cinder blocks and ricochet around the prison. "I'm looking for a Juan Altea or a Jorge Diaz?" He asked again, but no one responded. Four grimy, drawn, and unshaven faces just stared back at him.

Then, from the back left-hand corner, a man said, "Who wants to know?" Nick looked over and saw a lanky appearing, middle-aged man with a belt cinched around the lower portion of his right leg acting as a tourniquet. He had clearly lost a considerable amount of blood from the wound, evidenced by his sickly pallor and the moist stain in the dirt that encircled him. "My name is Nicholas De Julia. I'm a lawyer. I was hired by a Mrs. Maria Diaz to look for her husband, Jorge. Would you happen to be him by any chance?"

The injured man ran his hand over the wound on his leg once or twice while he thought about Nick's question. "My wife wouldn't do that. She knows better."

Nick closed his eyes for only a second. That's how long he gave himself to enjoy the moment. Jorge Diaz was alive. "Well I didn't give her much choice, Jorge."

"Yeah? How's that?"

"I explained to her that I knew someone who was actually out at Marquesa the other day, and that he saw what happened. After that, I kind of forced my assistance on her. So, don't be too mad at her when you get out of here, okay?"

Jorge pressed himself hard against the cell's back wall and sort of slithered to his feet. He stayed there for a moment to martial some strength and then dragged himself and his injured leg toward the bars. He almost made it, but not quite. Overcome by exhaustion, pain and weakness, Jorge Diaz stumbled and then fell forward. Nick reached through the bars and grabbed him under the shoulders, preventing him from hitting the ground with full force. Nick held on and was able to drag Jorge closer, propping him up against the bars.

"It's gonna be alright, my friend. I know it looks bleak but I'm gonna get you out of here. I promise you that."

Jorge weakly grabbed hold of Nick's hand and looked back at him. "I'm never getting out of here. And if you're any kind of lawyer at all you already know that."

"Look ..." Nick thought for a moment. He looked back down the corridor to make sure that neither the CIA agents nor the Marine soldier had crept within earshot. He then looked at each of the other men in Cell 5 and scrutinized them from head to toe looking for a tell, something that would give them away as undercover CIA agents. "Were all of these men in here when they brought you in?"

"What do you mean?"

"I mean have they added anyone to the cell since you were arrested?"

"No. They were all here long before me."

"How do you know that?"

"Because they told me so," Jorge said firmly. "Why do you ask?"

"No reason... just paranoid, I guess. That tends to happen when the CIA starts following your every move, you know."

"Why is the CIA interested in a lawyer?"

"Because I'm trying to help you."

Nick's directness took Jorge slightly aback. "Well I didn't ask for your help," Jorge said as he let go of Nick's hand.

"But you've got it, nonetheless. And please, don't start in with any of this I knew the risks, bullshit, because, quite frankly, we don't have the time. So, let's concentrate on your family for the moment, and how we're gonna get you back with them."

"Have you seen my boys?"

"I have."

"How are they?" Jorge asked with a grin because he was too weak to muster a smile.

"They're all doing fine."

Only then did the man with half a right leg begin to cry. "I miss my wife and my boys. They're everything to me. And I was a good father and husband. I took my duties to my family very serious."

"You did a great job. You should be proud." Nick said, continually looking over his shoulder. "And I don't mean to be rude, but I don't have a helluva lot of time here. Now your only chance of getting out of this pit is for you to come clean to me about what happened out at Marquesa." Jorge knew that "getting out of this pit," was not likely to ever happen. This wasn't as much a prison as a place where they stick people and forget about them. Detainees don't get trials, rights, or much of anything, actually. Regardless, Jorge didn't seem to be in a hurry to speak. Nick needed to change course.

"Listen, I got a visit from your fearless leader, Diego Martin... let's just say he stressed the organization's need for anonymity in no uncertain terms. So, I know how important secrecy is to you and your comrades, but the cat's already out of the bag. I've been to court and this whole situation has become front page news."

"Diego Martin did what?"

"He and some of your buddies roughed me up a little and basically threatened to kill me if I didn't just leave this thing alone. But, as it turned out, murder was only their initial reaction. By the end of the conversation, he agreed to help me. So, what I'm trying to say is that you don't have to worry about letting your friends down. They're okay with my involvement. We've agreed to work on this together."

"Really?" Jorge said sarcastically.

"I'm serious. I have their blessing."

Jorge looked Nick squarely in the eye. "Diego Martin is one of the sweetest men I've ever met. He's also one of the most successful land developers in all of Miami. Same goes for the rest of the boys. None of them would have said even a cross word to you, let alone threaten you."

"Then why can I still taste the gun they had in my mouth?"

"Neither Diego nor anybody else in the group even owns a gun. And where did you get this idea that we're running some sort of secret society?"

"Aren't you?"

"No. Everybody in Miami knows what we do. Hell, we file a flight plan with the FAA every time we go up."

Nick couldn't believe what he was hearing. "You mean to tell me that you filed a flight plan with the Federal Aviation Administration on the day you were shot down?"

"Absolutely. My partner informed them that we would be flying over the Straights looking for refugees. We always notify them." Jorge watched Nick trying hard to process this latest twist. "I'm telling you, it's no secret at all."

"Well then how come you and your wife were reluctant to accept my help."

"Because my wife and I happen to be illegals and we were scared to death of being deported. But that's our own personal problem, it's got nothing to do with the Brothers of Freedom. None of them are illegal."

"Son-of-a-bitch," Nick muttered under his breath.

"I'm afraid you've been had, my friend. I don't know who

you actually spoke to, but it sure as hell wasn't Diego Martin. Shit, Diego would have given you a ride to the courthouse."

"You don't say?" Nick casually remarked through obvious embarrassment.

"Believe me, I know. He loves publicity more than anything. Whatever hangs a lantern on the cause, he always says."

Nick thought for another moment. "You wouldn't happen to know his phone number off hand, would you?"

"Sure. You got a pen?"

"Just go 'head. I'll remember it."

"It's 407-519-1564." Jorge saw that Nick was rubbing his forehead as if he had one helluva headache. "Did you get that?"

"Yeah, I did." Nick continued massaging his temples and tried to refocus on his original objective, which was information. "Just so we're straight, you should know that the whole event led the nightly news. So, fortunately or unfortunately depending on how you look at it, you're famous." Nick raised his eyebrows and shrugged his shoulders. "So much for anonymity, huh? But nothing has come of it. Your wife and kids are fine. So, all that matters now is finding a way to get you out of here."

Although he wasn't happy having his family secret exposed, he did feel an unmistakable relief that he could now accept Nick's help. Jorge took one more deliberate look around at the squalid conditions, the disease and the barbarity. He looked down at his injured leg and saw that he was beginning to create a new stain in the dirt. He was only aware of the pain when he looked at his leg, and at that moment, it hurt a lot.

"So, what do you need to know?" Jorge asked.

"As much about the incident as you can tell me." Nick shot a quick look up the corridor. "But you have to make it fast."

"I'm afraid it's gonna be a shorter conversation than you'd like. The truth is that I don't know anything." Jorge met eyes with Nick. "I really don't."

"Just tell me everything you remember."

"Juan and I were making a routine flight. We had a spotter in the area ... Do you know what I mean by that?"

"No."

"We use certain fishing guides who work out of Key West as spotters on days when we expect a rafter. If they see one, they contact us and give us their position."

"Luis Mendoza," Nick said reluctantly.

"Yeah, that's who we had that day. Well, Luis contacted us and told us that a refugee --- a woman, was in the area of Marquesa Island. We proceeded north and...."

"North? From where?"

"Well, all of our flights start the same. We always fly over Havana and drop leaflets that encourage the Cuban people to revolt."

"Why the hell do you do that?"

"To piss off Fidel."

"That's it? That's the whole reason?"

"Pretty much."

"Did you put that in the flight plan you filed with the FAA?"

"No. We always leave one part out. Anyway, after we dropped the last leaflet we started to fly back toward Florida to look for the woman who was due that day. Maybe ten minutes later we got a call from Luis who spotted her near Marquesa."

"What happened next?"

"We flew right to the area and saw her on our first pass. We made a few come-arounds to determine our best landing strategy, and that's when we noticed the Coast Guard cutter in the channel. Right then we knew that it was over. And that's when it happened. Out of nowhere this fighter jet buzzed overhead, circled around and started to chase us."

"Did they ever try to make radio contact?"

"Never, they just started chasing us."

"And what did you do?"

"We shit ourselves. Our plane wasn't equipped for combat. We didn't have so much as a Swiss Army knife between us."

"Why didn't you just radio for help? Nick asked impatiently.

"Who were we gonna call --- a cop? We tried to evade it, but that didn't last long either. They launched a missile at us which sheared off the wing on Juan's side of the plane. That caused some jet fuel to spill into the cabin and ..."

"And what?"

"Somehow --- Juan just kind of --- burst into flames. I don't know if it was a spark from the electrical panel or what, but he was wet one second and engulfed in flames the next, and then almost at the same time, we hit the water." Jorge closed his eyes and was right back in the cockpit. "I even heard him screaming underwater, but then I think I passed out because the next thing that I remember is being pulled out of the water by the Coast Guard guys." Nick looked down at the raw flesh on Jorge's leg and could actually see his femur, which had splintered and come right through the skin.

"Has a doctor looked at that?"

"No. These guys told me that I shouldn't even bother to ask." Although Nick didn't say anything, he could discern a strong odor of cheese wafting above the rest of the foulness and knew that it was only a matter of time before Jorge lost the lower portion of his leg to gangrene. And if he were lucky, the problem would stop there. Otherwise, sepsis would fester and then spread, causing his organs to fail one by one. First his liver would shut down, then his kidneys, and shortly after that, his heart would quit. Nick knew all of this but saw no upside in enlightening his new client as to the vicious propensity of infection to spread.

"Jorge, is there anything else that you can tell me about what happened? Anything at all that might help me?"

"Not that I can think of." Jorge flicked his index finger twice at his ailing leg and was buoyed by the stab of pain he felt. "Mr. DeJulia?"

"Yeah?"

Jorge shrugged his shoulders and crinkled his face. "Do you really think that you can get me out of here?"

Nick shrugged back. "I'd be lying to you if I said that I knew for certain that I could. But I'll think of something. I always do."

"You sure?"

Nick smiled at him. "I am, actually. And it goes without saying, I'll tell Maria and your boys that you're alive, well, and will be home shortly." As Nick began to straighten up, Jorge reached back, grabbed Nick's hand, and shook it.

"There is one thing that you could do for me before you leave?"

"What?"

"Could you check on the woman that was brought in with me? She's a cell or two down that way," Jorge said with a head tilt in the opposite direction of where Nick's chaperons were waiting. "I heard her screaming something awful last night, but I haven't heard her since. I'm a little worried about her."

Nick checked his chances with yet another glance up the hall and slid a few feet to his left. He began asking innocuous questions of Jorge, who picked up on the scam and started talking incessantly. Nick slithered past the next two cells to the backdrop of Jorge Diaz yammering through his life history. Then, in the crux where the dividing wall met the bars of the third cell, Nick crouched near an ashen white, bedraggled woman, sweat soaked, too exhausted to cry, whose lower body was a bloody mess, cradling a blue infant. The baby still had the umbilical cord wrapped tightly around its tiny throat, but the dazed woman didn't seem to notice. She was slowly rocking back and forth, as if trying to put the baby to sleep. Immediately, pretense was ditched and he shot to his feet screaming. "Doctor! Get a Goddamn doctor right now! We need a doctor down here!" Nick stared at the top of the hallway but saw no movement at all. His panic went completely unheeded except for some of the detainees who, out of sheer instinct, began yelling for help in Spanish. Nick reached through the bars and placed his left hand on the woman's head for a second then ran through the din toward the front door. Nick ran at the CIA agents who had moved closer to the front door for some fresh air and got right in Agent Hundley's face. "They need help!" he yelled.

"They are detainees, terrorists and undesirables," Hundley said as he backed slightly away from Nick. "And they get all the help we're required to give them."

"There's a woman in there that just gave birth to a stillborn and my client got a gangrenous leg. How can you sit around and do nothing? Now, I want them removed from those sties and brought to the base hospital immediately."

"That's not my job." Hundley said with incredible dispassion.

"There's a woman in there with a blue baby and a man with half a leg who'll be dead within seventy-two hours. Is that alright with you? Because it's not alright with me." Nick took a beat, realizing that anger was getting him nowhere. "Please let them see a doctor." Nick could see that Hundley was at least thinking about it. "Please," he repeated.

Hundley looked at Lamonica and then the Marine standing next to them. "Have them sent to the prison hospital immediately. Now, are you through here, Mr. De Julia?" he asked Nick tersely.

"Not yet." Nick shot a quick look at each of the men in the room while he tried to think of something else to say. "I --- ah ---

never got a chance to speak with my other client."

"What other client?"

"The woman with the dead baby. The one who was picked up by the Coast Guard on the same day Jorge Diaz's plane was shot down. I represent her too."

"Bullshit." Obviously there was a limit to Special Agent Hundley's largess.

"I'm telling you, I'm her lawyer."

"Since when?"

"Since her relatives in Miami hired me last night."

Agent Hundley looked at Nick askance. "I read yesterday's transcripts from our wiretaps and the surveillance reports. I didn't see any mention of that woman or her family."

"Yeah, but don't forget that I did lose you guys for a little while there," Nick said with an almost embarrassed smile. "I want a few minutes to speak with her." Hundley looked unconvinced, but he was still listening. "Let me talk to her after she sees the doctor"

"I'm not sure."

"What can it hurt? At a minimum she's a witness to the events that are the subject matter of my complaint so, if need be, I'll seek judicial permission to interview her which means I'll just wind up dragging you guys back here tomorrow."

"Alright. After the doctor sees her you can have your conversation. Five minutes, no more. And I don't want to hear any shit about the time limit. Five minutes."

––––––––––––

Nick sat next to his new client's hospital bed waiting patiently for her eyes to open. In fact, Nick was on his seventh hour of waiting. Although he looked peaceful, Nick was having difficulty shaking the image of two stone-faced Marines zipping the woman's stillborn infant into a plastic body-bag that was five sizes too large. And it was Nick, unable to deal with the thought of the baby's tiny body sliding around, who had gently knotted the bottom of the bag just below the baby's feet.

Like everything else that had happened to him in the past few days, the whole event chipped away at his once implacable heart exposing a raw nerve of compassion. As for the woman, Nick only knew that she had been in severe shock and that she needed an emergency blood transfusion. Now, Hundley and Lamonica were allowing him to sit next to her in the recovery room and wait for his five minutes of interview time.

Despite all of his outward displays of confidence and bravado, Nick was drowning in self-doubt. The once cock-sure lawyer was now silently interrogating himself, and he didn't like the answers he was getting. He had come to the inescapable realization that he had made a mistake by sticking his nose in the cesspool that was the Marquesa incident. And it didn't matter a bit that his motives were pure. Truth be told, Nick thought to himself, my only success so far has been in giving a lot of good people an unhealthy dose of false hope. He felt like a schlock used-car dealer, passing out guarantees that were as wordy as they were worthless. But the odds-on reality was that there was no feasible way that Jorge Diaz was ever going to get out of prison. Nick wasn't even sure he could keep himself alive long enough to come up with an actual plan. And as the woman began to stir, Nick shook his head in self-disgust, knowing that the new Nicholas De Julia would certainly succumb to another set of sad eyes and offer a whole new slew of promises, the only difference being, this raft of lies would probably be in patch-work Spanish.

"Hola." Nick whispered with a smile. "Me llamo, Nick. ¿Como esta?" Apart from looking at Nick, the woman remained motionless. She didn't clear her throat, adjust herself in bed, or even blink the sleep from her eyes. She just stared at the stranger next to her and kept still. Nick decided to stammer through some more Spanish in a feeble attempt to win her over. "Cuando--obligato--un--esposa--la linea-tres...veces... ah... Como sa dici... ah... Oh hell, you don't speak English by any chance, do you? No, I didn't think so. No matter, really. To tell you the God's honest truth, I don't know what to say to you in either language." Nick reached out to take hold of the woman's hand, but she jerked herself a few inches away, remaining at a slight angle even after Nick slowly pulled back.

"Sorry about that," Nick said, holding up both hands. "I just wanted to show you that I mean no harm. I'm not one of them -- the people that brought you here, that is. No, I'm a lawyer." Nick dropped his voice down. "A very, very confused lawyer who's trying like hell to make some sense out of the whole mess." Nick leaned over to the metal bed stand and poured some water into a plastic cup. "Agua?" The woman shook her head about one millimeter to each side but did nothing else to disrupt her stare. Nick shrugged and downed the whole cupful. "Hell, if I was you, I wouldn't talk to me either." Nick began talking to himself. "I guess we're both wondering how a lawyer exiled in Key West winds up in a Guantanamo Bay prison camp trying to find out why the United States Government arrested a pregnant refugee after shooting down a private plane, killing one of its passengers." Nick looked down at the woman who remained silent. "That's okay; I don't have an answer either." Nick smiled. "So, is there anything you can tell me about what happened the other day? No wait, let me guess: You really have no idea what happened, right? There seems to be a lot of that going around lately. But somebody must know." Nick put a little more anger in his voice. "Stuff like that doesn't just happen. It's not an everyday occurrence in South Florida, you know."

A fresh wave of stomach pain hit Nick who closed his eyes tight and doubled over to the point where his head fell onto the side of the woman's hospital bed. As Nick waited for the pain to dull, the woman took her right hand and lowered it toward Nick's face. She hesitated for a second or two, waiting for another obvious wave of pain to pass, and then gently brushed some hair off Nick's forehead. Nick picked his head up just enough to make eye contact and gave a her a heartfelt look of appreciation then rasped a labored, "Gracias." The woman, with tears escaping from the far corners of both her eyes, reached out, took Nick's hand, and pulled him closer. Her touch was light, but she kept pulling until Nick's ear was just over her dry, blistered lips.

"I have a six-year-old daughter named Claudia. She lives in Havana with my sister, Celia Moralez. She works in Havana at a parador called Barredo. Please try to find a way to get word to my sister that I'm alright, and that I still want her and Claudia to try and get to America. Please, sir. I beg of you. I will die here a happy woman if I know that my daughter is free. I want nothing other than your help in this way. Would you, sir? Would you please do this for me?"

"Times up, De Julia. Let's go." Agent Lamonica was

standing in the doorway tapping his watch.

Nick leaned back and stared into the woman's pleading eyes until Special Agent Hundley came up alongside of him and nudged Nick towards the door.

CHAPTER 14

General Glendale cringed when he realized that the faint sound he heard was someone knocking on his office door; the General absolutely detested weak-wristed knockers. "Come in."

Walter Tipton turned out to be a weak-wristed door-opener as well. He peaked his small head around the corner and asked permission to enter even in the face of the General's mandate.

"Are you sure it's okay, sir. I can come back another time, of course. But the only reason that I was interrupting you now was because you told Deputy Director Anderson that you were to be disturbed whenever we finished sound segregating the tape from the airplane. And we've -- finished ---- sound seg-re-gating the tape. From the airplane, that is, sir." Tipton's voice had trailed off to near inaudible over the last half of his sentence. The young sound engineer pushed his half reading glasses back up his nose and nervously tapped his clipboard against his light blue lab-coat awaiting further instructions. The mere presence of a rookie, however, told the General that bad news was in his immediate future. If the engineers had uncovered so much as a shard of useful information, someone significantly senior to Tipton would have sashayed in hoping to lap up some credit. But such was obviously not the case.

"Is that the transcription in your hand?"

Tipton meekly looked up. "Yes, it is, sir. Yes, sir."

"Was the lab able to segregate the lawyer's voice from all other forms of noise on the plane?"

Tipton took a breath. "We were, sir. Yes."

"And what you have there is the transcription of what he said while he was on his cell phone?"

Tipton just nodded.

"Read it to me."

Walter Tipton looked as stunned as he was scared. "Oh, I'd really rather not, sir."

General Glendale ignored his plea and motioned for him to get on with it. Twenty-five-year-old Walter Tipton cleared his throat and flipped open his clipboard. He looked down at the transcript and saw that it hadn't improved since his first reading. A dispassionate, clinical reading of this particular transcript, young Tipton determined, was the only workable approach. Tipton took one last deep breath for luck and said:

"'Carwash. Working at the car wash, ----yeah. Come on 'yall and sing it with me, car wash. Whoa, oooh, oooh, oooh, talkin' 'bout the car wash, yeah.' He then apparently sings, what we believe was meant to mimic a few bass notes before he then begins the first verse, sir ..." Tipton waited a second or two, but the General didn't say anything, so he continued, even though to do so was killing him. "You might not ever get rich. But let me tell you it's better than diggin' a ditch. There ain't no tellin' who you might meet. A movie star.... or maybe even an Indian Chief." Tipton took another quick pause. "Car wash..."

The General again motioned with his hand, this time effectively conveying that Tipton should stop. "Is there anything else?"

Tipton gulped, and his voice cracked. "Mr. De Julia went on to sing what we've been able to identify as a...ah...Donna... Summer...medley, sir." Tipton hoped for some direction but didn't get any. So, he flipped open his notebook once again and said, "Bad girls, ohh beep, beep."

"Will —you — kindly — shut —up?"

"Yes, sir." Tipton flipped his notebook closed and stood at attention.

"Were you able to transcribe what he was typing on his laptop?" The General asked reluctantly.

Tipton, unable to meet the General's stare, pressed his eyes shut and nodded, "yes."

"Read it."

Tipton rubbed the sides of his throat as if he had swollen glands and again flipped open his notebook. He tried to say the first word but couldn't. He glanced up briefly at the General but realized that a reprieve would not be forthcoming.

"He wrote, sir, and just so there's no misunderstanding, I am now quoting --- *Do you think I'm stupid. You must think I'm stupid. Did you really think that I would write something I didn't want you to see?*" Tipton paused to, yet again, clear his throat. "*Maybe you are stupid. That must be it. So...*" Tipton tugged at his shirt collar. "*You must be extremely stupid, stupid, stupid....* Then there are a number of expletives, sir. Would you like me to..."

"I get the picture," General Glendale said with resignation in his voice as he adjusted himself in his chair.

"It continues along those lines, sir. With slight variations of the theme, if you know what I mean."

The General actually let the tiniest hint of smile escape before dismissing Tipton. Just as quickly, his smile faded into concentration. He sat in silence for a minute and then pressed one of the buttons on the intricate looking electronic panel mounted to his desk. "Anderson?"

"Yes, sir."

"A moment." He had barely let the button up before Anderson entered the darkened office. "Did you get a copy of De Julia's concert?"

"I read it. Yes, sir."

"He's smart, but a little too cute. Ego is his biggest weakness and that's something we're gong to have to look to exploit." Anderson nodded. "Where is he right now?"

"I'm afraid we've lost him, sir."

"What?"

"Excuse me, we briefly lost him --- in the terminal at the Miami Airport upon his return from Guantanamo, but we — reacquired him about an hour and a half later. He checked into a hotel in South Beach. He may be under the impression that he had completely shaken the tail because he checked in under his own name.

The General rubbed his tired eyes. "Where's the fat one?"

"You mean his associate ... Lenny Cicero?"

"Yes, Cicero. Where is he?"

"The last transmission we received from the field had him

driving through Miami. We learned through electronic surveillance that he told his secretary that he was going out for a bite to eat."

The General nodded. "He's going to meet DeJulia."

"Do you want me to have any of the surveillance teams move in?"

"No, not yet. We first need to know what card De Julia intends to play." The General nudged his tie knot up into his collar. "I think we should put Urdang on this." The General smoothed his crisp white collar over his tie.

"Urdang is working deep cover on another assignment, sir."

"I want Urdang to handle DeJulia." The General's retort had just enough bite in it to make Anderson notice. "Is that understood?"

"Absolutely, sir. I'll take care of it immediately." Anderson took one step toward the door, but then returned to attention. "Sir?"

"What is it, Kenny?"

"May I ask what you intend to do about Mr. DeJulia?"

"I'm not really sure what we can do at this point except keep an eye on him." He stared into space for a few seconds before returning his attention to his second in command. "Is that all?"

"Yes, sir."

"Dismissed."

"Yes, sir."

Nick sat on the patio of the Cardozo Hotel looking more like a movie star than a retired attorney. He wore a black tee shirt over a pair of tan linen trousers with a matching jacket folded neatly over his chair. A $300 pair of Revo sunglasses helped to conceal the bruises on his face, and his third scotch and soda helped conceal the bruises on his psyche. Nick took a minute to stretch out like a rich tourist whose only care was to pay attention to the endless parade of beautiful people that routinely walked along Miami's most famous street: Ocean Boulevard. And make no mistake about it, Nick picked the Cardozo Hotel precisely because it was along the main parade route. Key West had its share of good-looking women, but South Beach was unreal. It was as though the Ford Modeling Agency had purchased a city so its employees would have an idyllic place to tan. In fact, Nick was enjoying the scenery so much that he really didn't care that Lenny was twenty minutes late, especially given the fact that trailing close behind him was bound to be another group of CIA agents bent on destroying Nick's moment.

But alas, after a few more minutes of gawking, there was a thorn among the roses. Nick tilted his head down and looked over the top of his Revos to verify that among the beautiful, leggy blondes, walked a short, fat, bearded man, with a quick step. Lenny had arrived.

"Hey, Nick. You look like a million bucks." Lenny took Nick's hand and pumped it in his usual over-exuberant style. "How are you, how are you? Good to see you." Lenny let go of Nick's hand, grabbed him by both shoulders, and gave him a good shake.

"Good to see you too, Lenny. How's everything going?"

"Not bad," Lenny said as he sat down. "I can't complain, Nick, you know. I just keep rollin' along." Lenny opened up wide and gave Nick one of his special smiles.

"Would you like a drink?" Nick asked, flagging down a waiter.

"Ah ... okay. I'll have a Bloody Mary without the celery and go light on the Bloody Mary mix." The waiter looked confused. "Yes, very light. Very, very light."

"I see, sir. Will that be all?"

"Come to think of it, the hell with the Bloody Mary mix, just bring me a big glass of vodka with ice. Thank you." The waiter smirked at Lenny, crossed out all of his notes and walked away. "So, Nick, how was Cuba?" Lenny asked, adjusting his bifocals to get the optimal view of a red-head walking down the street.

"It was…interesting. How are Maria and the boys?"

"They're fine. I checked in on them this morning. Nothing unusual, you know? Everything seemed A-Okay."

"That's great, Lenny. Good work."

"Nothin' to it, Nick. Just earning my pay, you know?"

"Absolutely."

"So, Nick, what's our next move?"

"There is none. I've decided to drop the entire matter."

Lenny gave Nick a quick chuckle. "Come on, man, seriously, what's up next? And how come you called off my meeting with the

Diego guy?"

"I am being serious. I called off your meeting for the same reason I've decided to walk away, we're wasting our time and pissing off the wrong people in the process. I mean it took getting my ass kicked twice by two different groups before I realized it, but better late than dead, I figure."

Nick didn't think it possible, but he succeeded in wiping the smile off Lenny's face. "What about Maria and her kids? Aren't they depending on us? Don't we owe them a little more than this?"

"You going soft on me, Lenny? Or is it the money?" Nick rattled the ice in his glass and donned a smirk of his own. "Don't worry, Lenny, you can hold onto the money I gave you and I'll even throw in a week's severance pay."

Lenny was awash in relief. "Oh, sweet mother of mercy, you really had me going there. Wow, be still my heart," Lenny said, tapping is chest. "But tell me, not that I give a shit, but why are we calling it quits?"

"There's just too much of a downside. The government isn't gonna put up with my grief forever and I don't want to get killed over this, you know? Besides, I don't think that in the end I would be able to help these people anyway. So, all things considered, I'm just gonna shut down the whole operation. Both men stopped talking long enough to let the waiter bring Lenny his double vodka on the rocks.

"So that's it? You're just gonna go back down to Key West and forget about all this?" Lenny asked, taking a healthy gulp of his drink.

"It's not that I want to, Lenny. I don't really have a choice. I've got guys following me everywhere I go, they've got my phone tapped and, I'm sure, they have a team of IRS agents mining a thick stack of my returns looking for 'discrepancies'. And, to the tell you the God's honest truth, I wouldn't give a damn about any of it if I thought we had a real chance of getting Jorge Diaz out of prison, but that's not likely to happen. And I think it's time I realize that. The government holds all the cards, no matter what the game."

Lenny downed some more of his drink as if it were straight water. "When are you leaving, Nick?"

"Right now. I'm gonna take a cab over to my car in Little Havana and drive on back tonight. I just think that the sooner I put this whole lousy situation behind me the better off I'll be."

"What about Maria? Are you at least gonna tell her that you're quitting?"

"I'll call her when I get back to Key West."

Nick stood up, unfolded his jacket and put it on. "So, I guess this is it, Lenny. Thank you for your help."

Lenny stood up, ignored Nick's outstretched hand, and hugged him like Nick was headed off to war. "Take care, Nick. And stay in touch."

"Alright, Lenny. I will. And if you're ever in Key West you make sure to look me up." Nick pulled back from Lenny and started to walk away.

"Nick, can I at least give you a ride to your car?"

"No, that's okay. But I do appreciate the offer."

"Isn't there anything I can do for you?" Lenny looked sad, as if he was being forced to part with his best friend, and it wasn't lost on Nick. Maybe there was more to Lenny than the stains on his shirt.

"Come to think of it, there is one thing you can do for me."

"Anything, Nick. Anything at all."

"You can pay the bill. I'm a little short of cash," Nick said as he slid the folded bill to Lenny.

"No problem."

Lenny's smile reemerged as he sat down, lifted his drink in Nick's direction and drank a silent toast in honor of his friend. Lenny dug into his pocket as he watched Nick cross Ocean Boulevard and get into a cab. The two exchanged one final wave as the cab sped away. Lenny turned the bill over and just below the word "paid" was a hand scrawled note:

> *Lenny: Everything I just said is bullshit. I only did it because you were followed to our meeting and they were listening to every word we were saying. Rest assured, I'm not about to let these assholes off the hook. But I need your help, and we can't afford any mistakes. I left complete instructions taped under the lid of the first toilet in the lobby bathroom. I'm counting on you. And DON'T TRUST ANYONE.*

Lenny, glad that he really didn't have to pay for the drinks, sank the rest of his vodka and then headed into the hotel. He sauntered through the beige and white lobby of the Cardozo, pretending to make note of the art-deco design and high ceilings. He stopped at the lobby bar to ostensibly ask for the time, but what he really wanted was to see if anyone was following him. And he did so inexpertly, narrowing his eyes into slits of distrust that scrutinized every face in the place until he decided that the coast was clear. Only then did he make his move toward the bathroom, rubbing his stomach along the way as if to validate the need for the trip. Espionage was definitely not Lenny's wheelhouse, but he was trying.

After checking beneath all of the doors Lenny entered the first stall, locked the door behind him, and retrieved Nick's instructions. There, seated on the toilet, Lenny read all three pages. He didn't understand what Nick hoped to accomplish with his new plan, but he liked the "pain in the ass" quality that was at its core. Lenny was beginning to live vicariously through his friend and benefactor, as if it were the two of them matching wits with the government. As with most other things in his life, Lenny found the humor buried deep in Nick's plan, and for the next few minutes just laughed his ass off.

CHAPTER 15

Nick took Caroline Street into Old Town so he would end up on the lower end of Duval. There was simply no better way to recapture that Key West feeling than a trip along the main drag. He rolled past Captain Tommy's Bar and Sloppy Joe's Saloon, the Conch House Restaurant and the Gay Blade Men's Club. He continued on past the endless stream of sunburned tourists and drunkards as well as three transvestites each dressed as Madonna. Thankfully, Nick thought, some things never change.

Nick stopped briefly for a group of kids on motor scooters and saw that the blue Impala, which had been following him since Miami, had fallen two cars back. He pulled over momentarily, so they could catch up; after all, he figured, it was hardly a mystery where he was heading. So, Nick waved them through a yellow light and led them right to his home. Nick pulled into the driveway and then watched the Feds park across the street and gave them a little wave as he entered the house. The house smelled of perfume and Pinesol which, Nick determined, meant that Iris's house-sitting services included cleaning.

"You're back," Iris said softly as she stepped from the kitchen. She looked beautiful as always, but she also looked hopeful. The *I'm all yours* look she usually wore was gone and replaced by a much more touching yet problematic come hug me look. Neither Iris nor Nick moved closer. Iris was afraid of the response she might not get, and Nick was worried about the response he had already gotten. In actuality, Nick had forgotten all about Iris. He hadn't written a note to slip her or figured out a sly way that the two of them could steal a few minutes together without the Agency eavesdropping. And knowing what he planned to pull in the next twenty-four hours, there was really little doubt as to how he needed to handle Iris.

"I was so worried about you, Nick. I didn't know if ..."

"Shhhh. Shhhh."

"Why are you telling me to shush? I'm just glad to see you. I missed you so much."

Nick moved toward Iris, held her briefly by the shoulders, and then continued on into the kitchen. "It's no big deal. I'm fine."

Iris turned and watched Nick fingering through his mail. "I'm sorry if I seem excited but, the way you left and all ... I was concerned that maybe they saw me leave the gym or ...."

"That's enough." Nick said tersely. "There's no need for us to discuss it. Just let it go. I'm home. I'm fine. Let's just leave it at that." Nick continued to examine his mail to see if it had been tampered with.

"I didn't look at your mail."

"I didn't say that you did."

"I know, I'm just saying that I wouldn't do something like that."

"Oh, as long as you're just saying." Nick said sarcastically.

Iris tried to appear unaffected by Nick's callousness. "Would you like me to fix you something to eat? You must be hungry. Why don't you go and have a cigar and I'll..."

"Hey," Nick shot back. "You're not my housekeeper or my cook. Do you understand that? You know what you are to me and what I am to you, and I don't see any reason why we should change that now. Our relationship is what it is ... and nothing more."

Iris's beautiful blue eyes teared over. "Why are you acting like this?"

"I'm not acting any way, I.... just want you to leave."

"I don't understand."

"Well then I'll spell it out for you. I need you to leave, now. And take all of your things with you." Nick turned away so that Iris wouldn't see the look on his face. He cared about Iris, he just didn't love her."

"Alright, Nick," Iris whispered, her words sputtering through her tears. "I'll go."

"Good." Nick said with his back still to her.

Iris picked up her overnight bag and said, "One last thing, though."

"What?" Nick said with fake disgust.

"Don't you ever call me again. For anything, you ungrateful bastard." Iris's voice trailed off at the end as she turned, walked to the front door, and slammed it behind her. Nick ripped open his cable bill and pretended not to acknowledge that he had just ripped open Iris's heart. He knew that he had to distance himself from Iris for her own sake, he owed her that much, but he felt terrible all the same. And if everything went as planned, he wouldn't be around much longer to keep an eye on her. Nick also knew that there was work to be done and he didn't have time to wallow in self-pity. Without another thought about it, Nick grabbed his wallet and sifted through it, looking for the business card he had stolen from Captain Bra's boat several days earlier. Nick knew that his phone was surely tapped, but he felt no fear; Captain Bra had been operating south of the law longer than Nick had been alive. Surely a professional such as he would know enough to keep his mouth shut.

"Yo."

"I'm looking for Captain Bra Sanders."

"Speaking."

"How are you, Captain? This is Nick DeJulia. We had an abbreviated fishing trip a few days ago."

"Well I'll be. I didn't think I'd be hearing from you any time soon after that embarrassment. You know, with me running out of gas and all." Nick smiled. Bra really was a professional. "I'll tell ya, forty years in this business and it's the first time it's ever happened to me. Doubt if I'll ever live it down."

"It was nothing more than an oversight. I wouldn't let it bother you."

"Very gracious of ya.... appreciate that. So, what can I do for you?"

"Actually, I'm looking for a restaurant recommendation. I figured that anybody who has lived here for a couple hundred years has to know a good out-of-the-way place that doesn't attract a lot of tourists."

"I do indeed. Check out Blue Heaven. It's at the corner of

Taylor and Petronia, down in Little Bahama Village. Now we're not talkin' white glove treatment, you understand? But the food is great."

"Do you eat there often?"

"No," Captain Bra chuckled. "But I do plan on eatin' there a lot when they start serving meals for free."

"Tell you what, why don't you let me buy you dinner? I could use the company."

"Are you kiddin'? I'm the one that owes you."

"I insist. Really, I'd love it if you joined me. What do you say?"

"Alrighty. I mean, you know, if you insist and all."

"Great. Do you need me to pick you up?"

"No, sir. I live right around the corner from the place."

"Great. Why don't you head over there now, and I'll be by in about ten minutes."

"Okay, I'll grab us a table. See you there."

"You got it."

Nick walked over to his humidor and checked to make sure that the humidity was at an appropriate level. He then took two of the Punch Petit Coronas, courtesy of Adrian Olin, and headed off for the restaurant. Of course, Nick's companions for the evening tailed him the entire way. By the time Nick got to the restaurant the Blue Impala and its occupants were blocks away and there weren't any obvious agents in sight. But Nick wasn't about to buy into a false sense of confidence; quite to the contrary. The government was clearly stepping it up a notch if the surveillance wasn't obvious. So, this would be no time for carelessness. Nick had exactly the length of one dinner to devise a way to convey his plan to Bra without tipping his hand.

Nick walked up to the gate, peered in, and saw the captain on his second Red Stripe Beer. "Did you at least order me one?"

"I did. It's comin'." Nick sat down and skeptically took in the surroundings. "So, what do you think of the dining room?" Nick didn't answer until he had looked the entire place over.

"It's a backyard, Bra."

"Damn right it's a backyard. This place is classic Key West." Nick looked up and noticed that three sails had been tied horizontally in the trees overhead as a sort of makeshift canopy.

"What the hell do you do if it rains?"

"You grab your plate and run." Nick's eyes came down so he could take in the rest of the unconventional restaurant setting. There were rows of picnic tables and plastic lawn chairs precariously balanced on tree roots. Seven or eight cats ran from table to table, begging for scraps from the more liberal of the diners present. Two roosters and several chickens strutted around the property, pecking at crumbs on the ground with the roosters occasionally stopping to crow at the spotlight affixed to the top of the adjoining building.

"So, what do you think? Is this place great or what?"

"It's ... ah ... funky." One of the roosters suddenly changed direction and began pecking directly under Nick. "Not to mention a little unnerving."

"Ah, come on. He won't hurt ya."

"You're certain about that, huh?" Nick said, glancing under his chair to keep an eye on the bird.

"Absolutely. You know, this place is famous."

"Yeah? For what?" Nick asked, still staring at the rooster, which was now under the table.

"This spot right here used to be where they held boxing matches back in the thirties. Did you know that?"

"I must have missed that during my orientation."

"It's true. They used to hold boxing matches here every Tuesday and Thursday -- cock fights every Monday, Wednesday, and Friday. And guess who refereed the bouts?"

Nick noticed that the captain had some excitement in his voice. He was speaking quicker than Nick remembered and he wore a near constant grin. Nick assumed that it had been a while since Bra had been asked to go anywhere. "You."

"No. Papa himself. Ernest Hemingway. He lived just up that-a-way on Whitehead Street. Oh, old Papa loved the fights. And he would mix it up every once in a while, too. He was one tough son-of-a-gun, I'll tell you. I was just a kid, of course, but I remember it well."

"What's this fascination with Ernest Hemingway? I mean, for chrissakes you can't walk a block in this town without seeing a picture of the fat bastard, and you sure as hell can't order a sandwich that isn't named after him."

"I don't know. Every place has to be famous for something, we got assigned him, I guess."

Nick lifted his Red Stripe and tilted it toward Bra. "As good a reason as I've ever heard." Nick casually looked at every face in the crowd, wondering how many were there strictly to listen in on his conversation. It didn't really matter, though, he wasn't about to say anything worth hearing. "So, Captain, how's business?"

"Lookin' up ever since God put a brand new seventeen-foot Mirage with a 450 Evenrud motor in ole slip thirty-nine." Now it was Bra's turn to lift a beer in salute. "Here's to divine intervention."

"Well, the Lord does move in mysterious ways."

"And so can I in that new boat of mine." Bra squinted almost imperceptibly at Nick for only an instant to make sure the point wasn't missed. "She's a beauty I tell ya. Damn thing is so newfangled, I spent most of yesterday havin' to read the damn manual. Can you believe that? Been running a boat damn near sixty years and after all that, I have to read a manual to figure out how the radio works."

"What do you say we take her out tomorrow morning? I hear that the tarpon are running a little early this year."

"I'd love it. No one I'd rather fish with. And don't worry about payin' me. You took care of me on that last trip even though you didn't have to, so this one's on me. And I'll take you anywhere you want to go." Bra narrowed his eyes once again and locked in on Nick. "Anywhere at all."

"I was kind of hoping you'd know a few places that might be productive, for what we're looking to accomplish, I mean." Nick now had a glint of his own.

"I know a few out-of-the-way places. A couple are a little tough to get to, unless you know exactly what you're doin', of course."

"That's okay. I could do with a little adventure. As a matter of fact, I was thinking just this morning that all the places that I'm familiar with, are the same ones that everybody else knows about. So many boats and so many fishermen --- there's just too much pressure. No, no, no. I'm looking for something a little bit more ... secluded. Do you know what I mean? I'd like to go someplace a little daring, but worth the risk."

"I know exactly what you're saying. And ya see, that's what makes you smarter than most. You know when to leave it to the pros. Most of the guys I've taken out during my life thought that they knew it all. Always telling me where the fish were gonna be and how to approach 'em. But hardly one of 'em ever understood that I know the waters around here better than anyone."

"That's why I'm turning to you."

"Well I appreciate that, Nick. And in recognition of your faith and generosity in offering to pay for the meal tonight, I'm gonna let you in on a secret that maybe three guys in the whole world know."

"Yeah, what's that?" Nick said with a twinge of trepidation.

"After you finish your grouper and key lime pie -- you have to have a piece of the Heaven's key lime pie -- I'm gonna take you to a place that will tell us everything we need to know about tomorrow."

"Is that right?"

"It is. This place fills in all the answers. All we have to do is spend about ten minutes there, watch the water, look for a few clues, and then just be guided accordin'ly."

"Sounds great."

The two drank a few more Red Stripes and lapped up the rest of their meals. Two coffees and two pieces of key lime pie later, they were walking toward Nick's car.

"Ah, you don't wanna drive anywhere on a night like tonight, do ya?"

Nick flipped his keys into the palm of his hand and shoved them into his new linen trousers. "You're in charge, my friend. If you want to walk, we'll walk. But you've got to lead the way."

"No problem. Let's just keep headin' on down Taylor."

"Where are we goin'?" Nick knew the second he asked that he had made a mistake, but Bra quickly covered for him.

"You'll see. I want to surprise ya."

The tandem ambled over to the ritziest hotel on the island, The Casa Marina. Bra, moving quickly for a man of any age, guided Nick into the lobby. The room had an oddly pleasant, musty odor acquired through decades of perpetually open windows and doors. Several old portraits of the hotel's original owner, railroad magnate, Horace Flagler, stood guard over the seating area while lush tropical plants strategically set against the deep-brown wooden walls added a little life. But the combination of the two worked to achieve a distinctly upscale, tropical feel. The room reminded Nick of what a classy, 1930's hotel lobby in Savannah would have looked like. Bra, on the other hand, didn't seem to notice anything. He led Nick onto the patio where some of the island's wealthier tourists were reluctant to end what was certain to have been a memorable dining experience. The patio was lit only by torches, table candles, and a dim glow from the lobby. The conversations seemed as subtle, interrupted only by the sound of the Atlantic Ocean taking the occasional deep breath. And right to the water's edge is where Bra seemed to be headed.

"Is this the place, Captain?"

Bra shook his head. "Not yet. Come on. Keep up." Bra hung a right turn and started walking along the shoreline. Nick made note of how the waves kind of hissed as they gained strength, fell momentarily silent, and then struck the beach hard at the twosome's feet. The incoming tide didn't seem to bother Bra, but Nick sidestepped several waves in due deference to his new outfit. Eventually, they reached the Casa Marina's private dock. The hotel didn't allow boats to use the dock, though. It was strictly for guests, so they could walk the seventy-five yards or so out into the ocean to take in the view. The two walked the entire length of the dock. Bra dropped himself down on the very last plank, hung his legs over the side, and indicated that Nick should do the same.

"Come on, son. We don't have all night. Trust me, they can't hear us over the roar of the ocean and they sure as hell didn't think to bug the dock, so let's get on with it."

"I need your help."

"I gathered. What are you lookin' to pull?"

"I've gotta lose these fuckin' guys once and for all. But it isn't gonna be easy. I'm guessing that the coverage is gonna be a whole lot tighter this time."

"It's gonna be even harder than you think. It won't just be a couple of yahoos followin' us in a boat, I'll guarantee ya that. You know what?" Bra said, nodding and pointing to the sky. "I bet ya they're even usin' the blimps."

"The blimps?" Nick said inquisitively. "What the hell are the blimps?"

"Those little things you see up in the air that are shaped like blimps. I know you've seen 'em. They tell everyone that they're some sort of fancy-ass weather equipment, or some such nonsense." Bra paused to see if it was all registering. "Spy shit, ya know? So, we can keep an eye on El Jefe."

"Castro?"

"Yeah, how many El Jefes are there? But they use 'em for other stuff too. You know, drug smugglin', stuff like that. You can bet your last --- well ---- million --- that they're gonna have one right on us. And that's a problem. Kinda hard to out-run the eye in the sky, ya know?" Bra smiled. "But it sure ain't impossible."

"What have you got in mind?"

"Well, I ain't sayin' it's gonna be easy. But if we can avoid the guys that'll surely be floatin' behind us, we might be able to get away with it."

"What about these spy ... blimp ... things?"

"Well, the blimps do have one major flaw."

"And you know what that is?" Nick asked sarcastically.

"I do."

Nick took a beat and smiled at his wily compatriot. "And what would that be?"

"If they can't see ya, they can't track ya."

Nick nodded his head slowly, winked at Bra and lightly punched him on the shoulder.

"I got ya Captain. Brilliant."

"Ain't nothin' brilliant about it. Just common horse-sense, ya know? But to pull it off we're gonna need some pretty precise timin', a little help, and a whole lotta luck."

"Hey, I'm looking for you to be the quarterback here. Just lay out the game plan and tell me what needs to be done."

"Well in that case, huddle up."

Nick leaned a little closer to the captain and listened intently. Bra's idea was simple yet difficult all at once, and Nick liked it. They would certainly need more than a little help, but Nick had that covered. After running through the entire plan only once, Bra glanced over his shoulder and with nothing more than a slight hand gesture, brought the conversation to an abrupt halt. A couple of guys had positioned themselves at the other end of the dock. One of them had something in his hand, but neither Bra nor Nick could quite make it out, so, without saying another word, the two decided to err on the side of caution, and just go with what they had. Nick stood up first and then helped Bra do the same. Nick kept his hand on the captain's shoulder as the two started ambling back toward the beach.

"Hey, you want one of these?" Nick asked, holding out a

cigar with his other hand.

"Don't mind if I do."

"Here." Nick handed Bra the cigar, struck up his wind-proof lighter, and lit him up.

"Thank you." Captain Bra took a couple of long hard pulls. "Hey, hey, not bad. Not bad at all. Sure does beat the Backwoods smokes I've been buyin' at the CVS, I'll tell ya that much."

"I'm glad you like it." Nick still hadn't lit his own cigar. "And I appreciate your help."

"Are you kiddin'? I've been walkin' on air ever since the other day. It ain't somethin' that I can really explain. I guess you'd have to be my age to get it, but this whole thing makes me feel --- I don't know --- needed, I guess. I love it that someone sees that I still got a little left in the tank." Bra puffed on his cigar and stared at the sand for a long moment.

Nick smiled at his new friend "Okay, we gotta break it up when we hit the beach. I'm gonna go someplace for one more beer and I suggest you do the same."

"Okay." Bra then extended his hand. "Thanks for the smoke."

Nick grasped his hand and pulled him close into a hug. "Once you get back to town, slide the cigar band off and stick it in your pocket. There's a phone number on the back. Call from a phone you don't own and tell the guy who answers what's going on. He's expecting the call." Nick unclenched his friend and as Bra started to walk back up the dock, called after him, "6:30, right?"

"6:30. See you then."

Nick stayed put for a few minutes, enjoying his smoke and watching Captain Bra's skinny frame disappear along the beach. The odds against their success were staggering, but they had been mounting against him since he first learned that Jorge Diaz's plane went down. And although he had been pretty crafty so far, he knew that he couldn't keep it up. He was operating on borrowed time which was unhealthy given his adversary's historical lack of patience. No, he couldn't continue under the present scrutiny. Nick was certain that the best approach was to get lost and stay lost, at least for a while. And he knew that tomorrow was his last chance.

The gentle air that glides around on clear winter nights in the Keys makes everyone walk a little slower and breathe a little deeper. It's part of the magic of the place. Even the hardcore northern tourists who aren't comfortable unless they're worried, find themselves in virgin territory when that kind breeze washes over them. And that's when doctors consider opening coffee shops and physicists ponder the benefits of bartending. It was this intoxicating feeling of calm that had initially drawn Nick to Key West, and now he found himself waiting for it to kick in. Nick hadn't had a moment's peace in days, and he was starting to feel a little drawn down. More than anything, what he really wanted was a good night's sleep. But, all the same, he decided to have a night cap. So, Nick hung a left on Henderson Street, and headed for Dominic's, one of the better jazz clubs on the island, hoping to kill a little time and enjoy his cigar. There was nothing more he could do now anyway; the plan was set. Plus, Bra was off passing the word along so even a minor change was really impossible. No, the tweaking was over. It would either work or he was likely to spend many uncomfortable nights wishing it had.

Nick ordered a scotch and then watched the door, waiting for the next twosome of stiffs to appear and fail to blend in. But oddly, no one who fit the profile showed. Nick hadn't been to Dominic's in two or three years, so it wasn't likely that any Fed was already in the place, but one minute turned into ten, and still nothing. Reminding himself that concern was a waste of effort, Nick sank the rest of his scotch, ordered another and then took one quick glance around the room. There were only twenty or so patrons, a few waitstaff and a trio on the bandstand. A few people had come and gone, but nothing seemed out of the ordinary. He then remembered that he was dealing with the Central Intelligence Agency, and then looked with a little more scrutiny at the trumpet player.

"Excuse me." Nick turned around and saw that a young woman had taken a spot next to him. She was no more than twenty-five or six, with auburn hair, light-blue eyes and the type of porcelain complexion that would definitely be at odds with the noon-time, Key West sun. Her low-cut pink dress clung confidently in all the right places and she just loved that Nick noticed. Nick had seen better looking women in his life, but none that looked quite as comfortable on a bar stool with a white pump dangling from her foot.

"I'm sorry, were you talking to me?"

"Yes, I was. You're Nick De Julia, aren't you?"

"And who would like to know?"

"Oh, I'm sorry. I didn't mean to be rude. My name is Shannon O'Reilly."

"Shannon O'Reilly?"

"That's right."

"Well, your name certainly does fit your face."

"You don't know the half of it. What would you say if I told you that my diploma from Notre Dame reads Shannon Mary-Catherine O'Reilly, of Boston?"

"I'd say that St. Patrick's Day must be a very big event in your house."

"It is indeed. But then again, my father would take Arbor Day seriously if he thought it gave him a legitimate excuse to down a bottle of Bushmill." Shannon took her eyes off Nick long enough to take a sip out of her gin and tonic. She then wiped the condensation from the glass along the alabaster skin on her leg giving it a nice sheen.

"So, Shannon Mary-Catherine, why is it that you know my name?"

"Because I read a file on you this morning and followed you down here from Miami." Nick took a pause, unsure how to react. "I'm a reporter from the Miami Sun Newspaper. I thought what you did in court the other day was rather extraordinary and my editor agreed, so I asked if I could come down here and do an in-depth piece about what you hope to accomplish by all of this." Shannon flashed a smile that was meant to be more than friendly. It was the unmistakable look that certain women up to no good easily master and that most men can't resist.

Nick took a sip of his drink, looked right at Shannon and shook his head, No. "I admire your ambition, but I'm afraid that you're gonna be heading home empty-handed. Judge Fabre entered a gag order at the conclusion of that hearing. Sorry to disappoint you, though."

"Look, Mr. De Julia," Shannon reached out and rubbed her delicate hand over Nick's arm, "you don't mind if I call you, Mr. De Julia, do you? Or would you prefer, sir?"

Nick gently removed Shannon's hand from his arm. "Nick is just fine."

"Okay, Nick," she purred thoroughly undeterred from her course of conduct. "I can make you a very happy man in many ways," Shannon left her boast hanging, believing that like all men, Nick would have to ask, "How?" But Shannon Mary-Catherine O'Brien was about to learn that Nick DeJulia was not most men. Every touch and double engenders went unreciprocated, which was something that Shannon was not used to in the slightest and she couldn't get Nick interested in anything she was selling.

"Shannon, it's been nice talking with you, but I have to be going. I hope you enjoy the ride back to Miami."

"Look, Nick, if it's the gag order you're worried about, I'm sure we can work around it. All we have to do is focus the article on you and just allude to the case. Let's face it: you're hot... journalistically speaking, of course --- handsome, retired lawyer taking on the big bad government just to help some unfortunate refugees --- I mean, come on, this story has it all. And I'm willing to bet that there's a lot more to this than meets the eye." Shannon looked Nick up and down. "Oh, I bet there's a whole lot more." Shannon then turned her glass upside-down trying to coax out the last remaining drops of gin. "I read that story you planted in *La Cubano Journale*. I just wish you had given it to me. I could have done a much better job on it."

"What makes you think that the story was planted?"

"Please. If it's one thing that a reporter can smell, it's a freshly planted story."

"My compliments," Nick said as he tipped his glass towards her.

"Thank you, sir." Shannon said with raised eyebrows. "So, the question thus becomes, where do we go from here?"

Nick's voice went cold; the change slight but noticeable. "I'll tell you exactly where we go," Nick said, once again removing Shannon's hand from his arm. "I'm going home and you're going back to Miami. Understand?"

Shannon had never before been turned down cold when she decided to turn up the heat. But Nick left her no option. He threw fifty dollars on the bar and a wave to the bartender and walked out.

Nick moved around his house-like apartment like a caffeine addict on speed. He had less than a half-an-hour to grab his things, get dressed and stuff a bag with cash. The stakes were high, and Nick wasn't willing to start off behind schedule for any reason. Everything was timed to the second and couldn't be trifled with. So, Nick took one last inventory check, looked around for what could have been the last time, and was gone. He threw back the roof of his Porsche and tossed his rod, reel, bag and bank-roll on the passenger seat. And apart from the hundred and fifty-thousand-dollar sports car, Nick looked like any other guy in Key West who was up at that hour. He had on the uniform: a baseball cap, a red, long sleeved shirt, dark blue jeans, some Docksiders, and a pair of polarized sunglasses dangling from his neck. Nothing out of the ordinary, which was exactly what Nick was shooting for.

Captain Bra was just finishing up his own morning ritual, the same one he had been doing for half a century. It began at about 5:00 a.m. when he had coffee with the Harbormaster and ended at 6:25 when he lowered the engine into the water and started her up. This last phase had become dicey at best over the last few years but with the new motor, precision was once again a part of Bra's life. Unfortunately, so was being the subject of some pretty intense surveillance. Although it was anything but apparent, Bra could feel it from the moment he got to the docks. They were there, and in force, like a fog hanging over the marina. It wasn't unexpected by any stretch, but the palpable presence of the scrutiny was more than a little unsettling even for a multi-generational subversive like the Captain.

Nick rolled up with only three minutes to spare. He grabbed his gear out of the car, reached for the rag-top, but then hesitated. He looked up at the deep azure of the early morning sky and was reminded of the day's perfect forecast. *Don't give 'em a clue,* he thought. Nick drummed his fingers on the door and stared at his beautifully perfect biscuit interior. If this worked there was no telling how long he would be gone, and his car was certain to be ruined by eventual foul weather, pelicans, or God forbid, both. He had always left the roof back whenever he went anywhere in Key West on a sunny day, and this time wouldn't be any different. Nick did linger just long enough to say a silent prayer, but then stepped away and never looked back. He glided down the dock and tossed his gear to Bra.

"What the hell are you trying to do to me with this cutting it to the last-minute stuff? It ain't helpin' my blood pressure any, I can tell you that much."

"I'm sorry about that. Just had to make sure that I thought of everything."

"Wasn't that what last night was for?"

Bra waited for a response, but he could see that Nick had an *I can't believe it* look on his face. Bra turned around, shielded his eyes against the glow of the rising sun, and saw a young woman walking toward them with purpose. She was certainly pretty, but her determination made her less so in the early morning light. Nick grabbed Bra and whispered something in his ear.

"Are ya sure?"

"Yeah, I am." Nick looked up and saw that Shannon was only twenty or so feet away. "Just let me handle it."

"But how are ya gonna ..."

"I'll take care of it."

"But what if she ..."

"I said I'll take care of it. Trust me."

Shannon jumped into the boat without asking and sat on the cushion that covered the rear hatch.

"Captain Bra Sanders, please meet Shannon Mary-Catherine O'Reilly of Boston," Nick said wryly.

Bra smiled at the girl, tipped his cap, and without ever moving his lips said in a sing-song way, "We ain't got time for this."

Nick smirked at Shannon but was not amused in the least. "What in the hell do you think you're doing?"

"Going fishing with you. That'll give me plenty of time to get my story." Nick didn't appear flustered in the least. He glanced at his watch and realized like the true pragmatist that he was, that there was absolutely no time to argue or make a scene. Bra tapped Nick on the shoulder to get his attention, but it had little effect. Nick alternated his glare between Shannon and his watch.

"This can't happen, Bra muttered. Do whatever ya gotta do,

say whatever ya gotta say, but get rid of her."

"There's no time."

That's all Shannon needed to hear. Without wasting another second, she unfurled a baseball hat, put on some sunglasses and stretched her long legs toward the bow.

"You've gotta be kidding me?"

"No, it'll be alright. Trust me."

"No, I don't think it will. If you don't dump her right now, I'll throw her overboard myself."

"I said, trust me, and I'm not going to say it again." Nick looked right at Bra. "It won't be a problem."

Despite the bass in Nick's voice, Bra decided to try one last time. "What are you worried about.... making a scene? 'Cause you can put that right out of your mind. I've seen fifty guys throw pain-in-the-ass broads overboard in the last five years alone. Believe me, no one will even blink. Now I'm all for bein' a gentleman when you can, but you gotta admit this ain't one of those times."

Nick tapped his watch twice and motioned for him to get going. Captain Bra let out a worried sigh and then looked at his watch too. 6:30 exactly. He then looked like he was going to say something but changed his mind. "This ain't smart."

Bra walked to the back of the boat and grabbed hold of the stern line. "Excuse me, again, Darlin'," Shannon smiled at the old man and leaned gingerly to the side. "Thank you, and welcome aboard."

"Aren't you sweet?" It didn't take long for Shannon to get comfortable: she lounged back toward the warmth of the sun, her long legs stretched out, her feet crossed at the ankles. She then shook her hair off her shoulders and let it float on the rushing wind as Bra started to push up the speed once they reached the distant edge of Garrison Bight.

"Ya might want to hold onto somethin' there Missy. I'm gonna stand on it for a while." Without changing her expression, Shannon blew Bra a kiss and then wrapped her thin, French-manicured fingertips around the edge of her seat cushion.

Nick, on the other hand, looked anything but laid back. His eyes darted between Shannon's legs and the two Feds who were about four hundred feet away. He then whispered something to Bra, who in turn pointed to the storage compartment in the bow.

Nick slid along the small boat's periphery, steadying himself as he moved to the front of the skiff, lifted the hatch, and searched for the heavy-grade tarp that Nick had purchased for him to cover the boat when it rained. Nick checked to make sure that Shannon was still blissfully sunning herself before he gently removed both sections of tarp and laid it on the deck.

General Glendale sat at his command station and watched the satellite feed on the main screen at CIA Headquarters in Langley, Virginia. It was a grainy/green overhead image of two blips traveling in the same direction and remaining a certain distance apart. The agents who comprised the trailing blip radioed in every thirty seconds providing a clipped play-by-play of their subject's actions. An audio-tech specialist seated right next to the General would then pass along the updates, repeating verbatim the agents' terse transmissions.

"Mongoose One has visual on Snake. — heading due north at 35 knots. — keeping 600 foot perimeter as per instructions. — have visual. repeat, have visual. — maintaining separation. — visual of three occupants remains in tact."

The General listened intently but never took his eyes off the screen. "Did he say, *three* occupants?"

The young audio-tech used his index finger to press his ear piece in a little deeper. "Mongoose One, requesting visual verification of number of occupants." The General ignored the screen for a second and watched the audio-tech. "Mongoose One confirms three occupants."

"Get me closer."

The oldest of the satellite team momentarily abandoned his keyboard and spun his chair around. "We can program the satellite to narrow the image, sir, but we will lose our ability to track both the subject boat and the tail boat simultaneously."

"Do it." The General again turned to his audio-tech who continued to pass along updates.

"Mongoose at 36 knots. — visual intact. — separation holding at 590 feet. — all under control."

The General returned his attention to the screen which had gone blank while the satellite data was being reconfigured. "Come on, come on..." He muttered waiting for his close up.

"Snake adjusting course. — turning in easterly fashion. — normal appearing maneuver. — distance and speed remaining constant."

"What in the hell is taking so long?" At that moment, the screen lit up white and showed a fuzzy image of an older appearing male standing next to a younger appearing male, with a slight appearing female lying behind them. The General squinted at the image of the woman for only a moment before jerking a pair of glasses from his breast pocket. "Can you close in on the woman alone?" The giant screen before him flashed six or seven times until only the woman's face appeared. The General removed his glasses and stood up, then turned to stare at Deputy Director Anderson.

"Visual lost sir," two or three people yelled simultaneously as every monitor went black. "Visual lost entirely." The whole room was suddenly thrust into pandemonium. Everyone began slapping at their respective keypads as an outbreak of confused technical gibberish filled the room, but no one's voice rose above Deputy Director Anderson who immediately took charge.

"Does the tail still have visual contact?" He demanded of the audio-tech. "Does it?"

"Mongoose One reports loss of visual contact --- snake has pulled behind..." The audio-tech pressed his eyes shut and covered both ears trying to ignore the discordant din in the room. "A row of ..."

"A row of what?" Anderson demanded. "A row of what, goddamnit?"

"I can't make out the word, sir. It sounds like he's saying *mangoes*."

"That's mangroves." Anderson said matter-of-factly. "Reconfigure the satellites. Pull 'em back. Get a wider angle so we can see where the hell they are." Senior personnel barked at their underlings who repeated the orders aloud. "Tell the tail to close. Close now. Full throttle close until visual is reestablished."

"Mongoose One this is base. — Abort game plan. — Emergency close until visual of Snake is reestablished. — Repeat, emergency close until visual of Snake is reestablished."

"Where the hell is the feed? Pull it back... pull it back!"

———————————

The last of the natural light dissolved behind them as Bra spun the skiff around the first bend and officially entered the Green Room. Like a blind man speed reading brail, Bra hit a few switches and negotiated the next two turns without having to pull back on the power at all. Both Nick and Shannon defensively cupped their ears as the engine's whine became trapped in the thickets of mangroves and root structures that entombed them. Normally, Bra wouldn't even attempt to navigate the maze that was the Green Room's interior without at least a spotlight, but being invisible for the time being was worth the risk. Without warning, Bra cut the power to near zero.

"What the hell is going on, Nick?" Shannon asked with an obvious waver in her voice. She pulled her hands from her ears and felt at the blackness in front of her. "Nick?"

"I'm right here," Nick said as he sat beside her. "Don't ask any questions. If you want the story that will make your career just do as I say. Now, get on the deck."

"Why do I have to..."

"I told you no questions; there's no time." Nick grabbed hold of Shannon behind the neck and guided her into the well of the boat. "Now get in a fetal position. Do it."

Nick couldn't see Shannon's outline, but he reached down and felt her to make sure that she had complied. "Now put your hands over your head and let your arms cover your face." Shannon heard a woosh, and then felt a type of cold rubber blanket descend unevenly over her. Nick worked to tuck Bra's rain tarp all around Shannon's curled-up body, making sure that she was adequately mummified, and then took a second tarp and wrapped her up again.

"Now, listen to me and don't say a word, okay? We're about to do something that's a little dangerous and the tarp is nothing more than a precaution. It'll keep you from getting scraped up so as long as you lay completely still and stay that way until I tell you that it's alright." Nick tucked the last bit of tarp underneath Shannon's left side, lay on top of her and said, "Bra.... Now." Shannon heard the muffled buzz of the engine pick up just a little and felt the skiff move slightly forward. The boat bobbed from side to side for a second or two and then Shannon felt some water splash into the boat as it began scraping along the mangrove roots. The scratching sound was high-pitched and unnerving, like a dentist's drill, but neither Bra nor Nick noticed; each nervously alternated between looking at the blackness in front of them and the blackness behind them.

"Nick." Shannon's muted voice was barely audible through two layers of rubber.

"Shhh. Not another word. It'll all be over in a few minutes."

All of a sudden, Bra's raspy voice yelled, "Oh, shit!" Not a second later the boat struck something immovable, causing Shannon to slide forward despite the full weight of Nick who was still on top of her. She then heard the motor rev for a second before stalling out completely.

"What the hell was that, Goddamnit?" Nick asked in an angry whisper.

"We drifted between two mangroves; the bow's stuck."

"Come on Bra, get us the hell out of here."

Shannon could faintly hear Bra straining to push the skiff free.

"I can't budge her. She's wedged in there too tight."

"Son-of-a-bitchin'-bastard, we don't have time for this. Rock it free."

Again, Shannon heard Bra's moans but only felt the boat move slightly from side to side.

"I can't, I tell ya. She's wedged too far in."

Shannon then felt Nick lift himself off her. "Just start the motor and put it in reverse, Bra. I'll push us free." Shannon heard the two men shuffling their positions and then felt Bra place his hand on her twice-covered shoulder.

"It'll be okay, sweetheart, just stay still." Bra hit the motor once, twice and a third time before it finally kicked over. Almost simultaneously, Shannon felt the skiff rock deep to the right and then backup. She could hear very faint muttering, but couldn't make out exactly what was being said, primarily because Bra kept revving the engine.

"There ya go ... atta boy." Bra said as the boat drifted backward. "We're off. Good work." Bra stroked where he thought Shannon's head would be and again whispered some reassurances. "Nothin' to worry about, sweetie, we're okay now. We'll be out of here in a minute. Just sit tight."

"What in the hell is going on?" General Glendale was now maroon from an anginal bleed caused by a combination of hate, stress and impatience. Spit shot out of his mouth with every syllable. "Status. Give me a Goddamn status report."

"Mongoose One — requesting status — repeat, requesting immediate status."

The General watched as the huge screen blinked in rapid succession creating a strobe effect in the room. Then all eyes returned to the spindly young tech who seemed to push his earpiece even further into his ear. "Snake has ..."

"Knock it off with the damn names for chrissakes and just tell me what's goin' on." Anderson commanded.

Much to his credit, the audio-tech remained focused on his job. "The tail boat lost him in a tunnel, sir."

"A tunnel? They lost them in a... tunnel." Anderson muttered. "They're in the middle of the Atlantic-fucking-Ocean --- and they lost them in a ... tunnel."

"That's affirmative sir." The tech said with noted trepidation. "And the tail boat is lost within the tunnel. They have no visual."

"Sir," the leader of the satellite team spoke up without taking his eyes off the screen. "I believe we have something."

No one had even noticed that the screen had stopped blinking and now showed what appeared to be a long and meandering, black, cylinder spread across the white that was the ocean surface.

"Now what in the hell is that?" The General asked, squinting at the image.

"It would appear to be a closely aligned string of islands, sir, or an inordinately amassed thicket of mangroves which could create a type of tunnel. And if so, that would explain why the satellite lost them."

"But that means that they have to still be in there, correct?"

The screen blinked several times as the satellite team leader again widened the angle, "What we're seeing now is a view of the ... tunnel ... for lack of a more accurate term, and a half-mile radius on all sides. There is nothing else moving, so I would say that it is safe to assume that both boats are still within, sir."

"Well, then keep the feed right where it is." The General sat back down for the first time since the melee began, and like everyone else in the room, waited. The dizzying fray had calmed to a silent and much more aggravating stillness. Billions of dollars of genius and technical advancement rendered impotent because of some trees. Even the audio-tech decided to begin censoring the updates which had now become depressingly repetitious: Lost in dark, no visual. No one dared say anything for fear of consuming the last inch of General Glendale's fuse. Instead, all eyes bounced between the tunnel's entrance and exit waiting for a grainy/green blip to alight. Only the clockwise sweep of the satellite scope and the digital timer at the bottom of the screen seemed unaffected by the tension. Still, nothing.

"Sir," the audio-tech's voice was almost giddy. "The tail boat believes it has reestablished visual contact."

"Believes? Well do they, or don't they?"

"They can see a light being used by what they believe to be the subject boat. They are following the light and ..."

"Sir." A younger member of the satellite team stood up and pointed at the blip coming out of the northern end of the tunnel and picking up speed.

Anderson, proving his worth immediately swung into action. "Get me a close up. Forget the tunnel. Concentrate on the boat." He then turned to the audio-tech. "Don't slack. Keep the updates coming, son. Where's my close-up?"

"Sir." The same junior-grade satellite guidance specialist now pointing at another emerging blip.

"Mongoose One is out of the tunnel and has reestablished visual. — Snake is within two hundred and fifty yards. — Requesting instructions. — Close or maintain periphery? — Repeat, requesting order to close or maintain periphery."

General Glendale held up his hand and remained silent until the screen flashed for the final time and showed three individuals, one at the bow, one at the helm and one on the stern. "Maintain periphery," the General said as he settled back into his chair at the center of command. "Reconfigure the satellite to pick up the subject and the tail."

———————————

Shannon hadn't waited for permission, she just wriggled herself out from under the tarp and sat back down on the rear hatch. She took a minute to notice that Bra had the boat at full throttle, and that Nick was standing near the bow with his back to her. She then glanced over her shoulder just long enough to see that they were about five hundred or so feet in front of the only other boat in the area.

"You okay, honey?" Bra asked without turning around.

"I'm fine," Shannon said, tinged with both anger and impatience.

"Don't worry," Bra said, grabbing just a glance at the boat behind them. "We'll explain everything once we stop. You better just hold on now."

Even though it didn't seem possible, Bra edged up the speed a little more and kept it there for the next forty-five minutes. He wound his way north across an endless succession of flats out of Key West, past Stock Island and then Shark Key, but still showed no signs of stopping. And if not for the cold metal reality of Shannon's 9-millimeter pressed up against the back of his neck, Bra would have kept going until he really did run out of gas.

"That's enough. Stop the boat." Shannon pressed the pistol into the soft flesh on the back of Bra's neck to convey her sincerity. "Come on, stop it."

Bra hesitated for a moment and then gradually cut the power, bringing the boat to a controlled halt. He then turned slowly with his hands in the air and faced Shannon who had struck a wide stance, holding a gun in one hand and her CIA identification in the other. "Whatever you say, honey," Bra said with a grin. "Now, I'm far too old to die like this so you just stay calm, okay?"

Shannon brushed past Bra toward the bow, grabbed hold of Nick's shoulder to spin him around, and found herself face to face with the real Diego Martin. Shannon was in an absolute daze and her expression showed it. Her mouth hung agape as she checked him out from his Cheshire smile to his Docksiders. He wore a red fishing shirt, a tan fishing cap, and a pair of blue jeans... Nick's identical outfit. It took less than a second for her to figure it out, and a second more for her to signal for the tail boat to close. Then, with her thumb, she depressed the crown on her watch and turned the underside to her lips. "Base, this is Urdang. It would appear that Houdini made me for an agent and then promptly escaped.

CHAPTER 16

"Yo."

"Hi, this is Nick De Julia. Is Sweets available?"

"Yeah, hold on for a second." Nick heard the guy drop the phone and then yell for Leander Sweets Lovell. Of all the clients Nick had ever represented, Sweets was his all-time favorite. He was a career criminal to be sure, but there was just something loveable about the guy. Nick used to say that Sweets was the kind of crook who would rob you at gunpoint, but make sure that you had cab fare home.

"This is Sweets talkin'."

"Sweetie-boy how ya doin'?"

"Who's talkin' there?"

"It's the guy who's kept you out of an orange jumpsuit for the past twenty years."

"Hey, hey, hey ... How are you counselor? Long time no talk."

"I know, it has been a while. You been staying out of trouble I hope?"

"Yes indeedy. I have turned over a new leaf, my friend. No more smokin', no more dopein', no more' drinkin'. I'm spendin' time with my family. I'm tellin' you, man, it's a whole new me. Hell, I'm even off probation."

"Bullshit."

"I know, I know... pretty much been on probation since birth, but not no more."

"Hey that's great to hear. I'm happy for you."

"Thank you, thank you, thank you. And you know what? I owe it all to you, my friend. Remember what you said to me as we were leaving the courthouse that last time? Huh?"

"Yeah, I asked if you had anything to do with the sudden disappearance of the state's key witness."

"No after that."

"I said that you had too much on the ball to be wasting your life as a shiftless, no good, second rate, stick-up man."

"And?" Sweets sounded almost giddy.

"And that if you didn't turn it all around your tomb stone was gonna read: Here lies someone who managed to be a piece of shit from wire to wire."

"That's right. And in case I never told you before, thank you for the love, man. I felt it from you that day and I never forgot it. You talked to me like a friend and it touched me, man, it touched me. And I'm happy to say that I've been straight up ever since."

"That's really something, Sweets."

"Yes, sir. No more crime for me, man. No more runnin' afoul of the law, you know what I'm sayin'? That part of my life is done, it's over, it's history."

"Congratulations."

"So, what can the new and improved Sweets Lovell do for one, Nick De Julia?"

"I need you to commit a crime."

"No problem. Whatcha got in mind?"

"Remember all those cigars you used to get for me?"

"Yeah, yeah, yeah, yeah. The Cubans you're talkin' about?"

"Right."

"What about 'em?"

"You told me that you used to take a couple of trips a year to the Bahamas and then sneak over to Cuba to get the smokes, right?"

"Yeah, that's right. I was cuttin' out the middle man back in those days. So what?"

"I need to know how you did it."

"Did what?"

"Snuck into Cuba. I mean, were you hooked into some sort of syndicate down there? Did you pay off someone in the Bahamas who had a boat? Did you have a fake passport, what?"

"What's goin' on, man? Why you wanna know all this shit?"

"I really don't have the time to go into it, pal. Suffice it to say that I got myself mixed up in this case and, believe it or not, the Feds are after me. I need to get lost for a while. I figure I can't do any better than Cuba."

"So, where you callin' from?"

"I'm at the Nassau airport. But, to be honest with you, getting this far was no easy chore."

"Cuba, huh?"

"Yeah."

"Look, man, I ain't passin' judgment or nothin', but has it dawned on you that everyone and his crippled-ass uncle is trying to get the hell *out* of Cuba? I mean, do you really think that trying to get into that country is a smart move on your part?"

"Actually, there's someone there that I need to see."

"Okay, man. I'm sorry I asked. Ain't none of my business anyway and I'm sure you got your reasons."

"Hey look, Sweets, I feel like shit involving you in this, especially now that you turned your life around and all, but I'd appreciate your help all the same."

"Are you kidding, man? I'd do anything for you. Anything at all."

"Thanks."

"You got it. No problemo."

"So?"

"So what?"

"So how do I do this?"

"Alright. Pay attention now. Have you got a pen?"

"Yeah I do. Go ahead."

"Alright. Now, the first thing that you have to do is walk over to the Cubano Air Terminal and buy a ticket."

"Buy a ticket?"

"Yeah, that's first. But then comes the hard part."

"What's that?"

"You get on the plane and fly there." Sweets gave it a second to sink in. "Think you can handle that?" Sweets asked, trying unsuccessfully to stymie a laugh. "'Cause if not, I can run through it again."

"No, I think I've got it."

Now Nick could hear Sweets laughing his ass off. "You crack me up, man. Did I ever strike you as some sort of criminal genius or somethin'? Syndicate my ass. What syndicate is gonna help a shiftless, no good, second rate stickup man? All these years you thought I was the Pablo Escobar of the cigar world?" That I had planes and drop zones and shit? No wonder you paid so much for those damn things."

"What about all that stuff you told me ––– about how hard it was getting in and out of Cuba and that was the reason that the cigars cost so much?"

"Well that was just basic salesmanship, you know what I'm sayin'? Just watchin' the bottom line."

"Hey, no bullshit --- that's it?"

"Absolutely. Sorry to disappoint you, though. I know you were hoping for better and all, but that's it. Make your reservation and go, man."

"How can that be? I thought it was illegal for Americans to go to Cuba."

"You crack me up, man. Which one of us is the lawyer? It ain't illegal to go to Cuba. It's illegal to spend money there – that's it. And the Bahamians don't give a damn what you do, and neither do the Cubans. I mean they'll look at your passport when you land in Havana but that's all; they won't stamp it or nothin'. You just have to tell 'em how long you plan on stayin', but that's about it. –– I'm serious, man. No one's gonna bother ya."

Nick was rubbing his eyes in embarrassment. "And that's it, huh?"

"Ain't nothin' else to it. More than anything them Cubans want US dollars, so they make it as easy as pie for tourists to go there and part with their cash. But remember, they can't do no business with any US companies, so you can't use no credit cards. You got to pay cash for everything. But that shouldn't be no problem for you, man. You were always long on green if I remember correctly."

"Thanks, Sweets."

"I do what I can for ya. You know that."

"Sure. I'll see you."

"Hold on there for a second, counselor. You listen up. Whatever it is that you're doin', I strongly recommend that you give it up. You ain't cut out for crime, man. You got too much to lose, you know what I'm sayin'?"

"This coming from the man who introduced me to the saying *crime don't pay unless you do it every day?*"

"I'm just tryin' to return the favor, man. That's all."

"I'll keep that in mind. Thanks."

"One last thing."

"What."

"Them Cubans don't give a shit about you goin' in, but they can get a little freaky about you goin' out. I mean it ain't like here. If you stay one day longer than you're supposed to, they'll go lookin' for your ass. So, don't go messin' around, okay? Go easy. And good luck, man."

Nick hung up the phone, rolled his eyes and took a seat. Clearly, he needed to take a moment and regroup. When you reach a point where you can't see the forest because the forest is in the way, a breather is long past due. Gone was the cocky smirk of contentment which Nick loved to put on display, he felt confused and almost regretful; virgin territory for someone of Nick's ilk. He leaned forward, put his elbows on his knees, and silently reminded himself that all worry was wasted time, but continued, nonetheless. Was Shannon CIA or really a reporter like she said? What if I do get Jorge Diaz out of jail? I don't know what kind of person he really is, he knew the risks and threw the dice to the back wall anyway. Maybe Sweets was right. Maybe it ain't worth screwing up my life for. What will I have really accomplished? And at what cost? Nick pulled his head from his hands and really thought hard about that last question. It was one that he never permitted himself to contemplate before. Do what needs be done and move on. End of story. Regret had absolutely no utilitarian value at all -- - a complete waste of valuable time. Ethics were only important to the good lawyers, not the great ones. Still, the question nagged at him. He knew the answer deep down, but even during this rare moment of soul searching he chose not to deal with it. Instead, he reminded himself of the blood oozing out of Jorge Diaz's leg and that pathetic Cuban girl, sitting on the dirt floor of her cell, clutching her stillborn infant. And Maria and her handsome boys whose lives are possibly forever changed for what? *Why?* He asked himself as he stared at the Cubano Air ticket desk.

CHAPTER 17

"Can I offer you anything?" General Glendale looked unusually at ease, almost welcoming in fact.

"No thanks. I'm good."

"Okay then." The General reached over, picked a file off his desk, and started leafing through it. "I want you to know that your country appreciates your efforts over the last few years. Your contribution has been significant. I commend you."

"Is that really why I was brought here, to be commended?"

"No. I just wanted to meet you and discuss a few things. That's alright, isn't it?" The General never even bothered to look up. "And from the list of payments I see here, I'd say that you've done well for yourself. I trust that all of the payments have been made in a timely manner, yes?" Now it was General Glendale's turn to wait in vain for an answer. "Yes, you've done very well," the General repeated for emphasis as he scanned yet another page.

"Sir, can I just say that ..."

"So, have you had an opportunity to talk to your colleagues about this most recent occurrence? You, of course, know to what I am referring."

"Yes, I do. But I'm afraid that ..."

"And what have you learned?" The General closed the file slowly and aimed his blue/gray stare at his guest.

"I know how they pulled it off, but I don't know where De Julia went."

"Really? And tell me, how did they pull it off, as you say?"

the General asked through another fake smile.

"De Julia got word to Diego Martin that he needed to shake you guys. They planned the whole thing out in advance. De Julia told Martin what to wear and where to be. They made the switch in the Green Room — that's what we call that area where the mangroves grow into one another to form a kind of tunnel. Anyway, Martin gave De Julia a snorkel so he could stay under water until your tail boat passed. He also hid a jet ski in there so De Julia could get out."

"What happened then?"

"Martin arranged to have a sea-plane land about a half-mile away from the tunnel, and De Julia just doubled back out of the Green Room and met up with them. Apparently that all went down while you were still chasing the old guy."

"And where did they take Mr. De Julia?"

Luis Mendoza looked down at the floor for a second and then off to his right. "I really don't know," he said unconvincingly.

"I'm sorry? What did you say?"

Luis paused again. "I said that I don't know where they took Mr. De Julia."

General Glendale tossed the file on his desk, walked around to where Luis was sitting, and took the guest chair next to him. "Do you know what we call an informant without information? A felon. Or have you forgotten about that? Possession with intent to distribute, wasn't it?" The General took yet another vicious pause. "Yes, I believe it was. And please feel free to correct me if I'm wrong, but you were caught with such a large amount of cocaine that it was considered a federal offense. Yes, I'm fairly sure that's right. Remind me, what are you looking at again?"

"Twelve years."

"Well, that was the minimum mandatory sentence, I believe. It could wind up as high as twenty-five, isn't that so?"

"Hey look, I've done what you asked. I've been feeding you guys busts for years. Not just drugs but immigration stuff too. I never held out on you, not once."

"You never had a choice. You've been feeding us information to keep yourself out of federal prison, and you're gonna keep doing it or that's exactly where you'll wind up. But only after I let it be known to your buddies at the Brothers of Freedom that one of their own has been --- how shall I put it ---

rather talkative."

"Why did you shoot that plane down?"

"And where do you get the balls to ask me a question like that? I think that you're forgetting to whom you're speaking."

"Murder was never part of our arrangement."

"And matters of national security are not the type of thing that I feel impelled to discuss with low-level informants such as yourself." The General leaned his head slightly toward the door. "Mr. Anderson." Instantly, Deputy Director Anderson entered and took his post at the General's side. "Mr. Anderson, it would appear that Mr. Mendoza's services will no longer be necessary. Please take him into custody and alert the US attorney for this district that our ... what shall we call it ... ah ... arrangement with him has terminated due to his refusal to cooperate per the terms of his plea agreement."

"Okay, wait a minute." Luis was now smiling at both gentlemen. "I'm sure we can work something out here."

"And what would that something be, Mr. Mendoza?" The General asked with a mock tone of inquisitiveness.

"I can find out where they took him. I'm just gonna need some time."

"I don't give a damn where they took him, I only care about where he is."

"I understand."

"I don't think you do. Two days."

"Pardon?"

"You have two days to find out the information I'm looking for or I'll have a warrant issued for your arrest."

"Hey, I'm not even supposed to see any of those guys until next week, and even then, I'm not sure that I can get you that kind of information without raising suspicion. It's not something that they'd normally share with me."

"That would be your problem, Mr. Mendoza."

"I'm gonna need more time than you're giving me."

"Well, if time is a concern, I suggest you stop wasting it." General Glendale stood up and Deputy Director Anderson helped Luis do the same. He then escorted him out of the office to an awaiting agent without another word being said.

Anderson looked at the General and decided to think out loud. "I guess we have to discern that if DeJulia contacted the real

Diego Martin then he must have figured out that the guys who roughed him up in Miami were really with us." Anderson shook his head in disgust. "I'm not sure how, but that must be what happened." The General looked expectedly annoyed but didn't respond. "Do you really think this kid will be able to find out anything?" Anderson asked the General.

"He's a sneaky little bastard. He should be okay, but I want a twenty-four-hour-a-day tail on him. As for this Lenny Cicero character, I want two teams on him. An undercover tail and a second team with parabolic microphones. I want to know every word that comes out of his mouth. Clearly, he's the weak link. Sooner or later, he's bound to screw up."

"What about the old man and this Diego Martin fellow. Were we able to get anything out of them?"

"Nothing that we didn't already know. And for what it's worth, I don't think that De Julia would have informed either of them of his intentions, he's too smart. We'll have better luck with the informant, so let them go. And despite our... difficulties," the General said, nearly choking on the word, "I don't think that De Julia is any closer to knowing the real truth, and that's all that matters. So, if playing James Bond makes him happy, so be it. I don't care if he thinks he's winning, so long as he's not."

"Is there anything you want me to do?"

"Get in touch with every air traffic controller within a fifteen-hundred-mile radius and see if an unscheduled flight popped up on any of the scopes. I also want you to check whether any pilot who we know to be associated with this Brothers of Freedom group filed a flight plan for today. And let me know what you come up with."

CHAPTER 18

The plane pulled in low, giving Nick his first real glimpse at old Havana, glistening in the amber hue of a fading sun. He wasn't sure what he had expected, but the city, even from a cloud's distance, looked anything but forbidding. Like a once beautiful woman, Havana maintained a certain allure, a vibrance that time can chip away at but never quite conquer. Nick could practically hear the laughter of the dozen or so children jumping from the city's seawall into the Atlantic surf, timing it so they hit the water just as the waves crested and crashed. Maybe it was the thrill of heading to a taboo land, or maybe just a byproduct of shedding big brother, but Nick felt the buzz of anticipation. Something good will come of this trip, he thought to himself.

Once on the ground it was a matter of minutes before the entire plane load of adventure seekers, most of whom were American, gathered on the tarmac. A small contingent of unarmed military personnel then quietly herded the group toward the corrugated metal enclosure that was the Cubano Air Terminal. Nick was actually taking in the surroundings when one of his fellow passengers, who looked like he was in Havana for an international skateboard competition, tapped him on the shoulder and pointed at the soldier directly in front of them.

"Hey, check it out, dude."

Nick pulled his Revos down a bit to clearly see that the soldier in question was wearing a Nike tee shirt underneath his olive-drab military issue.

"Communism in the 21st Century, hey, dude?"

Just as Sweets had predicted, Nick was in and out of Customs without a question being asked or his passport being stamped. All they did was copy down some information off his paperwork, wish him well, and point him toward the Cuban version of a cab stand. As per American custom, Nick went to the first cab in the cue and, despite the car's questionable mechanical health, got in the back seat.

"Hablo Ingles?"

"So, so," the cab driver retorted, with a waggle of his right hand.

"Good enough. Where's the best hotel at?"

"Best is hard to say. Right now, the better hotels are in Miramar, which is only about five kilometers outside of Havana. The Melia Cohiba, the Havana Beach Club, the Novotel ... All very nice."

"Fine. Any of those will do. And your English is very good, does everyone here speak so well?"

"Si, yes, everyone in Cuba learns in school for many years."

From the second the cab driver turned off the meter and pulled away from the airport, Nick marveled at how Cuba seemed to be a country awash in contradiction. Brand new Mercedes S Class sedans sped past oxen drawn carts. Kids wearing parachute pants in the design of a US flag were sitting beneath billboards that celebrated the Victorious Revolución. Women in ratty house dresses walked hand-in-hand with children in pressed yellow and white school uniforms. Key West was quirky, but Cuba, at least to an American, was nothing short of surreal.

"Hey, kid ... can I ask you a question?"

"Si, Señor."

"What do you think of Americans?"

Without so much as a pause he said, "American people... very good. American government... not very good."

Nick thought for a moment. "What do you think about Castro?" he asked, fully expecting the cab driver to avoid the question as if the car was bugged.

"He is very good man with very bad ideas. No good for the people, you know? He always say — will get better — will get better — will get better... But things never get better. Life here is very hard, except if you are in the government. If you are in the Cuban government, life is very, very good."

Nick didn't show it, but he was taken aback by the cab driver's

176

candor; outspokenness was not supposed to be a Cuban commodity in great supply.

"What's your name?"

"Vladimir, sir."

"So where are we heading, Vladimir?" Nick asked slightly amused at the name.

"I thought I would take you to Novotel. Is the newest Hotel on the island and is very nice. I think you enjoy."

"I'm sure it'll be fine."

"And what about cigars, sir? If you are interested in purchasing any, I can get them for you cheap. My cousin works in the factory. Very good, very good. Same cigars as in the government stores but much cheaper. I get you some, yes?"

Nick's visit was less than fifteen minutes old and he already found his first capitalist.

"Why don't we hold off on that for now? I'm gonna be here for a few days so there's no real rush."

"Very good, sir. But you let me know, yes?"

"Absolutely," Nick muttered as he grew increasingly preoccupied by Vladimir's emerging driving style which was reminiscent of someone in the hunt coming down the stretch at Daytona. As Nick searched nervously and unsuccessfully for a seatbelt, Vladimir darted in between perceived openings in the late-afternoon traffic. The Russian-made piece-of-junk he was driving kind of looked like a Hyundai's sickly little brother, but actually was fast enough to be dangerous.

"So, where you from, Nick?"

"New York," Nick said with noticeable trepidation.

"Ahh, El Duque Hernandes," Vladimir yelled out as he tucked his chin to his shoulder to imitate the pitching style of the Cuban born member of the Yankees. "Do you know of El Duque?"

"Of course. Helluva pitcher."

"Oh, yes, very good, very good." Vladimir's smile beamed as he now demonstrated a penchant for leaning on his horn which, oddly, never seemed to make anyone angry. Most people would turn around in no particular hurry and smile at him despite the continual blare.

"You mind if I ask you another question, Vladimir? And there's no reason to turn around when answering, by the way."

"¿Qué?"

"Keep your eyes on the road, kid."

"Yes, sir. Of course."

"What is a paradoer?"

"Parador," Vladimir said, correcting Nick's pronunciation. "A parador is a home which the government allows to be used as a kind of a restaurant."

"Have you ever heard of one named Barredo?"

"Barredo, yes. Is very good."

"Would you like to meet me there for dinner later on tonight?"

"Really?" Vladimir asked, clearly excited.

"Why not? I'm sure I could use a translator. Wouldn't want to end up eating monkey ass, you know?"

"I am your man, sir. Thank you. What time?"

"Why don't we meet at nine o'clock?"

"Very good. Shall I pick you up?"

"Depends. Is it far from this Novotel place?"

"No, sir. Is actually close by. Not even one kilometer's distance."

"Then I'd rather just walk and take in a little of the local flavor."

"Thank you, sir. Thank you so much."

Vladimir finally pulled off the highway and into a ritzy looking suburb which more closely resembled Palm Beach than the ravaged Cuban neighborhoods occasionally featured on CNN. Twelve-foot-high wrought iron gates and stone walls outlined each tropical estate with huge, Spanish-style mansions set at the far ends. Circular driveways, some wrapped around ornate fountains, gave each of the properties a palatial appearance. Even Vladimir slowed to a pace car's speed in seeming deference to the area's considerable curb appeal.

"Hey," Nick said, "Who the hell lives here?"

"High government officials."

"I wouldn't doubt it if Castro himself lived here."

"He does."

"No shit? This is Fidel Castro's neighborhood?"

"One of them. He has many homes."

Nick gawked for several more blocks and realized why he never heard of *high government officials* floating into Key West.

Vladimir pulled into the palm tree lined Novotel parking lot and up to the main entrance. The hotel itself was brand new and magnificent. Sandstone walls, marble floors, tropical works of art and rich, floral patterned furniture blended perfectly into what would be considered a five-star hotel in the free world. Smiling bellhops thirsty for American dollars raced to open doors and carry luggage for the arriving tourists. In fact, everyone in the place was smiling. Everyone, that is, except Vladimir. He stayed right at Nick's side, possessively guarding what the locals desire most: A visiting benefactor. He waved off a number of rushing bellmen and hustled Nick over to the front desk. Then, in Spanish, assumed the role of Nick's travel agent, trying to negotiate a favorable price. The young girl behind the counter was less interested in Vladimir's inquires than in Nick himself, whom she stared at in a not so wholesome way.

"How many nights you stay?" Vladimir asked Nick.

"Three."

"Trés." The girl behind the counter then responded in a dialect of Spanish that was far more pleasing than Vladimir's clipped translations.

"Is seventy-five dollars a night, okay? I know is expensive, but hotel is very new." Nick shrugged and thought to himself that on a strict cost per-night basis, maybe communism wasn't all that bad.

"That's fine." He reached into his pocket and without a second thought, pulled out his customary roll of green. As if hypnotized, Vladimir's and the desk clerk's expression went slack. Nick's pocket money was equal to roughly twelve years' wages for the average Cuban, literally. Seeing that their looks were a combination of amazed and respectfully envious, Nick became self-conscious. Not that he'd be mugged or targeted for a robbery or anything like that, but just that it had been a long time since Nick was made aware of just how much he had. An amount of money that wouldn't support him for a month back home was all the money in the world to Vladimir, the desk clerk, and by this time, two nosey doormen. If only they could see what I have strapped to my waist, Nick thought to himself. But he deftly peeled three hundred-dollar bills from the stack and buried the rest in his pocket. Nick then turned to finalize his plans with a still dazed Vladimir.

"Come on, snap out of it. So where is this Barredo place?"

Vladimir quickly shook his head from side to side. "It's on Vijello Blvd. I don't know the number but there is a sign."

"Okay then. I'll see you there. Nine o'clock?"

"Si, Señor. Nine o'clock."

Nick took the elevator up to the fifth floor, walked into his smartly appointed, brightly painted room, and noticed several things right away: There was an ashtray on every flat surface in the room, including one on the sink in the bathroom; the Sony television in the armoire was wider and newer than any you'd find at a local Hampton Inn; and there were instructions posted on the wall explaining the series of numbers one would have to dial to call the US. All in all, not exactly the third world, backward-ass, cut off from the rest of civilization kinda place that Nick had expected. So, he turned on ESPN — not ESPN Español — but actually ESPN, and then picked up the phone. He studied the chart for a second and then tried to remember if Lenny had caller ID. He flipped open his cell phone and, seeing that he had service, figured why take a chance.

"Talk to me."

Nick rolled his eyes much the same way he did before starting most conversations with Lenny.

"Where are you?"

"I just had some dinner and now I'm walking up Duval Street. Why?"

"Is anyone following you?"

An aggravated Lenny dropped the phone to his side just long enough to give an obligatory glance up and down the street. "Goldie Locks --- this is Papa Bear --- the coast's clear." Unfortunately, Lenny's statement was as incorrect as it was sarcastic.

"What happened to Diego and Bra?"

"They got arrested and then let go. No big deal. They're both fine."

"And what about Captain Scarborough? Anything yet?"

"No, nothing. They've been diving around the clock, but nobody's seen a thing. Should I tell him to quit?"

"No. Tell him to give it a couple more days"

"You got it." Nick could sense the edge in Lenny's voice from the outset; it was not a sound that he was used to hearing.

"So, how are you doing?" Nick asked somewhat cautiously.

"How am I doin'? Lousy, that's how I'm doin'." The Feds across the street were picking up Lenny's end of the conversation just perfectly through a hand-held, parabolic microphone, the tip of which was ever-so-slightly peeking out of their sunroof.

"What's the problem?"

"What's the problem, he asks." Lenny ran his hand through what little hair he had left. "Nick, for chrissakes, ----- the President of the United States?"

Nick cringed. "Heard about that, huh?"

"Heard about it? No, I didn't hear about it. I read about it in the New York freaking Times. God only knows how they found out about it."

"I sent them a copy of the subpoena."

"Oh, that's just beautiful. Not only do you forge my name without telling me, but you forge it in order to subpoena the President of the United States."

"It's just for a deposition."

"A deposition that I have to take. Me — Lenny Cicero — the Pride of Aruba. Are you out of your Goddamn mind? You really expect me to depose the President with less than two weeks to prepare?"

"Lenny, would it really have made a difference if you had two years to prepare?"

"Hey, hey, hey. I never said I was a trial lawyer. I do Muni-court shit, zoning, evictions, disturbing the peace cases. Why the hell did you have to send the subpoena in my name any way?"

"I wasn't sure when I'd be back, and I wanted to get the ball rolling on this thing. You know, give 'em a little something to think about. So, I ...."

"No, no, no, no. I don't wanna hear it. You get your ass back here right now and deal with this shit. You hear me?" Lenny screeched.

"Will you relax? It might not even get to that point. I'm sure they'll move to quash."

"They've already filed a motion to squash."

"Quash."

"Well whatever the hell it's called," Lenny screamed, "they've filed it along with two dozen other motions, one of which seeks my death by lethal injection."

"Will you calm down?"

Lenny continued to feverishly rub his head. "He sends a deposition subpoena to the White House and a copy to the New York Times under my name, and then tells me to relax. Do you know the last time I took a deposition? Do you? Never! That's the last time I took a deposition."

"Alright. I got it. I'll be back as soon as I can. Just put the whole thing out of your mind."

"Yeah?"

"Yeah."

"You promise?"

"I promise. Just stop yelling."

Lenny took a much-needed sigh of relief capped off with a little chuckle. "Alright then."

"So, when is their Motion to Quash scheduled for?"

"Day after tomorrow."

"You're shitting me?"

"I shit you not." Lenny paused and then actually pointed at the phone. "You can get back by then, right?"

Nick rubbed his eyes shut. "Lenny, I gotta tell ya, that's a little sooner than I had anticipated."

"What are you saying here?"

"That I'm afraid you're gonna have to handle the motion on your own."

"What?" Lenny yelled.

"You heard me."

"What are you insane? You expect me to appear before Judge Fabre? You know how she feels about me."

"We don't have a choice. There's no way that I can get back that quick."

"Why the hell not?"

"I just can't, Lenny."

"Tell me why."

"Just take my word for it, alright?" Now it was Nick's turn to sound annoyed.

"Well where does that leave me?"

"Opposing their motion the day after tomorrow."

With Lenny, no argument lasted more than a couple of minutes. There just wasn't that much that warranted prolonged unhappiness. So, in typical Lenny fashion, he smoothed out his beard, shrugged his shoulders, and accepted the realities of his situation. "Alright, Nick, go on."

"What does that mean?"

"Tell me what to say for Christ sake."

"Not a problem, just let me give it some thought, okay?"

"So, you're gonna get back to me?"

"Absolutely."

"You swear to God."

"Yeah, whatever. Just leave it to me."

Lenny cocked his head to one side. "I can live with that."

"I'm thrilled to hear it. Happy now?"

"I wouldn't go as far as to say that I'm happy --- I think that it would be more accurate to say that I'm appeased for the moment."

"Fair enough." Nick, let out a long, disgusted sigh. "So, any other disasters I need to know about it?"

"Well, now that you mention it, there was one other article in the paper that sounded a little hinky."

"Dealing with what?"

"Well --- you, actually."

Nick felt a strange feeling in the pit of his stomach, as if a bad turn of fate was in his immediate path. "What was it about?"

"I'm not entirely sure. It was this whole long, cryptic article, but the gist of it was that the government believes that you're involved in some sort of shady overseas activity. I just assumed that it was all planted to make you look bad. And I'm sure anyone else reading it would think the same." Lenny could suddenly sense the tension on the other end of the phone. "Trust me, buddy, we're not talking Pulitzer territory here." Still no response. "It was real crap, you know what I'm saying?"

"What did it mention, specifically?"

"Just that you had done something that the Justice Department was looking into."

"Is that it?"

"Pretty much. Except that the American Bar Association and the FBI were made aware of whatever it was." Lenny waited, but Nick didn't say a word. "Is this something that worries you?"

"I gotta go, Lenny."

"Hey, wait a second. What's up with all this?"

"Nothing. But I've really gotta get going."

"Well at least tell me where you're at?"

Nick thought for a second. "Where are you right now, exactly?"

"I'm standing out in front of Sloppy Joe's. I was just heading in for a nightcap. Why?"

Nick took another pause to weigh the risks and benefits and decided that perhaps it would be safer if at least one person in the world knew where he was. "Alright. Now when I say this, I don't want you to repeat it out loud or ask me any questions, okay?"

"Sure. Whatever you say, Nick. You know me... mum's the word."

"Lenny, do we understand each other?" Nick's voice was thick with pent up anger.

"Yes, we do. I've got it for cryin'-out-loud."

"I'm in Cuba, and I don't have time to explain why. Just ... go enjoy your drink."

"What the hell are you doin' in ..."

"What the hell did I just say?" Nick yelled, effectively cutting Lenny off. "Don't repeat it out loud --- ever. Jesus Christ, Lenny ..." was the last thing that Lenny heard, before Nick tapped "end" on his phone call and, quite possibly, his career.

For someone like Nick who prided himself on methodically calculating all the angles and probabilities when dealing with any dilemma, a blindside shot was particularly painful. He had contemplated his one major vulnerability when he started this whole thing, but never really thought they'd actually unearth it. But if it was so, the great Nicholas DeJulia was staring down the double barrel of disbarment and disgrace. To be out of the arena, he felt, would make his greatest unspoken fear come to pass: Nick would be like everyone else, coasting through life from paycheck to paycheck, accomplishing nothing, and waiting on retirement. And as he strolled through the side streets of Miramar on a warm and welcoming Cuban night, shed of his armor-plated bravado, Nick looked like a man who had just lost love.

He stopped for a moment to try and revive the cigar that he had ignored to death, and only then came to the sudden and unfortunate realization that an already horrible night still had plenty of time to get much worse. Nick was not heading to Barredo for dinner, but to fulfill a promise that was certain to break another person's heart; a task that he did not relish.

As Nick checked the concierge's directions against where he found himself, he suddenly noticed that the opulent mansions of

Miramar had been mysteriously replaced with rows of decrepit one story homes where the window treatment of choice appeared to be bed sheets. Instead of lush tropical landscaping, this particular neighborhood boasted a pack of scrawny dogs loitering around garbage barrels searching in vain for food. Although some of the homes had car ports, there wasn't a single car anywhere to be found. Plentiful, however, were pot holes. Pot holes the size of moon craters pitted the entire street. It was hard to detect whether they were the result of years of neglect or mortar fire. Call it force of habit, but Nick wondered how many slip and fall cases he could have if he practiced in Havana. And based on his last phone call with Lenny, perhaps it was a consideration worth more than a passing interest.

The biggest difference between the swank end of Miramar and the current spot, though, was laughter. This dingy little hamlet was alive. Despite the hour and the fact that it was a weekday night, no one seemed to be indoors. Groups of adults sat out in front of every home, playing cards or dominoes, listening to Cuban jazz, talking, smoking cigars and laughing. The neighborhood kids were out playing, running, and chasing one another around, but all of that changed as soon as one of them spotted Nick. In a flash, they all crowded around, tugging on his shirt and rattling off questions in exuberant Spanish. Nick tried but had difficulty understanding them, partly due to the language barrier and partly because they were all talking at once. But soon one voice drowned out the others. He was the tallest and probably the oldest member of the group.

"Americano?" he asked Nick, after quieting down his comrades.

"Sí. I'm an American."

"Where you from?" the boy said through a gap-toothed smile.

"Nuevo York," Nick responded.

As if right on cue, all of the children, even the girls, yelled out, "El Duque! El Duque!" Then everyone, including Nick, struck a pose to imitate the high kicking, chin tucking, hurler, which made each child laugh all the harder. Nick then passed out several one-dollar bills very much to the squealing delight of his new friends, before turning back to oldest boy.

"Dónde Barredo?" Nick asked, effectively conveying his question even though butchering all rules of syntax.

"Ah, Barredo ... Come, come, come." Much the same way

Vladimir had laid claim to Nick, this boy shoed away all his friends and led his new American pal to the corner where he could point to the parador's front door.

"Barredo," He said, continuing to point. "Is very good. You like."

"That's what I hear."

"Americano, you need cigars? My mother works in factory. I can get you fine price."

"No, I'm good." Nick thanked the boy, and then was somewhat disappointed when he asked for more money. Reluctantly, Nick slid him another buck.

"Buenas noches, my friend. Glad you make it." Vladimir wore a pair of white jeans, a shirt that looked more Jamaican than Cuban, and a smile that would have made Lenny envious.

"I'm sorry I'm late. You should have gone in and gotten us a table."

"I can no go in without you. I get in trouble."

"What are you talking about?" Nick asked cynically.

"Cubans can no go in any place of business if not with a tourist. Is the law."

"I don't get it."

"Castro does not allow Cubans to be in restaurants, or bars, or clubs, or stores unless they are invited by a tourist. Is only then okay."

"Sounds like bullshit to me."

"Bullshit, no bullshit ... is the law." Vladimir tapped the underside of his wrists together, which was Cuban sign language for handcuffs. "No good to break the law for Cubans."

"Or visiting Americans, I'm sure." Nick put his arm around Vladimir so as to leave no doubt that they were together and walked in the front door. The house was modest but clean. Each room was separated by black wrought iron gates instead of doors, giving the entire place a type of courtyard feel. An official-looking certificate issued by the government and authorizing that the home be used to serve food for turistas hung next to framed pictures of Fidel Castro and Che Guevara; more than likely the three came as a boxed set but Nick knew better than to ask.

"Welcome. Welcome." A fast-approaching old gent said in Spanish before offering Nick and Vladimir a man's man handshake.

"Una mesa para dos." Vladimir, eager to prove his utility, quickly requested a table for two. He then said something else to the host that Nick didn't catch at all, but just after they sat down, Nick saw the old man slip Vladimir a few dollars.

"Hey, what's that about?"

"No entiendo."

"Sure, you entiendo. You've entiendoed every word that I've said so far, so knock it off and tell me why that guy gave you some money."

"Is a finder's fee. He gives money for every customer I bring."

Nick shot Vladimir a slight smile and whispered, "But you didn't tell me about this place. I told you I wanted to come here."

"Si, Señor, but Mr. Castaneda does not know this." Vladimir, thinking that Nick would approve of his New York style guile, waited for a congratulatory wink or a nod. "Life is very hard in Cuba, my friend. You always have to do what you can to make money." Clearly, Vladimir was not only embracing capitalism, but was preparing for a career in automotive sales once the embargo ended.

Nick, unfazed, picked up his handwritten menu and said, "I'm sure life is just as tough for Mr. Castaneda, you know?"

Vladimir smelled trouble and after a quick risk/benefit analysis, moved to immediately defuse the situation. "I see that you are right, Señor. I never think of it like that. I will give the money back." No sense pissing-off a guy who could be his meal ticket for the next three days over two dollars, Vladimir thought.

"Just hold onto it. I'll take care of Mr. Castaneda."

Vladimir's smile returned instantly. "Gracias, Mr. Nick. Muchas gracias." He then picked up his menu and practically began to drool on the table. "Mr. Nick?"

"Yeah."

"Can I have anything on the menu?"

Vladimir's body language was that of a person who hadn't eaten in months. The mere proximity of real food had an obvious and very real effect on him. He looked like a lottery winner who had yet to receive his check. But his question was genuine, and he now waited anxiously for Nick's response.

"Sure. Why don't you order the best thing on the menu for the both of us, and a couple of drinks too."

A waiter who was no more than eleven or twelve years old and no doubt the son of the owner, came over to the table and offered to take the order. Vladimir decided to forego the special of the day, whatever it was, in favor of *Langoustes, frijoles, y arroz.* He then tucked his cervietta into his shirt and not-so-patiently awaited the arrival of his drink.

"So, what are we having?"

"Ah ... lobster, beans and rice. You'll like very much. I am sure of it."

"I hope so, because if it's lousy you're paying for it."

"Qué?" a deathly concerned Vladimir asked.

"I'm just kidding, my friend. How do you say 'joke' in Spanish?"

"Chiste."

"Well then, I was just chiste-ing with you."

"Thank God. I have no money. Life here is very, very hard."

The young waiter brought over two drinks that looked like cloudy gin and tonics with a green weed floating on top. Nick watched as Vladimir used his straw to pound into the bottom of the glass, causing it to become down right murky.

"And what are we drinking here?"

"Is a mojito."

Nick examined it a little more closely and noticed an inch or so of white sediment at the bottom of the glass. "It doesn't taste like any Mojito I've ever had. What's in it?"

"Is rum, soda, lime juice, sugar and yerba buena. Try it."

"What's yerba buena?"

"Is — ah— good grass."

Nick lifted the drink, took a sniff, and was relieved to learn that Cubans apparently considered mint to be good grass. So, mimicking Vladimir, he tapped at the layer of sugar at the bottom of his glass before taking his first sip. "Damn good. Refreshing." Nick took another sip, and then started to choke. "And sweet." Nick coughed until his face was red. "My God."

Nick regained his composure "So what do you do for a living, my friend?"

"I work at university. I am a painter."

"Oh yeah? Is that a full-time job?"

"Is supposed to be, but I no work in months."

"Why not?"

"No paint."

Nick now laughed and coughed in alternating bursts.

"Good evening gentlemen. I am Celia. I hope you're enjoying your drinks?" The young woman's voice was as soft as it was sweet. So sweet, in fact, that Nick was in no particular hurry to see her face as anything was bound to be a letdown. When it came to women he had long lived by the axiom: Never trust a profile, so he wasn't about to bank on a voice.

She was more Spanish than Cuban looking, with deep brown eyes, perfectly rounded cheekbones and lips that parted ever so slightly when she smiled. From her delicate frame to the glow of her tawny skin, Celia Moralez was that rarest combination of all things beautiful.

"The mojitos — are you enjoying them?"

Nick put his fist to his mouth and cleared his throat one last time. "They're terrific. Thank you for asking."

"Thank you for dining with us. If you should need anything, just let me know."

Nick nodded and smiled. "I'll do that."

"Enjoy your meals." With that, she turned and walked away. Nick watched her talk to some other diners for a moment or two and then disappear into the kitchen. Only then did he notice the all-knowing, Cheshire look on Vladimir's face.

"Que un caliente, eh?"

Nick stuck his tongue in his cheek. "No entiendo."

"Yes you entiendo. You entiendo every word I say so far, my friend."

Impressed with Vladimir's quip, but unable to think of the Spanish equivalent of touché, Nick just smirked and winked.

"Well, take it from Vladimir, there is no reason to settle on the first thing you see. You should shop, shop, shop. Plenty of other women in Cuba just like her. There is one around every street corner, believe me." Vladimir raised his glass up to his forehead and then took a long swig.

"Vladimir, my boy," Nick said, "that's one of the biggest mis-truths in life. There are supposed to be women like that on every corner, but there aren't. Truly beautiful women are like Haley's Comet: They're out there for sure, but they don't come around very often." Nick still hadn't taken his eyes off the kitchen door for fear of missing what would certainly be a graceful re-entry. "Do you know that woman?"

"She is the owner's daughter."

"Does she live here?"

"Of course. This is a parador. Everyone who works here is family."

The kitchen door swung out and Nick craned his neck for a good look, but all he could see was Celia's outstretched arm and perfectly manicured fingertips holding the damn thing open. Then, with a measured step, came an adorable little girl. She had short, black, curly, hair, and a very proud look on her face, pleased that she was being permitted to carry a platter of food to some customers. Celia filed in behind the little girl, placing her hand on the small of her back for support. The little girl delivered her platter of food to the table but needed Celia's help to serve it. She then curtsied for the older couple and ran back into the kitchen.

Dinner was surprisingly good, especially the lobster. Although it looked strange, rounded like a hamburger patty and at least an inch thick, it tasted delicious. Not that Vladimir chose to savor every morsel. His approach was more along the lines of hungry lion meets slow impala. Nick hardly noticed. He was far more interested in stealing glances at Celia. The way she moved, her smile, the way she danced past the flamenco guitar player in perfect rhythm, her tendency to physically touch anyone she was speaking with, it all appealed to Nick. And she seemed to make everyone happy. Each patron, the waiters, the cab drivers who were hanging around hoping to pick up a fare, they all lit up when she offered her attention. She was the kind of woman whose presence made others feel better about themselves. She was... captivating.

But Nick wasn't there to get a date. Quite to the contrary, he was there to be the bearer of exceedingly bad news. Suddenly, he flashed back to the Guantanamo prison and Celia's sister, sweat-soaked, bloodied, and pitifully rocking her dead baby. It was an image that Nick wanted to forget but couldn't. And it was at that very moment he realized the same pit of human despair wasn't on the other side of the world, but on the other side of the island.

"You okay, man? You no look so good." Apparently, Vladimir had mustered the will to set down his fourth mojito just long enough to notice the concerned look on Nick's face.

"It's no big deal. I was just thinking about something that I have to do."

"But something you don't want to do, yes?"

"That's right. It's something that I definitely don't want to do."

"Do you know what Cubans do in those situations?"

"No."

"We have another mojito and worry about it later."

Nick looked askance at his new friend and decided that dinner was now over. He stood up and placed a neatly folded one-hundred-dollar bill on the table, which was equal to the tab plus a four hundred percent tip. Vladimir then grabbed the check to look at the total.

"Mr. Nick. Why you pay so much? Is only twenty US."

"The rest is Mr. Castenada's tip. I told you that I'd take care of him."

Vladimir, seeing the apparent error of his ways quickly produced the two dollars that he had scammed from the host. "I give it back. I give it back right now. I tell him what I did. You give me the tip, yes?"

"No, no, no," Nick said, forcing the money back into Vladimir's hand. "That's the way this one went."

"Please, Mr. Nick."

"No," Nick said firmly. He then leaned in close to his young companion and said, "Let me give you a little piece of American advice."

"Sí, Señor."

"Never screw a friend. 'Cause it always comes back to bite you on the ass. Entiende?"

All Vladimir could do was stare at Mr. Castenada's good fortune lying on the table. He tried to think of a persuasive rebuttal, but the half-gallon of rum he had consumed made that unlikely. Nick then flashed his eyes quickly toward the door and Vladimir knew that the gravy train had reached its final destination. He thanked Nick for the dinner and then asked if Nick would be so kind as to give him cab fare home. Clearly, Vladimir failed to see the wisdom of Nick's advice. Amused though by his moxie, Nick escorted him outside, gave him five dollars, and watched an ashamed Vladimir slowly walk past three cabs and into the steamy Cuban night.

Truth be told, Vladimir's bullshit was only slightly more obvious than Nick's. As he stood in front of the restaurant still trying to catch glimpses of an ever-in-motion Celia Moralez through the open windows, he decided that the bad news could wait. It would be a sin, he thought, to wipe a smile off such a pretty face on such a beautiful night. He understood, of course, that his decision to postpone the unpleasantness was nothing more than a fragile truce between the stronger and weaker aspects of his personality, but he really didn't care. Satiated by one long last look at Celia, who walked onto the front porch for a breath of fresh air, Nick got into a cab, and headed back to his hotel.

CHAPTER 19

Nick lay in bed, arms folded behind his head, staring at the stucco ceiling. All night long his pleasant thoughts of Celia were chased out of his mind by the realization that Lenny Cicero was back in Florida in charge of this law suit. Information remained the goal and Nick felt like he was failing miserably. For all of his backbone and one-ups-man-ship with some rather formidable foes, Nick had now thoroughly convinced himself that he hadn't really accomplished much at all. Outsmarting the Feds gave him a bit of an ego boost for sure but was he really any closer satisfying his own curiosity about the incident, or to helping Jorge Diaz or Celia's sister? Was any of this chase leading to the truth, or was this particular truth just unreachable, huddled at the bottom of a classified abyss right alongside a multitude of other shameful government moments perpetrated in the name of National Security? But the one issue above all others that sat at the center of his mind, was why? Why would the U.S. Government shoot down a private plane and why would they be going to such lengths to cover it up?

It had been a week or so since Nick had become involved in the matter, and even though he hadn't made much progress, he felt like he had no choice but to plow forward. "One thing at a time," he muttered to himself. He was in Cuba to deliver a message, and as he threw the covers off, he silently vowed that not another day would pass with him in derogation of his objective.

The sun had yet to rise, but Nick was already on the move. He retraced his steps from the evening before, but this time his pace had purpose. Affected by neither the mansions nor the slums, Nick walked quickly toward a café that was just across the street from Barredo. He watched as several bleary-eyed men speaking in raspy tones received a shot glass filled with maybe two ounces of coffee which looked to be three shades blacker than a moonless night. One at a time, the men paid for their coffee, downed it in one gulp as if it were a nip of whiskey on a cold day, and then headed off to work. When it was his turn, Nick asked for five cups, paid a dollar (got back change) and set up shop at one of the four outdoor tables overlooking Vijello Boulevard. A waiter, yammering something in Spanish that sounded distinctly cautionary, rushed toward Nick with a bowl filled with brown crystal clusters. Given that courage was the order of the day, he threw back the first cup of unsweetened Cuban coffee. Without so much as a single facial concession to the bitter sting searing his throat, Nick promptly plunked two crystals in each cup and waited for them to melt.

For an hour at least, he bravely sipped the acidic black sludge and pretended to read the day's edition of Granma, Cuba's official newspaper. But in actuality, showing the patience of a sniper, Nick was staring at the front door of Barredo, waiting. At 6:10 an upstairs light went on and by 6:30, he could see several people moving about, but none of the silhouettes glided quite the same way as Celia. Nick snapped his newspaper for effect and stayed trained on the house until she finally stepped onto the porch, looking every bit as beautiful as the night before. And best of all, she began walking directly toward the café. Much to his disappointment, however, she walked right by without even noticing him. But that had its upside as Nick got to take in a new and equally attractive view. Proving that Cuban men also appreciate the female form, two grubby construction workers offered her their place in line. Equally impressive, at least to an admiring Nick De Julia, was how she politely declined. Moments later, with a petite coffee cup in hand, Celia walked by Nick's table, but this time, he reached out and gently grasped her free hand. Far from being startled or put-off, she stopped, smiled and said "good morning" in Spanish.

"It's nice to see you again," Nick said.

"Again?"

"Yes. We met last night." Nick yanked off his sunglasses and was relieved when Celia did, in fact, remember him.

"Of course. Lobster, beans, and rice."

"That's right. Very good."

"And did you enjoy your meal, Señor?"

"Very much."

"I'm glad to hear it. If there is anything else we can do for you during your stay in Cuba, please do not hesitate to ask."

"Actually, there is one thing."

"What is that?"

"I would love it if we could have coffee together."

Celia looked down at the four empty cups. "Am I the first person or the fifth person you've made that offer to?" she asked with a smile.

"You're the only person," Nick replied. "Come on ... please?" Nick added, tapping the chair next to his.

Celia hesitated for only a second, smoothed the back of her skirt, and sat down. Nick offered her a brown sugar crystal, but she put her hand over her cup to signify a "no thank you." She then pursed her full lips, blew on the coffee exactly twice, and downed the whole cup in one swig.

"Are you enjoying your paper?"

Nick couldn't help but laugh. "Not really. I'm afraid I can't speak Spanish very well, let alone read it."

"Is okay. You're not missing much. It's a government newspaper, so it only has those stories that the government wants us to read."

Nick wasn't sure how to respond, so he didn't. It felt odd to be nervous, but in strange way, he liked it.

"Can I ask you a rather personal question, Señor?"

Nick straightened right up. "Certainly."

"What is your name?"

Nick rubbed his forehead and covered his eyes in embarrassment. "I'm so sorry. My name is Nick. Nick De Julia."

"It is a pleasure. I am Celia Moralez." She then reached across the table and grasped the back of Nick's hand, wrapping her thin fingers around until she was gently squeezing his palm. Nick, almost imperceptibly, pulled his fingers in so as to grasp the tips of hers. Celia's skin was as soft as her voice and her touch as gentile as her demeanor.

"So, you are from America?"

Nick nodded, unsure how his admission would be taken. But Celia seemed unfazed.

"Would you mind terribly if I asked you one more question?"

"Not at all. Ask me anything."

Celia sat up straight and took a good look all around her. Then the two of them, in unison, leaned close. "Is it paradise?"

Nick, enjoying the proximity to Celia's smell, was a bit taken aback by the question. "Is it paradise?" Nick scratched at his chin to buy some time. "That's a tough one. I would have to say that it's becoming more like paradise dot-com these days."

"Qué?" Celia looked confused and Nick immediately felt like a jerk. Her question was one of hope and Nick killed the moment with good ole-fashioned American cynicism. Recognizing his screw-up, he quickly moved to recover.

"I'm sorry, I was kidding. 'Is America paradise?' Well, comparatively speaking I'd have to say that it's still a wonderful place to live. I mean, don't get me wrong, America definitely has more than its share of problems, I'd be lying if I said otherwise, but on the whole, you can live anywhere you like and rise as far as your talent will take you — which is still a pretty good deal." Nick could see Celia's eyes flash with interest. "The land of opportunity, you know?"

"Is much different from here. In Cuba, you can only be what they tell you to be. But in America, a person can be anything, sí? It is the person that gets to choose."

Nick nodded. "Anyone can be President."

She took another quick look around and then dropped her voice down to a throaty whisper. "Cuba is a jail for anyone who has — how you say — ambition. In Cuba, ambition is like contraband – both will get you into trouble."

"Ambition is rewarded in America. But you should also know that everything has a down side, even success."

"How can success be bad?" Celia asked with her own cynical tone.

Nick answered honestly, "Well, people sometimes reach a point when they have so many possessions that they become the possessed, having to work longer and harder just to pay for everything. And then your family life suffers because you're always working, and even when you're not, you're worrying about work.

It's a vicious cycle — like a marathon with no finish line, so you can never win."

Celia placed her hand on Nick's arm. "Are you talking about you?"

Nick, afraid of looking badly in her eyes, just made a face and gave an equivocal head bob. "I didn't mean to get too deep on you there. Sorry about that."

"Is not necessary to apologize. I enjoy talking to you." She smiled briefly and then looked down at the coffee cup she was nervously twirling. Nick, almost to a point of actually resting his head on the table, bent far forward to interrupt her stare.

"So, tell me, who was that beautiful little waitress with the pin-curls?"

"That would be my niece, Claudia." Celia was suddenly radiant with pride. "She's my sister's little girl, but I look after her now."

Nick had his opening. The time had come to tell her the cold truth; to fulfill the promise that he made in a scurvy makeshift hospital, to a grieving woman. He knew exactly what he had to do, but just couldn't.

"What happened to your sister?" Nick asked, ashamed of himself.

Rather than answer the question directly, Celia stalled by trying to take a sip of coffee despite nothing being in the cup. And then, as she ran her fingertip along its inside rim, said: "Let's just say that she was a slave to ambition. Entiende?"

"Entiendo."

Celia began to gather herself. "I'm afraid I have to go now."

"Would it be okay if I asked you a personal question?" Nick blurted out, desperate to hang on to her company for a bit longer.

"Is only fair, I guess." She looked directly at Nick and flashed a smile so beautiful that even Peter Roget would have had difficulty finding words descriptive enough to do it justice.

"Have you ever considered leaving the island?" Nick decided to forego the metaphors in favor of directness.

"I would have to honestly say no. This is my home. I have my family, my friends, and our little restaurant that I love. There is really no reason for me to leave." Celia took a moment to read Nick's expression. "You were expecting something different?"

"No, not really. Well … maybe. I guess I just thought everyone wanted to leave here."

"What makes you think that?" she asked looking almost hurt.

"I don't know. I guess I've always had this mental image of Cuba as being a very repressive society."

Celia just shrugged and then got up to leave.

Nick, trying to prolong the conversation but not really knowing how, blurted out, "You're not on your way to a date by any chance, are you?" Celia paused and Nick could see a hint of a smile. "It isn't easy to admit but I'm a very weak man, and there's just no telling what I'll do if I find out that you're cheating on me. I just don't think I could take that kind of rejection."

Celia took a half a step forward and then stopped long enough to look at Nick like he was crazy. "Why don't you come by for dinner tonight. I'll make you something special."

Nick stood up, nodded and said, "Can I let you in on a little secret?"

"Si."

"I was coming whether you asked or not."

Lenny wiped his brow with his chubby, paw of a hand as he walked up Green Street toward Captain Tommy's Bar. It was unusually hot for early March, and that's exactly what Lenny decided to use as the rationale du jour for a mostly liquid lunch. Unlike Nick, he didn't bother trying to figure out whether he was being followed, filmed, or under some sort of frozen surveillance. Actually, Lenny had pretty much decided that he was fed up with the case and every aspect of its attendant bullshit. The Feds could have escorted him into the bar for all he cared. More than anything, he just wanted to spend an old-fashioned Key West afternoon -- one where you tell a lot of lies, drink too much, and chase girls that you'll never catch. Even the thought of it made Lenny break into a near jog.

Captain Tommy's had become his favorite bar since getting to the island. It had everything Lenny liked: Lively conversation, cheap drinks, and plenty of girls in bathing suits who liked to party. Lenny threw the doorman a hearty wave and then took his now usual seat, the one under the red thong and garter belt stapled to the ceiling. And before he could even wiggle into a comfortable spot on the stool, Lenny had Captain Tommy's withered arm around him.

"A Stewart's and vodka for my good friend and a Bud for me." Captain Tommy slurred to the bartender. Lenny had been in town two days and already achieved good friend status.

"What's up there, Captain? How are you?" Lenny asked through a rather dour tone.

"Worried. I had you pegged as someone who's never in a black-ass mood? What gives?"

"Ah, it's nothin'."

"Yeah? I ain't buyin'." Lenny let out a quick chuckle as he looked over to see that Tommy had a remarkably long ash hanging from the filter of a spent Marlboro. "What gives?"

"You know Nick De Julia?"

"Sure. Comes in all time. Quiet, but pretty nice on the whole."

"Yeah, well I'm finding him to be one gigantic pain right in my fat ass. Always making me do some cockamamie shit."

"Well, I sure am sorry to hear that. Anything I can do?"

"Nah. Don't concern yourself. My bad moods never last long." Suddenly, Lenny's face unfurled and he let out a more traditional, high-pitched cackle.

"Lenny Cicero?" Two well-built guys, each holding out some very official looking credentials, appeared suddenly on either side of Lenny. "We'd like to have a word with you, sir."

Lenny, seemingly unfazed, looked beyond the agent to his right and continued to speak to Captain Tommy as if they were alone. "Ya see what I mean? This is all because of that scrawny little bastard. I swear I can't get a minute's peace." Of course, Lenny punctuated his comment with a quick burst of laughter.

"Sir? A word?" The agent repeated, this time with a bit more impatience in his voice.

"Yeah, yeah, yeah ... You guys are always in such a rush."

"Here you go, Lenny." A burly bartender daintily put down a napkin and then placed Lenny's drink in front of him.

"Thanks. And you can put this on their tab," Lenny said with a head tilt toward the suits. After a short sip, Lenny wheeled around on his stool, hopped off and said, "Let's go talk," as if he were actually enthusiastic about the prospect. With one agent in front of him and another behind, the odd-looking threesome walked out of the bar and up to a van parked at the intersection of Green and Duval. One of the agents slid the side door open, but only Lenny entered. There, seated comfortably in front of three rows of flickering video monitors, was the second in command at the CIA.

"Attorney Cicero. It's a pleasure to finally meet you. My name is Anderson, I'm the Deputy Director of Operations at the CIA. I'm sorry to be interrupting your afternoon."

Lenny gave the Deputy Director a full blown, gums exposed grin and then pumped a hearty handshake. Although he looked thrilled to be there, Lenny was scared to death.

"Can I offer you a drink? Coffee, water, soda?"

Lenny held up his now sweating glass, which was still half-filled with his favorite concoction. "I brought my own."

"So, you did."

"Mr. Cicero there's no reason to be nervous. I wasn't sent here to harm you in any way, believe me. No, I'm actually here to help you."

"Isn't that nice?" Even Lenny knew that his comment sounded stupid, but he was too scared to think clearly.

"It's not a matter of us trying to be nice, Mr. Cicero. It's more along the lines of our desire to do something that will be --- let's say --- mutually beneficial."

"Ah sure ... reciprocation ... absolutely. One hand washes the other I always say."

"So, then I take it that you're amenable to reaching some type of accord in relation to this whole unfortunate matter?"

"Well I'll tell ya ... as far as I'm concerned, the answer is a great big: You betcha! But as I'm sure you've figured out by now; my opinion doesn't really mean much." Anderson flashed a fake smile. "I'm afraid that Nick's the one running the show, if you know what I mean? I'm more of a ridin' shotgun type of guy."

"Yes, I've actually heard that he's more of the — ah — how shall I put it ...?"

"The brains of the operation? Most definitely. Don't have to sugar coat it. I know the score."

"Well, then maybe I should be speaking to Mr. DeJulia?"

"Absolutely. That's what I would recommend. He's really the guy you need to come to terms with on this whole thing. And despite the grief he's been giving you guys, he's actually a real reasonable guy."

"Well I'm certainly glad to hear that." Anderson began cleaning his glasses with the backside of his tie. "So?"

"So what?"

"Would you happen to know where he is? — So I can contact him to discuss our proposition."

Lenny gulped down the rest of his drink. "I'm afraid I can't help you there either. I have no idea where Nick is." Lenny held up his right hand. "Swear to Christ."

Anderson inspected both lenses against the van's dome light and then put them back on. "Now why do I have such trouble believing that, Lenny? Can I call you Lenny?"

"Of course. Lenny's fine. That's what everybody calls me anyway. You know ... Lenny."

"Well, buying your bullshit for the moment ... Do you know of a way that we could get a message to your friend?"

"Listen, Mr. ... Anderson is it? I'd really like to help you out here, believe me, but I honestly don't know where he's at or when he's coming back, or if he's coming back for that matter."

"I see. Well, on the off chance that he phones in, you know, just to touch base or check in, maybe you could pass along a little bit of information?"

"I'm not expecting a call, but if it should happen..."

Anderson paused. "It's kind of a lengthy message. You think you might want to write this down, so you don't forget any of it?"

"No, no, no." Lenny let out a belly laugh. "If it's one thing I've got, it's a steel trap memory. I won't forget a word of it. Shoot." Lenny immediately wiped the smirk off his face and concentrated on the Deputy Director intently so as not to miss a single word.

"Very well. First off, please tell Mr. DeJulia that he's got a helluva tax attorney. We've been over about a decade and half's worth of returns without a single red flag. Quite an accomplishment I must admit."

"He'll be glad to hear that, I'm sure."

"I bet he will be. But you, on the other hand, might want to have a little word with yours."

Lenny swallowed hard. "Is there a discrepancy?" Lenny asked while adjusting both sides of his glasses.

"I'm afraid it's a tad bit more than a discrepancy. You see, our people tell us that your deposits never seemed to match up with your reported income for any of the past ten years, which leads us to believe that you've been taking in a lot of cash from your immigration practice."

"Cash?" Lenny muttered through a cracked voice.

"Yes. Considerable sums of unreported cash, or at least that's how the indictment will read."

"Mr. Anderson, just for the record, I officially deny any wrongdoing, but off the record, how much are we talkin' here?"

"Somewhere in the vicinity of about two-hundred-thousand in back taxes, penalties, and interest. And that's only going back ten years, mind you. Imagine what we're gonna find if we trace it back to when you first opened your firm." Now Lenny wasn't smiling at all. "Are you sure you don't want to write any of this down?"

"No, I don't think that I'll be forgettin' about this any time soon."

"Suit yourself."

"Is that it?"

"For the time being. I mean, we don't have enough evidence at present to link you to this internet gambling operation we're looking into, but that is subject to change too."

Lenny threw his arms up in the air. "Now I have no idea where your headin' there, but I can tell you for certain that I've got nothing to do with anything like that."

"Well forgive me for not taking your word on that, okay, Lenny?"

"I'm serious. You've got the wrong guy there."

"Really?" Anderson sat way back in his chair. "Well then answer me this: How well do you know Nicholas DeJulia?"

"Barely at all. He hired me to be local counsel in this crazy airplane case he's chasin' after. And that's the extent of it."

Anderson shook his head as if he didn't believe a word Lenny was saying. "And he never cut you in on this computer bookie thing he's got going on?"

"I haven't got the faintest idea what you're talking about."

"I'm talking about a very intelligently conceived, multi-million-dollar business that Nick set up in The Cayman Islands." Anderson paused to watch the information seep into Lenny's consciousness. "That's right, my friend. We've been tracking it for months. I mean, don't get me wrong, his fingerprints aren't anywhere on the day-to-day operation; no, he's way too smart for that. But all the signs are there." Anderson reached over and grabbed a manila folder. "Six trips in the past year; a lifestyle that far exceeds his means; a limitless pool of cash; guy even owns a laundromat in Marathon Key."

"So?"

"Well, let's just say that it launders more than clothes, alright?" Anderson shut the folder and then tossed it on top of some computer equipment. "Face it Lenny, this guy is the profile." Lenny put his empty glass up to his forehead and tried to cool down a bit.

"Mr. Anderson ... and I hope I'm not out of line here ... but is all this really necessary? I mean, isn't there something that can be done here to avoid any type of ..." Lenny grabbed at his throat. "...unpleasantness?"

The Deputy Director crossed his legs, grabbed both arms of his chair, and nodded slowly. "I can think of a few ways."

Lenny's eyebrows perked right up. "'Ways'?"

Anderson's trace of a smile slowly dissolved into a serious scowl. "Why don't we just knock off the crap right now. All of it." The Deputy Director's whole tone of voice suddenly changed. He was no longer glib, but rather, matter-of-fact and stern. "We've maintained from minute one that this was a sensitive matter that touches the very heart of our national security; a situation that could have global ramifications. But you guys wouldn't listen. You knew better. You just jumped aboard the blame America first bandwagon and filled everybody's head with conspiracy theories. You were more comfortable helping these low–life law breakers than your own country."

Lenny rubbed his beard several times. "And if I was to convince Nick to ... say ... let it go?"

Anderson, doing his best to channel General Glendale, stared at Lenny for a long moment. "Do you think you can?"

"I have no freaking idea, but I'm gonna try like hell."

"Well, if you were successful, then all of your problems would just," Anderson wiped both his hands together, "go away."

"Everything goes back to normal?"

"Everything. Your tax problems will be no more, and Nick will be free to vacation in the Caymans as frequently as he likes."

"What about Jorge Diaz and that pregnant lady rotting away in Guantanamo?"

Anderson brought a clenched fist up to his gritted teeth. "Here I am thinking that you're finally catching on and you go and ask a silly question like that."

"It's just that I know Nick's gonna ask me, that's all." Lenny blurted out, holding his hands in front of him in a defensive posture.

"Well then let me be really clear about it you rotund little bastard. You have three days to drop this matter in its entirety, or our deal is off." With the Deputy Director's threat still ringing in his ear, the van's side door slid open and Lenny was forcibly invited to take his leave. Anderson repeated, "Three days," as the agents hopped back in and slammed the door shut.

Always a man of enlightened self-interest, Lenny yelled: "Hey how about a continuance on that Motion to Quash thing?" just as the van pulled away.

Lenny was also pragmatic. The mere thought of cutting loose the albatross that was the case in exchange for IRS clemency was the no-brainer of all time. Unlike Nick, he didn't get off on the fight. A challenging case to Lenny was one that gave him heart burn, and such was the situation now. No ... the path of least resistance was definitely Lenny's main thoroughfare through life and one from which he hated to detour. Not even the money that Nick was throwing his way seemed to be enough anymore. Lenny never did quite see the end game here anyway; now more than ever, the whole thing seemed not only pointless, but increasingly self-destructive. He actually did love the idea of helping people, but not quite as much when doing so put him in the crosshairs.

He hiked up his pants and walked right through the drunken happiness that was all around him. To the chorus of *Lenny's* ringing out, as per a recently adopted custom, he managed a passable smile as he resumed his throne at the end of the Captain Tommy's Bar.

"Stewart's and vodka."

"Hey, what the hell was that all about?" Lenny nonchalantly looked to his right and saw a concerned looking Luis Mendoza. Lenny didn't answer right away, and Luis picked up on the hesitation. "You know I'm with the boys, right? I mean I assume Diego told you about me."

Lenny then did what he did best — smile. "He did. But I gotta tell you, I'm getting to the point where I need a scorecard to keep up with who's who."

Now Luis smiled. "I'm with the good guys," he said with a

hand on Lenny's shoulder. "So, what was did those guys want with you?"

"Ah, it was nothin'. Just an unavoidable by-product of workin' with Nick freakin' DeJuia."

"What's that mean?"

"It means that while he's off screwin' around somewhere, I'm left to mop up his mess."

Luis saw an opening. "Where does this guy get off leaving you with the short straw all the time? You shouldn't be putting up with that crap."

"Yeah well, don't cry for me Argentina ... If you knew what he was payin' me you'd be singin' a different tune, believe me."

"I don't see it, man. I mean, he stirs up a whole mess of shit, gets everybody pissed at him, and then lets Diego and that old man get arrested while he takes off to places unknown. It don't make no sense." Luis took a moment to look around the bar and then dropped his voice down. "And what's he really accomplished? I mean, let's face it: he's got everybody convinced that he's gonna do somethin' to help, but so far, from where I'm sittin', he's done nothing."

Lenny glanced over at Luis looking inordinately serious. "Look kid, I'm the first one to admit that I don't know much about most things, but Nick doesn't strike me as someone I'd wanna bet against."

"Oh no? You really think that he's gonna expose the government for what they did? Forgive me, man, but I don't see it happenin'." Luis took a swig from his Bud and then made believe that he was interested in looking around the bar.

"You don't see it happenin', huh?" Lenny repeated sarcastically.

"Not one damn bit. And I ain't alone neither. I've talked to Diego and a few of the other guys, and they think the same way as me. We all put our faith in your boss, but now we're startin' to think that that wasn't such a hot idea."

"Maybe it's just that none of you are smart enough to understand what he's really up to. Did you ever stop to think of that?"

"Hey, I'm open to that possibility. I sincerely doubt it, but I'm willing to listen. Why don't you go ahead and explain it to me?" Lenny stared right back at Luis but didn't say a word. "That's what I thought. I'll bet you fifty bucks that you don't even know where he is, let alone what he's up to." Luis pulled out his wallet, fingered through his bills, and then slapped down two twenties and a ten.

Lenny took a long pull on his drink, wiped his mouth on the shoulder portion of his shirt, and slid Luis's money back toward him. "I know exactly where he is, kid. Don't fool yourself."

"Yeah?" Luis said rather cynically as he put his beer bottle down on the money. "Where?"

"It doesn't matter."

"Yeah, it don't matter 'cause you don't know shit."

"I already admitted that. But I do happen to know that one little piece of information."

"Well then I'm all ears."

Lenny stretched his arms out and looked all around the bar before leaning in close to Luis. "Now I'm only telling you this because Nick might still need some help, and I want you and the boys to be ready at a minute's notice. But what I definitely don't want, is you spoutin' off about this to anyone who'll listen. You got it?"

"I hear ya."

"I'm serious, kid. If I tell you this, I don't want you breathin' one word of it to anyone other than Diego. Agreed?"

"Hey I know how to keep my mouth shut, man. You don't have to worry about me."

"Well I do worry about you because I barely even know you. Capice? And another thing, don't start askin' me a lot of questions about it. I'll tell you where he's at, but that's it."

"Whatever makes you comfortable, man."

Lenny now looked anything but comfortable. He adjusted his glasses, cleared his nostrils with his thumb and index finger, and then pushed his drink away before taking one last inventory of those about him.

Luis turned his palms up and with an impatient smirk said, "So where the hell is he?"

Lenny leaned in until his beard scratched up against Luis's left ear, and said in a whisper, "Rapid City, South Dakota", right before grabbing   Luis's   fifty   bucks   off   the   bar.

CHAPTER 20

Nick remained seated as Celia escorted the last of the evening's patrons out of Barredo. She had talked him out of the lobster and into the *Especial*, which in the heart of Manhattan would have been titled something along the lines of: Red snapper dusted in semolina with orange/mango chutney. But in Cuba, it was simply: Fried fish with fruit. Regardless, it was delicious. Even more satisfying, was the company. For the majority of the meal, Celia ignored her hostess responsibilities so she could spend a little time with her new favorite customer. She and Nick shared his meal, consumed two bottles of bad wine, and never once suffered through an uncomfortable silence. The conversation flowed from serious to humorous as easily as it moved from topical to whimsical. It was the type of night that flew by, and one which neither wanted to end.

Nick stood up in a gentlemanly way as Celia returned to the table with two brandy snifters. He thanked her and then the two touched glasses before taking their first sip. "Did you enjoy your meal?"

"Very much. Thank you."

"Was nothing. But I do have a surprise for you. A gift."

"You're kidding? You bought me a gift?"

"Si." Celia handed him a pale yellow and red metal tube. "This is the very finest cigar made in Habana. Is a Montecristo Tubo."

"I've never even heard of a Montecristo Tubo."

"I was promised by my uncle that it is the very best. The uninformed think Cohiba first but he tells me otherwise. And he should know. He's worked in the Corona factory for forty-seven years as everything from a picker, to a roller, to a reader."

Nick unscrewed the top and let the dark brown cigar slide into his palm. "What's a reader?" Nick asked as he put the cigar up to his nose to take in its subtly sweet aroma.

"A reader is someone who reads to the workers in the factory."

"Really?"

"Si. Rolling cigars is very boring work. So, each factory has someone whose job it is to read to the workers over the loudspeaker. He reads the day's newspaper, the baseball scores, and even novels in the afternoon."

Nick paused and asked with all the first-date politeness he could muster, "Is it alright if I smoke in here?"

"Is okay to smoke anywhere in Cuba. Go on."

From the very first puff, Nick felt certain that all the Cuban smokes he had ever paid top-dollar for stateside had to be counterfeits. This was perfectly moist and fresh, with a taste best described as cigar nirvana. It had hints of leather and coffee that politely lingered after each exhale. And the wrapper had a certain something on it that tasted sweet and made Nick's lips tingle. But its single most enjoyable aspect was that the cigar was a gift from Celia. Thoughtful was always the one quality that meant the most to Nick. The extravagance of any gift never really impressed him; all extravagance requires is money. But a thoughtful gesture, no matter how small, always got to him.

"Is good?"

Nick looked over at Celia's little-girl smile and her warm eyes and felt nothing but shame because he was lying to her, fear that he'd have to leave soon, attraction like he hadn't known for a long while, and genuine interest in the person she appeared to be. As she patiently waited for an answer to her question, Nick decided to fall back on the one thing that never let him down: Instinct. He placed his cigar in the ashtray, leaned over, grabbed hold of the back leg of her chair, and dragged her across Barredo's flagstone floor until she was a mere breath away. Celia looked shocked, but not altogether unhappy. "Thank you," was all Nick said, as he leaned over and kissed her on her slightly parted lips.

CHAPTER 21

Nick lay awake since dawn but hadn't moved at all for fear of waking Celia. Both were lying on their left side and Nick had his lips right up against the top of Celia's head. Her skin was warm and soft, and still smelled of perfume. Her hair hung low across Nick's chest and her head in the crux of his elbow; the exact position in which they had finally fallen asleep only a few hours earlier. The previous night had been as close to a perfect first date as Nick had ever experienced. But now reality was starting to seep back into his thoughts. He was never comfortable with a case lying dormant, not even for a few days, and that's exactly what was going on back in Key West. After all, Lenny was a great guy but not a person Nick could trust to mind the shop for very long. But even that was a secondary worry. Nick was acutely aware that every moment he now spent with Celia would make coming clean about her sister that much more difficult, and even worse was the fact that somehow, he had this gnawing feeling that he would be viewed as a liar. He hadn't actually lied to Celia, but that distinction was certain to go unappreciated, or at least that's how Nick saw it in his mind.

Although Celia's bedroom showed its physical flaws in the bright early-morning light that poured through the threadbare curtains, Nick saw none of it, choosing instead to focus on the pictures of her family that lined her dresser, the neatness of her desk, and the sheen of her skin. He didn't remove the sheet that covered them out of a morning-after sense of propriety, but moved back an inch or so, just enough so that their bodies were not up against each other and began to gently blow cool air on her back. Celia let out a slight groan, stretched her back, and then threw her hair to the side. "Buenos dias, Señor," she said in a thirsty voice before leaning over and kissing Nick on the chest.

"Good morning."

Celia pulled her legs out from under the sheet but left it draped over her chest and mid-section. "Is going to be hot today." Nick just nodded. "Is something wrong?" She asked as she ran her hand through Nick's hair, dragging her nails gently across his scalp on the way out. "Do you not like the heat?"

Having limited time, Nick saw no upside in witty retorts. Unvarnished, un-lawyerly honesty was his only shot, and he decided to take it. "It's not the heat. I was just thinking about how much I enjoyed last night. And how much I've enjoyed meeting you."

"Me too." Celia paused, trying to read Nick's expression. "Is that bad?"

"No, it's not bad at all, it's just ---- a problem."

"I don't understand."

"The truth of the matter is that I have to leave soon."

"Si."

Nick looked away from Celia as he continued. "And there's a very real possibility that I might never see you again ---- and I wish it were otherwise."

Celia smiled coyly. "Well, maybe will not be the case."

"How's that," Nick asked with a discernible note of caution.

"I'm afraid that I may have ---- mislead you... just a little," Celia said, holding out her index finger and thumb about an inch apart.

Now Nick was concerned. "About what?"

"About the kind of person I am." With that shot still whistling over Nick's bow, Celia swung her legs around to the side of the bed and pulled a shirt over her. She held Nick's hand for a second and then practically leapt off the bed. Nick then watched as she walked over to her closet and parted some dresses that hung there. Then, out of a bank of shoeboxes, she reached down to a row near the bottom and pulled out two. In a silent moment that seemed to go on forever, Celia sat next to Nick, while staring at the boxes. She ran her red fingertips over the tops, pausing only to smooth down certain portions of blackened scotch tape before suddenly dumping out the boxes' contents. Nick could not have been more confused as he found himself awash in two dozen or so blocks of neatly stacked one-dollar bills.

"I don't get it. What is all this?"

"It's money that I've been stealing for the past four years." Celia paused for a second, afraid of Nick's reaction. "I'm sorry that I couldn't trust you right away, but if they ever found out that I did this ..." Celia looked away for a moment and then began caressing the bills. "They do that, you know. They send people to pose as tourists to get information. You can't trust anyone in Cuba." Celia looked up at Nick, smiled, and placed her index finger gently on his lower lip. "Especially handsome strangers." She and Nick both smiled nervously at one another. "It's not all for me, though, it's for Claudia too. She's my responsibility now, and I'm determined to take care of her." She began stacking the cash back in the box. "Is hard to believe that it has taken four years to get this much. But I never want to risk suspicion, so I only take a portion of the tips that Americans sometimes leave; but never from the price of the dinners."

"How much is here?"

"Seven hundred and forty-seven dollars. All I need is about two hundred and fifty more and I can pay a man who promises to arrange everything."

"And what exactly does a thousand dollars buy you in Cuba?"

"Passage to America in a boat with a motor. Five Hundred each for Claudia and me." Celia completed stacking her hard-stolen money and then sealed the boxes. "My sister, Marta, could not wait. The two of us started taking money from the very beginning, and it was always the plan that the three of us would leave together. Me, Marta and Claudia. But time always moved too slowly for her, Cuban life was too small. So, she left on a raft several weeks ago, and no one knows if she made it." Nick felt the familiar lump in his throat starting to expand. Celia crossed the room and shoved the box back into place. "My sister made me promise to try and go to America as soon as I had enough money, so that Claudia and I could travel by boat. Rafts are too dangerous for adults, forget about children. And I will never take a risk with Claudia. So, I think it should take about one more year and half, and then I should have enough." Celia returned to the bed and threw herself in Nick's arms. All at once, her toughness and resolve disappeared. She suddenly looked scared and began frantically kissing Nick. "I am sorry I lied to you." Nick craned his neck backwards, placed his hands on Celia's shoulders, and gently pushed her away.

"What is it? What is wrong?"

Nick rubbed his eyes for a moment and then reached down into the pocket of his jeans which were on the floor next to the bed. He pulled out an impressive roll of hundreds and handed it to a stunned Celia. "Forget a year-and-a-half; you can leave in an hour-and-a-half if you want to."

Celia said something in Spanish that ended in "aquí," and the cab driver skidded the car to a halt. They were in the middle of downtown Havana, right in front of the old Capitol building, a beautiful relic which, from the outside at least, was an exact replica of the U.S. Capitol. The building's façade and foreground were painstakingly maintained, which was in stark contrast to the rest of the neighborhood.

Celia grabbed Nick's arm and led him down a succession of narrow side streets and cut-throughs, right into the bowels of Old-Havana, where nothing was well-maintained. Buildings were missing not only doors and windows, but whole sections. Poorly clothed children splashed in an ever-present trickle of sewage that ran along each and every gutter, and in the pools of dirty water that collected in each of the omni-present potholes. Everything in the city had a layer of dirt on it --- the buildings, the streets, --- even the people. But with an artist's eye, Nick still saw an unmistakable beauty beneath it all. In the midst of a world that was literally crumbling around them, everyone managed a smile and seemed to somehow wring a little joy out of the day. There was a sense of acceptance that was evident, not resignation, but acceptance. As if life itself was all they had, but that it was enough. The entire scene was the antithesis of life in the United States, where people with multi-million-dollar bank accounts seek therapy because they're unfulfilled.

Looking all around to see if they were being watched, Celia

pulled Nick toward one of the few homes in the area with a door and then rapped twice. A young man no more than eighteen years old, with a pocky complexion and a pissed-off look on his face swung the door open. He wore jean shorts, sneakers, and a Chicago Bulls tank-top with the number 23 on it. After inspecting both callers and the neighborhood street, he seemed convinced that nothing was awry, and motioned for them to come inside.

An even younger boy sat in the corner of the room at a card table and appeared to be affixing official green and white, Republica of Cuba, labels to a stack of counterfeit cigar boxes that lined the walls. He moved quickly, grabbing a box, spinning it into place, slapping the label on, and then smoothing it out, all in one motion. By the time Nick looked away from the little guy and then back again, he was almost finished with another box. Nick gave a wink of admiration to the one-man assembly line and got a gap-toothed acknowledgement in return. One thing was becoming crystal clear to Nick: not only capitalism, but entrepreneurialism was alive, well, and thriving among Cuba's youth.

"So, would you like to buy some cigars, Señor?" Gone was the young man's scowl of distrust and in its place beamed a customer-friendly grin. Nick turned around and shot the young salesman an equivocal look. "Maybe."

"You cannot get better quality anywhere in Cuba, I assure you. My brother works in the Partagas factory and he gets them for me. They are the same as you get in the government stores but not as much money."

"Are they really that good?"

"I guarantee it. If you are not happy, just bring them back and I will return your money."

"You should think about doing an infomercial, kid. You've already got the lingo down pat."

"Qué?"

"It's not important."

The boy looked at Celia and appeared momentarily confused. "So, do you want a box or no?"

"Alright you sold me. And since there's no telling when I'll be able to get back here, why don't you make it two boxes. I have one friend in particular who'd really appreciate a box of cigars from the Partagas factory."

"You have a friend that is familiar with that factory?" The

young man snapped his fingers at the little boy and then rattled off something in Spanish.

"He's actually a former countryman of yours. His name is Pombo, and he's been living in the states for quite a while now. Owns a little cigar store in fact."

The young man took the boxes from the little boy and re-smoothed all the stickers to assure a finished appearance. "How did your friend get from Cuba to America?"

"He did it on a homemade raft."

"He is very lucky," the young man said as he handed the cigars to Nick. "Most people who leave on rafts never make it to land again. Is sad but true."

"You know, I should have introduced myself. My name is Nick."

"Hola, I am Rafael."

"Nice to meet you."

"Same is true."

Nick dug into his pocket and pulled out some money. "Say, Rafael, answer me this... If it's so dangerous to leave the island by raft, why do so many people do it?" Nick asked, continuing to count out some money.

"I don't know, sir. Maybe they are desperate to leave for their own reasons and they don't have the money to pay for a safer means of transport."

Nick's eyebrows perked up as if he had just heard something unexpected. "Is there a safer means of transport?" Nick looked at ease but was silently hoping that there weren't any larger Cubans in back who might prefer to skip the deal and just relieve him of his money. Confident that he could take the two in front of him, and seeing no other real choice, he pressed on. Rafael, on the other hand, seemed content to ignore Nick's question and to stare at his bankroll.

"I asked if there was a safer means of transport."

"Sí, Señor," Raphael said, never taking his eyes off the cash. "For the right price you could make the trip on a boat with a motor. One operated by a captain that's used to making the crossing. Of course, such a thing cost too much for most Cubans."

"Why's that?"

"I'm sure the Señorita has told you that life here is very

difficult. The everyday person is not permitted to keep very much money. Twenty dollars per month is considered top pay in Cuba, and that goes to high government officials. I know a heart surgeon who only gets sixteen."

"Just for conversation's sake," Nick casually asked, "how much would it cost for someone who did have the money?"

"Is standard five hundred dollars each person. But with a minimum of two persons."

"And what about two people and a child? What would that go for?"

Rafael continued to look at all Nick's money but didn't want to overreach and blow the deal. "One thousand five hundred," he said in a cracked voice. "But only if the child is very small."

"And if someone was to pay, say...two thousand for the same number of people, how soon could something like that be arranged?"

"I would have to inquire, Señor, but the people would have to be prepared to go with very little, maybe only one day's notice. They could not bring luggage, and they would have to be responsible for their own water, but no more than one gallon per person."

Nick peeled off three hundred-dollar bills in front of Rafael's salivating eyes and put the rest in his pocket. Nick held the bills out in front of him. "Can you make it happen as soon as possible?"

CHAPTER 22

Deputy Director Anderson knocked only once and then waited for the customarily terse, "Come". He opened the door and approached the General who, remaining true to form, didn't even bother to look up from his file. But Anderson was unaffected, having grown used to the General's penchant for discourteousness.

"So, where are we?" The General asked as he made a note in his file.

"Very little media attention and none of it even close to problematic. None of these Brothers of Freedom have filed any flight plans of late and we're continuing to monitor all of the air-traffic south of Miami."

"And De Julia?" For this, General Glendale gave his second-in-command full attention.

"A couple of our boys had a chat with his accountant and found out where all his money is presently residing. It took a little doing but we've got it worked out so that we'll be able to see whatever he does with the accounts, including where he wants any money to go. That should give us enough time to get our people to just about anywhere."

The General nodded. "Good. What else?"

"We've contacted every air-traffic controller within a thousand miles and only came up with one unregistered flight which blipped-up shortly after we lost him. We haven't been able to find out where the flight originated from, but it landed in the Bahamas. I sent down specialists to interview airport personnel and I've already got our embassy people and customs agents checking disclosure forms filed within the last few days."

"What about the motion to quash their subpoena of the President?"

Mr. Anderson hesitated. "The hearing on our motion has been continued."

"What?" The General said, reaching for an octave that challenged his range. "The last update I had made it clear that the Judge was refusing to grant any postponements."

"That's what the Judge initially indicated but apparently this Lenny Cicero character had a heart attack. We tailed him to a doctor's office late last night and then picked up the call for an ambulance. We were able to confirm the destination to be the Fisherman's Hospital in Marathon Key."

General Glendale stared meditatively for a moment and then said, "You say he was brought by ambulance?"

"That's correct, sir."

"How long a drive is it from Key West to Marathon?"

Anderson smiled at his boss. "It was long enough to properly prep his hospital room, sir."

"Good," the General said with a nod of approval. "Very good. So, what's his status?"

"He's stable, but he's going to be there a few days at least. After that it's anybody's guess when he'll get medical clearance to continue on with the case."

"Were you able to get anything out of him down in Key West?"

Anderson handed his report to the General. "Not really. I hit him with the tax stuff, and it scared him well enough, but he still didn't give up De Julia. For what it's worth, I'm convinced more than ever that he knows where De Julia is."

"What makes you think so?"

"He fed one of our informants some crap about De Julia being somewhere in South Dakota, but none of it panned out. I mean we looked into it briefly, but it was clearly an attempt to throw us off the trail."

Again, the General paused a moment to take it all in. He then offered his subordinate the ultimate compliment by asking his opinion, "So what do you suggest?"

"I think we should just keep listening for the time being.

217

Something's bound to break."

"Alright. But just make sure that I get updates from all of our field operatives on a two-a-day schedule. Understood? This still has the potential to be an incendiary situation, so let's make damn sure that everybody stays sharp. We can't afford any let-ups."

Anderson shook his head confidently. "We won't have any, sir. You have my word on it."

"Good." The General took another second to collect his thoughts and then refocused on his second-in-command. "Is that it?"

"Actually, sir, there is one more thing. We tracked down De Julia's former law partner."

"Where was he?" The General somewhat rudely interjected.

"We found him at a hotel bar in Saint Martin."

Even though he clearly respected Anderson, he still occasionally tested his acumen. "What was he drinking?"

Anderson laughed a fake laugh and then stole a quick glance at the back of his file. "A scotch and soda, sir."

General Glendale winked at Anderson, and then tipped an imaginary cap toward his subordinate for a job well done. "So, tell me, did Mr. De Julia's former partner have a strong self-preservation instinct?"

"He did indeed, sir." Mr. Anderson passed along a second file and then proudly waited for his kudos, taking great delight in how the General's smile seemed to widen after each sentence read.

"This is good," The General muttered without looking up. "Oh yes, this is very good. ---- And you already leaked it through Cicero? Excellent."

"Thank you, sir."

"No, no, thank you, Mr. Anderson," the General offered, still buried in the minutiae of the report. "This is it. --- This is the leverage we've been looking for." The General finally looked up, simultaneously slamming the file closed.

As Anderson turned for the door, the General had one final thought.

"One more moment."

"Of course, sir."

"Perhaps we should withdraw our motion to quash the President's deposition subpoena."

The Deputy Director thought for a moment but couldn't see

the General's angle. "Why, sir?"

"Well, with Cicero in the hospital and DeJulia out of the country, perhaps a better tact is to produce the President and argue that they missed their chance." The General paused and then added, "When was the original date of the deposition set for?"

"It was to take place in a few days."

"Let's try it. Have our counsel send a letter to Cicero withdrawing our objection but insist that the deposition go forward as originally scheduled, and let's just see what happens."

Although skeptical, Anderson deferred to his boss. "Consider it done, sir."

CHAPTER 23

Since leaving the Cuban version of a travel agent, Nick and Celia hadn't exchanged so much as a word. The realities of the situation were setting in as Celia contemplated the very real possibility that she would never see her family, friends, or home ever again. Nick could sense her angst. He initially felt like he was doing her a favor, but it no longer seemed so. His customary throw money around and get it done attitude had likely placed her plans on a track too fast for her liking.

The two had walked all the way from the entrails of Old Havana to the Malecon, a seawall that separates Havana proper from the Gulf of Mexico. The Malecon is like a breathing work of art that offers an atmosphere best suited to lovers, tourists, photographers and artists. Celia and Nick, on the other hand, were only there because it meant that they could walk no farther and remain dry. Still, neither said a word. Celia looked north and let the sea breeze push her cotton dress tight to her figure. Feeling that the onus was on him to speak first, Nick decided to dispense with the customary *is something wrong?* smokescreen and get right to it.

"I feel like I owe you an apology." With that, she finally turned to look at him. "I thought it was what you wanted but now I feel like I pushed you into something you weren't ready for. It's an affliction I suffer from: I think I can solve everyone's problems." Now Nick turned away. "So, if you want to call the whole thing off, I'll certainly understand." Celia, seconds away from crying, grabbed Nick from the side, and put her head in his chest. Nick kissed her forehead and whispered, "Honestly, this is your decision alone. If now is not the right time, keep the money and leave whenever you like." Celia breathed back most of her tears, and then motioned for Nick to take a seat on the seawall.

"I know that I am not acting like I should. You were very kind to me today, offering your help and money in the way that you did." Celia leaned over and kissed Nick lightly on the cheek. "I am grateful." Celia flashed her little girl smile, the one that Nick hadn't seen all day, and said, "I am just afraid. Afraid of getting caught; afraid of not making it; afraid of endangering Claudia; and... afraid of going home and facing my family for the last time, unable to tell them what I'm doing or where I'm going," Her eyes again filled with tears. "It's just frightening to think that one minute I may be with them like always, and then twelve hours later be gone forever without a word being said."

"Why can't you tell them? They'll love you regardless, won't they?"

"That's not the issue. I won't say a word because I love them. It's for their protection. As soon as it is learned that I fled, everyone in my family will be interrogated. So, this way no one will have to lie. And even though they'll understand, and very much want me to be happy, it will be hard to leave like that." Celia laughed a little, although clearly still deep in thought. "Where you are from, people don't have to make decisions like this."

"I never thought of it that way. I ...don't know what I was thinking this morning," he said, shaking his head in shame. "I was insensitive to the realities of your situation." Despite what anyone had ever said to him, Nick had never considered himself a selfish person, but he was starting to see things in a different light. Perhaps selfishness dressed up like altruism is selfishness all the same. And that little realization brought him right back to the issue of Celia's sister. Nick still hadn't told her a thing about what really brought him to Cuba, and he knew damn well why. If Celia Moralez had been unattractive, or in need of a diet, he would have told her the truth straight away, but such was definitely not the case. For a cocksure legal genius, he was absolutely at a loss as to what to do.

Celia, still preoccupied with her own moral dilemma, stood up, and then placed her hand on Nick's shoulder to stop him from doing the same. "I have to go home and see my father and brothers." Celia then ran her hand gently through Nick's hair, as she had done while they were lying in bed only hours earlier, dragging her nails along his scalp on the way back. "Why don't you come by for dinner?"

"I'd like that," Nick said sincerely. "I'd like that very much."

"Me too."

Nick looked her in the eye and ran his hand along her face, "You're beautiful."

As Celia walked away Nick had a terrible sinking feeling, as if he'd never see her again. Despite being the veteran of two marriages and numerous relationships, meaningful and otherwise, Nick had never before known such a feeling of profound...concern. He then jogged past Celia, turned to face her and started to walk backwards.

"If you let me come with you, we can talk a little, walk a little --- do whatever you want to do. 'Cause you never know --- you might feel like talking and then if I'm not there, where will that leave you? You'll be talking to yourself and that's just dumb, people will mock you." He slipped behind her. "You just walk at your own pace as if you're alone, you'll never even know that I'm here." She played along for twenty or thirty feet but then stopped suddenly, causing Nick to bump into her. As they both laughed, he reached around and warmly hugged her from behind.

"I forgot to tell you that sudden stops do pose a problem under this plan."

CHAPTER 24

"Wake up, Mr. Nick. Mr. Nick wake up." Nick's body jerked to an upright position, startled by the unexpected shaking. He immediately grabbed for the sheet and pulled it up over his midsection and then looked over at Celia who, as good fortune would have it, was already covered up to her neck. Standing next to Nick, and clearly enjoying his scrambling act, was Celia's niece, Claudia. Nick grabbed his watch from the nightstand and saw that it was 6:15 am. He rubbed his eyes for a second or two and then reached down and pulled Claudia onto the bed. The little girl, still in her pajamas, which consisted of one of her grandfather's tee shirts knotted at the sleeves and waist, had obviously been awake long enough to acquire a milk mustache.

"What is it, sweetheart?" Nick asked through a yawn. "Did something scare you?"

Ignoring Nick's question, Claudia smiled at him, reached over and ever so gently tapped her fist against his chin causing him to feign unconsciousness, a little game that had played to many laughs the night before. While Celia tried to spend a little more time than usual with her father and brothers, Nick and Claudia had bonded over card tricks, smoke rings, and a game Nick called "Knockout Shot." So as not to disappoint his new friend, Nick opened his eyes suddenly and said, "Now I knock you out," just as he touched his clenched fist to her tiny face, causing Claudia to outstretch both arms and then fall backwards right onto her Aunt Celia. To be certain, Nick was not at all comfortable with Claudia catching him in bed with her aunt, but all he could think to do was act as if it was no big deal and draw attention away from his embarrassment. Celia, on the other hand, was a trifle more direct.

"Claudia why are you in here so early? And didn't I tell you to always knock before entering someone's room?"

"I did knock but no one heard me." The little girl said sweetly in her defense. "There's a man downstairs who wants to see Mr. Nick and he asked me to get him." Claudia smiled and then lunged at Nick. "And now I knock you out."

But this time, Nick was only out for a second. "Claudia, what man wants to see me?"

"I don't know. He's just a man."

"Well what does he look like?"

Claudia fell back into the crux of her aunt's arm. "He looks like everybody else."

Nick looked more than a little nervous. He pulled his jeans toward him and put them on under the sheets. Only then did he stand up and quickly throw on a shirt and shoes. "Where is the man, Claudia?"

"He's on the front porch." The little girl sweetly replied while closing her fist in preparation for another attack. But Nick beat her to it, sneaking in a clean shot as he leaned over to kiss Celia.

"I'll be right back," Nick whispered to Celia before pointing at Claudia. "And you're knocked out until then." At that moment, Claudia dove forward into Nick's pillow and lay there as if having been shot.

Nick was nervous but nonchalantly opened the door only to see that there was no one there. He stepped onto the porch and looked all around but still, nothing. Just as he turned to reenter the house, Nick heard a short shrill whistle coming from the direction of the café. He wheeled around and immediately recognized Michael Jordan's jersey. It was his travel agent, Raphael, enjoying a café con leche, and waiting on Nick.

Nick purchased a coffee, filled it with sugar, and sat at another table with his back to Raphael.

"So, what's the story?"

"I have arranged for you to meet the man who will be bringing you to the states."

"When?"

"Right now, but only if the terms are agreeable."

Nick blew on the coffee and, drawing off past experience, took a small sip. Then, while still looking away from his contact, said, "What the hell are you trying to pull? I thought that we had already come to terms."

"Not quite, I'm afraid. When I told the captain that he would be transporting two Cubans and an American, he doubled the price. He wants three thousand. And my percentage will come out of that."

"And did you tell him that I was paying you an extra $500.00?"

"You said that is be between us."

"Yeah, but that was before you and your friend decided to try and tuck it to me."

"What does this mean – tuck it to you?"

"It means that you are trying to get more money simply because you think that I have it. But let me tell you something my friend: Having it and parting with it are two very different situations." Something didn't add up. Nick leaned back in his chair, lifting the front legs off the ground, and pushed back until his chair struck Raphael's.

"First you tell me that everyone in the whole country is broke, that you know brain surgeons who work for about a dollar and a half a month, and then you tell me about a guy who's willing to smuggle a couple people to the states for two thousand dollars. And now, today, this same guy wants three thousand to make the crossing. And you said that it was somebody used to making the crossing. So, then I'm left to think: Why wouldn't this guy just have stayed in the states if he had been successful making it across even once? You see what I'm gettin' at here? Why would a Cuban take that kind of chance?"

"Because, Señor," Raphael said somewhat reluctantly, "he's not a Cuban. He is American."

Nick quickly downed the remainder of his coffee and then waited for the bitter sting to relent. "An American, huh. Well that certainly would explain the way he negotiates. How is it that an American can come and go in a place like Cuba?"

"That is really something that you should ask him, Señor. I only concern myself with my own business. So please tell me: Would you like to meet the captain or no?"

"Where is this guy -- the American?"

"He keeps his boat at the Marina Hemingway. Is about 15 kilometers from here."

"And he's there now?"

"Si, Señor."

Nick finally turned around, tapped Raphael on the back of the head and said, "Let's go, kid. Lead the way."

The decrepit cab hobbled onto Calle 248 for the ten-mile crawl to the Marina Hemingway. Nick spent most of his time working on a tangled twist of wires hanging from what used to be the dashboard, trying valiantly to resuscitate the car's air-conditioning system. Between the searing heat, the drenching humidity, and the cabby's inattention to personal hygiene, air circulation had become an imperative. It wasn't until several minutes after the driver and Raphael had written off the project to the point where they stopped even offering suggestions, that Nick figure-eighted two frayed copper strips, and air suddenly began to cough into the car. Unfortunately, the smell emanating from the long since dormant vents was hardly an improvement. Nick considered it a moral victory all the same.

From the moment the nattily dressed security guard lifted the wooden gate and stood at attention, the contradiction that is modern day Cuba only deepened. The entire complex had resort-like beauty, complete with a half-dozen restaurants, an outdoor bar, tennis courts, pool, jacuzzi, jet-ski rentals and rows of canal-side townhouses, each painted bright white beneath red tile roofs.

"Come, come, come." Raphael implored, pulling Nick past a Cuban band entertaining the outdoor diners and toward the marina itself. From the first look, it was obvious that the Marina Hemingway had everything necessary to be considered a first-class marina. Everything, that is, except boats. Over two hundred slips neatly lined the massive aquatic arena, each with ample room, a drinking water supply and electrical power. But a solid one hundred and ninety of them appeared to be suffering the ill effects of the recent half-century downturn in the Cuban economy. The ten or so boats making use of the place were all moored in a row, in the slips nearest to where the opening of the canal met the blue/green water of the Gulf Stream. Stranger still was that eight out of the ten boats that he and Raphael approached flew US flags on their masts. And as they got a little closer, Nick noticed the ports of registration painted on the back of each boat. Port Charlotte, Florida. Bar Harbor, Maine. Point Judith, Rhode Island. San Diego, California. Baltimore, Maryland --- and so on.

For the most part, the boats were all nice-sized and well-maintained. All, that is, except for the first boat in the queue. Hailing from Muscle Shoals, Alabama the "Aqua Mule" was a twenty-foot powerboat with little to no trade-in value. The aluminum railing was pitted, the teak floor was worn and weathered gray, the few brass fittings that existed looked brass no longer, and the propeller on the single outboard motor showed more than a few scars, dings, and dents. Over the years, moisture had seeped beneath the dials and gauges on the console, hopelessly clouding them and rendering each instrument effectively useless. The boat had only a small area below deck, but large enough to allow three people a cramped escape from the sun if need be. And that was about it. The boat on the whole was as ugly and out of shape as its owner.

Hank Lodish sat near the back of the boat, swigging a Lone Star Beer at 7:15 in the morning. He wore only jean shorts, the waistband of which was in full surrender to his impressive girth. He had a greasy mop of tan and gray hair, a bushy mustache that blended in well with the hair coming from his nostrils, and a meaty nose on which sat a pair of square glasses tinted brown. The soles of his feet, which were up on the outboard, were black from dirt while his toenails appeared black from infection. The only other thing that Nick made note of as he approached the port side of the boat, were the two circular scars over Lodish's right chest wall.

Raphael stepped in front of Nick in order to make the introductions: "Señor, Lodish, this is ..."

"Nick. My name is Nick." Clearly, Nick wasn't thrilled about the prospect of becoming overly familiar. Maybe it was owing to his filthy appearance or the fact that Lodish initially ignored Nick's outstretched hand until he could take another sip of his beer, or maybe it was just the product of a sixth sense, but Nick knew then that he would hate the fat bastard.

"You can call me Hank," he drawled. Nick just nodded. "So,

I understand from my little amigo here that you and some of your friends are looking for a boat ride."

Nick cocked his head to the side and shrugged his shoulders. "Maybe."

"You got the money?" Lodish asked brashly as he rolled his tongue back and forth along the inside of his lower lip.

"Yeah, I've got it. I just don't know whether I want to give it to you."

Lodish looked over at Raphael. "What in the hell kinda bullshit is this? I thought you said that it was a done deal?"

"Well he was wrong," Nick interjected. "And not one cent changes hands until I get some answers." Nick, as always, customized his words and tone of voice for each particular situation, and for Mr. Lodish, every word offered would be high and tight. "Now how is it that you can just come and go here without a problem? Are you greasin' somebody?"

Lodish drank down the last half of his beer, swished his tongue back and forth one more time and then crumpled the can. "I ain't used to gettin' interviewed. Know what I mean?" He said just before tossing the can into the pristine canal.

"Just answer the question, smart ass."

Lodish laughed at Nick's moxie, flipped open his cooler, and reached down deep for a cold one. "Anybody can come into Cuba by boat. You don't need a visa or nothin'. All you do is call the Cuban Coast Patrol up on channel 16 and tell 'em that you're comin' in."

"And then what?"

"Ya pull your boat in and tie her off." Lodish looked Nick up and down. "Now will you need me to explain how to do that, too?"

"What about getting out?" Nick asked tersely.

"Well," Lodish squinted off into the distance. "That's my business."

"Not if you're interested in my three thousand bucks it isn't. So, let's dispense with this he-haw shit and get right to it. I need to know exactly what's gonna go down or I'll make arrangements elsewhere, alright? I haven't got a lot of time to screw around here."

Lodish wasn't used to dealing with anyone quite as straight-ahead and willful as Nick, and he really wasn't sure how to react.

But he was certain of one thing: he didn't care for the discussion to go any further in front of Raphael, and he told him so indelicately. "What the hell are you doin' still hangin' around here, you little bastard," Lodish yelled as he struggled against gravity all the way to upright. "Get the hell out of here." Raphael showed some real grit by standing his ground with a knotted jaw and clenched fists then turned to Nick as if awaiting instructions.

"Wait for me at the front gate," Nick said, and like a dutiful son, Raphael threw one last scowl at the unkempt captain, and then walked away.

"You didn't answer my question: Now it might be okay with the local government for Americans to just sail on in here, but it sure as hell isn't alright for Cubans to sail on out. So how do you plan to pull this off without getting noticed?"

Proving that he wasn't altogether dumb, Lodish decided to try another approach. "Why don't you just sit down, have yourself a brewski and we'll run through it until you're all nice and comfortable with everything." Lodish then winked at Nick and tapped the seat cushion next to him.

Nick reluctantly complied, "Alright, let's hear it," Nick said, waving the information forth with his right hand.

"First of all, ya ain't got nothin' to worry about. I've been makin' this run three to four times a year for as long as I can remember. And believe me, there ain't nothin' to it."

"Yeah? So, why'd you get shot?" Nick asked cynically, pointing to the entry wounds on Lodish's chest.

"That happened somewhere else over somethin' else, believe me."

"Yeah, well I don't believe ya," Nick said, mimicking Lodish's drawl. "So just get to it. How's it's gonna work --- and please spare me the good ol´ boy bullshit, alright? 'Cause quite frankly I haven't got the time nor the inclination to listen to it." Nick was used to intimidating bullies, and today would be no different.

"Let's just say that I'm in tight with a few guys who work for the Cuban Coast Patrol, and whenever I go back, I just make sure that I leave when they're workin'. And if I happen' to be carryin' somethin', well then they just kinda look the other way. It costs me a few dollars for sure, but it's a cost of doin' business is the way I look at it."

"And how often have you done this?"

"If you're askin' how many times I've taken people across, well then, the answer is next to never, actually. Not a lot of Cubans got that kind of money."

"I thought you said that you've been making the trip three or four times per year?"

Lodish did that thing with his tongue again. "What do you think, that carrying illegals is how I make my livin'? Shit...if that's what you *dee-duced*, then I'm afraid you're not too bright, son." Lodish laughed loudly and took a big mouthful of beer.

"I'm still waiting for an answer. Why do you go back and forth if you're not smuggling?"

"Who said that I wasn't smugglin'?" Lodish wiped his wet lips with the heel of his hand and then wiped that on the side of his shorts.

Then it hit him, and Nick winced in disgust. "Cigars." Lodish smiled, pointed at Nick, and then pulled his finger back to the tip of his tri-leveled nose.

"That's right. I'm the mule that makes sure that all them Wall Street types get their Cohibas." Maybe Hank Lodish wasn't stupid at all. "So, I figure, if I have to be in the water anyhow, I might as well have some company, provided they can come up with enough money to make a difference." Lodish lifted his beer can to his lips. "Ain't no skin off my ass."

Nick had a terrible feeling about Lodish and an even worse one about the setup in general, but seeing that viable alternatives were in short supply, he felt boxed in. "So, would we shove off from here?"

"Hell no," Lodish jutted out his chin and pushed both eyebrows far up onto his forehead, probably thinking that the look somehow emphasized his point. "There's a canyon along the main highway about twenty miles south of Havana, heading toward Veradaro. Ya can't miss it. Got a big ol´ rusted out suspension bridge goin' across it; only one like it all along that stretch of road. Now that's where I'll be takin' delivery of my shipment later on and will have it all loaded up by 8:15; we'll take off from there at 8:30."

"I'm not sure that we can pull everything together that fast."

"Well you sure as hell don't have a choice, now do ya? Boat leaves then and I ain't waitin' 'till 8:40. One gallon of water a piece and no luggage."

"Is that it?" Nick asked.

"Not quite. I need half the money now." Lodish flexed his chubby, grimy fingers in Nick's face.

"What assurances do I have that you won't just take off with it?"

"Because I am a professional," Lodish said, unconvincingly, "and I have a reputation to protect."

Nick smiled and Lodish followed suit. Within an instant, they were both laughing. "Yeah, well the hell with that," Nick said, wiping the smile right off Lodish's face. "Now we might as well get this out of the way before this deal goes any further --- I don't like you, and I don't trust one God-damn thing about you. So, I'm not givin' up a dime until each of us is actually in the boat." There was no way in hell Nick was gonna let some fat redneck call the shots all the way to Florida. But Lodish was smart enough to know which one of the two had the leverage in this negotiation.

"So, you're a tough a guy, is that it? One of them New York hard-asses? Well you seem to be forgettin' one thing: It's my boat. And that means it's my rules, okay? Now I don't give a rat's ass whether ya like me or not." Lodish then stood up and Nick did the same. "I also don't mind tellin' ya that it's only worth my while if I can take half the money now and triple the amount of product that I'll be haulin' across. And that way I can turn your fifteen hundred into five times that once we hit Florida." Lodish forced his chin out and sent his eyebrows skyward. "Are you understandin' how this works now? 'Cause if you don't, I can run through it a little slower this time?"

Nick leaned back, happy to put any additional distance between himself and the burly Alabamian, and then reached into his pocket for a fold of pre-counted cash. He slapped it into Lodish's thick hand and without another word, climbed out of the boat.

"It's nice doin' business with ya," Lodish yelled to Nick's back. "And don't take none of this stuff personal now. I get the feelin' that we're gonna end up gettin' along just fine. Ya hear me?" Lodish paused for only a second. "And the rest of the money is due once everyone is in the boat."

CHAPTER 25

"This is it," Raphael said matter-of-factly as he, Nick, and Celia peered over the edge of the bridge. "Leave the car on the side of the road. It is far too dangerous to try and drive down the embankment. Just try to pull it somewhere over ------ there," he said, pointing just south of the bridge. "But you pull it behind that heavier brush to the right. I will pick it up later."

"You're not gonna be here when we leave?" Nick asked.

"No, Señor. I supply some of the cigars to your captain, but I do not make the delivery. He arranges for someone else to do that. But I will come here to pick up your car. That I do for you as a favor." Nick just smiled. "Now, I think don't walk over the boulders down to the water, is very dangerous at daytime but worse at night. Instead, you should walk back up toward the road until you get to a path that's just after that first big boulder."

Nick wriggled his feet until he was sure of his footing, gripped the edge of the bridge, and then leaned forward until he and Raphael looked like a tandem circus act. "Point to the path again."

"Is right --- there." Celia grabbed hold of Raphael's shirt, as he remained trained on the spot as if he intended to shoot at it. "Do you see?"

"I got it," Nick responded. "That's a helluva a grade, though."

"Qué?"

Nick stepped off the edge and wiped his hands. "I said that it's steep."

"Si, but it will be alright. Just stay on the path and slide your feet forward. If you pick them up, you risk stepping on a rock and falling. No, better to slide... sideways if you can. And slow."

Nick glanced over at Celia and saw her looking out over the rocky bank in a type of meditative stare, the kind of blank expression that hid well a person's inner thoughts. "You okay?"

Celia stirred from her private moment and managed a brief yet beautiful smile. "I was thinking that I should carry Claudia. Otherwise it would be too dangerous for her."

Nick wanted to believe that that was her only concern. "You know, the view is a whole lot better over here." Nick walked Celia to the other side of the bridge where the two squinted into the glare of the open ocean. Nick then moved in behind her and draped both arms over her shoulders and across her front, pulling her close until her back was up against his chest.

"I used to go to the docks at Cojimar and look out over the ocean for hours, trying to picture what America would look like. At night, I would try to rearrange the stars that sat on the edge of the horizon to look like city lights from Los Angeles or maybe New York." Nick kept her close, content to just listen. "And it was always on a day like this that I would dream most of leaving. Look how calm it is. How beautiful, the way the water shimmers in gold because of the low morning sun. The ocean when it is like this --- could never hurt you." Celia filled her lungs with an ocean breeze as if trying to steady her nerves. "On days like today, I think that I can see everything I've ever wanted." She then tilted her head back and smiled at Nick. "One week ago, nothing seemed possible. Now, all has changed. And you've given that to me --- and to Claudia. For that I will always be grateful. Always." Celia leaned back again and kissed Nick on the cheek. "After tonight, there won't be anything left to fear. And once I see Claudia standing on an American shore, I will know that I succeeded, that I fulfilled the promise that I made to my sister. All I need to know is that Claudia has a chance at a better life, and I will be forever happy."

Raphael cleared his throat to get a little attention. "I am sorry to interrupt, but it is not smart to stand here too long. Attention is not our friend," he said as he got in behind the wheel of the car.

Then, to Nick's dismay, Celia noticed that he had gotten quiet. "What is wrong? Do I talk too much?"

Nick ignored her question and just muttered, "Son-of-a-bitch."

"What?" Celia asked. "What is it?"

"I have to tell you something." Nick turned Celia to face him. "The thing is --- that --- I --- never meant to be in this position."

"What position?" Celia asked nervously.

Nick took a deep breath, looked at Celia, and sighed. "I don't want you to think that I lied to you. But all the same, you have to know that we didn't meet by accident. I came to Cuba...to meet you. Not someone - you. Because the thing is ...." Nick paused to fully take in Celia's beautiful face one last time. "I met your sister...briefly, and...." Celia's eyes glazed over, and her expression was that of someone in a hospital who's waiting to hear whether or not a loved one would survive. "She never made it to Florida, or any piece of land in America. She was apprehended by the Coast Guard just outside of Key West." Nick took a second to try and assess Celia's reaction. "They caught her and sent her to prison."

Celia's bottom lip started to quiver. "Dónde?"

Nick, still holding on to her shoulders, looked down at the ground, and then directly at her once again. "She was sent to a detention center at Guantanamo."

"My sister is here?"

"Just for now." Nick quickly interjected. "But I swear to you, Celia...I swear to you, I will get her out."

"You knew that she was here, and you never told me?" Celia asked through a quiver in her voice.

"It's not that I didn't want to tell you. I tried --- believe me. But the more I got to know you, the more I wanted to keep getting to know you and then I just became concerned that if I told you the truth..."

"You are a liar." Celia said in a deadly serious tone.

"I never lied to you; I just hadn't yet told you the whole truth. Big difference."

Celia suddenly looked mad. "A liar is a liar --- and will always be a liar."

"That's not true. I ..."

"Leave me alone." She pulled free from Nick's grasp and began heading for the car, angrily wiping away her tears.

"I will not leave you alone." Nick grabbed her once again,

but Celia shoved him away with a shrilled "No."

"Don't do this. You and Claudia are one lousy day away."

"No, we aren't. We were a day away. But now, we are nothing." Just as quickly as her anger had emerged it dissolved back into sadness. "How could you lie to me? How could you just let it all be a lie?"

"It was not all a lie." Nick yelled back, not quite grasping that contrition is less effective when screamed. "How we met was a lie, but that's it. How I feel about you is real. The fact that I'm not leaving without you is real."

"Enough," Celia said just above a whisper. "Do not say anymore." Again, her eyes filled with tears as she ran toward the car, grabbing the door handle just as Nick caught up to her. "Love cannot grow from lies." She sounded firm, but didn't try to get into the car, a fact that Nick took as a sign of hope. "So please, leave me alone now."

"I won't."

"You will have no choice." Celia shot back.

Nick struggled to regain his composure, but still looked mad. If she had only known him better, she would have realized that he was mad at himself, not her. "Just think, Celia. Just think about it for one second. I didn't have to tell you this. I could have kept it from you for the rest of your life and you would have never known the difference. But I didn't. Now doesn't that count for anything? Why don't you just think about that for one minute." Nick could hear how angry he sounded, so he stepped back, exhaled some tension through his gnashed teeth, and tried to calm down. "Let me make it as clear as possible," he said very deliberately as he struggled to constrain himself, "just so there's no misunderstanding here. I very much regret how we met, but not *that* we met." He paused yet again to read Celia's expression. He gently put his fingers on Celia's chin, pulling it around against her wishes until they were face to face. "Now tonight…we are going to the States." Celia again tried to look away, but Nick forced her chin to stay in place. "That's right. You, me, and Claudia."

"How could I ever do that? All along I thought I was bringing my sister's little girl to her. But now it would be like taking Claudia from her."

"Claudia," Nick raised and lowered his voice in a single word, "is precisely why I know that you will show up tonight. You love that little girl more than anything and you made it pretty clear a few minutes ago that getting her to the States is what's most important to you. So, no matter how much you may hate me at the moment, I know that you'd never take it out on her by being selfish. That's not who you are. That's not who you'll ever be." Nick let go of her chin and moved his hand down onto hers, which was still holding tight to the door handle. "I will be here tonight at 8:15 as planned, and I will not leave without you."

———————————

Nick stared out the window. "I should have just kept my mouth shut," were the first words that he had uttered in over an hour, and the old man behind the wheel used it as an opportunity to break the long and uncomfortable silence.

"¿Qué dijiste, Señor?" He asked brightly.

Nick, not wanting to appear rude, glanced over at the gracious gentleman who had offered him a ride some fifteen miles back, and shook his head "no", effectively waving off the question. It wasn't until he resumed his stare out the window that he finally recognized that the car hadn't moved an inch in the last thirty or so minutes. They had made it back to Havana proper without so much as tapping on the brakes, but now they were in bumper-to-bumper traffic. As Nick stuck his head out the window a little further, he saw that throngs of people had gathered for one reason or another, all fixated on whatever was going on toward the city center. Cheers suddenly broke into his consciousness as he noticed a sea of Cuban flags being waved about.

"Do you have any idea what's going on?" Nick asked, forgetting that his companion seemingly spoke no English.

The old man smiled at Nick warmly and said, "No sé. No hablo ingles."

Nick went into his pocket and pulled out his last two twenty-dollar bills. He hesitated for a second and then, figuring that he had plenty more in the hotel room safe, held out one for the old guy's troubles along with a "Muchas gracias." For the first time since he had been in Cuba, Nick actually got a refusal. The kindly gent said something in Spanish that sounded pretty but was emphatic, nonetheless. Nick just smiled the way he did when life threw him a curve, and then made the man take both twenties. One wink and an "adios" later, Nick took to the street.

Like being hit with punch, Nick was immediately taken aback and awed by the entire scene. And as he started to make his way through the crowd, he realized that it wasn't a crowd so much as a massive gathering of electrified exuberance, with a feel that was one-part outdoor concert, one-part political convention, and two parts riot. A large stage had been erected next to the statue of José Martí and huge, flowing Cuban flags hung from derricks on either side of it. Closest to the stage were thousands of school kids, each in the traditional mustard and white colored uniform, and behind them, several military battalions standing in rigid formation, which represented the only calm in this churning human sea. Members of the Cuban police, who wore a distinctly different uniform than that of the Cuban military consisting of pale blue shirts, dark blue pants, and gray berets, walked throughout the crowd in sets of two passing out miniature Cuban flags and what appeared to be leaflets. Nick took one of each and smiled respectfully at the heavily armed gentlemen despite the fact that he was being jostled from side to side by a large group of overjoyed young men.

Nick hit a point where the throngs of people had grown so thick, that he couldn't continue on, as dozens of people began forcing the group as a whole to one side or another. Nick began to feel angst as it became impossible to move in any direction other than that in which he was being pushed. One particular wave pinned his arms against his side and he actually felt his feet lift off the ground as he was subsumed by the hysteria around him. This one particular bit of inertia was stronger and more persistent than the previous, thrusting Nick far to his left and straight for a metal light stanchion. He careened off the pole and was deposited face first onto the scalding macadam. Nick had started to feel claustrophobic while being thrown helplessly from side to side, but now he was out-and-out frightened. Lying on the ground was the very worst place to be when in the middle of a melee, and he knew it. So, Nick bounced himself off the ground, bumped into several more people, but got himself back to upright. And then, like a tidal wave that finally passes, the entire scene drew calm. The yelling stopped, as did all of the crowd's motion; it was like someone had merely thrown a switch to "off". That someone, was Fidel Castro.

The Beard himself was one of two men standing in the center of the platform, and he had begun speaking in a rather staccato, halting fashion. The scene was now nothing short of surreal. In the span of a word or two, the crowd had gone from uncontrollable to orderly.

Nick, breathing heavily, looked down and saw that his elbow was bleeding, but he was fairly sure that nothing was broken. He also noticed that what he thought was a billboard was actually a video screen which now boasted a moving pictorial of one of the last communist dictators in the world. The speakers crackled and whistled as Castro launched into some rhetoric that Nick couldn't follow. Happy to be back under his own power and having no idea if and when the fracas would start up again, Nick decided to waste no time and began making his way toward the rear of the pack. But something about the moment made him continue to look back at the screen and try to decipher what was transpiring. He saw Castro point to the soldier standing next to him numerous times, say something that sounded reverential, and then wait for the thunderous applause to die down. He heard words such as "victorio" used twice, and "Miami" used in a derisive way almost every other sentence, each time in conjunction with "counter-revolución." "Estados Unidos" and a word that sounded like "agitators" was also thrown around. Something wasn't right, and it gripped Nick to the point where he forgot about his escape strategy, turned around, and like everyone else, listened.

For nearly twenty minutes, Castro, looking old and gray with thick bags beneath both eyes, thundered away as if it were January 1, 1959. Despite his stooped shoulders and slowed-by-age movements, his tone was bright and whatever he was saying consistently registered with the faithful, as each scripted pause gave way to frenetic flag waving and cheers of approbation. And even though Nick could only catch parts of sentences and certain other individual words, it was obvious that this was an organized moment of national pride. The buildup and collective chest-thumping continued until Nick saw Castro unfurl a colorful ribbon, place what was most certainly a medal around the young soldier's neck and kiss him on both cheeks. Then, Castro held the soldier's hand up in the air as if he had just won a title fight, a military marching band began to play, and cannons blew off ceremonial charges. This sent the crowd into delirium and, to a slightly lesser degree, Nick started to get bounced around all over again. But unlike before, he was suddenly nonplussed by the assaults as if he were too deep in thought to care. He replayed the words that he could make out and tried to place them in the context of the moment. Different scenarios and theories began to ricochet through his mind until his attention fell entirely on the folded piece of paper that was still in his right hand. Amidst the body shots and shoulder thrusts, he opened it up, looked it over, and said, "Holy shit." Just as quickly, he crumpled the paper, pushed it into his back pocket, and frantically began looking for the fastest way to safety. He fought through the still celebrating masses and didn't stop until he was blocks away.

"Holy shit," Nick repeated as he now paced back and forth in the doorway of an abandoned, downtown Havana office building. He looked up and down the street for no particular reason and then pulled his phone from his belt. First glancing at the numbers scotch taped to the back, he dialed out straight away.

Lenny was drumming with two pencils against a metal bedpan when his cell phone rang. Even though he seemed in the musical moment, he threw his makeshift sticks in the air and knocked his snare/portable toilet to the ground as he fumbled to answer the call. "Nick?" Lenny yelled with a distinctly uncharacteristic hint of desperation in his voice.

"Lenny, I didn't expect to get you on the first try, but you're not gonna believe this."

"Nick, I'm so glad you finally called, 'cause we're both in a shit-load of trouble."

"What kind of trouble?"

"They know everything. And I mean everything. From the internet thing to the Laundromat to some --- accounting oversights, --- they got us both nailed to the freaking wall."

Nick narrowed his eyes and furrowed his brow in a confused look of utter disbelief. "What the hell are you talking about?"

"The Feds," Lenny yelled in his nasal whine. "They grabbed me a couple of nights ago, threw me in some van and told me how they know everything that you've been up to, and how you've been …."

"Lenny, Lenny, Lenny," Nick screamed with escalating anger. "Slow down and tell me what the hell you're talking about. What internet thing?"

Lenny, still wearing a hospital Johnny and lying in bed, let out a heavy sigh of exasperation and said, "The internet gambling business that you've been running out of the Caymans and the laundromat that you're spin cyclin' your money through --- they know all about it. And they said that if you didn't drop this ridiculous matter right away that they would prosecute the both of us right after we're disbarred." Nick still hadn't moved an inch as Lenny continued his rat-tat-tat recap of what had transpired since he left. "But here's the thing Nick, all is not lost because I have their word that they'll forget about everything --- everything --- if we just let go of this stupid, asinine, case." Lenny paused for congratulations but didn't get any. "Did you hear what I said? They're gonna drop the whole nine yards, and we don't have to do a Goddamn thing except walk away."

"Lenny, listen to me, okay? Don't say another word and just listen. The Feds are conning you. There is no internet --- whatever, and I sure as hell don't own a laundromat. I mean, don't you see that they're just trying to scare you into cooperating?"

"Hey look, Nick, it's not all about you, okay. They pulled my tax returns and found all sorts of --- well --- irregularities, and I'm sure they're not conning me about that. I know for a fact that those are real 'cause I put 'em there. So, don't bother playin' coy about your stuff. Now we either give up the ghost on this one, or you mark my words, they're gonna tuck it to us --- hard." Nick could hear Lenny breathing heavily on the other end of the phone. "So, what do you say, can I tell 'em that we're willing to come coco?"

Nick thought for just a moment and then asked in disgust, "Where the hell are you?"

"Will you please knock it off? It doesn't matter where I am. Haven't you heard one freaking word I've said?"

"Lenny, I'm not fooling around. Where are you right now?"

"I'm lying in a hospital bed fresh off fakin' a heart attack."

Once again, Nick was forced into asking a plaintive, "What?"

"I couldn't think of any other way to get out of that Motion to Squash...thing...so I talked to my buddy, Doctor Razzo and a couple of hundred bucks later, boom, he was swearing to God that

I just had a minor heart attack. And I gotta tell ya, I ain't far from it. And it's a good thing that I pulled this, because I got word today that the Feds withdrew their Motion to Squash and instead want to go ahead with the deposition of the President as planned. So, I figure that I'll just write a letter to the court tomorrow and tell them that I'm in the hospital and just seek a continuance. But none of that matters anyway because we both can be scot-freaking-free of all this if you just let me make the call."

"First of all, I don't want you to contact the court about the deposition. Just leave it as it is. Did they try to change the date or the place?"

"No, it's set for the day after tomorrow at my office," Lenny said through his bewilderment.

"Just leave it alone."

Lenny waved his arms in the air and decided to try another tact. "Tell ya what; tell ya what. Why don't you just leave everything to me? I'll take care of the whole shootin' match. All you have to do is grab yourself some smokes, give El Jefe a big wet one from me and get your ass home."

Nick winced and grabbed a handful on his own hair. "How long have you been in the hospital?"

"What difference does it…"

"Just answer me you asshole."

"Three days. Why?"

Nick pulled his eyes shut in frustration, squeezed the phone in his right hand, and then said, "I'm flying home the day after tomorrow through the same route. I'll talk to you then." Nick had barely finished speaking before he threw the phone on the cobblestone street as hard as he could. "Goddamnit," was all he said, as he jammed his heel onto what was left of the handset and began running toward his hotel.

———————

Deputy Director Anderson ran through the corridors of CIA Headquarters with purpose. In fact, most people in his path actually heard his Bostonians slapping against the tile floors far in advance of having to sidestep him. The file he carried looked awfully thin to be important, but the way he clutched it tight to his right side said otherwise. That and the fact that he waved his credentials in front of him so as to gain quick access to the restricted areas, pretty much sealed that the Deputy Director had news that couldn't wait. Even his knock on the General's door had a distinct urgency to it.

"Come."

"Sir, we've had a breakthrough. We just intercepted a transmission between DeJulia and Cicero." Anderson outstretched the file toward the General with one hand as he pressed against the stitch in his side with the other. General Glendale, not wanting to appear as undignified as the now panting Anderson, waited a second, took the file in a very measured way, but didn't open it. The General bounced it in his hands three or four times to let Mr. Anderson regain a modicum of composure.

"What am I going to see when I open this up?"

"We believe that De Julia is in Cuba, sir."

The General closed his eyes in abject disgust. "Do we believe, or do we know?"

"We know that he was there and are reasonably confident that he's still there."

"Basis?" The General asked, still without having opened the file.

"A short while ago, Cicero received a cell phone call from someone he identified as "Nick." During the course of the call, Cicero said things that could indicate that De Julia is in Cuba. I immediately instructed our field personnel in the Bahamas to circulate De Julia's picture around the Air Cubano ticket counter, and they got several positive ID's. We then checked their records and found that a ticket was issued to a Nick DeJulia on the day he disappeared. We then contacted the U.S. Interests Section in Havana and asked them to crosscheck the name with the Cuban Ministry of Tourism."

"And?"

Cuban Customs does show that on that same day, a man named Nicholas De Julia produced a passport and filled out paperwork indicating that he was on vacation and planning to stay three days. Now all hotels in Cuba are required to submit guest lists to the Ministry of Tourism on a daily basis. And when we checked that, the name De Julia did not appear --- but there was a room at a place called Novotel registered to a Mr. Ruderman."

"So?"

"DeJulia's college roommate was a man named Gary Ruderman."

The General took it all in, unsure whether this was good news or bad. "Were we able to hear De Julia's end of this phone conversation?"

"No, sir. He's using prepaid phones; there's no way to trace his calls. But we did hear Cicero's end of the conversation."

"Could you discern anything of value?"

"Cicero made several references that lead us to believe that DeJulia is there, but nothing about what, if anything, he's uncovered." The General did not respond. "I have agents staked at the Air Cubano terminal in the Bahamas prepared to arrest De Julia upon his arrival for illegal travel to Cuba." The General peered over his half-glasses, dismissive of Anderson's proposed solution.

"Mr. Anderson, if De Julia has in fact unearthed something that could prove embarrassing or otherwise detrimental to this administration or our country as a whole, ---- well then the question goes begging: Why would we ever want him back here," General Glendale posited, turning his palms to the heavens, "in a land where even prisoners have the right to speak out and be heard? Wouldn't it be better, given that silencing him has been our number one objective, if Mr. De Julia --- didn't come back at all?" The General thought out loud.

"Yes, sir." Anderson dutifully answered.

"Why don't we, very quietly, notify the Cuban Government that a wanted criminal has entered their country under the name Nicholas De Julia and is on the run from charges of cocaine trafficking. Tell them that he is known to use the alias of --- What was that name again?"

"Gary Ruderman, sir."

"Right, Ruderman. Tell them that he could be traveling under either name and that if captured," the General cocked his head to the side and thought for a second, "we would have no interest in extradition."

Anderson understood that coded message and knew that the Cubans would as well. There was no way that an American criminal would ever eat even one meal at the expense of the Cuban

Government.

"Is there anything else you would like me to tell them, sir?" Anderson asked, standing at attention.

"Yes." The General looked off for a moment as a trace of smile formed. "Tell them that he's from Miami."

CHAPTER 26

Ideas, scenarios, possibilities, and predictions weaved their way through Nick's mind until they formed a tightly knotted mass of confusion. He had no real assurance that Lodish would be in the canyon at 8:30, that Celia would look beyond her anger and show up as planned, or that he could still count on anonymity in Cuba. And most problematic of all, Nick had no way to gauge the reach of the CIA if Lenny did, in fact, give him away. As if that weren't enough to contend with, he realized thirty seconds into his cab ride that he had given away the last dollar he had on him.

"Hola, amiga. I have a poco problemo."

"What is it?" The female cabbie said in perfect English, finished off with a tinge of sarcasm.

"I'm sorry for the broken Spanish. I've only been here a couple of days."

The lady looked in what was left of her rearview mirror a saw a nervous man trying to look calm. "You've been here only a few days and you're in trouble already --- that's Cuba, Señor."

Nick laughed along. "I'm afraid that I'm about to be in trouble with you too."

"Why is that, Señor?" she asked, turning onto the road that runs along the Malecon.

"I don't have any money --- presently." The woman again met Nick's eyes via the mirror. "I mean I have money, don't get me wrong; it's just that I don't have any on me --- right now. It's at the hotel."

"Which hotel?"

"Novotel."

The woman kept looking at Nick for a moment and then shrugged her shoulders. "It's Okay, Señor. I had no money when I woke up this morning, and if that does not change, so be it."

"Muchas gracias."

The woman uttered a less than enthusiastic "Um-hum," which sounded just cynical enough to remind Nick of home. She then began to yammer something about US/Cuba relations going back to Batista, but Nick tuned her right out. He kept pondering his own dilemma, as a replay of Lenny's screw up made him sink lower and lower into the back seat. Not at all prone to paranoia, Nick felt odd looking all around to see if they were being followed. To the backdrop of the cabbie's diatribe on the long-reaching effects of the US embargo, he began to mutter to himself. "Come on now, get a hold of yourself. There's no way that this can be a problem. Even if they're sure where I am, what can they really do? I'm not going back on a commercial flight. I signed into my room under a different name. They never even stamped my passport. It's not like they can call up the Cuban Government and tell them to arrest me? It's not illegal to be here from a Cuban standpoint. There's no embargo against Americans traveling here." Nick was actually starting to feel better. "No, I'm worried about nothing, and now is definitely not the time for panicked thought. No, no, no," Nick said, running both hands through his hair. "Focus on what I need to do. That's all. A to-do list --- just like always --- just like every other case. Okay. First, I need to get my money. Second, I have to lay low until tonight," he said with a glance at his watch, "and then make sure I can get a cab that can take me out to the bridge." Nick stared down at the floor for a long moment and then, reluctantly added, "And I should get a gallon of water --- just in case." He bit down on his bottom lip and shook his head to try and get the mental picture of a crying Celia out of his mind. "I hope to hell she shows."

The cab driver, content to blather on about the regrettable collapse of the Soviet Union, took the long route back to Miramar, but Nick didn't really mind. He had time to kill. Besides, it gave him an opportunity to hone his to-do list, smoothing out the subtle imperfections, burrs, and blemishes that always lie in wait to sabotage. But as the cab reached the last traffic light, Nick casually looked over to his left, and in an instant, the entire game plan went right out the window. Nick slid further down into the seat and pretended to scratch his temple, effectively hiding his face.

"Drive. Just drive straight."

"But Señor, Novotel is over there." The woman said, looking to her left, only then realizing just how many police cars blanketed the hotel parking lot.

"I don't care. When the light turns green, you just keep going straight."

"Si, Señor. Whatever you say." Nick's eyes met the woman's one more time in the rearview mirror, and then he saw her drape her left arm over the top of the steering wheel; a posture she had never taken before, and one perfectly suited for jerking the car to the left. Nick's eyes darted between the still red traffic light, the policemen buzzing about in front of the hotel, and the cab driver's whitening knuckles; there was nothing but road ahead of him and whole lot of water to his right. Like a cornered snake, Nick didn't waste time, and, with like quickness, he pulled the Montecristo cigar tube from his pocket, and pushed it up against the back of the cab driver's neck.

"Now you either keep driving straight, or you're gonna make me do something that we'll both regret. Comprendo?" Without another word, Nick watched the woman slowly slide both hands onto the sides of the steering wheel. "Good. Now if you want to see tomorrow you make sure that we just go straight." When the light turned green, the woman, now near tears, drove right past the Novotel entrance at about fifteen miles per hour. Nick, although still pushing the metal tube into the woman with enough authority to convince her that he meant business, ducked down until he felt the car pick up speed. Coming up just enough to peer out the back window, Nick saw a number of police officers interviewing members of the staff while others ran in and out of the main lobby. All in all, it was an imposing sight and one that struck at Nick's very core. He had underestimated the reach and resourcefulness of the CIA, and this was the price.

"What the hell do I do now?" he wondered aloud as he nervously checked his watch. "Six and a half hours. Six and a half Goddamn hours." Once again, he was forced to martial his thoughts, trying only to concentrate on the problem at hand. "Step by step; think." Nick quickly decided that traveling on a main street was no longer advisable given the certainty of his growing popularity. Working hard to subordinate the fears that raced across his mind, he turned his attention to the immediate surroundings, looking for a deserted side street to pull down.

"Make your next right," he told the woman behind the wheel. "The one immediately after that yellow cinderblock wall." A few turns later, Nick found himself in a godforsaken area far worse than any he had previously encountered. "This is good. Pull over here," he said, removing his cigar tube from the poor woman's skin. "Okay, now get out, nice and slow." Again, the sobbing woman complied. Nick felt badly scaring the poor lady like this, but a compliant driver had suddenly become the difference between life and death, so he felt it fell into the category of "you gotta do what you gotta do." He kept his tone of voice sharp and his volume high. "Now don't you turn around, but I want you to look at your watch. Go ahead, look." Nick searched his mind for the word in Spanish. "Mira, mira." He yelled. "Que hora es?"

The woman's hand shook as she raised it. "Dos meno venti."

"Okay. Now I don't want you to move from this spot for one hour. Comprendo? Don't move until tres meno venti. Si?"

After two false starts, the woman finally got out an audible "Si," just before Nick put each of the motor's seventy-five meager horses to work. He had been careful to alternate turns on the way in so he would have no trouble finding the exit. Right, left, right, left, did put him back on the highway toward Havana, but without a map he would be at the mercy of his memory. But even that was a problem to be solved in the future. Getting past the fifty cops hovering around the Novotel parking lot was the problem for the here and now. Imploring himself yet again to think, Nick decided that his best bet was to figure out the worst-case scenario and guard against that first. "What can screw me?" Nick ran his hand through his sweat dampened hair several times while his mind whirred through the possibilities and probabilities. "Alright, the present danger is being spotted; and the cabbie can ID me. So, I have to assume that she didn't buy the tough-guy act and has already notified the cops by phone. So, the car, something easily identifiable, is a liability. But without it, there's no FREAKIN WAY," he screamed, "that I'll be able to make it to the bridge by 8:30." Nick closed his eyes tight, despite still driving, and tapped the steering wheel with his fist several times. "Okay, that means the key is getting back to Havana. It'll be easier to dump the car there, then I need to find some other way to get out there tonight." Nick pulled around a slower moving car but then brought his speed under control, remembering that even a routine traffic stop could end it all.

Nick looked up ahead and saw that he was approaching Novotel. Even from a half mile away, he could easily see the police lights flashing up against the building. But there wasn't a roadblock, or even a car pulled over anywhere along the highway. Everyone still appeared to be milling around the hotel entrance and strewn throughout the parking lot. So, Nick kept it at 35 miles per hour, laid his left arm out the window like he was completely at ease, and headed straight. "Just look straight ahead," he told himself. Then, over a little hill, dead in front of him, came five or so police cars with lights flashing and sirens blaring, heading right for him. They were a few hundred yards ahead but bearing down fast. Everything ran through Nick's mind. Stop; turn around; go right through them. Nick's eyes shot from left to right, from the rearview mirror to straight ahead. Then, from his right, about a hundred feet up, a police officer ran out, stopped right in the middle of Nick's lane, faced him, and with both hands, demanded that he stop. Again, Nick's thoughts raced. Go around him; run over him; give up. Seeing that the officer wasn't budging, Nick knew he had to make his decision, so he pulled his foot off the accelerator and paused for a moment, truly unsure of whether he'd hit the brake or put the throttle on the floor. After one more panicked look all around, he jammed his foot down, locking the brakes. The tires smoked and the car fishtailed as Nick held onto the shaking steering wheel. He actually felt the back of the car start to hop just before he brought it to a complete stop, five feet from the officer who still hadn't moved. The officer looked him right in the eye and screamed at him in Spanish. Nick slowly took his hands off the steering wheel and showed the officer his palms. The officer yelled at him one more time, and then turned his back to Nick so he could wave the still speeding police cars into the Novotel parking lot. After the last car passed, the young officer looked at Nick one more time, patted his chest to indicate just how close to a heart attack he had actually been, winked, and motioned that Nick should continue on. Without missing a beat, Nick mouthed a "Lo siento," to the officer and headed straight for

Havana at a blistering twenty-five miles per hour.

Nick looked at his watch for the thousandth time and saw that he had made it to seven o'clock. After dumping the car in one of the busiest sections of Havana, just a block or so from the *Hotel Nacional de Cuba*, he headed straight for the entrails of the city. With his head down and hands in his pockets, he had walked briskly by every clean, well-lit establishment in search of a place where patrons were few and respectable people were unlikely to frequent. Chin Lu's Chinese Bar was just such a place. The entire room had no more than four tables and five or six bar stools. There weren't any windows, very little in the way of lighting, and each of the four bare walls was painted a dark red. But the best part of all was that the bartender didn't seem to mind that Nick drank only ice water for going on five hours now. In the whole time that he had been there, only one other person had come and gone. It was perfect. The big question, though, was what lay outside Chin Lu's front door. Nick was still twenty miles from his destination and without a cent in his pocket a cab ride was out of the question. But by now, dusk had begun to provide some cover, and that meant it was time to move.

Despite not having a tab to settle, Nick walked over to the bartender, who had been reading a book nearly the entire afternoon.

"Excuse me."

"Another glass of aqua fria, Señor?"

"No, I think I've had enough. But I was wondering if you wouldn't mind doing me a favor?"

"How much of a favor did you have in mind, Señor?"

Nick held out the carefully folded letter that he had spent most of the afternoon working on. "Would you see to it, that this letter gets delivered to a parador called Baredo? It's just outside of Miramar."

The bartender took the letter, turned it over and saw only the name "Celia" written on the outside. He then looked up at Nick and laughed. "I see you met a woman during your visit."

"Believe me, my friend, she's not just a woman."

"A real beauty, eh?"

Nick smiled. "In every way imaginable."

The bartender tucked the letter into the breast pocket of his shirt and then buttoned the flap over it. "I will be happy to do you this favor, Señor."

Nick nodded appreciatively and then said, "I'm sorry, but I don't have any money to give you."

The bartender quickly waved off the apology. "Señor, I had no money when I woke this morning; I will have no money when I go to bed tonight; I will have no money when I wake tomorrow. To do this favor for you, shall not cost me in the least." Nick couldn't believe he heard this sentiment twice in one day but didn't question his good fortune in this regard.

Nick shook the man's hand, squeezed his shoulder, and then stepped out into the twilight. With his one thousandth glance down at his wrist, Nick realized that he had less than ninety minutes to get where he needed to be. And unlike some of his other dilemmas, which required focused thought in pursuit of the best possible course of action, there was really only one option at present: Nick needed to steal a car, and fast. Instead of walking toward the city center, he continued on into the more dangerous outskirts, where western hemisphere poverty was at its absolute zenith. There certainly were more cars closer to Havana, but more policemen too. So, Nick kept walking toward the ragged and ravaged neighborhoods that bespoke the failure of la revolución, hoping to find something to hot wire. But one block turned into two, and then three without any prospects. Time was fleeting and his odds weren't improving. After nearly a half-mile jaunt the only two cars that he came upon had men in them, and even though he still carried his trusty cigar tube, they didn't look like the type who'd fall for it. Nick was quickly learning that without bribe money, maybe he wasn't that resourceful after all.

The deeper he got into the maze of torn up streets and bombed out buildings, the more he felt the gnaw of panic in his gut. As seven o'clock became seven-thirty, he truly began to sweat, figuratively and literally. He was fully consumed with the realization that the only thing worse than Celia not showing up, would be for her to be at the bridge thinking that he didn't show up.

Nick quickened his pace from a jog to an all-out sprint; his strides echoing through the narrow streets caring little that a sweat soaked American running through this area of Cuba was bound to draw more than casual attention. Nick kept on in search of opportunity like a man possessed, but still nothing; not a single car for six straight blocks. Now breathing heavily, he stopped just long enough to check his watch: 7:40. It seemed as though time itself was quickening its pace, forcing Nick to run even faster.

He sprinted past three more side streets before he finally found a prospect. It was an ancient-looking Ford parked outside one of the more dilapidated two-story buildings on a dead-end street. After only a few days it had become apparent to Nick that buildings in Havana were constructed to withstand everything except a prolonged hurricane of inattention, and this structure was a prime example. The building appeared to lean out towards the street in a threatening way, as if challenging Nick to move the car before it was crushed in an avalanche of mortar. But on the upside, there wasn't an operational streetlight to be found and not a single person in sight. In fact, the only sounds came from a nearby barking dog and two people somewhere within the building who were screaming at each other in angry Spanish. 7:45; this could be my last chance, Nick thought to himself as he headed for the car like it marked the finish line of a hundred-yard dash. His shoes squeaked to a halt just as he reached his hand in the open driver- side window to pop the hood. He quickly moved to the front of car and began to finger around in the dark for the trip latch. Despite his wrist being at an odd angle, Nick managed to steal a quick glimpse, 7:46, and then shot a look at the building that loomed over him where the ongoing argument had escalated into something that would qualify stateside as a domestic disturbance. After sticking his face right up against the rusted grill, he finally found the tag end of the latch, pulled it, and threw the hood up practically in one motion. Nick then knelt on the front bumper and leaned in; there, staring back at him --- was nothing. The car had no motor, no engine block, and no mechanical components whatsoever. It had been stripped for parts right down to the bare metal. Nick stayed motionless for a long moment mesmerized by the cavity that was the engine bay, before slamming the hood in frustration. Ironically, the latch didn't catch, and the hood just glided right back up. 7:47.

I messed up, Nick thought to himself, I'm not gonna make it. And then, just when it seemed like it couldn't get any worse, a flash of blue got his attention. The sweep of the lights made huge circles at first, briefly illuminating the buildings at the top of the intersection, but as the police car moved closer the circles of light drew tighter and brighter. The car was moving slowly down the same road that Nick had just come from, as if it were tracing his steps. And worst of all, it was about to block the only way out. Nick looked all around in a frenetic panic. He had a lot of talents, but the ability to un-dead-end a street was not one of them. As the circles drew tighter still, Nick realized that he was trapped. He could hear the car's tires rubbing against the road and the squeak of its shocks as the car bounced in and out of the omnipresent potholes. It would be at the top of the street in a matter of seconds, perpendicular to where Nick stood frozen, and blocking the only way out. After one last fruitless look around, he jumped into the front of the Ford and pulled the hood down to within an inch of closing. Before he could even adjust himself, a flicker of blue intermittently lit up the street and even seeped into Nick's metal coffin via the tiny slit of an opening he stared out of. I hope to hell I shut it in time, he thought to himself, knowing that his only real chance was for the small dead-end street to appear desolate at a glance; maybe then the cops would pass on patrolling it in favor of some other dingy little avenue.

So, Nick stayed trained on the building across the way, hoping against hope that the garish blue light would give way to the much more accommodating dark of night, but not before he could use it to catch one more look at his watch, of course: 7:48. Just keep goin'. Just keep goin', Nick repeated, but nothing seemed to be happening. The rhythm of the lights never changed in any respect, as if the car had parked at the top of the intersection. "Come on move, you rat bastard, move," Nick said somewhere between a whisper and his regular voice, trying to will his situation into improvement. But then, he heard the unmistakable squeal of old, worn-out brakes, and in that instant, everything changed. The lights danced all over the street, the police car's engine revved louder and louder, and his heart sunk lower and lower. All he had was a one-inch high line of sight, and even that was interrupted when the police car skidded to a halt directly aside him. A million thoughts shot through his mind, but he settled on one: There's no way he was going down without a fight. So, he slowly and quietly rolled onto his back in the center of the compartment and drew his knees to his chest, thinking that the instant the cop began to raise the hood, he'd kick it open with all the force he could conjure and try to catch him off guard. There, in a contorted and tensed up ball, Nick stared at the bottom of the trunk lid, waiting for it to move even the slightest bit. As the officer's footsteps approached, Nick pointed the soles of his feet directly at the hood, hoping to time it perfectly and explode against it. He blocked everything else out except the sound of the officer getting closer and closer, and then --- passing the front of the car and continuing on until Nick couldn't hear him at all. He remained motionless and kept listening, but now only heard the couple that was still arguing. Nick relaxed his legs, rolled around until he was facing forward, and cautiously lifted the hood just slightly at first, and then a little more until he saw that he was the only one on the street. The officer had gone into the building, presumably to stop Señor whomever from killing his wife. Wasting no time, he struggled out of the car and took only a single step toward the intersection before it hit him --- The police car was still running. Seeing that it was now 7:50, and without a second of hesitation, Nick added "grand theft auto" to his ever-widening criminal resume. He jumped behind the wheel, threw it in reverse, and fishtailed his way back up toward the through street.

Finding his way out of this residential labyrinth would have been daunting at high noon with a map, but cloaked in darkness, it seemed damn near impossible. And given the fact that he was driving a borrowed police car, the task was certain to be that much more difficult. So, Nick harkened back to Lodish's directions, recalling that the bridge was "twenty miles south of Havana, heading toward Veradaro," and decided to pin all his hopes on the tiny compass glued to the dashboard of the car. Suddenly, keeping the "S" right in the middle of the top line became the most important thing in his life, and he wasn't exactly subtle about it. Nick inelegantly barrel-assed around turns and accelerated whenever he found himself on any portion of the road that arguably resembled a straightaway, all the time bouncing his eyes between the compass, the road, and the police radio mounted just below the dash. Nick still couldn't speak Spanish, but something told him that he would be able to discern when they started talking about him.

With no traffic lights nor stop signs to obey, Nick flew through intersections without so much as tapping on the brakes; and at one point, he even figured out how to turn on the siren, thinking that would make his present driving style actually less conspicuous. But no matter how fast he drove, time itself seemed to keep pace. And worse yet, Nick had no way of knowing if he was even heading in the right direction.

After two or three of his more daring maneuvers, one of which had him on the sidewalk for a time, the road seemed to open up, giving Nick his best chance to gain some ground --- but toward where? Just as Nick squinted at what he hoped would be an actual highway sign off in the distance, his attention was suddenly pulled down toward the radio, where he deciphered a report of a stolen police car. Nick's adrenaline level was at absolute max; the prospect of being hunted by communist party police officers sent a chill right up his sweat-soaked spine.

Seeing a wooden roadside sign that confirmed that he was in fact heading toward the resort community of Veradaro, filled him with a new resolve. As he whooped and hollered in the car Nick started to recognize things: A baseball stadium; a billboard with a headshot of Che Guevara in his trademark beret; and a rusted out old Packard on the side of the road. All of which told Nick he had a chance. The highway would lead him right to the bridge, but would he make it? 8:15.

He turned off the siren and the headlights but kept his right foot squarely on the gas until the car made a sound as if it might throw a rod or shoot a piston right through the hood. So, he eased up a bit, but still urged the car on, rocking his body toward the steering wheel imploring it to, "Come on, come on."

After speeding through a hilly region, Nick could see the ocean to his left and nothing but empty road ahead of him. It wasn't until 8:22 that he saw the first flashing blue light in his rearview mirror at least half a mile behind him but coming hard. Driving without headlights did obscure the car as intended but in reality, made the turns, twists, and mere bends in the road adventures in and of themselves. Straight-a-ways, on the other hand, were met with nothing but acceleration. Making it to the bridge on time wasn't enough anymore; with half the Havana police force in tow, every second was critical. Nick had to give himself enough time to get there, ditch the car, and make it to the boat, all before his pursuers reached him. And with a half-mile lead, he'd only have thirty seconds at most.

He was going to make it to his destination on time or die trying. It was that simple. So, he turned on his headlights, and slammed his right foot all the way to the floorboards, internally vowing to keep it there regardless of what sound the car made in protest. The engine hesitated for a second, gathered up some power, and then seemed to blast the car forward. The speedometer needle raced to the right and the escalating pitch of the motor drowned out everything except the voice inside Nick's head that kept repeating, *Stay with it, don't let up. Stay with it...* The steering wheel was the first thing to start vibrating soon followed by the rest of the car, but Nick held on. Stay with it, don't let up. Stay with it... And just when it seemed as though the engine would explode, Nick jammed both feet onto the brake and jerked the hurtling car to the left, narrowly missing a small herd of goats that had found their way into the middle of the road. He tried to pull the car right back, but inertia won out, causing the car to careen into and then along a metal barrier that protected motorists from a precipitous cliff-side drop. Sparks rained into the driver side window and spilled onto the hood; the unnerving squeal of metal scraping along metal sliced through the night; the unpaved shoulder made the car rock from side to side. And all the while, Nick's foot had somehow made its way back to the accelerator. With all of his weight shifted to his right, he gritted his teeth and let out a sustained grunt as he forced the car off the guardrail and back onto the road. Dirt, rocks and debris spattered from the rear wheels and smoke streamed from the length of the driver's side, while Nick fought to get the whole of the car's mass heading in a single direction. And just as the car seemed to bounce and shimmy for the last time, there it was --- the bridge, no more than a quarter mile away; its silhouette tall and dark black against the cloudless evening sky. Even though it didn't owe him a thing, Nick asked the car for one last burst of energy and got it.

Knowing that the race is never over until you run through the tape, Nick wasn't about to pull up short. He had risked his life for the meager cushion he now enjoyed, and another few seconds tacked on could only help. So, in a final bold move befitting the actions of a man on a quest, he decided to ignore Raphael's prudent counsel and his own common sense by pointing the car toward the area just to the right of the bridge, steeling himself as best he could, and driving directly over the side. The back of the car flew high into the air as it left the edge, forcing the nose down hard onto the embankment. And it stayed down, grinding along the slope until the car's rear completed its inevitable descent. But the back fell askew, with the left tire hitting slightly before the right, causing the car to bounce, teeter, and almost flip onto its side. Nick did everything he could to hold onto the wheel, but he, like the car itself, was simply at physics' mercy. His body, pushed from side to side, slamming into the door and hitting his head on the roof in alternating blows; his legs, continually banged against the dash and the underside of the steering column. The ground seemed to rise up, hit the car, and then disappear with the same type of brutal rhythm as that of a boxer with a great jab. Nick would have had no way of knowing, but the very first time that all four wheels were on the ground simultaneously, was when the car ground to a dusty halt at the very bottom of the embankment.

Nick took a quick breath to make sure that the car had really come to rest, and then took a quick inventory to make sure that all his limbs had completed the journey as well. He tried twice to open his door but, remembering the goat incident, knew not to bother a third time. He dropped his head to the side and pulled himself through the open window.

Although he felt beat up, he also knew that he wasn't in between rounds. So, after one morbid peek at the drop that he just survived, Nick ran to the spot that Raphael had earlier pointed out and saw the small light on the bow of Lodish's boat, which was about ninety feet offshore. And that's all he saw. Nick scanned the shoreline, up and down, but couldn't make out a figure anywhere. An exasperated and disheartened, "No," was all he muttered. And then, he heard a short, sweet whistle come from directly beneath the superstructure. Nick stepped down a few more feet, leaned over, and saw Celia holding Claudia.

Again, ignoring Raphael's advice, Nick ran down the path, hopping over the smaller boulders and vaulting over the bigger ones, never stopping until he reached Celia. The two hugged with Claudia sandwiched between them.

"Why did you do that?" Celia asked, referring to his rather showy arrival.

"I don't have time to explain. The police are following me. We have to go --- now."

"Why are they following you?"

"Celia, please," was the only response Nick offered.

Celia then thrust Claudia into Nick's arms and said, "You have to swim her to the boat. I'll get the water."

"Forget about the water; there's no time."

"No. We need it just in case," Celia said as she began running back up the path.

"Celia, no," Nick hissed with restrained frustration, but to no avail.

"We'll make it. Just get Claudia to the boat," she yelled with her back turned.

Nick watched her for a second and then flipped Claudia onto his back, telling her to wrap her arms tight around his neck. He turned around one more time to see Celia moving quickly toward the top of the path. Reaching into his back pocket, he took out the folded-up flyer and stuck it in between his teeth. After walking into the water as far as he could, Nick began doing the breaststroke, keeping his carriage high so that Claudia wouldn't get so much as a gulp of water.

For his part, Lodish waited at the side of the boat and urged Nick to hurry up. And when he finally did get close enough, Lodish reached down and picked Claudia right off his back and into the boat; he then grabbed Nick by the shoulders and pulled him in as well.

"Where in the hell is that crazy broad goin'?"

Nick took the folded piece of paper from his mouth using only his fingertips and then shook it free of any excess moisture. "She went back for the water."

"Look, I've been here too long. We gotta get the hell outta here, now."

"We're not goin' anywhere until she gets back." Nick could see how skittish Lodish had become and knew not to say anything about the pending arrival of the *policía*. "It'll be okay, trust me."

Nick looked back at the hillside but couldn't make out much of anything at all. His first thought was that he was just having trouble seeing through the darkness, which in an odd way gave him a slight measure of solace. But then he caught the rustle of some tall weeds and a glimpse of movement, which turned out to be the outline of a petite female clutching three gallons of water tight to her sides, and his worry returned. If he could see her, so could anyone from the side of the road, a realization made even more frightening by the loudening whine of police sirens.

"What in the hell is that?" Lodish asked, staring up at the underside of the bridge. "Why are the police headin' this way?" He looked down at Nick and then grabbed a fistful of wet shirt. "Were they following you? Did you lead them here you stupid bastard?"

Nick, not even realizing that he was doing it, repeatedly pushed Lodish away with his right hand and waved Celia on with his left. "Forget the water, just run."

The sirens grew louder and louder until everyone's attention was pulled to the top of the hill. Lodish killed the motor and the bow light, while Celia dropped the water jugs down and crouched behind a boulder. Nick, instinctively grabbed Claudia, knelt down, and told her to shush. Unable to see any of the cars or the road itself, all Nick could do was listen as the upsurge of the sirens reached a crescendo, and then began to fade slightly as the cars, one by one, raced across the bridge and away from the canyon. All the cars, that is, except one: The final car seemed to come to a stop in the middle of the bridge where it stayed for several seconds before slowly rolling back to the spot where Nick had left the road. The siren was off, but the overhead lights still flickered against the boulders and brush. It lit up Celia in short bursts of blue, but Nick held out hope that the steep angle would help keep her hidden. The tinny sound of a Cuban police car's door opening echoed faintly through the canyon as did a brief conversation between what appeared to be two officers. Nick let go of Claudia and continually motioned for Celia to stay down. He had no way of knowing whether she could even see him, but it made him feel better all the same by doing something that could possibly help.

One of the officers implored the other to, "vamos" twice, but Nick could tell that the inquisitive one was undeterred. A few Spanish echoes later, the overhead lights were traded for a white spotlight that swept across the bank and the hillside, coming to rest on the abandoned police car that Nick had neglected to drive into the weeds.

One of the officers said something with some urgency in his voice and the other repeated it over the police radio. At that same moment, the light that had been resting steadily on the car began to light a path for the officers as they very slowly and cautiously attempted to descend the hill.

In the thick night air, the only thing that Nick could see clearly was a rapidly shrinking window of opportunity. He pointed himself in what he believed to be Celia's general direction, and mouthed the words "Come on", punctuated by rapid arm gestures that desperately waved Celia forth. "This is our only chance," he added, trying almost to will her into action.

Celia looked over the rock one last time to make sure that the officers had reached a point that would not allow them to quickly get back up or down the hill, then turned and took a long look under the bridge, as if she were looking directly into Nick's eyes. There was even the hint of a smile on her face when she slowly blew a kiss toward the boat.

"No, no, no," was all Nick could muster as he watched a beautiful, petite silhouette making a break toward his stolen police car. Almost instantly the officers began yelling at the moving suspect as they quickened their descent down the hill as best they could. And then, just as Celia dove in through the driver's window, the two officers opened fire, shooting three quick shots, one of which ricocheted off the car. Nothing seemed to move afterwards, though, except the echo of the shots across the water. The once sweeping spotlight now steadily blanketed the car. All anyone could do was stare and hope.

"Mr. Nick?" Claudia whispered for the first time. "Where's Aunt Celia?"

Before Nick could even think up a lie, Celia hit the ignition, turning the car over on the first try, threw it into gear and peeled away, creating a dirty haze behind her as she took off down the dirt path and away from the road. The officers opened up a sustained flurry of gunfire that now filled the canyon with enough noise so as to overlie the sound of Lodish's boat motor propelling the craft at full throttle in the opposite direction. Nick swung his head around and hissed a "No." through gnashed teeth only to see that Lodish was holding the wheel with his left hand, and a gun with his right, which was pointed directly at Claudia.

"Sit down or I'll blast her head right off," Lodish yelled, continually turning around to look briefly at what was in front of him. "I'm not foolin' with you," he added, keeping up the intensity in his threats. "I'll shoot her where she stands if you don't sit down right now."

Nick turned to watch the last vision of Celia's car driving down the dirt path into the black Cuban forest, and then back around to look at Lodish, who held a gun rather steadily for a lunatic simultaneously piloting a boat. Without much of a choice, Nick wrapped his arms around the little girl, and dropped to his backside near the stern. With the buzz of the motor at full throttle only half drowning out Lodish's litany of threats, Nick looked back into the darkness and felt his soul sink. A million things raced through his mind like usual, but this time there was no clarity or cohesion to any of it; he didn't have a plan, an agenda, nor any to-do list darting through his thought process. In actuality, he couldn't even concentrate beyond the realization that sooner or later the guy with the gun was bound to learn that no more money would be forthcoming, and God only knew what the consequence would be then.

Nick rubbed his eyes in a feeble attempt to somehow stave off the waves of desperation that were washing over him. And when he finally pulled his hand away, he looked down at Claudia, just as she sadly looked up at him. In that instant, it hit him. He was now responsible for the very life of a seven-year-old girl. He didn't have the luxury of being unsure. So, Nick forced a smile, caressed her cheek with the back of his index finger, and whispered, "Everything is going to be fine. I promise you. Everything will be okay ..."

CHAPTER 27

As soon as Nick heard Lodish cut the motor, he paused to let the boat stabilize, and then stood up, sliding Claudia behind him. Although he was no longer pointing it at them, Lodish still held the pistol in his right hand. Nick quickly scanned the cockpit of the boat for anything that could be remotely used as a weapon but came up empty. Then he noticed that Lodish seemed overly occupied and most definitely concerned with a set of lights off in the distance, moving toward them from the left.

"What's going on?" Nick asked pointedly.

"That's the Cuban Coast Patrol heading toward us," Lodish said as he pulled open a small door on the console and shoved his gun inside.

"Don't you think that someone might have made them aware of what happened back there?"

Lodish cut all the lights on the boat, grabbed a pair of binoculars and fixated on the approaching craft. "Flash your lights...come on, damn it, flash 'em …" Lodish said into the darkness.

"Hey, what the hell is going on? I thought you knew these guys."

"Oh, I ain't got a good feelin' about this …. somethin' ain't right." Lodish, completely ignoring Nick's comments, stayed trained on the boat. "Son-of-a-bitch …" He dropped his binoculars and ran to the back of the boat towards Nick and Claudia. Sit on the gunnel, both of you, right now."

"What the hell's a gunnel?" Nick yelled back.

"Just sit on the back rail. Get your Goddamn feet off the deck."

Nick grabbed Claudia and jumped on the back of the boat. Lodish went as far as he could toward the stern and then bent down to grab hold of a silver ring that was bolted to the deck. With a quick pull and a forceful hoist, Lodish lifted the entire deck up exposing the inside of the hull. Wedged in between the sloped sides were two pieces of plywood that had been nailed together so that one section overlapped the other. But because the beam of the boat was so narrow, the plywood couldn't have been more than eight or nine inches below where the floorboard would lay.

"Get in there and lay flat, the two of you."

"There isn't enough room in there for one person," Nick yelled back. "There's no way."

Lodish frantically alternated between looking at Nick and the still approaching boat, which was seemingly picking up speed. "I said get the hell in there, both of you. Now."

Reluctantly, Nick slid himself onto the plywood ledge, and then grabbed hold of Claudia just as Lodish tossed her to Nick's right. Without another word, Lodish began to lower the deck on top of them. Unsure of whether the deck would actually strike his face when fully lowered, and a second before he would find out, Nick tapped Claudia on the chin and said, "I knock you out." With that, the deck fell into place, and the pair was thrust into total darkness. The fit was so tight, that Nick couldn't even turn his head in either direction, with the underside of the deck just touching his eyebrows and the tip of his nose. Likewise, his hands, arms and legs were trapped at his side as if he had been shoehorned into the compartment. Within a few seconds, he could feel his body temperature spike, as the heat of his breath was being forced back around his face making each successive inhale an increasingly claustrophobic event. Rapid, frightening thoughts began to flash in and out of his mind, with the notion of Lodish leaving him and Claudia motionless in this coffin-like cocoon being the most frequent and disturbing. More than anything, he felt an overwhelming urge to slam his hands, arms and head against the floorboards until they gave way, allowing him to take a much-needed deep breath of cool sea air. Nick felt Claudia's little finger wrap itself around his. Then, as if sent by God as a diversionary tactic to help him stay sane, Nick's focus shifted to the sounds of a Cuban Coast Patrol officer speaking to Lodish. They had boarded the boat and now, seemingly, and stood directly over Nick's face.

He could hear short bursts of angry sounding Spanish questions being directed toward Lodish in quick succession, but instead of answering whatever it was they were asking, he alternated between asking the men to calm down, and reassuring them that all was well --- an ill-conceived strategy that was failing quickly. Then Nick heard a new voice screaming something in Spanish, to which Lodish responded by yelling as loudly, something about receipts and documentation. But the officers were apparently unswayed as the next sound that Nick heard was the muffled, yet unmistakable thud of what was certainly Lodish hitting the deck.

The scene fell calm for a long moment. Nick's paralyzing sense of claustrophobia was magnified by the most heart-wrenching whimper coming from Claudia. On the one hand, if the deck lifted, exposing he and Claudia, a worse fate would be staring down at them; on the other hand, the tightness in his chest, the arresting sense of motionlessness, and the knowledge that the little girl was apparently too scared to even cry, were bringing him to the breaking point. Every fiber was telling him that he had to escape this suffocating isolate or else... He let out a pained sound, gasped for air, and slammed his face against the floorboards that covered him, opening a nasty gash right in the middle of his nose. Then, he turned his palms up and pushed against the deck with every bit of strength he had, just as he heard the sound of a boat motor going from loud to a sustained fading. At first it didn't budge, and all Nick could think was that the deck had been somehow locked into place, which opened the floodgates of absolute, all-out anxiety. Nick tensed his entire body, growled desperately, and exploded against the underside of the deck. It wasn't for a second or two, but he felt the deck dislodge and begin to lift up just enough so that he could turn his hands around to more of a bench press position. From there, he rested for a second, and then gave it all he had one last time until moonlight and fresh air swept into the chamber. Nick had to yell at Claudia to stir her from her paralyzing response to the whole ordeal, but when she was finally roused to move, she did so quickly, crawling completely onto the deck. For Nick, the angle made it more of a struggle, but he was able to slide his torso out, before taking another rest. Not even caring whether the Cubans were still on the boat or not, Nick lay with his head on the topside of the deck, content to look up into endless space. It took about thirty seconds of sustained deep breaths until he was able to wriggle himself completely topside and see firsthand that he and Claudia were alone. In fact, it was the little girl who pointed over Nick's shoulder toward a Cuban Coast Patrol Boat that was heading back toward land, no doubt with a very pissed off American.

Nick tried to gather himself, knowing that he didn't have to time to figure anything out or even conceive a plan that went beyond wiping the blood from his nose and speeding the boat in the opposite direction. It took him about thirty anxious seconds to find the ignition, and about as long to figure out the throttle, and after yanking Claudia in between him and the console, they were off. Nick tried to keep the boat moving steadily forward with little regard as to just which direction forward was. But even that didn't turn out to be the easiest of endeavors for the newly commissioned captain; something about his piloting style seemed to roil the sea, as it constantly rose up in protest during the early going. Nick would go from full throttle to nearly cutting the power entirely every time he hit an uncooperative hole in the water, which was often. So, in an uncharacteristic tip of the cap to self-doubt, Nick cut his speed in half, and got a much needed nod of approval from the Gulf Stream.

Without a word passing between them, Nick and little Claudia stayed focused on the blackened sea in front of them for the next hour and a half. Time and time again, a constrained Nick would nudge the speed up, only to be reprimanded by a force that he clearly didn't understand. Fearful that he was going to unwittingly do fatal damage to the boat, he pulled the throttle back yet again, and vowed to leave it there --- until daylight at least.

Sometime around 11:30 it hit him. Nick pulled the throttle all the way back to point where the boat was idling. He wanted to shut it off entirely to preserve fuel, but the sound of the motor running gave him a certain sense of security that he didn't want to abandon.

"Why are we stopping, Mr. Nick? Won't it be better to just keep going?"

Nick slowly took in the darkness, all 360 degrees of it, before bending down on one knee and facing Claudia. "Sweetheart...the truth is... I have no idea where we are right now. And I'm afraid that if we keep going in what could turn out to be the wrong direction, it might become a really big problem."

Claudia nodded in agreement that almost seemed like genuine empathy. She didn't cry, or whine, or blame Nick for anything; she just asked one question: "Would it be better to wait for the sun to come up?"

Nick smiled and kissed her on the forehead. "That's what I'm thinking. So why don't you try to get some sleep, and I'll keep an eye out to make sure that everything is fine."

"No, I'll stay with you... to keep you company."

"That's not necessary, sweetie, I'll be fine."

Claudia thought for a minute and said, "Then let's take turns. That's fair ..."

Nick took a quick look around and then back down at Claudia's determined little face. "Alright. But I'll watch first. You get some sleep, and I'll wake you when it's time to switch. Deal?"

"Deal." With that, the two unlikely partners shook hands. "Where do you want me to sleep?"

Nick turned around and noticed that the small cabin in the front of the boat was packed with cigar boxes from floor to ceiling. "I think in here would be best," Nick said, motioning to the cabin. "Just let me clean this out for you." Working furiously, Nick began to throw tens of thousands of dollars worth of premium Cuban smokes overboard without the slightest hesitation. He didn't even notice the large cachet of Punch Petit Coronas that he was consigning to a watery fate. And even though he didn't have to toss all of them into the drink, he did.

"There you go," he said, pointing to the little V shaped mattress that followed the contours of the boat's bow. Claudia looked below but didn't move. Sensing her fear and realizing that only a few hours ago the two of them had been trapped in claustrophobia, Nick took the pressure off her. "You know, why don't you let me go below first and see if there's a light switch, okay?" Nick winked and headed below into the tiny little compartment, flicking on the light without any trouble. "Is that better?"

Again, Claudia just looked, but did move a little closer this time.

"You can leave the light on, and I'll keep the door open so you can come out anytime you want." Nick scooped her up in his arms and carried her down the two stairs into the boat's cuddy and placed her on the mattress. He then bent down to kiss her forehead, "Now I'm gonna stand right on the top step, so you can see me, okay?"

Claudia, never having let go of Nick's neck, pulled him close. "Is Aunt Celia alright?"

Without missing a beat or showing the slightest bit of doubt, Nick said, "She's fine, and I promise you that we'll see her soon. Now you have to get some rest, so you can take the watch in a few hours. De acuerdo? I'm countin' on you now."

Claudia nodded, and as soon as Nick stood up, quickly flipped herself around so that her head was closest to the door.

Nick walked back onto the main deck and took a long, hard look at the blackness that surrounded their tiny boat in every direction. "Ninety miles," he muttered under his breath. "That's always the number you hear. *Cuba is ninety miles off the coast of Florida.*" Nick took another 360-degree spin around. "But where the hell is Florida." Without GPS or even a compass to offer the simplest of assistance, Nick was at a loss, and he definitely didn't want to start running haphazardly towards any angry Cubans, or anywhere else that would be further away from the US.

For the briefest of moments Nick looked up at the stars but was forced to admit to himself that the only subject that he knew less about than boats was astronomy. He then looked down at Claudia and thought about how he missed the days of having friends in high places that could bail him out of a jam. Then, with a quick glance at the boat's radio, Nick actually said aloud, "But then again… I do have some friends in low places as well." With that, Nick turned the radio on and turned the dial until he was on the lowest channel. He clicked the button on the handset, and said, "Bra? Do you read me? …. Bra, do you read me?" Without a response, he went up one channel and repeated himself, "Bra? Do you read me? Bra, do you read me?" Nick fully intended to repeat the process for every channel, remembering what his new friend had told him back in Key West. And it all paid off, once Nick hit channel 19. "Bra, do you read me? Bra?"

"Who in the hell is calling me?" a voice on the other end of the radio rasped in an annoyed tone.

Nick pumped his fist in the air for a second and then responded.

"Bra is that really you?"

"Of course it's me, who the hell else would it be? But the bigger question is, who are you?"

Nick thought for a second. "It's your boat mechanic." He then released the switch and waited. One second turned into five, which seemed like an eternity.

"Well it's nice to hear from you, but I can't say that I'm in need of your services. A friend of mine actually bought me a new boat and it runs like a scalded cat."

Nick touched the handset to his head as if to send a telepathic thank you to Bra. "Well I guess that's too bad for me. I'm just finishing up a job where I'm at and I was planning on heading back to Key West to see what my prospects were like there."

"Oh, there are a lot of boat mechanics around here these days. I'm not sure that you could make a go of it here at present."

"Thanks for the information. I'm actually expected a little further north, but I think I'll come back to Key West first to take care of a few things."

Now it was Bra's turn to think for a second, as he tapped the receiver on top of his Red Stripe. "Are you sure you can find work where you're thinking of headin?"

"Not really." Nick shot back, looking at 360 degrees of water.

Bra nodded and smiled ear to ear. "Alright, well I certainly do wish you well, and if you need me, I'll stay on this channel."

"Good to talk to you. Take care." And with that, Nick lifted the button on the receiver's handset, and immediately began to try and will things to happen. "He understood. He's a smart old bastard, I'll give him that. He got it. It's only a matter of time and he'll find a way to help."

Nick looked down at Claudia who had actually gone to sleep. "Don't worry about a thing, Honey, I've got a friend who's on the job," Nick said as he bent down to stroke her forehead.

CHAPTER 28

Bra jumped into his truck and rolled over to the marina as fast as he could without drawing any attention to himself. It was somewhat odd of him to be there at night, but he didn't have a choice; he did his best to look nonchalant as he took a fly rod out of its tube and quickly assembled it, attaching the reel with impressive speed and dexterity. With all the calm he could muster, Bra then strolled down the dock toward his boat. Nick's paranoia was starting to rub off, as he just assumed he was being watched. And in actuality, he was right.

"What the hell is he doing here at this hour?" one young agent working the night shift said to another.

"Damned if I know," the other responded as he lifted a pair of night vision binoculars to his eyes. "Looks like the old guy's going fishing."

"What should we do?" the less experienced agent asked.

The other kept the binoculars tight to his face and watched Bra for another moment. "Let's not take any chances. Call it in and let's put an aerostat on him just in case. But I'm sure it's nothing -- he's probably just gonna try to catch some tarpon rolling through the channel. You know, at night is really the only time that fishing guides can actually fish if you think about it. They work all day, you know?"

"You don't think we should follow him?"

"The day guys know about boats. Not us. We wouldn't even make it out of the harbor at night. Plus, it really doesn't matter as long as we keep an eye on him, right? And what's better than the eye in the sky? Go ahead, call it in."

The two low-level agents went about doing their job as Bra jumped on a friend's boat for a second and seemed to retrieve something. But just as quickly, he hopped out and headed down toward his boat. In less than a minute, he was untied and idling out of the marina. Only after he passed Garrison Bight without anyone behind him did he feel comfortable enough to dial up channel 19.

"Mr. Goodwrench, are you out there, my friend? This is Bra calling Mr. Goodwrench."

"I knew I could count on an old rumrunner like you," Nick said with a smile in his voice.

"Ah, what the hell. Once a crook, always a crook I figure. So, where you been, buddy?"

"Nick hesitated and then asked, "Are you using the radio on your boat?"

"No, I am not. I 'borrowed' a walkie talkie off a young fella's boat down at the Marina. I also grabbed his cell phone if that would be better?"

"I'm afraid that isn't going to help us; I don't have any cell reception where I am."

"So, where in the hell are you?"

"That is precisely the problem. Where am I?"

Bra thought for a moment as he looked down at the brand-new ICON radio set amid the impressive instrument panel on his new boat, courtesy of Mr. DeJulia.

"Do you have power?"

"Yes."

"Well then listen up. I want you to keep your transmission button depressed for about a minute, but don't say nothin'. Just pin the throttle and keep quiet. Then cut the power and let up on the button so you I can talk to you. Don't ever say anything until I tell you it's okay. You got it?"

Nick thought for a long second and took in another 360-degree view of ocean. "But I'm not sure in which direction I'll be heading."

"Hey look – you called me asking for help, right?"

"Right." Nick responded reluctantly as if being scolded by a teacher.

"Well then stop being a pain in my ass and just do what I tell you, alright? Now move."

Nick bent down and shook Claudia awake. "I have to run the boat for a little while, Sweetie. But don't worry, de acuerdo?" Before she was even finished nodding, Nick did exactly as Bra described for exactly one minute according to his count, and then throttled back and set his radio to receive. Bra stared at his radio and then reached under the instrument panel for a map, which he spread out under a small light. He took a pen, circled an area and let out a hardy, smoker's laugh. Whenever he would speak to Nick from this point forward, he would shut his boat radio off entirely and only use the walkie talkie. "I see we've been busy."

"What?"

"It doesn't matter. Look, cut the power down to an idle, and the turn the boat about 45 degrees to your left. Once you've done that, it's the same drill from here on out. Keep the transmission button down while you're running but don't say anything. When you ease off the power, set the handset to receive and then wait for my instructions."

Without any hesitation or further conversation, Nick did as he was told.

"Can you hear me?" Bra asked a minute later.

"Yep."

"Good. You're heading right where you need to go. And don't worry about a thing, I'm gonna guide you right to me."

"How?" Nick yelled to compete with the wind speeding by his head.

"Remember that radio you put in my boat for me?"

"Yeah. So what?"

"It gives the coordinates of your transmissions so that I can tell exactly where you are and where you're going. I'm just going to keep running myself in the same direction that you're traveling, and we'll just meet up in a few hours. Just remember to ease up on the transmission button every couple of minutes so I can correct your course if need be. Comprendo, my friend?"

"Alright, Bra. I'm in your hands." Nick, now out of habit, did a quick 360. "And by the way, --- thanks --- a million."

"I'll have you in by first light."

For the next five hours, Bra had Nick performing "one full revolution to the right," and "hand over hand three times to the left," etc., keeping him dead on course, but five hours pounding away at the sea with an uncertain destination was taking an emotional toll on Nick. Every time the hull of his little boat would slap against the water, Nick would feel a panicked angst deep in his stomach. His inexperience at the helm of a boat, coupled with the pitch-black night made for a certain amount of drama that Nick could have done without. For his part, instead of heading toward Nick right away, Bra went straight for the place where he felt the most secure; his personal sanctuary was the back country of Key West, with its maze of secluded mangrove islands and lees. He figured that if he indeed was being watched, this approach would be viewed as nothing out of the ordinary.

The General buzzed Mr. Anderson into his office, but never even looked at him. His chair was turned completely away from his desk, and he seemed to be staring at the portrait of Abraham Lincoln, which stood vigil over the room.

"Sir," Mr. Anderson said cautiously. "I just wanted to update you on some recent developments." Although the Deputy Director paused for a response, none was forthcoming. "Sir, the older gentleman in Key West began to act somewhat suspiciously, so one of our field agents requested, and I authorized use of several surveillance tools. Then on my own initiative, I authorized monitoring of all radio communication, be it cell phone or traditional radio contact, on every frequency within one hundred miles of Key West. Given the late hour, thankfully there was not an overwhelming amount. At any rate, sir, we did pick up some chatter between this man and De Julia. We were then able to hone in on De Julia's position. He's piloting a small boat in the Gulf of Mexico. It would appear, based on their conversations that the older man claims to be leading De Julia toward Key West. Our actual tracking of his progress would show that he's considerably off course." Anderson then handed the General a transcript of several conversations and his written recommendations. "Those are obviously just suggestions, sir. If you would like, I could have the Coast Guard intercept De Julia within twenty minutes of you issuing the order. They are already on alert and have a vessel prepared to move in. Toward that end, sir, we're actually set up to act on every aspect of what you see there," Anderson said, pointing toward the notes he had handed the General. "Everyone is waiting for the go ahead. Clearly, we can charge De Julia with 'Trading with the Enemy', given his travel to Cuba, along with everything else we presently know about. With a little effort and digging, I'm sure that the charges could easily grow." Anderson paused yet again, but there was still no acknowledgement of any kind from the General. "Sir, I need to know how you would like to proceed." After taking one very deep breath, the General finally, albeit slowly, spun his massive chair around to face his second-in-command.

"I received this about 10 minutes ago." The General handed the Deputy Director a single sheet of paper, which he quickly read. "Does that answer your questions pertaining to our strategy, Mr. Anderson?"

"I see that it does, sir. Would you like me to see to this personally?"

"I would. Quite frankly, I'm not sure I've got the stomach for an approach this dangerous to our overall national well-being." The General's eyes finally met Anderson's as he shook his head in disgust. "But what the hell, I guess the times really are changing. Tell everyone to stand down, except for team…" The General glanced down at Anderson's recommendations, "…three. Tell them to move in immediately. They are to do so, however, in accordance with the directive which you are holding. Understood?"

"Of course, sir. I'll attend to it."

CHAPTER 29

"How you doin', Nick? Are you handling it okay?"

"I'm just doing what you tell me, but I've been at this for hours and hours and I still have nothing but a lot of water in front of me. Do you have any idea when I should start expecting to see you?"

"Any second now you're going to see land off on the horizon. Just keep heading for it." Bra waited but didn't get a response. "Just trust me and hit the button again so I can check your course." Bra could tell something was wrong and didn't sign off as per the system. "Are you alright, my friend?"

Nick pursed his dried-out lips and rubbed the back of his aching neck. "Not really. This whole thing has turned into a freaking fiasco. I don't even know what to do anymore. I've got some precious cargo here and I'm not really sure how to handle it."

"What is it?"

"Well, let's just say that I finally know what it's like to be a father for the first time in my life; or at least that's kind of been the situation since last night." Nick stole a glance at Claudia, who was still sleeping. "And I'm --- scared, I guess. Scared that this whole thing is going to blow up in my face, and nothing will have been accomplished after all."

Bra was more than a little confused by Nick's statement but did know that if he had wanted to be specific, he would have been.

"Hey Nick, do you believe in God?"

Nick squinted at the radio, unsure of the meaning or timeliness of the question. "I certainly do at the moment, why?"

"Did you ever hear the story about the guy who was trapped on the roof of his house because of a massive flood?"

"I don't believe I have. ---- But does the story have any relevance to my current situation?"

"I believe it does."

"Well then, I'm all ears."

"Okay, there's this guy forced up onto his roof because of this biblical type flood. And needless to say, this guy's scared out of his mind 'cause he can see that the water's still rising. He knows that it's just a matter of time at this point. So, given that he's up against it, and things look as bleak as they could be, he decides to say a little prayer. *Lord*, he says, *please save me from this horrible fate. I've lived life with a pure heart, and although I ain't perfect, I believe I deserve a break.* At that moment a man rows a boat up to the side of the house and says, *Hey Mr., jump down here. I'll fish you out of the water and row us to safety.*"

"So, you're trying to tell me that: It's always darkest before the dawn? Is that the idea?"

"No. 'Cause the guy up on the roof says that he won't do it. He yells back down to the guy in the boat that he can feel the presence of the Lord inside of him, and that he's suddenly filled to the brim with true faith. *The Lord will save me; I believe it in my heart*, he yells as the guy rows away. The man on the roof stands up and sees that his feet are starting to get wet because the flood just keeps getting worse. He spreads his arms out wide and yells, *I know that you'll save me Lord. I believe it in my heart.* Within seconds, a tremendous surge of water knocks the guy off the roof and into the drink; the man struggled and struggled, but ultimately drowned."

Nick cocked his head to one side and thrust his tongue into his cheek. "I gotta tell you, I'm not feeling too good about that story, Bra. I guess I was kind of hoping for a better ending, you know?"

"But I ain't finished. You see, when the man finally meets God in heaven, he says to him, *How could you do it to me? I believed with all my heart that you'd save me. I stood there and proclaimed it to the world at the top of my lungs, I just don't understand how you could forsake me like that.*"

"And did God respond?" Nick said derisively.

"Yeah, he said, *I gave you a whole life to do whatever you wanted. You turned to me when that life had only seconds left and asked for help. And in under a minute I sent you a boat. Now you want to blame me because you were too stupid to get in?*"

"So, the moral of the story would be…?"

"The moral of the story is that a breakdown in communication can cause all sorts of problems, and I don't want that to happen to you. So, my friend, let me be clear: That land that you'll be seeing in the next thirty seconds, is Route 1, just south of Islamorada. Bang a right when you get there and pull beneath the first bridge you come to. I ain't God but I sent a car for you. Some of your Cuban buddies from Miami should be there waitin' for you."

"Where are you?" Nick said, thoroughly confused.

"A long ways away from you. And hopefully, you're a long ways away from the nearest spy blimp. But listen up, son. I can't be certain of that, okay? I did the best that I could, but I'm afraid you're on your own from this point forward. Good luck."

"You sly son-of-a-bitch," Nick said through a laugh. "You're something else."

"You bet your ass I am." At that moment, Bra tossed the walkie talkie into the ocean, and began the trip back to Key West and what was certain to be a very interesting reception.

Bra's words had not even finished resonating in Nick's mind, when right there, through the lifting haze, was the outline of a bridge off to his immediate right. The old-timer's audio navigation had gotten him half way to Miami with enough time to meet his deadline. Nick let out a rebel yell as he jammed the throttle forward and sped toward land. Claudia, not having any choice because of all the noise Nick was now making, woke up and stood next to him. It was actually the little girl who pointed toward a flashing light that was coming from the northern end of the bridge. Nick swung the boat around and within seconds, they could see three men, waving them forward. Apparently, Bra had used his "borrowed" cell phone at some point during the evening to call Diego Martin, explain the situation, and enlist his help. He also accurately figured out how long it would take each to get to some mid-point for a rendezvous and coordinated the whole thing perfectly.

Nick ran the boat right onto the shore as three burly, dark-skinned gentleman rushed into the surf to help him. One of the men took Claudia without asking a word and just whisked her to an awaiting car, which immediately sped off; two others helped Nick up an embankment and shoved him into the back seat of second car, assuring him that arrangements had been made so that Claudia would be safe.

"Where are we heading?" Nick asked while looking through the rear window in hopes of catching a glimpse of Celia's niece.

"Where do you think? You've got a deposition to take, don't you? It's our job to get you there. So, just relax and gather your thoughts, we'll have you there in no time."

CHAPTER 30

A dirty, uncharacteristically disheveled, and exhausted Nick De Julia stared at the back of the seat in front of him, reflecting on what had transpired over the last two weeks, and how he would approach the last leg of this odyssey. So much had happened that he really wasn't sure where he was going to start. He had taken hundreds of depositions during his career, but never one quite like this. President William Huggins was described as being the type of "smart" that reaches another level; one that goes beyond the mere well-read, well-rounded products of an Ivy League/Rhodes Scholar education. He was also known to be wily, intuitive, shrewd, practical, and charismatic. In other words, he was an adversary the likes of which Nick had never come across. Normally, Nick would weave intricate traps to ensnare witnesses into damning admissions or lock them into positions that were unsupportable. But he wasn't sure that an approach like that would bear fruit with someone who was certain to be three steps ahead of him. And after barely a consideration, the intimidation approach went out the window as well. Nick couldn't imagine a man with access to "the bomb" was likely to fold under questioning.

"Hey, do either of you guys have a cell phone on you?" The passenger tossed one over his shoulder, which Nick caught and began to dial in one quick move.

"Lenny Cicero here," he said with a rasp.

"How you doing there, partner? It's your old pal, Nick."

All of a sudden, the rasp was gone. "Nick, where in the hell are you? No, no, forget it, I don't even want to know. But you should be aware that I already have an ambulance on the way to pick me up, because I most definitely feel another coronary coming on."

"You didn't try to cancel the depo, did you?"

"Of course not. What do you think I am, an amateur? I was gonna wait until I got to the hospital."

"Why don't you cancel the ambulance; just tell them that it turned out to be indigestion and with the help of a little Pepto Bismol, you're expected to make a full recovery."

"But what about the deposition?"

"Looks like I'm going to be able to take it after all."

"Thank you, God, thank you." Lenny threw his glasses on his desk, leaned back in his chair, and dropped the crux of his arm over both eyes. "I am getting entirely too old for this shit."

Nick heard the comment and gave a Lenny a second to compose himself. "Ah --- Lenny, are you okay to talk for a second?"

"Just give me a minute, will ya? --- I'm not sure I was lying about that heart attack stuff. Whoa, do I need a drink."

"Lenny," Nick yelled into the phone.

"I'm here, I'm here. What is it?"

"Is the deposition still going to be at your office?"

"No. The Secret Service came by last week and said that it was too much of a security risk for the President. They changed it to the Cardoza Hotel, but said that I couldn't tell anyone, which I haven't. I guess they didn't want any press there. I was told to say that it was canceled, and that we weren't sure if it would ever go forward."

"Who the hell told you to say that?"

"How the hell should I know? Some guy with a badge, a gun, and friends at the IRS for all I know. And why are you yelling at me? It's not like you've been around to consult with. I don't know what I'm doing. I just say "yes" to whatever anybody asks. I mean that's pretty much my life's strategy at this point. You know, a few years ago ..."

"Lenny, just --- spare me. What time?"

"It's set for 11:00." Nick looked at the car's dashboard clock and felt relieved that he would make it. "Are you going to need any help?"

"No, Lenny, clearly you've done everything humanly possible up to this point," Nick said with pointed sarcasm.

"Well, I'm not one to normally look for praise, but it's about time that you gave me a little pat on the back." Nick rolled his eyes knowing that Lenny was actually serious. "And I don't know if this is a good time to bring this up or not, but I didn't get my check this week."

"Consider it in the mail, Lenny."

"Thanks a ton, Nick. And if you need anything else, you know where to reach me."

"Yeah. Miami General." Nick clicked the phone closed. "The Cardozo Hotel in South Beach, as quickly as you can."

As the car rolled its way down Ocean Boulevard, Nick contemplated how nice it would be to fake a heart attack just once in his life in order to avoid doing something that was sure to be anything but enjoyable. Truth was that for all his cocksure bluster, Nick didn't have any idea at all how things would play out. In fact, he really didn't even have a game plan. He was sure that Lenny's cell phone blunder exposed his being in Cuba, and it was as likely as anything that he would be arrested as soon as he entered the building. Regardless, he had come too far to pull up short of the tape. Besides, too many people were depending on him. So, Nick righted himself in the backseat, and tried in vain to freshen his appearance.

Apparently, the subterfuge worked, because there wasn't a single reporter or cop car anywhere to be seen. Only one man was in front of the hotel. He was a trim and well-appearing man who made a beeline for the car the second it pulled up. "Mr. De Julia? I am Mr. Anderson, Deputy Director of the Central Intelligence Agency." Nick donned a mock smile and then extended both wrists, as if to make it easy for Anderson to handcuff him. But Anderson just carefully shook one of his hands and said, "I've been asked to escort you to the Presidential Suite; will you please come with me, sir?"

Nick dutifully followed Anderson through the lobby, which

appeared empty, making Nick think that the Secret Service was quite adept at the "Secret" part of the job. He followed the Deputy Director through the tan and white accented lobby, with its beautiful sandstone walls outlined by dark mahogany. Everything seemed normal, except for the fact that the elevator attendant was six-foot-three and wore sunglasses. And although the tandem traveled up only five floors, it was a surreal ride all the same. Mr. Anderson had an elegance that belied his civil servant status; tall, sharply dressed and neatly coiffed, he looked more like a banker than a CIA Agent. Nick, on the other hand, had a scraggily growth which was more gray than black, a slightly torn fishing shirt and a terrible case of chapped and blistered lips. The two men stood shoulder to shoulder, facing the elevator door, listening to an instrumental version of the song, "It's Five O'clock Somewhere". When the door finally opened, Nick could see a corridor lined from side to side by a gauntlet of men with rigid posture and earpieces. He filed in behind Mr. Anderson, following him to the end of the hallway, and when the two men entered the suite, Nick walked in like he owned the place until he realized that the room was empty. There was neither a court reporter nor the phalanx of Assistants Attorney General that Nick expected.

"What's going on?" Nick asked, still looking around the room.

"The President asked if he might have a word with you in private."

Nick thought for a moment, and said, "And you don't mind me talking to your --- well --- the government's client, without you...or anyone else present, for that matter?"

"It's at the President's request, Mr. De Julia. Follow me please." Mr. Anderson walked Nick to the opposite end of the suite, where he knocked on a door only once, and then walked in. President William Huggins was on the phone, but greeted Nick with a nod and a wave, courteously gesturing for him to sit down. The President politely said goodbye to whichever head-of-state he was speaking and briskly walked toward Nick. He was a much taller man than Nick had appreciated when seeing him on television, and his full head of silver hair didn't seem to move at all. Nick had always wondered if the President wore a hairpiece, and despite the face-to-face meeting, he still wondered. But what seemed most 'out of place' concerning the President's appearance, was the warm expression that had yet to leave him.

"It's a pleasure to meet you, Mr. De Julia. I'm Bill Huggins." Nick was more than slightly taken aback by the President's friendliness toward him, and really wasn't sure how to respond. He also suddenly became extremely self-conscious about his own rather grimy appearance, a feeling that the President picked up on. "Please don't concern yourself; there never was going to be a deposition today."

"Is that right?" Nick asked, still a little unsure about his status.

"No, I'm afraid not. I do realize that my predecessor was deposed twice while President, but that was because he seemingly had a penchant for sexually harassing women, which I can assure you — I do not." Nick couldn't help but smile a bit. "What you were proposing struck a little too close to the nerve that is our national security for it to be doable. The position that I hold enjoys a great deal of protection in this area, as you should know, and I'm afraid we played along for effect, but it was never actually on the table as an option."

Nick paused. "I find myself wanting to ask why you're here, then."

The President took a slow and deliberate sip of coffee. "Because I thought it time that you and I met. Over the objection of the head of the CIA, a gentleman who very much wanted to meet you," the President said, as if he had helped Nick dodge a bullet, "I flew here from Washington just to speak with you. And while we're on the subject, please realize that I could have sent anyone from a staffer to a cabinet member, but I thought it important enough that I show up myself. Consider it a show of respect. I'm hoping that it wasn't a miscalculation on my part, so don't interpret my presence here as weakness." The President paused to see if he had Nick's attention. "I also knew that trying to intimidate you was likely a waste of time; men like you don't rattle. So, in other words, I came here to talk to you man to man."

Nick was listening intently. "I take it then that you know where I've recently been?"

The President nodded. "Sounds like you had a hell of an ordeal while you were over there."

Nick licked his dry lips for a moment while he thought of how to respond. "You could say that."

The President unbuttoned his beautifully tailored suit, and

with discernible grace, dropped his lanky frame into a chair opposite Nick. The President's smile didn't dim at all, if anything, it broadened as he settled in.

"Just so we're clear, I believe that I'm up to date on everything that you've been through from the beginning." The President cocked his head slightly to the side. "I know everything that you've been doing for the last several years, actually. So, with that as the backdrop, I'd like to make you an offer."

Nick didn't appear nervous but was definitely dialed into the conversation. "And what would that be?"

"To have a conversation unlike any you've ever had in your life. One where you don't have to worry about what someone is really trying to say." President Huggins waited for a second to gauge Nick's receptiveness. "I mean, I could have you arrested right now and brought up on a myriad of charges, but that's not what I want. I'd rather we just be frank with each other. And to put a finer point on it, what I am proposing is to talk entirely off the record. For you and I to have a conversation free of even the slightest tinge of concern about truthfulness. But I'm a little hesitant that you'll be able to live up to your end of that bargain."

"And what makes you think that? Did one of your files say that I'm not a man of my word?"

"No, actually one of my files calls you a master negotiator. And that is what worries me. What I'm proposing here is that we dispense with all posturing and just talk to each other about this problem that we mutually share. We come at it from different perspectives, for certain, but we share this problem all the same." The President kept his gaze locked on Nick. "Are you capable of such a conversation?"

Nick didn't agree right away. He thought about it for a long moment. If anyone else was proposing such a discussion, Nick would think that he was about to be hustled in a major way. But this man's seeming sincerity was seductive, and utterly believable. Nick also had to briefly grapple with the fact that he, for the first time perhaps in his life, was not the clear-cut alpha-male in the room. And it wasn't the Office of the Presidency that awed Nick, it was the man. President Huggins's presence was powerful, and he really did appear honorable. So, with a deliberate nod, Nick decided to go with his instinct. "Agreed." Nick then reached into the breast pocket of his shirt and pulled out the only two cigars he brought back from Cuba. "Would you care for one?"

President Huggins smiled, and reached into his own breast pocket, producing two of the exact same cigars. "I was actually going to offer you one. These are your favorites, I understand."

"Well in that case, let's smoke yours, because something tells me that after today, you're going to have an easier time replenishing your stock than I am."

"Fair enough." With that, President Huggins handed Nick a cigar and a gold lighter with the Presidential Seal on it. The two men lit up and each enjoyed the first few pulls on their respective cigars without any more talk. Nick could also see that this was not the President's first cigar, a fact which made him seem even more trustworthy.

"So, Mr. De Julia --- Can I call you Nick?"

"Please do."

"Thank you. So, Nick, I have to say that I have enjoyed reading about your exploits. You're a man to be admired. I particularly got a kick out of the laptop stunt you pulled on the plane. I'm sure that caused some collective heartburn over at Langley."

"Well, just to prove how honest I intend to be, please let me say that the 'laptop stunt' was more about me being a jerk than anything. But based on what you said when I walked in, I take it that I didn't outsmart them about everything?"

"Well that's true, I guess." The President took a quick draw of his cigar. "The Constitution aside, the United States Government is rather omnipresent. It's hard for anyone to get away with much." The President thought for a second. "Well, much that matters, that is."

"All the same, I feel like I've been on the right side of this thing since the beginning," Nick said, without averting his eyes.

"Do you? And what makes you so sure of that?"

Nick put his cigar down, reached into his pants pocket, and pulled out a folded and knackered piece of paper. "This tells me that I'm right." Nick decided to take the President up on his offer and hit him with the truth straightaway. Nick reached over the coffee table and handed it to the President, who very deliberately unfolded and smoothed it out.

"Can you read Spanish?" Nick asked.

"I can."

"And is what's written there accurate?"

The President read every word and then said, "It is true — more or less."

Nick took a long drag on his cigar, taking just a moment to revel in the fact that through sheer will and determination, he had finally gotten to the truth of this mysterious incident. "Let me see if I have got this straight: We, the United States of America, allowed the Cuban Air Force to shoot down an unarmed, civilian aircraft, within our borders, which was being operated by two American citizens?"

The President never looked away, and certainly did not seem apologetic. "We didn't. I did. And would you like to know why?"

Nick paused. "I really would."

"Because it wasn't just the right thing to do under the circumstances, it was the only thing to do under the circumstances." The President's voice did not have even the slightest waver; it was as authoritative as it was commanding. "We live in a very different world these days. One where a single misstep could cause a worldwide ripple effect. So, that said, let me turn it around — what would you have had me do? Retaliate and shoot down the only jet their mighty air force owns? Confirm our perceived desire to dominate smaller countries? Give recruiting material to the jihadists around the globe so they can denounce our imperialistic actions? ...Please," The President said, his words dripping with derision.

"What about your oath? The one you took when you got the job?" Nick asked with a much more pointed tone of voice. "The one where you swore to protect the citizens of this country against all enemies."

The President left his cigar in his mouth and turned both palms toward the heavens. "What the hell do you think I was doing? Are you really serious with that? What are you going to say next: that I don't want word of the incident to spread because I'm worried about losing the Florida vote? Come on, you're a whole lot smarter than that."

"The individual who was killed was an American citizen."

"He was an American citizen engaged in an illegal act, and one which he was routinely warned to avoid for fear of this precise type of reprisal."

Nick let that sink in. He thought he had been in the big

leagues as a lawyer in New York, but he was clearly wrong. The President was far more formidable than any previous adversary. But as the President had previously pointed out, Nick didn't rattle.

"Well, then let me ask you this – if what they were doing was illegal, why didn't you simply arrest them?"

The President pondered the question for a second. "Because we chose not to."

"But *why*, is the question. Is it because you liked them doing your dirty work for you —— dropping flyers over Havana encouraging them to revolt? You used these guys and didn't even blink when it went bad. So, I guess I still don't see your point. For me, the bottom line is that an American citizen was killed by a foreign nation's act of aggression, within our borders...on your watch."

The President's retort was immediate. "And a whole lot more would have died if I had done something about it. And please spare me the righteous indignation over this senseless loss of life. You want to talk bottom lines – those guys knew the risks and accepted them. They also brazenly capitalized on the fact that we weren't prosecuting them for violating international airspace laws, or for aiding and abetting the proliferation of illegal immigration. And let me tell you about risk —— I'll say it again, they were explicitly told that Cuba's Air Force might engage them if they continued along with their course of action. And I know that much is true because we told them so. That's right, your callous government who only cares about its own self-interests, warned them for months that they were going to be fired upon if they didn't stop doing what they were doing. The Cuban Government told us that they would not tolerate violation of their airspace any longer and were prepared to take action. We, in turn, told the Brothers of Freedom that we could not and would not protect them if they persisted, no different than when we announce that we can't and won't protect Americans who voluntarily choose to go to war-torn regions like Iraq or Ukraine. Not even one Marine's life is worth risking saving arrogant idiots who ignore explicit instructions to cease and desist in such matters." The President showed the first glimpses of anger. Nick sat silent for a minute, letting the practical side of his own conscience evaluate everything being said. Subconsciously he shook his head from side to side. "You disagree?"

Nick exhaled and rubbed at his eyes. "I guess the thought of knowingly allowing another country to attack our own citizens within our borders doesn't seem very...well...American."

"Fair enough; so, I'll ask you again, what should I have done under these circumstances with everything else going on around the globe as the backdrop to the decision?" The President tapped the ash off his cigar but didn't look away from Nick. "I'm wide open, what do you have?" The President raised his eyebrows as if to say, I'm all ears. "Not so black and white, is it — even in hindsight?"

Nick was not ready to concede the point. "Why didn't you tell the Cubans that you wouldn't permit it when they informed you of their intent?"

Now it was the President's turn to shake his head 'No', "As I've said, I was not going to endanger one member of the military, or our population at large because of this group, even if their ultimate goals are morally defensible. They routinely violated international law and I was not about to make our government complicit."

"So why the cover-up? If you're so certain that you're right, why not come clean about the whole thing and let the court of world opinion decide?"

"Because of perception, Nick. We don't need any other nation, rogue or otherwise, thinking that we've lost our will to fight. You have to pick your battles very carefully. I mean, you see that, don't you?"

"You don't think terrorists talk? You're not concerned with the precept that what we tolerate we encourage? Maybe next time it won't be just a couple of Americans you deem dispensable."

Nick shot the President a wry look. "Didn't you give me an eloquent preamble when I first came in here about having an entirely honest conversation? Now you're going to sit there and deny that you considered these two gentlemen dispensable?"

"I don't see my position as anything but consistent. The decisions were not made based on whether or not these gentlemen were --- and I'll use your word --- dispensable. We did, in fact, try to save their lives."

"And how did you do that?"

"By giving them a year's worth of notice that they were sealing their fate. Who are they to step away from that now? They

287

knew the risks because we told them what the risks were, and they persisted anyway. Don't you see?"

Nick found himself holding on to the last threads of his argument but was forced to consider its futility. "I would say it depends on how you look at it. I can easily say that they were trying to help a group of horribly repressed people overcome a fascist regime. I mean, isn't that what we do all over the world? Don't you see that?"

"I do, but the 'we' in your statement is the considered policy of the United States Government, not a couple of yahoos with a pilot's license."

"Well maybe they thought you needed help, because you've been doing a pretty poor job for the last fifty years with that particular fascist regime."

Each man took a second to cool down and gnaw at his cigar. "Perhaps you do have a point there, but it doesn't change anything. We've both stated our positions rather frankly, and I really don't see any point in going further. So, given all that we've said here today, I need to know your intentions." Nick had rarely in his life been at such a clearly defined crossroad. The President's intellect was formidable and his arguments persuasive. He could also see that Nick's contemplation was not for show, it was real. Feeling as though he was close to the sale, the President decided to try and lock it down. "I would like you to drop this entire matter right here, right now. If you would agree, I'd consider it a true act of patriotism, and you will be compensated."

"And if I don't agree?" Nick said through a steely-eyed stare.

"Well, permit me to say that I sincerely hope that's not the case, but if that's your decision, I'm afraid that our response will be rather far-reaching. You will be prosecuted for tax evasion and for your involvement with illegal internet gambling. We have all the proof that we would ever need. We know how it was set up, when it was set up, where it was set up, and how you launder your profits. Your former partner, Marty Littrell, who is living in Vero Beach by the way, will likewise be prosecuted but offered immunity to testify against you. Jorge Diaz will remain a detainee at Guantanamo as will that young lady who was apprehended on that same day."

Nick looked down at his cigar, and President Huggins lowered his head in an effort to lift Nick's gaze back up. "And perhaps most importantly, that little girl that you brought with you from Cuba will be immediately placed in foster care in an undisclosed location, but ultimately, she will be returned to Cuba."

Nick gently picked some dead skin from his lips in an effort to buy a second. "How do you know about her?"

"The men that picked you up this morning in Islamorada were CIA agents. The Agency intercepted your communication with your friend from Key West. And when he attempted to contact Diego Martin, that call was intercepted as well. No one knows that you are here except Agency personnel and Mr. Cicero. How's his heart condition, by the way?" The President said with a wink.

Nick let the quip pass, thought about it all, and decided that there was certainly no reason to engage in denials. "Looks like you have me painted into quite the corner."

"It doesn't have to be that way at all. I meant what I said earlier: I admire you. And I know full well that you are not likely to drop this matter to avoid personal problems, no matter how significant they may be. But I'm hoping that your loyalty toward your country and the other people involved in this whole mess will make you think twice. And if you really do take the time to mull it all over, Nick," The President got up and sat next to Nick on the couch, "what will persisting with this thing really accomplish? The truth will come out that I protected our nation against greater harm -- that the event was deemed to fall under the secrecy codicils of our national security plan and thus there was no cover-up -- that if it was a mistake, that I erred on the side of caution. When you strip it all away, do you really think that the majority of Americans will be angered that one Cuban-American got killed while in the process of endangering us all?" The President took his fist, and lightly tapped Nick on the knee. "Don't do it. Just drop it. And if anyone asks, just say that you're convinced that it was, in fact, a matter of national security, and that you are bound by confidentiality not to disclose what you've learned. Trust me, it will all go away in less than three news cycles."

Nick threw his head back and blew a tremendous plumb of smoke up into the rafters. "So, you're trying to tell me that I've lost my first case?"

"Not at all. I'm telling you that you've won another one, but you just can't tell anyone. And I mean exactly that. You can have everything you want. Jorge Diaz will be immediately released and relocated with his wife and children under the witness protection program. The decedent's family will be quietly compensated and relocated under the same terms. The little girl ..." The President waved is hand toward Nick for the answer.

"Claudia."

"That's right; Claudia will be reunited with her mother, who will also be let out of Guantanamo immediately, shipped stateside and fast-tracked for citizenship. And your own --- transgressions, including those of your associates, will be wiped away, never to be brought up again." The President leaned forward and snubbed out his cigar. "You've won, and what I just offered you is far more than any jury could. So that leaves only one reason why you would consider turning this deal down..."

Nick looked up with all the bravado he could muster, "And why's that?"

"Because your ego won't allow you to seem as though you lost." The President took a sip of water and let his statement just hang in air. "Thus, the question is: Is this about all the people you purport to be trying to help, or is this just about Nick DeJulia?"

Nick slowly pushed himself out of his chair and walked over to a beautiful bank of windows overlooking the Atlantic Ocean. He continued to indulge in the calm enjoyment of his smoke and contemplated what he was being asked to do. Eerily, he found himself again facing the same type of issue that got him suspended from the practice of law in the first place. Should he do the wrong thing for all the right reasons, or the right thing for all the wrong reasons? But after all that had happened, he had truly lost track of which was which. Nick also now believed that President Huggins was the genius negotiator. He was able to fully articulate his position, drop in facts that Nick didn't previously know and effectively threaten him, but outside of anyone's earshot. It was actually a tactic Nick had used many times – people are always more willing to give in if no one else knows the reason why. But not even that realization was bothering him at the moment. His attention was more toward wishing for a simpler life; one where he wasn't plagued by inner demons constantly driving him forward into difficult circumstances. Maybe his partner, Marty Littrell, had been right all along. Maybe, Nick thought, he had mastered everything in his universe except for himself. The same competitive drive that made him so successful was also the seeds of his undoing in the law, and now, it was threatening to do him in yet again. And then he actually mouthed Marty's quote. "When you know what you're doing is going to hurt you, but you do it anyway, that's the height of stupidity." Nick wiped at his face as if to wipe away the realization of past mistakes, and in the next moment began to think about Celia. It dawned on him that everyone involved in this case, including himself, would actually be better off if he took the deal, except for Celia. Repayment for her selflessness was not part of the compensation package currently on the table. Nor was a reunion between the two a likely scenario.

Showing the true depth of his perceptive powers, as if reading Nick's mind, President Huggins added: "But I cannot help you in any way with getting anyone else out of Cuba, so please don't ask me. In fact, I was told personally by one of our men in the American Interests Section in Havana that the Cuban Government obtained your picture off a hotel security camera and published it to their customs agents with instructions to forbid your entry into the country. And I assume after today's conversation, you are aware that we cannot protect you in any way if you should later decide to disregard that fact?"

"Is the woman alright?" Nick asked, even though he feared the answer.

"I honestly don't know," The President said with a note of compassion.

Nick nodded his head and actually believed yet again that President Huggins was telling him the truth. He then opened the door leading to the balcony, and gently tossed his cigar over the side.

"So, what's it going to be, Nick? I need to know," President Huggins stole a glance at his watch, "And unfortunately, I can't wait any longer."

CHAPTER 31

Nick De Julia sat on his observation deck much the same way he did every night. He smoked in silence and pondered every aspect of his life; the good, the bad, the ugly, and the regrettable all received equal time. But unlike before, his mind would now most frequently wander south, to a place where even the ravages of time and poverty can't seem to dull the natural beauty that is everywhere. During this nightly reflection, he would always rationalize that he did it for Celia. He knew how she risked everything so that Claudia could have a chance at freedom and knowing that Claudia and Celia's sister were brought together by Nick's decision would always ease his conscience a bit. But he would never be at peace with himself until he could actually speak to Celia and tell her that everything had turned out the way she wanted, and he was responsible for that.

Every night, the same thoughts would haunt him. It had been nearly seven months since it all ended, but that didn't make him feel one bit better. The Brothers of Freedom hated him for dropping the matter, but Randolph Charlton loved him because the insurance payment on the destroyed plane was significantly higher than the plane's actual value. And even though numerous families were back in tact, all thanks to Nick's efforts, he still felt low. He had no idea where Claudia and her mother had been relocated to and that really bothered him. He had grown close to the little girl in a short time and now really missed her, almost as much as her aunt. Lenny had gone back to being the most popular lawyer in

Delray Beach and Marty Littrell had set up a new operation somewhere on the Treasure Coast, or at least that's what Nick had heard.

Nick had run everything through his mind again and again ever since he agreed to the President's proposal. For months he tortured himself with regret, wonder, and equivocation. Despite viewing the whole ordeal through every conceivable perspective, he still wasn't sure he had done the right thing. And on this particular night, as one hour of introspection turned into two, Nick simply couldn't take it any longer. He picked up the phone and dialed a number that he had long ago memorized by heart; it was the number of a real friend.

"Howdy."

"Bra...It's Nick."

"Hey, buddy. It's great to hear your voice. Haven't seen you at the dock or in the bar in I can't tell you how long. How ya doin'?"

"I can't complain. How about yourself?"

"I'm still alive, so I guess you can say that I'm playing with the house's money at this point. But I will tell you, Buddy, things sure have been dull since you've been laying low. I really miss the excitement of what we had going on. I didn't understand half the time what in the hell you were up to, mind you, but it sure made life interesting." Both men laughed. "So, what's on your mind?"

"I was just thinking that it would be nice to get together for dinner."

"Sounds great. Provided you're buying, that is."

"Don't I always. How does tomorrow night fit your plans?"

"Well I'll have to check with my social secretary, but I'm guessing that it's alright. So, what do you say, Blue Heaven again?"

"I was thinking more along the lines of a new place."

"That's fine. What's it called?"

"Barredo."

"Never heard of it. Is it in Old Town?"

"No, it's a little south of Old Town."

"No shit. About how far?"

Nick blew a perfect smoke ring over his railing and watched a gentle breeze carry it toward the shoreline. "Oh, I'd say about ninety miles."

THE END

ABOUT THE AUTHOR

Darin Colucci is a successful personal injury attorney recognized by Newsweek.com as one of the finest lawyers in the country.

He's also the author of the self-improvement book: Everything I Never Learned in School: A Guide to Success, which won a 2017 Eric Hoffer Award. He makes his home in Duxbury, Massachusetts where he lives with his wife, Lorna and son Jackson.

Departure Tax is his first novel.

www.ingramcontent.com/pod-product-compliance
Lightning Source LLC
Chambersburg PA
CBHW030028180626
46810CB00001B/268